# Fatal Infraction

A Mike Stoneman Thriller

# Fatal Infraction

A Mike Stoneman Thriller

Kevin G. Chapman

Cover design:  Bespoke Book Covers

*For Sharon, whose constant encouragement and deep commitment to these characters makes these books so much better than they would be without her. All my love.*

# Chapter 1 – Team Chemistry

EVERYONE AGREED THAT JIMMY should not have slept with Nate's girl. Within the team, some things were out of bounds. As the quarterback and leader of the offense, Jimmy should have known better – or at least kept it a secret. Nobody was surprised when it blew up.

Nate Bedford, a five-year veteran wide receiver, was nearly dressed when Jimmy Rydell strolled into the locker room at the practice facility. A dozen players lounged in the comfy chairs in front of the video game consoles, shouting at the screens and at each other. A dozen more were in various stages of undressing or dressing. They were halfway through their three weeks of voluntary spring practices. Jimmy was accompanied by four offensive linemen who had been lifting weights with him after the organized drills ended. Jimmy's shirtless upper body glistened with sweat, emphasizing each cut in the dark muscle of his chiseled physique.

"Lookin' good, Jimmy," linebacker Billy Davis called out as he wagged a finger at the quarterback.

Nate nudged Austin Riley, a rookie free agent who was trying to make the team. "Look at him. Showin' off. There's more to life than muscles." Riley smartly said nothing and turned away.

Jimmy took two steps toward Nate, holding his workout jersey in his left hand. "Some people prefer some muscle instead of your skinny white ass. I know Candi does."

"You shut yer mouth!" Nate's Louisiana accent always became more pronounced the angrier he got. He took a stride toward Jimmy, fire in his eyes. A large arm, belonging to the all-pro center Kevin Mahwah, reached out and blocked him momentarily.

"Keep a lid on it, Nate."

While Nate stopped, Jimmy kept walking. Five feet of carpet and one low wooden dressing bench separated them. "You got a problem with me? Huh, Nate?"

"You're damn right! Somebody's gotta teach you some respect."

"You want a piece of me?" Jimmy flung his jersey to the floor and held up a hand, gesturing for Nate to step forward.

Nate showed off his cat-quick reflexes by stepping onto the bench and launching himself toward Jimmy in the same motion. As a quarterback, Jimmy was accustomed to large men hell-bent on his destruction assaulting him. He took a quick half-step back, planted his left leg, and landed a right jab dead center on Nate's nose before the two athletes went tumbling to the floor in a knot of arms and legs.

Nate was an inch taller than Jimmy, but leaner and lighter. When Jimmy rolled on top of him, a dazed and bleeding Nate had no chance of gaining the upper hand. Jimmy delivered two sets of right-left combination punches to the side of Nate's face before a gang of teammates grabbed him by the shoulders and pulled him off.

Nate struggled to his feet, a stream of blood from his nose covering the front of his face, neck, and white polo shirt. As he gained his balance, he spewed a torrent of expletives and lunged toward Jimmy, but two large pairs of arms held him back. "You bastard! You don't touch Candi again, ya hear me?! I'll kill you! I'll cut your dick off!"

Everyone in the locker room was silent as the two men stared at each other across ten feet of empty space. Nate had caught nine touchdown passes from Jimmy the prior season. The team was counting on him to be their primary deep threat in the season ahead. Chemistry between a quarterback and a wide receiver was both essential and fragile. This wasn't good. But it was private. What happened inside the locker room stayed between the players. That was an unwritten rule. Of course, so was the rule about not sleeping with other players' girlfriends.

Jimmy shrugged off the hands that were lightly restraining him and waved dismissively toward his most reliable receiver. "Candi's all yours."

"Yer damn right she is!"

Jimmy walked away toward the showers, accompanied by three of the offensive linemen with whom he had entered. Everyone else exhaled and returned to the normal buzz of conversation, now a bit more hushed. Someone tossed Nate a white towel, which was quickly stained red as he attempted to wipe the blood off his face and shirt. He said nothing, but glared at Jimmy's back until the quarterback rounded a corner of green-tinted marble tile and disappeared from view.

Every player in the room had an opinion about Jimmy – and about Nate. Most were worried the two teammates might not be able to put this incident, or their underlying conflicts, behind them in order to move forward on the field. None of them imagined it would be the last time they saw Jimmy alive.

◆◆◆

## Jimmy Rydell Found Murdered

**By Dexter Peacock, Sr. Correspondent and Kristi Olson, Staff Writer**

June 1, 2019 12:15 p.m. ET

Jimmy Rydell, Heisman Trophy winner and number one overall pick in the 2017 NFL draft, was found dead today, the victim of an apparent murder. Rydell's naked body was discovered this morning on the carousel in Central Park. A spokesperson for the NYPD would say only that the investigation is underway and no suspects have yet been identified.

In January of 2017, Rydell led the Mississippi State University Bulldogs to an unexpected SEC championship. Rydell's record-setting 43 touchdown passes earned him both the Heisman Trophy and the Davey O'Brien Award as the nation's top quarterback.

Before his first professional season, Rydell was involved in several off-field incidents, including a fight with security officers in a New York nightclub and an arrest for driving while intoxicated in New Jersey. He became a controversial figure when he took a knee during the singing of the national anthem prior to the opening game of the 2018 season, despite a league directive that all players should stand. Rydell was fined, but not suspended, for the incident and continued to display his support for the Black Lives Matter movement on and off the field. A knee injury ended his rookie year after eleven games, in which the team went 5-6.

Rydell's 2018 season was similarly marred by off-field incidents, culminating with his embarrassing arrest in a Manhattan strip club after he shot himself in the foot with a registered gun. He later pleaded guilty to misdemeanor weapons charges, for which he was serving a period of probation and public service at the time of his death. Rydell returned for the last three games of the 2018 season, winning only one of those games, but playing well. In a recent interview, team General Manager, Chip O'Meara, said he was optimistic going into the 2019 season with Rydell at quarterback.

Last May, Rydell was arrested and charged with a misdemeanor when he and actress Brenda Cooper were filmed swimming in the fountain in Central Park near Columbus Circle at 2:00 a.m.

Team owner, Woody O'Meara, said in a statement this morning that the entire organization is shocked and saddened by the tragic death of their quarterback. "Despite his troubles off the field and his injuries, Jimmy Rydell was a young man of tremendous character and amazing talent who will be missed by everyone in our locker room and front office."

Since the end of the 2018 season, rumors have circulated linking Rydell and two other New York players to a league-wide investigation into possible point shaving. Rydell had declined to comment on the rumors and the league denies that there is any ongoing investigation. However, inside sources told *The New York Times* that federal agents are working on the case and that involved individuals linked to the Gallata crime family are under investigation. A spokesperson for the NYPD declined to comment on the existence of a link between the Rydell murder and the ongoing federal probe.

Funeral services for Jimmy Rydell will be held at Riverside Church on Thursday, beginning at 3:00 p.m. The team has made a donation of $100,000 in Rydell's name to the Boys & Girls Clubs of Greater New York, a charity for which Rydell did substantial fundraising work during his troubled time in New York City. Mr. O'Meara will also match all donations from fans up to an additional $100,000. Fans are urged to make donations via the link on the NFL's website: www.NFL.com /JimmyRydell in lieu of sending flowers.

# Chapter 2 – Welcome Back

Saturday, June 1, 2019

NYPD HOMICIDE DETECTIVES Mike Stoneman and Jason Dickson sat across from each other in the small conference room on the third floor of their precinct on 94th Street. Captain Edward Sullivan leaned into the pock-marked wood table, trying to get his face closer to the chrome speaker box positioned in the middle. Sullivan, whom everyone in the precinct called Sully, was growing increasingly impatient with the conversation. His bosses were focused on politics and public relations rather than police work. Sully's always ruddy face was turning a darker shade of crimson, which Mike and Jason knew from experience was a signal to back off until the pressure released.

Being in the precinct at all on a Saturday was unusual. Being there with Sully and being on a call with Police Commissioner Earl Ward was nearly unprecedented. Mike and Jason only worked on a Saturday if they were on a significant case. This one certainly fit the bill. They had not been dispatched to Central Park, where the body was found. Instead, Sully had called and told them to meet him at the precinct. A forensics team was at work in the park, but it was pretty obvious to the responding officers that the body had been dumped there, not killed there.

Mike leaned back in his chair, a notepad on his lap. He wore his usual work outfit of tan slacks, a well-worn blue dress shirt with a conservative striped tie, and his signature navy blue sports jacket. Since it was a Saturday, he was wearing his loafers and he had skipped his morning shave. Mike's face was placid, but still showed a few more lines than he liked to admit. He stretched his left arm over his head – a remnant from the physical therapy exercises he was still doing daily. He had finished the 22-week program less than a month earlier after having shoulder surgery the prior December. His therapist recommended that he keep up the exercises. He lowered the arm and ran his fingers through his wavy brown hair, which was sprinkled with gray, especially behind his ears. He had just celebrated his fiftieth birthday, but he was in denial concerning the creeping advancement of age.

Jason sat straight up, as always. His six-foot-three muscular frame was as imposing as ever, although he was not wearing his normal pressed suit and crisp-collared shirt. He looked like he had received the call from Sully while out on a sailboat, although he did not sail. His khaki slacks, blue-and-white polo shirt, and dockers were a far cry from his general fashion-plate look. He was the only Black man in the room, and the only Black detective in the Manhattan North Homicide Division. He stood out in any crowd.

Jason's left arm was wrapped in an Ace bandage above the elbow. He was still healing from a gunshot wound received two and a half weeks earlier onboard Epic Cruise Lines' *Colossus of the Ocean*. The other detectives in the precinct had not stopped ribbing him about getting into a gunfight while on a vacation cruise. Jason thought the trip with his girlfriend, Rachel, along with Mike and his recent romance, Michelle McNeill, seemed more than two weeks earlier. It had turned out to be less relaxing than they had hoped.

Sully's face was getting redder by the minute. Jason made eye contact with Mike and shrugged, silently mouthing, "Shit show," to his partner.

"There's more press on this than on the royal wedding," Kimberly Williams said with unmasked anxiety. Williams was the head of communications for Mayor Frederick Douglass. Her job was to make sure the mayor's media profile was positive and that any public statements from city agencies, including the police department, were politically appropriate.

"I'm not concerned about the damned press!" came the angry voice of Commissioner Ward. "We have a dead athlete, a city full of freaked-out residents, and a ton of evidence that's getting stale while we sit around and argue about the optics and the publicity angles. Nobody seems to have seen Jimmy since Wednesday, so there's a big gap to fill here. I want Stoneman and Dickson over at Rydell's apartment building with a squad of uniforms right now!"

Sully agreed. Mike and Jason sat passively, not speaking. They pretty much knew how this was going to end, so adding their commentary would not shorten the call. After several more minutes of discussion about the pros and cons of letting the NFL's internal security guys participate in the investigation, Ward finally cut off the conversation, told Williams that he would speak to the mayor directly, and gave Sullivan the order to get his team on the case right away.

Sullivan punched the button to end the phone call. "OK you two, take four uniforms and get over to Rydell's building."

Mike stood up, hearing his knees creak. He had been hoping for a relatively quiet first month back to work after their less than restful vacation, and after the excitement of the week before that. The shootout at the Alexander Hamilton Hotel in Brooklyn seemed like a year ago, but it had only been four weeks. Sully and other detectives didn't want to hear about how exhausted they felt. They refused to believe that six days on a cruise ship with an unlimited premium drink package could have been stressful – the bullet wound in Jason's triceps notwithstanding.

As they walked out after Sullivan and headed for the stairs down to the street, Jason remarked, "I don't know how you root for this team."

Mike shrugged. "It's genetic. My dad was a big Joe Namath fan. He taught me to chant J-E-T-S before I could say my name. My childhood bedroom was all green and white, with green jet planes hanging from the ceiling. I now consider it to have been child abuse to saddle me with a rooting interest in a team that does nothing but break my heart and drive me crazy. But the Gang Green is in my blood."

Twenty minutes later, Jason parked a nearly new Lincoln in the loading zone on Riverside Boulevard in front of Park Towers, the sparkling high-rise where Jimmy Rydell lived. The plan was to interview the staff, check out the apartment, and then get over to the team's practice facility in Florham Park, New Jersey. Team owner Woody O'Meara and his son Chip, the general manager, had agreed to talk to them as long as they arrived before 4:00. Since they needed a car for the trip to Jersey, they had checked out an unmarked departmental car and drove to 69th Street. A black-and-white squad car pulled in behind them and four uniformed officers piled out.

"I could have walked here from my apartment," Mike grumbled as he climbed out the passenger door.

"Then you would have missed that enjoyable meeting."

Mike couldn't suppress a chuckle. "Alright. Let's get this done efficiently. There's a uniform upstairs securing the apartment, right?"

"That's what Berkowitz said. They sent one over as soon as they found the body."

Mike knew homicide detective Steve Berkowitz was a detail man. He had no doubt that the apartment was secure. Whether it was a crime scene remained to be seen. "How long do you figure it will take us to get to Jersey later?"

Jason stepped aside for a man emerging from the building, walking two Golden Retrievers. "Might take an hour. The later we start, the longer it'll take."

A doorman in full uniform, including white gloves, held the glass-and-chrome door for Mike and Jason and welcomed them to Park Towers. The uniformed officers stayed outside. Mike had given them instructions to interview anyone entering or leaving to see if they knew Jimmy Rydell and if they had seen or heard anything unusual concerning him since Wednesday.

Park Towers was one of a dozen huge apartment buildings that had sprung up like bejeweled mushrooms along Manhattan's West Side over the past decade. Like the others, it was built on reclaimed parkland between the newly created Boulevard and the Hudson River, with spectacular views of New Jersey. This particular building was closest to the southern end of Riverside Park, which ran from 129th Street all the way down to 72nd Street. The southern end of the park had been refurbished to reflect the developers' desire to create an instantly upscale neighborhood. They even commissioned a statue and a memorial for Eleanor Roosevelt, which now sat north of the nearby park entrance.

The two detectives strode across the marble-tiled lobby, flanked by potted palms, and approached an imposing front desk formed from polished blonde wood. Mike flashed his badge and announced that they wanted to speak to the building manager. The desk attendant, in a uniform the same as the doorman's but without the white gloves, held Mike's stare without expression. Dealing with celebrities, paparazzi, and police was not an unusual occurrence. The man was dark-skinned, with large, bushy eyebrows. Mike could not put an age estimate on him; somewhere between 35 and 60. He spoke with an Eastern-European accent.

"Is this related to Mr. Rydell?" When Mike nodded, the man, whose nameplate identified him as Cesar Conarrubias, walked through a doorway into a hidden back room without another word.

While they waited, Jason turned to Mike. "Any chance we get the autopsy report before Monday?"

"What makes you think I have any inside information?" Mike deadpanned.

"Oh, I don't know. I figured maybe somebody who's sleeping with the ME might be in a position."

"I haven't spoken to Michelle," Mike replied with a smile. "But, knowing how hot this case is, I would expect her to be working the weekend on our dead quarterback. Too bad she doesn't get overtime like we do."

Before the discussion could continue, Cesar the deskman returned, followed by a somber-faced man in a pressed business suit. He was a few inches shorter than Mike's 5'10", with slicked-back black hair. He spoke to the detectives with a practiced confidence. "Detectives, I've been expecting you. I'm Charles Stafford, the building manager. We're all stunned about Mr. Rydell. We want to fully cooperate. What can I tell you?"

Jason extracted a notebook and pen from his inside pocket. "When was the last time anyone on the staff saw Jimmy?"

"As near as we can tell, the dayside desk attendants recall Mr. Rydell coming in early in the evening on Wednesday. That's the last time anyone remembers seeing him."

Jason took down the names of the two men and one woman who were working the lobby on Wednesday. All three of them would be back at work Monday afternoon. Stafford volunteered to get their home addresses and phone numbers if the detectives wanted to speak to them sooner.

Jason then asked Cesar, "He has a reputation for throwing huge parties up there. Is that true?"

"Yes, sir. That is correct, but mostly on weekends. Mr. Rydell has many guests, but many nights he has none."

"OK." Jason made a note on his pad. "What about Thursday morning? Were any of you working then?"

Stafford pointed toward the door. "Henry was here. He works Wednesday to Sunday."

Mike and Jason exchanged a glance, then Mike said to Stafford, "Can somebody else cover the door for a few minutes while we talk to him?"

"Of course," the manager responded, but he made no move to make it happen.

"Now?" Mike prompted.

"Oh, of course." He motioned to the other man behind the desk to relieve Henry.

"What's the security camera setup?" Jason looked toward the ceiling, scanning for the familiar smoked-glass domes of surveillance cameras, but did not immediately see any.

Stafford smiled and puffed out his chest, then went into what Jason figured was a prepared spiel for prospective tenants and real estate brokers. "We have a state-of-the-art security system here. All the apartment doors are equipped with electronic locks that can be opened with a smartphone app or a keypad or pocket fob, and include a rotating access feature allowing entrance on a scheduled or one-time code for domestic help. There are automated motion-sensitive security cameras in the common areas and elevators as well as in most hallways. We have 24-hour security in the lobby, and each apartment is equipped with an external door alarm if the door is opened without authorization while the resident is inside." He finished the confidently delivered recitation, then glanced toward the front entrance, where Henry was on his way across the expansive lobby.

"So," Jason said, waiting for the building manager to look back in his direction, "we should be able to see Jimmy on the security system from the moment he entered the building until he went into his apartment, and then we should be able to see whether he exited the unit or whether anyone else entered, is that right?"

Mike gave his partner a soft elbow to the rib. "Should be the easiest murder investigation in history."

"Well, actually," Stafford said hesitantly, lowering his previously proud chin. "Mr. Rydell objected to having a camera in the penthouse vestibule, for privacy reasons."

"What does that mean, exactly?" Jason asked impatiently.

Mike jumped in to take a stab at a translation before Stafford could equivocate further. "I think it means there's no camera between the elevator and Jimmy's penthouse, is that right?"

"Unfortunately, that's true."

"Yeah, figures. Couldn't be easy. Alright, we'll reckon with that when we go upstairs. What about the gym? I understand Jimmy was famous for his middle-of-the-night workouts. Are there cameras there?"

Stafford's shoulders slumped further. "I'm sorry, Detective, the residents here include a number of celebrities, who don't want video of themselves sweating in the health club. So, no, there are no cameras in the gym."

"What about the entrance doors into the health club?" Jason pressed. "There must be security there."

"Not exactly," Stafford said slowly. "The health club is accessible only by residents who have already cleared security into the building. For the same reasons the residents don't want cameras inside the club, there is no video of the residents in their workout clothes entering the spa doors."

"Great," Jason sighed. "But there would be video of anyone using the elevator to get to the health club. Where is it? Basement?"

"Yes," Stafford said quickly. "The health club is on the lower level. If you take the elevator, then you'd be on video."

"Is there another way to get there besides the elevator?"

The building manager's face appeared pained. "Well, yes. You can access the spa via the fire stairs."

"Fine," Jason said, barely hiding his annoyance. "Is the gym open 24 hours?"

"Not generally. Except, well, for Mr. Rydell. We allowed him access any time. He preferred working out alone. He had the code to the door and could get in and out even outside the posted hours of operation."

"Are there electronic records of when the doors are accessed?"

"No," Stafford said quickly. "We don't keep track. There is really no need. And the cleaning staff goes in and out at all hours, using the same code."

Mike spoke softly in Jason's direction. "It just keeps getting better and better."

Jason tried another idea. "What about the apartment doors? You said they were electronic locks. Do you have a record of when the door locks are opened, and by what method?"

"No. The building management does not have that. If a resident used the smartphone app to unlock the door, their phone might record it, but we don't have it. Again, it's a privacy issue."

"Of course it is," Jason grumbled. "So, we should have him on a camera coming in the building, going into the elevator, and exiting the elevator in his penthouse lobby. But after that, we would only have more video of him, or any other record of his activities, if he got back into the elevator. Is that about right?"

"That's right."

"But he couldn't leave the building without being seen on camera, right?"

Henry the doorman had made his way over and was standing silently, listening. He reached out his hand to get Jason's attention. "Unless he left through the service entrance."

Stafford spun in Henry's direction, having not realized he was there. The building manager's face showed extreme displeasure that his underling had spoken out of turn. "Henry, please let me do the speaking to the police."

"I'd like to hear what this man has to say," Jason quickly interjected. "You're Henry, right?"

"Yes, sir." Henry was a tall, thin Black man in his 50s. His short black hair was neatly cut and his face clean-shaven. Dressed in his doorman uniform, he looked like a butler for a wealthy estate. He spoke with a mild southern accent.

"What were you saying about the service entrance?"

"Well, Sir, Mr. Rydell and some of the other residents want to avoid people who hang around the front entrance, looking for autographs or taking photos. They sometimes use the service entrance on the side of the building, or the breezeway, to come and go. There are stores on the street and the breezeway door is often open when deliveries go in and out. Some tenants use that door and take the stairs or the service elevator inside."

Jason raised an eyebrow. "I'm sure you were aware of that, right, Mr. Stafford?"

"That's not approved procedure," he snapped, shooting daggers out of his eyes toward the doorman. "I suppose it could happen, but it is not permitted, strictly speaking."

"Well, speaking not strictly," Mike said to Henry, "if I were a resident and I wanted to slip out the service entrance, how would I get there?"

Henry hesitated, looking at his boss nervously. When Jason prompted him, Henry said, "If you use the service elevator, you can get there through the breezeway. Or you can use the fire stairs that exit to the same place. Or you could take the rear fire stairs that exit directly to the street."

"Is there a camera in the service elevator?" Jason asked, turning back to Stafford.

"Of course."

"What about in the fire stairs?"

"No, not in the stairwells."

"What about this breezeway, by the service entrance?"

"Yes – there's a security officer who sits down there and checks the trucks and deliveries in and out, and there is a camera on that door."

Jason made a few more notes. "How do you get out of the building from there?"

Henry helpfully piped up, "You can exit through the service doors, if they're open, or through the fire door."

"Great. Well, Mr. Stafford, we're going to need to look at what video you have available. We'll send over a team to work with your security staff to review the recordings. Have your folks already started looking?"

"No, Detective. I instructed our security team to leave that to the police."

"Thank you. We appreciate it. We'll get a team over later today." Jason then turned to the doorman, who was shifting his weight from side to side nervously. "Henry, Mr. Stafford tells us you were working Thursday morning, is that right?"

"Yes, sir."

"What happened Thursday morning?"

Henry explained that Jimmy's routine was to come downstairs around 8:00 a.m. to meet his driver and bodyguard, a man he called "The Duke." Henry didn't know The Duke's last name, or if Duke was actually his first name. All he could say was that The Duke was with Jimmy most of the time. He was always upstairs when Jimmy was having a party, and he drove Jimmy everywhere, including to and from practices across the river in Jersey. But, that Thursday, Jimmy never came down.

"That figures," Mike mumbled, knowing Jimmy's driver's license had been suspended after a DUI arrest.

"Tiger brought his coffee and bagel, like usual," Henry said, "and The Duke was there, like usual, but Jimmy wasn't there."

"Who's Tiger?" Mike asked.

"He's a kid who hangs around. Mr. Rydell likes him. Mr. Rydell gives him money to get him coffee and a bagel every morning. He has a shoeshine stand and hangs out on the sidewalk during the day. He don't bother nobody. He's a nice kid."

"OK," Mike said, cutting Henry off, "let's get back to Jimmy. On Thursday, Jimmy was late, so what happened?"

"The Duke said he would go upstairs to get him, like maybe he slept late or forgot he had a practice. He went upstairs, then came down again, but said Mr. Rydell wasn't there. We looked all over for him, called his phone, but couldn't find him. After a while, The Duke said he'd go to Jersey and see whether Jimmy showed up there. That was about it."

"Had that ever happened before?"

"No, Sir. Mr. Rydell sometimes went away. He told us about a trip to Las Vegas; that was just before he gave all the doormen a thousand-dollar tip. But he always let us know, so we would hold his packages. And he always told Tiger when he was going to be gone, so he wouldn't bring his morning coffee. But not this time."

Mike turned to Jason. "I guess we'll have to add this Duke guy, and maybe the kid, Tiger, to our list of people we need to talk to. We need to finish up here and then get over to Florham Park, so that'll have to wait."

"Let's get upstairs and see if Jimmy left us any messages."

# Chapter 3 – Meet The Duke

A FEW MINUTES LATER, Mike, Jason, and Mr. Stafford were all in the penthouse elevator. Stafford had reluctantly provided information about Jimmy's rent and monthly fees, which included the normal building services along with a slate of extras. Jimmy had maid service twice a week, laundry and dry cleaning pickup and delivery, and on-demand catering for his parties. The total monthly expense was huge, even for somebody earning a professional athlete's paycheck. Mike wondered how much of Jimmy's big signing bonus ended up paying for annual expenses.

Stafford reluctantly conceded that Jimmy's management agency was sometimes late making his payments. But the building owners liked the cachet of having the star quarterback living there, which attracted other high-end celebrities. So, they cut him slack when he needed it. They all figured Jimmy had to be good for it.

The group stepped off the elevator on the top floor into a vestibule about the size of a standard elevator lobby area in a high-rise, except that theirs was the only elevator door in sight.

The area was decorated with a thick oriental rug covering blonde hardwood flooring. An ornate wooden table dominated one wall, topped by a huge floral display in a crystal vase, which partially obscured a large oval mirror in a gilt frame. The opposite wall featured several pieces of abstract artwork. At the end of the space was a double door made from carved wood, with an electronic security pad to the right of the frame. There was no number or name. It was the only door except for an emergency exit tucked into the far corner, presumably leading to the fire stairs. A uniformed NYPD officer, who had been there guarding the door for the past several hours, snapped to attention when she saw Mike and Jason.

Mike turned his head toward Stafford as they exited the car. "Could somebody access this entrance area through those fire stairs?"

"Only if somebody on this side opened the door. It's locked from the stairway side."

Mike caught Jason's eyes and tilted his head toward the fire door. Jason covered the ground in three large strides, pushed open the door using a large metal bar in the center, then disappeared into the fire stairs. The door slammed shut behind him. A moment later, the door reopened and Jason passed through.

"What the—" Stafford blurted out.

"Duct tape over the latch," Jason said without waiting for a question. "Low-tech, but effective. Somebody wanted that door open."

"Yeah, well, for all we know it was Jimmy who wanted easy access for visitors from inside the building," Mike muttered. Then, to Stafford, "You said there's no camera in this entrance area, right? So, if somebody came through the fire door, we'd have no video record?"

Stafford reluctantly nodded. "But there is still a tight security seal on this door. Nobody could get in without having the fob or the app, knowing the code, or being let in from the inside."

Jason scowled. "That narrows down our list of suspects to anyone Jimmy gave the code to, or loaned the fob to, or anyone he knew well enough to open the door for. Plus, anyone who was already in the building on a night when Jimmy left his door open."

Mike shared Jason's disappointment, but tried not to display it. "OK, let's get inside." Mike motioned for the officer guarding the door to step aside. Then he turned again to Stafford. "You have a pass code?"

Stafford entered an 8-digit code into the security pad and waited for a green light to appear. The door emitted a distinct click as the lock disengaged, allowing Stafford to swing open the right side of the double door. Mike told the officer to stay outside, then stepped across the threshold, followed closely by Jason and Stafford.

The interior was a model of modernist furnishings and artwork. A sunken living room spread out to their left, ending at floor-to-ceiling windows looking west across the river toward New Jersey. Sunlight streamed in, bathing the polished wood floor and the leather sofa and chairs. Beyond that, the open floorplan exposed a formal dining space with a huge mahogany table encircled by ten high-backed chairs beneath a crystal chandelier.

Before they could take in all the details of the luxurious space, a deep voice with a slight Southern accent bellowed out from beyond their field of vision, "Who's there?"

Mike and Jason exchanged a puzzled expression. Stafford called back, ignoring Mike's raised hand, which was intended to stop him. "It's Charles Stafford, the building manager. I'm here with the police."

"I'm in the kitchen."

Mike reached out to hold Stafford back from taking a step forward. "Who the hell is here?"

"Damned if I know," the building manager responded.

Jason pushed Stafford backward gently. "Wait here." Jason and Mike were both annoyed that the possible crime scene was contaminated. The two detectives walked down a hallway, which turned right and opened into an expansive kitchen, with sparkling chrome appliances and a bright white marble floor.

A muscular White man was sitting on a bar stool at a food preparation island. He held a sandwich in both hands in front of his mouth as he chewed and glanced up, seemingly unconcerned about the arrival of the cops. He slid down from his stool and stood, glaring imposingly at his guests. He looked like a professional body builder. Jason was accustomed to being the biggest and most intimidating figure in the room, but this man dwarfed him in every physical respect. He outweighed Jason by easily fifty pounds – all muscle. His biceps bulged against a tight gray t-shirt that barely contained his broad shoulders. He had a crewcut of blond stubble on his head, held aloft by a massive neck. His chiseled body featured a slim waist and thick thigh muscles that strained against the fabric of his forest-green shorts. He was as ripped a real human as Mike had ever seen.

Jason stepped forward confidently and spoke in his deep voice, with a heavy helping of cop-authority. "I'm Detective Dickson, NYPD Homicide. This is my partner, Detective Stoneman. This is an active crime scene. Who are you, and how did you get in here?"

The mountain of muscle looked confused. Jason and Mike both wondered whether he would fit the stereotype and be as dumb as he was big, but they both knew never to make that assumption. They also both noticed the acne around his neck and figured it for an indication of steroid use, which was consistent with the muscle mass.

"I'm Duke Drepp. I got permission to be here. Whaddaya mean *crime scene*?"

Before Jason could respond, his attention was diverted by the appearance of a woman padding into the room from the left. She looked as if she had recently rolled out of bed, with disheveled, slightly matted blonde hair hanging loosely around her shoulders. She wore no makeup, but still had large, dark eyes and plump lips. Her body was barely concealed by a man's dress shirt, unbuttoned, which fell to mid-thigh. She placed her hands on her hips, causing the front of the shirt to open wider and expose the majority of her breasts.

"Duke?" she called out, annoyed, "I thought you were making me a sandwich? And who are these guys?" The woman stared at the detectives, not at all embarrassed by the amount of skin she was showing.

"NYPD, Miss," Jason said. "May I ask you what your relationship is with Jimmy Rydell?"

The woman stared at Jason with a confused expression, then turned her head toward Duke Drepp. "Duke, why is this guy asking about Jimmy? Is this Jimmy's fucking apartment?"

The big man shrugged. "Yeah, it is. Jimmy lets me crash here whenever he's out of town. I'm his security detail, but yeah, it's not my place."

The woman shrieked, "You asshole!" and scampered back the way she came, disappearing around the corner before Jason or Mike could tell her to stop.

Duke watched until the woman was out of sight, then turned back to Jason. "What the fuck are you doing here?"

"You're Jimmy Rydell's bodyguard?" Jason shot back.

"Yeah. That's me. What happened? What shit did Jimmy get into this time?"

Mike stepped forward, still keeping Jason between himself and The Incredible Hulk. "Mr. Drepp, I'm guessing you haven't been watching the news today?"

"No. And don't call me that. Everybody calls me The Duke."

"Well, Duke, Jimmy's dead."

Mike watched closely as The Duke processed the information. His facial expression didn't change much. "Dead? No shit?"

"No shit," Jason replied. "Why are you here?"

"Like I said, I hang here with Jimmy all the time. He doesn't mind if I use the place when he's out of town. He took off on Wednesday, so I figured he wouldn't mind if I brought – um – Chelsea up for the night." He held out his hands, palms up, as if surrendering for his indiscretion.

"When did you expect Jimmy back?"

Before The Duke could answer, Chelsea burst back into the room, now wearing a tight silver dress with matching 4-inch heels and carrying a sparkling sequined purse. She walked quickly to The Duke and planted a slap across his face.

The Duke barely registered the blow. "See how impressed she is?"

Neither Mike nor Jason laughed at the attempted humor. Mike said, "Miss, we're going to need to get your contact information so we can take a statement from you. Please give it to the officer at the door." He put two fingers in his mouth and whistled loudly as he took two steps to the kitchen's entrance.

He waved to the officer, who had peered her head inside and yelled for her to take contact info from Chelsea.

Chelsea turned and stormed from the room, her heels clacking across the hardwood. The men watched her leave. Then Jason took a step forward so he was directly in front of The Duke, tilting his head up to keep eye contact. "Jimmy Rydell's body was found this morning on the carousel in Central Park."

The Duke's face now registered obvious puzzlement. "What the fuck?"

"You're telling us you hadn't heard?"

"No. I've been . . . busy this morning."

Jason made a show of looking at his wrist. "It's two-thirty."

"Yeah, well, we were up late and I guess we slept in. Is that a crime?" The Duke glared at Jason, who held his ground.

"When was the last time you spoke to Jimmy?"

The Duke turned his body away from Jason and reached for his sandwich. "I dropped him off out front Wednesday around 5:30. I haven't talked to him since." He then took a healthy bite, staring evenly at the two detectives.

Jason didn't wait for him to finish chewing. "We're conducting an investigation. This apartment is potentially a crime scene. I'm going to have to ask you to wait outside while we conduct a search of the premises." Jason stepped sideways, creating more room for the huge man to pass by and motioning toward the hallway leading to the front door. "There's a uniformed officer in the entrance area. You can wait there with her." He turned around, searching for the building manager. "Mr. Stafford?"

Stafford poked his head around the corner. "Yes?"

"Please escort The Duke outside. Then you can come back and accompany us during our inspection of the apartment, but please don't touch anything."

When the front door closed behind The Duke, Mike turned to his partner. "If I needed a bodyguard, I guess I'd want somebody who looked like that."

"I don't know," Jason responded, "I might go for a bit more agility and a little less bulk, but I have to admit he's an intimidating sucker."

"Let's see how badly our crime scene is compromised."

They spent the next fifteen minutes walking through the apartment and taking notes, as well as a few photos on their cell phones. Stafford confirmed that the penthouse had laundry and maid service. Jimmy's clothes were collected twice a week by his maid and sent out for laundering. They were delivered back to the apartment by the maids, who came in on Wednesday and Saturday. He pointed out that he had prevented the maids from disturbing the room.

"It's like living in a hotel," Mike noted.

Mike insisted they treat the area as a crime scene, which slowed the process. Despite Mike's grumblings about the scene being contaminated, Jason pointed out that they were fortunate Jimmy's maid service had not touched the place since Wednesday night. There were no signs of a struggle – unless The Duke had cleaned it up. Everything was about where you would expect it to be if the resident had stepped out voluntarily.

In the master bedroom, Jason was impressed with the man's closet, which was filled with snappy suits. Expensive casual clothes were carefully arranged in his drawers. There was a gap in a row of sneakers lined up on a beveled rack underneath the suits, and a pair of sneakers sat on the floor next to a padded bench. Also on the floor next to the bench were a pair of pants, a polo shirt, and underwear. Jason deduced that Jimmy had changed clothes and then not remembered or had time to put the dirties in the hamper. "Looks like he was planning on being back," Mike observed.

A large suitcase and an overnight bag sat in an orderly grouping at the bottom of a smaller closet.

"Doesn't look like he packed for a trip," Jason noted.

Mike examined a wallet laying on the top of a chest of drawers. It was loaded with cash and credit cards. Next to it, a Rolex watch and a diamond pinky ring rested casually. "I'm gonna rule out robbery as a motive."

In the living room – with the huge windows overlooking the Hudson River – Jason noticed two framed photos of Jimmy. One showed him with a much older White man wearing a Mississippi State sweater. He recognized the man as Roland James, Jimmy's college coach. In the photo, Jimmy was being presented with a framed uniform. He saw the same uniform hanging on the wall. In the second picture, Jimmy was surrounded by a group of about 15-20 teenage boys. The background wasn't obvious. Jason snapped quick pictures with his phone.

They systematically examined the apartment. They didn't find a cell phone, which was not a big surprise. It would have been more unusual if the phone were there and the owner were missing. Jason would send in a request to his carrier for phone records and another to his bank for financial records. It would take a few days to get them, and the requests couldn't even go in until Monday. They were already way behind where they should have been for an investigation into a murder that may have happened several days earlier.

Jason confirmed with Stafford that Jimmy could have gone up and down the fire stairs at any time without being seen. Stafford pointed out that it was forty-five floors to street level. Jason countered that Jimmy was a professional athlete.

They picked up The Duke on the way out and waited for the elevator. Mike told the officer at the door to wait for the forensics team to arrive, although he didn't expect much useful evidence to come from the forensics sweep. It didn't appear that Jimmy had been killed there – or that he had been abducted.

As they waited for the elevator, Jason said, "I guess you didn't guard Jimmy's body well enough, eh?" Mike recognized the technique – trying to get the witness riled up so he would say something without thinking. He questioned whether The Duke ever did much thinking.

"I wasn't here. I had the night off," he responded, more calmly than Mike expected.

Jason turned his body toward the huge man and stepped forward, putting his normally imposing form inches away from The Duke. "We're going to want to talk to you. Right now we need to get out to Florham Park. Can you meet us there?"

"Not today," he said into Jason's forehead, not giving up an inch of ground. "I gotta go take care of a few things."

"Fine. Give me your phone number so we can contact you when we're ready to talk." Jason tipped up his head and stared levelly at The Duke. They stayed in that posture for several tense seconds before The Duke stepped back, reached into his back pocket, and extracted a black wallet, from which he produced a business card. The card identified him as "Vernon 'Duke' Drepp – Professional Personal Security." Jason took the card and pocketed it.

After a silent elevator ride to the lobby, Mike and Jason bade good-bye to Mr. Stafford.

They were running late. Mike checked in with the uniformed officers outside and told them to keep canvasing the residents. The Duke, who had walked outside right behind them, headed for an SUV parked on curb to their left on Riverside Boulevard.

As Mike and Jason walked toward their parked Lincoln, a high-pitched voice called out, "Hey, Duke!"

Jason located the source of the voice as a Black teenager sitting on an old wooden chair pushed up against the side of the building. There was a black shoeshine kit on the ground in front of him. He looked rumpled, with dirty black hair sticking up in spiky peaks. He had unusual facial hair; like he was trying to grow a goatee but it was only coming in around the edges, leaving a circle of wispy whiskers around his chin with a bare donut hole in the center. He was thin and wiry, wearing faded blue jeans and a green hoodie despite the warm June temperature.

The Duke stopped and turned to the youth, who shouted out, "Did you find out where Jimmy went?"

The Duke waved at him but didn't say anything.

Jason walked over to the boy. When he identified himself as a police detective, the kid became nervous. "You're Tiger, right?" Jason asked.

The boy stared at the ground and shuffled his feet, not wanting to make any eye contact with Jason. "Yeah, that's me."

"When did you last see Jimmy Rydell?" Jason didn't have any time to waste.

The kid then looked up defiantly. "Jimmy didn't do nothin'."

"I didn't say he did. I just want to know when you last saw him."

"I guess it was Wednesday morning."

"Where was that?"

Tiger dropped his head again, then said, "I brought him his coffee and bagel. He was coming out of the building with The Duke, like normal."

"OK. We knew that already. Thanks, Kid." Jason turned to walk back to the Lincoln. They needed to hit the road if they were going to make their meeting with the club officials across the river in New Jersey.

When Jason opened the car door, Tiger called out, "Hey, I wanna talk to you some more." The kid then looked at The Duke, who had stopped next to his black Escalade and was watching the encounter. Tiger then stared at the sidewalk.

Jason waved at Tiger and called out, "We'll be back."

When they were pulling away, Mike asked, "What did the kid say?"

"Nothing we didn't already know. Not much chance he killed Jimmy and disposed of his body without the doormen seeing him."

Mike chuckled. "Yeah. One suspect we can rule out."

## Chapter 4 – Meet the Boss

ON THE RIDE TO NEW JERSEY, Mike flipped through the news and sports radio stations. Everyone was talking about Jimmy Rydell. The hosts on WFAN loved talking about Jimmy. Their callers loved criticizing him. Sports fans were not known for their objectivity. Today there were as many crazy theories as there were callers. Several people picked up on the speculation in the *Times* article that the murder could be related to a point-shaving scheme. Other callers were certain Jimmy had been assassinated by white supremacists who wanted to silence his protests for racial justice. When Vinny from Staten Island suggested that the backup quarterback, Tim Flacko, might have murdered him, Mike switched to WINS, a straight news station. The host there was also talking about Jimmy but was just reporting the facts.

Only a few hours after the body was discovered, nobody really knew anything. That didn't stop everyone from talking.

An hour after leaving Park Towers, Mike and Jason pushed through the smoked-glass doors of the NFL training complex in Florham Park, New Jersey. The team was about halfway through four weeks of workouts known as Optional Team

Activities or OTAs. These practices were limited, but important, especially for rookies and free agents trying to make the squad.

The practice fields arranged all around the central building were deserted, save for two placekickers taking turns at 50-yard field goals. It was just after 4:00 p.m. and the majority of players had finished their workouts and departed. A perky brunette behind a glass reception desk greeted them and immediately directed them up a wide staircase to the top floor of the two-story structure, where they were met by another female aide.

A moment later, they were shown inside the office of Woody O'Meara, team owner and retired Wall Street hedge fund tycoon. The large space was carpeted with green field turf and jammed with mementos of the man's successful life. The walls were lined with photos of him with an all-star cast of celebrities from actors to sports stars to politicians. The furnishings were dark leather and glass. The wall opposite the door was composed of full-length picture windows with a view of the main practice field. Mike could see the yellow goalpost standing out against the blue sky as a brown football sailed end-over-end between the uprights. He had only a moment to take in the surroundings before turning his attention to the four impressive men who all stood upon their arrival.

Their hosts had been arranged in plush chairs around a football-shaped glass coffee table, adorned with a green-and-white china tea service. Woody O'Meara was easily recognizable, with his white hair and thin frame. He was comfortable in his own domain, wearing khaki slacks and a green polo shirt. Mike and Jason had done enough homework to easily recognize O'Meara's son, Chip, who was the team's general manager. The son was thicker and shorter than his father, wearing a tailored suit with a tightly knotted silk necktie. Also present was the team's very recognizable head coach, Eddie Malone, wearing green sweatpants and a white polo shirt. He had a whistle hanging on a lanyard around his neck. Malone had a pronounced paunch and a perpetually scowling face. They didn't recognize the fourth man, but the elder O'Meara quickly introduced him as Craig Linderman, the team's General Counsel. Normally, Mike and Jason did not like questioning potential witnesses in the presence of their lawyer, but they weren't entirely surprised that the corporate executives would not meet with the police alone. They exchanged handshakes and took seats on a soft sofa opposite the two O'Mearas.

"Thank you for staying late to speak to us," Mike said to get the conversation started.

Malone grunted, "Hummph – during OTAs, I'm here twenty-four seven."

"Sure, but I'm not," the younger O'Meara scolded.

"Are the players all gone for the day?" Jason asked, nodding toward the coach.

Malone responded in a slight drawl. Jason knew he had started his coaching career at LSU and that he was originally from Louisiana. "There may be one or two in the trainer's room still. And I think the kickers are still out there. But pretty much everyone else is gone. Today wasn't a formal OTA day, so it was just voluntary workouts, weight training and such."

"What about tomorrow?" Jason pressed.

"Same story. Not a mandatory reporting day, but most of the players will be here."

"Detective," the lawyer spoke up, "are you suggesting you want to interview the players?"

Mike nodded. "Yes, we will. It's standard in an investigation like this to interview coworkers and friends. I expect many of the other players on the team qualify as both."

Chip snorted, "I only wish they were all his friends."

"Did he have any enemies?" Mike inquired calmly, following up on the GM's comment.

The lawyer shot Chip a scolding look but said nothing. Chip squirmed in his seat, thinking about his answer, then said, "He had plenty, if you ask me. Between his antics off the field and his pre-game disrespecting of the national anthem, plenty of teammates don't – didn't – like him."

"Enough to murder him?"

"I doubt it, but you never know." Chip sat back in his chair, satisfied with his answer and smirking toward the lawyer.

"Let's back up," Jason cut in. "The last time Jimmy was at practice was on Wednesday, right, Coach?"

"That's right."

"Did anything unusual happen on Wednesday?"

The coach hesitated until Woody nodded. It seemed the group had already discussed how they were going to answer this question. "I didn't see anything myself," he said, looking Jason directly in the eye. "But I heard from a couple players that there was a scuffle in the locker room on Wednesday afternoon where Jimmy was involved."

"Who else was involved?"

The lawyer cut in before the coach could respond. "Detectives, since Mr. Malone wasn't there himself, anything he heard would be hearsay, so I think it's best if he doesn't repeat things he heard second-hand."

Mike looked at Woody, rather than at the lawyer, when he responded. "This isn't testimony. We're just trying to find out anything we can that will help us track down the person who killed your quarterback. We'll certainly want to talk to the players who were there, but there's a tight window for us to follow the clues. Jimmy's been missing since Wednesday, so we've already lost a few days. We're not holding anyone legally responsible here – we just want to get whatever help we can get from you."

Woody smiled at Mike, then spoke to Malone while looking at his counsel. "Let's try to cooperate here as much as we can. I came in today for this so we can ensure full support for the police and this investigation. Let's not start splitting legal hairs, shall we?"

Malone seemed happy to answer after the owner had given him permission. "From what I understand, it was Jimmy and Nate who got into it, which is not a big shock. They've had some differences on and off the field."

"Nate Bedford?" Mike asked.

"Yup."

"Any idea what the altercation was about?"

"Well, I can't say for sure, but I heard there was a girl involved."

Mike looked at each of the men sitting opposite him, but none showed any sign of speaking. "Anything more specific?"

"Nothing I feel comfortable saying with any certainty." Malone locked his mouth shut and chewed on what Jason assumed was gum, causing his jaw to throb rhythmically.

"OK, we'll interview the players tomorrow. Are you aware of any other off-the-field issues with Jimmy in the past few weeks?"

The four team officials looked at each other. Chip finally spoke. "We're not aware of anything in particular, Detective.

Jimmy had various issues in the past, as you may know. But in just the past few weeks, we're not aware of anything new."

"Fine," Mike said. "When was the last time you personally saw Jimmy?"

"Wednesday, just after lunch. He was in my office, down the hall."

"Why was he in your office?"

Chip shrugged. "It was a routine discussion. It was Jimmy and his agent, Aaron Taylor. We were talking about restructuring Jimmy's contract, to give us some salary cap space. I have discussions like that all the time with players and their agents. It's no big deal. And, Detectives, that's confidential information, so please don't tell the press about it."

"Did you come to an agreement about the contract?"

"No, actually, we didn't. It was just a preliminary discussion. We were going to have another conversation about it, but of course, that never happened."

"What was Jimmy's mood when he left the meeting on Wednesday?"

"He seemed fine. He left things mostly to Aaron. He didn't say much."

"OK. Can you give me Mr. Taylor's phone number? We're going to want to talk to him also."

"Sure," Chip said, reaching for his phone. He gave the number to Jason while Mike discussed the schedule for Sunday with Malone. At first, Chip objected to interrupting the players during their workouts, but Woody repeated his earlier statement about wanting to cooperate.

"It's not an organized practice," Woody said. "Besides, I'm sure the other players will want to do anything they can to help find whoever . . . murdered their teammate."

Mike took note that Chip didn't seem particularly broken up about the loss of his starting quarterback. Woody, on the other hand, hung his head and seemed quite emotional about the situation.

As they stood up to leave, Jason asked a final question. "On Thursday, when Jimmy didn't show up to practice, why didn't the team report him as missing so we could start this investigation earlier?"

Chip spoke up quickly in response. "Frankly, Detective, Jimmy's absence was not unusual enough for us to take serious notice. The OTAs are voluntary under league rules, so he wasn't required to be here. I'm not allowed to fine him for skipping it. Plus, if the press got wind of the club reporting him missing, it would start a firestorm. After I found out about the scuffle in the locker room on Wednesday, it really didn't surprise me that Jimmy would blow off voluntary workouts on Thursday. So, I didn't make a big deal about it. There was no team practice on Friday – we're not allowed to have organized activities on Fridays or weekends, although most of the players do show up for voluntary workouts. But, again, Jimmy was not required to be here, so we didn't want to make a big deal about his absence."

Mike snapped his fingers. "Say, today we met a guy named Duke, who says he was Jimmy's bodyguard. You guys know him?"

"Sure," Chip responded, just as quickly. "You probably know Jimmy had a penchant for getting himself into trouble in nightclubs and such. So, we assigned him a bodyguard to help keep him away from bad situations and to make sure nobody tried to ambush him. The Duke also acts as his driver, since Jimmy had his driver's license suspended. In fact, it was The

Duke who first told us that Jimmy didn't show up Thursday morning to be driven to practice."

"I guess he didn't do a very good job of keeping Jimmy out of trouble," Jason noted acidly.

"Well, the guy can't be with Jimmy twenty-four hours a day."

"We're going to want to speak to Duke also. Will he be here tomorrow?"

Chip pulled out his phone and tapped the screen. "I'll make sure he is."

As they walked down the big staircase toward the lobby and the exit, Jason said, "So much for my weekend plans."

"With Rachel?"

"Yeah. We have tickets to see a Broadway musical tomorrow afternoon. I guess she can take her sister instead."

Mike held the glass door open for his partner. "You don't seem disappointed about missing the show."

"Mike, you know I'm not much of a musical theater fan. But Rachel is, and I'm trying to be the good boyfriend. I even called a certain theater agent we know, Max Bloom, and had him hook me up with good seats. They're third row center, so she's really looking forward to it."

"You two are spending a whole lot of time together since the cruise. Seems like whenever you're not on the job, you're with Rachel. I guess you're moving ahead full steam."

"I am. It's been great. I don't want to do anything to screw it up. I really love her, Mike."

"You'll have to do something for her to make up for missing the musical," Mike deadpanned. "Maybe a piece of jewelry. I know a tall blonde woman who can set you up."

Jason laughed as he slid into the driver's seat. "I've actually been thinking about that."

# Chapter 5 – Frozen Evidence

-

JASON DROVE THE LINCOLN TO BROOKLYN, where he disembarked at Rachel Robinson's home. Mike drove back to Manhattan and parked the departmental vehicle on 68th Street in front of his apartment building, in a space all other drivers avoided because it was perilously close to a fire hydrant. He left his police "on duty" placard on the dashboard and strolled into The Dorchester. After greeting his two doormen, he ascended to his 10th floor one-bedroom. He thought about Jimmy Rydell running up forty-five flights to his penthouse and felt slightly inadequate that he wasn't taking the stairs. He quickly punched 6 and took the stairs for the last four floors.

Fifteen minutes after he took off his shoes and poured himself a neat serving of The Balvenie Caribbean Cask 14, his cell rang with Michelle's ringtone.

"Hey, there," he answered suggestively. "Where are you?"

"I'm home," she replied brightly. "I have a pot of sauce on the stove and a pack of fresh fettuccini in the fridge. You feel like a late dinner?"

"Are you finished with the Jimmy Rydell autopsy?"

"No, Mike. I never started it."

"What?" Mike held the phone away from his head, staring at it like it was an alien scanning device. He punched the speaker button. "I thought you had permission to expedite it, given the celebrity of the victim and the urgency of the investigation."

"I do. And I will conduct the autopsy as soon as it's possible." Michelle stopped talking, silently goading Mike into asking.

"Alright. I'll bite. Can you please tell me why you haven't even started the autopsy?"

"The body has to thaw out first."

"Thaw out?"

"Didn't you hear?"

"Hear what?" Mike was now standing, his phone held in front of him and his scotch glass in his left hand.

"I assumed you got the initial report, Mike. Sorry about that. When the body came in, it was mostly frozen."

"Frozen? Christ. There's a puzzle. But I guess he's been missing since Wednesday night, so maybe it makes sense. Can't you heat him up and do the autopsy?"

"Nope. The body has to thaw slowly. We have to keep the exterior refrigerated at thirty-eight degrees so the outer layers don't start to decay while the inner layers thaw out. It's going to be a few days."

"Shit! That's going to slow us down, and we don't have extra time. We're already two days behind."

"So, Detective, you've determined the time of death without me?"

"No, Doctor." Mike hoped his voice reflected a mirthful rather than accusatory tone. "I'm just assuming he was probably killed between six o'clock Wednesday night and eight o'clock Thursday morning, based on when he was last seen alive and when he was first noticed to be missing."

"And the cause of death?"

"I saw a photo." Mike attempted to navigate to his email on his phone. He had received one with a photo of Jimmy's body attached. He tried to tap on the email, but opened the one above the one he was aiming for. "Crap!" he grunted, then emitted a low growl while he closed the incorrect email, opened the right one, and tapped on the paperclip icon to open the attachment. When the photo popped up, he squinted down at it. He and Jason had speculated, based on the bruising around the neck and the enlargement of the eyes. "We're thinking strangulation," he said confidently.

"So, what do you need me for, then?"

"I need you to cook me that great sauce of yours and then keep me warm at night."

"OK, I'll let you conduct the autopsy, whenever the body is defrosted." Michelle didn't laugh. Mike had a momentary pang of panic, thinking she might be pissed off at him.

"Michelle, you know there's a thousand things you may find that will help the investigation, even if the cause and time of death are known. Maybe there'll be traces of skin under his fingernails."

"Don't you forget it!" she retorted, this time with a playful lilt. "But for now, I have to wait, and you boys will have to be patient."

"You know we don't do patience well."

"I know. But there's nothing I can do."

"Were you at least able to do a visual inspection of the body?"

"Oh, yes I did," Michelle said with more enthusiasm than Mike appreciated. "I don't often get stiffs in such good shape."

"Were there any obvious indications of wounds, aside from the neck bruising?"

"No. No gunshots or knife wounds. No other bruises of significance. He's a football player, so there are some scars and some bruises consistent with his physical activity, but nothing obvious that could have caused his death." She paused, having said as much as her cautious doctor instincts would allow without performing the full autopsy. "So, get your cop ass down here before the sauce burns and we can talk about it all over pasta."

"You need a bottle of red to go with that?"

"Got it. What? You think I'm serving dinner in a barn?"

Mike burst out into a deep laugh. "I'll be there in twenty."

# Chapter 6 – Jimmy Football

Sunday, June 2

SUNDAY MORNING, MIKE AND JASON were back in the Lincoln on the way to Florham Park. Sully had questioned whether they might have handled a few of the player interviews on Saturday night, but Mike pointed out that it would be much more efficient to get them all in the same place. Plus, since they were already on overtime, they were trying to save his budget. That shut him up with a grumble.

The 24-hour news cycle was still fully focused on the mystery of Jimmy Rydell's murder. Without any new facts to report, the speculative theories became more and more far-fetched. A memorial of flowers, stuffed animals, and footballs sprang up outside the carousel in Central Park.

Kristi Olson's morning story in *The Times* again mentioned the rumored federal probe into point-shaving in NFL games. But she had no additional evidence to suggest Jimmy was involved, or even that the suspected probe existed.

Mike finally snapped off the sports talk radio. "Did Rachel get her sister to go to the show with her today?"

Jason, who was driving, nodded but kept his eyes on the road. "Yeah. Diana was apparently pretty psyched about it. I hear *Kinky Boots* is supposed to be pretty good, but I'm just as happy to skip it."

"Instead, we're off to dive into the soap opera that is Jimmy Freaking Rydell."

"Your boy Chip just couldn't stay away from him on draft day, I guess."

Mike glared at his partner, who was not looking at him. "First, Chip is not my boy. I'd be happy to have somebody else running my team. He's Woody's boy, which is why he's the GM and not running a casino into the ground. The old man's trying to groom him to take over when he's ready to step down, so he made the kid the GM. Chip thinks he's a genius, but he was born on third base and thinks he hit a triple. It was Woody who was in love with Jimmy Rydell, not Chip."

"You're pretty well versed in this, Mike. You'd think you were a rabid fan or something." Jason smiled as he continued to stare ahead at the curving lane of the Garden State Parkway.

"I have regrettably spent far too many of my valuable hours contemplating who should be the next draft pick for my Green Monsters. It's one of the great things about having Michelle around – it saves me from obsessing about meaningless bullshit that I have no control over."

"Does that include the Mets?"

"Hey, let's not go crazy. I'm not going to be able to beat that addiction so easily. Jimmy Rydell has been a train wreck since the day he was the number one pick. Lots of people questioned Woody's taking him, despite the Heisman Trophy. I mean, it *was* impressive how he took Mississippi State to the national championship. Nobody saw that coming. I read an article where

Woody gushed about how he loved the kid's story. Jimmy was in and out of foster homes and had a rugged childhood. I'm not sure why Woody, who was born into a rich family, had such a connection with a poor Black kid like Jimmy. He decided he wanted the kid on his team. He saw Jimmy as a leader and ordered Chip to trade up to get him."

"I didn't follow all that," Jason replied. "I didn't really care about the guy until he took a knee during the national anthem. I know he took a lot of shit over that. I feel for the kid, and respect him for doing it, knowing it was going to hurt him and open him up to the crazies."

"I've told you I disagree with you about respecting the flag and the national anthem, but you're right about him opening himself up to the crazies. I read that he got death threats. I'm sure there were plenty of folks ready to confront him whenever he went out."

"For sure. There's more white supremacists out there than you think."

Mike paused. "There are plenty of crazies out there who aren't total racists. But I guess that's why the team set him up with a bodyguard."

"You've never really seen racism in action, have you, Mike?" Jason turned his head to glance at his partner, before returning quickly to driving mode.

"I've been around the block a few times."

"Yeah, but it was a white block. I'm sure you've seen a lot, Mike, but you're a spectator, looking at it from the bleachers. You've never been down in the mud, looking up at it."

Quiet spread out like a stain inside the car while Mike decided how to respond. "You have a perspective on this I can't possibly have. I'll let you use that when we're talking to these guys. You can relate to the Black players better than I can, and if there are any closet racists among the White players, you'll probably get under their skin, which can be useful. Let's see where it gets us."

Then Mike changed the subject. "So, it's been almost three weeks since we got back from the cruise. Are you still taking your time before making any big life decisions?"

"Three weeks is a long time, Mike. That bullet wound in my arm is almost healed. I'm going to have a nice scar, but Rachel kinda likes it. She says it reminds her how I risked my life to protect her."

"She's still not letting go of that, eh?"

"No. She's like a bulldog. We've been spending all our time together since then. In fact, today will be the first time she's going out without me – and that's only because of the last-minute change of plans. I was going to take it slow, but Rachel isn't a patient woman. She clearly wants us to get engaged."

"I can't say I'm surprised. I like her. And Michelle loves her. But her biological clock is ticking. And if I can hear it, then it's pretty loud."

"I know. She's worried I'll string her along for a year and then dump her like her last boyfriend did. Then she'd be back at square one. She's not shy about telling me that getting married and having children is what she wants. I'm afraid I'll lose her unless I move."

"It's your life, Partner. I still think you shouldn't make a huge life decision so fast."

"You said wait a few weeks and see whether my heart still wanted it, Mike. Well, it's been three."

"OK. But, if you go ahead, you're gonna need a ring."

"I already thought of that." Jason reached two fingers into the pocket of his crisp robins-egg-blue dress shirt. They were both dressed for work since they were going to be deep in the investigation all day, and there would be press in the area. He handed Mike a thick white business card, trimmed in gold leaf. It was from the All-American Gem Company and had the name *Helene Rosen* written in gold script.

"Is she back already?"

"Yeah. I talked to her on Friday. Her guy, Henrick, got his visa and reopened his booth on 47th Street. She told me she had an emerald Rachel would love."

"Emerald? Is that Rachel's taste?"

"I remember how much she loved Mrs. Bloom's emerald ring on the cruise. I would go with a diamond, but Mrs. DiVito-Rosen said she remembered Rachel saying emeralds were her favorite stones."

"And you have to believe her," Mike said, then hesitated. The two partners then said at the same time, "Because she has a photogenic memory." They laughed loudly. Mike pointed to the road sign announcing their exit in one mile. "I guess you have to go with that. So, you're really going to buy a ring and propose?"

"You can't tell Michelle," Jason said seriously. "It's going to be a surprise. If Michelle spills it to Rachel, I will be pissed off at both of you for a year."

"Fine. You're asking me to keep secrets from Michelle. Wonderful. But of course I will. How long will I have to keep this big secret?"

"I have a reservation at *Le Renard Courrant* on Thursday night."

Mike turned his head toward Jason, puzzled. "What the hell is that?"

"It's the hottest new restaurant. It turns out Sophie from the records room has a niece who works as a hostess there, so she was able to get me a reservation. Rachel knows we're going there for her birthday. I have it all planned out how I'm going to surprise her."

"Well, nice job of planning – and keeping it a secret. What kind of food do they serve at this place?"

"It's a vegan French place."

"What does that mean?"

"I have no idea. I looked up the menu online and it's all in French. But it's the hottest place. I'm sure the food will be great."

"Have fun." Mike pointed again at their exit, which was coming up fast.

# Chapter 7 – Locker Room Testimonial

UNLIKE SATURDAY AFTERNOON, when the practice facility was mostly empty, on Sunday morning it was Grand Central Station with muscles. During the spring OTAs, players were permitted to work out without pads and without contact drills. All participation was technically voluntary, but every player who was serious about either making the team or making the team better was present.

There are only forty-five active players on an NFL team's roster during the season, but there were nearly a hundred milling about the practice facility, wearing shorts and cut-off t-shirts. There were also dozens of coaches and team officials, trainers, fresh-faced interns, and members of the press. Hundreds of fans, decked out in team jerseys and logo apparel, sat on metal bleachers or roamed behind the makeshift barriers separating them from their heroes.

The June sun was already beating down on the practice fields at 9:30 a.m. Mike's shirt collar immediately developed a dark stain. Jason, as always, looked cool. After a mild spring, summer was arriving early. The forecast was dry and hot for the next week, with a chance of isolated thunderstorms. They walked under a green canvas awning and pushed through the glass doors into the central administration building, where they were immediately greeted by the same brunette whom they had met the day before. She introduced herself as Tammy.

Tammy led them back out the door toward a pop-up tent with a green canvas roof, sitting on a patch of grass halfway between two practice fields. There was an arrangement of weight machines and other workout equipment sprawled out on a platform of interlocking black padded mats a few yards beyond the shelter, where a very sweaty group of players were hefting barbells. Tammy escorted the detectives to a portable table with four chairs arranged around it.

Before she walked away to fetch the first player they wanted to interview, Jason asked, "Until last Thursday, was Jimmy here for all the OTA workouts?"

Tammy responded immediately. "Absolutely! He was the last player off the field every practice day, and the last one out of the weight room on workout days. He was the quarterback, and he was working hard."

"That doesn't mesh with his reputation," Mike observed wryly.

Tammy lowered her eyes and smiled at the ground, with an expression Mike couldn't identify. It might have been remorse or melancholy. "Well, Detective, there are a lot of things about Jimmy that seem paradoxical." She turned and walked away crisply in her tight white pants and her hunter-green silk blouse.

By the time Mike and Jason had grabbed themselves bottles of water from the silver bucket filled with quickly melting ice on their table and extracted pads and pens from Jason's briefcase, the clip-clop of Tammy's heels approached on the concrete sidewalk. Behind her, offensive lineman Kevin Mahwah loped along with his eyes fixed on Tammy's ass. The huge man settled himself into a chair opposite the two detectives, took a towel from around his neck, and wiped the sweat off his face.

Mahwah was in his sixth professional season and had been named all-pro twice. He was the leader of the team's offensive linemen, known to fans as the *Jet Fuel Squad*. His mane of flowing golden hair and square chin with a pronounced cleft made him a media darling. At 6'6" and 320, he was a mountain with bright blue eyes and a winning smile. He relaxed into his seat and crossed his legs, looking confidently at the two policemen without a hint of trepidation.

Jason, as planned, took the lead. "We're very sorry about the loss of Jimmy Rydell." He paused, but got no reaction from Mahwah. "We're investigating the circumstances of his death, which we're presuming to be a homicide. Thank you for voluntarily speaking to us. Can you tell me when you last saw Jimmy?"

Mahwah's stone-face fluttered for a moment as he uncrossed his legs and leaned forward, placing his forearms on his massive thighs. "I'm guessing the reason y'all are here is that you already heard about the fight." Mahwah had a slight southern accent that Mike pegged for somewhere in the Carolinas. He knew the center had attended college at Duke, as had Jason. That was partly why they had selected Mahwah as their first interview.

Jason relaxed his posture and leaned back. "Yeah, we heard. I know how it is sometimes in the locker room. Coach Peterson once dressed me down good for slamming a wide receiver into the whirlpool in the trainer's room."

Mahwah raised an eyebrow. "When did you play?"

"From '07 to 2010. Peterson was only there a few years when I got there. I wasn't first team until senior year. The scholarship got me a degree, so I have no regrets. But like I said, I know how things get. We just need you to tell us what you saw and heard so we can try to piece it together and figure out whether it might have had any connection to his death."

"Nate's a good ol' boy, for sure, but there's no way he killed Jimmy." Mahwah sat up, glaring at Mike rather than Jason.

"I appreciate your perspective on that," Jason soothed. "Let's just go back to Wednesday and you tell us what happened."

Over the next twenty minutes, the big center emptied his memory under the gentle prodding of the two detectives. After the practice drills on Wednesday, the players hit the outdoor weight area, which they called "Muscle Beach," until about 3:00 p.m. Then, Mahwah announced to the other offensive lineman that he was leading a run around the complex. This was his usual routine, to help bond all the members of the Jet Fuel Squad. Jimmy went with them. These guys were his defense against serious injury every time he dropped back for a pass, so he treated them with respect and often lifted with them. They ran a three-mile circuit, finishing up in the locker room. He headed for his locker. He didn't see how it started, but the next thing he knew, Jimmy was down on one knee planting punches into the face of Nate Bedford.

"Were you surprised to see that?" Jason prodded.

"Well, Nate and Jimmy were never friendly, but when Jimmy went and screwed Nate's girl, well, that was out of bounds, man. I wasn't surprised they had it out."

Mike looked up from his notes. "So, you think the fight had something to do with a girl?"

"Oh, yeah. No question. Like I said, I didn't see how it started, but I heard afterwards Jimmy said something about Candi . . . and Nate took offense . . . and that's what got it going.

But, you know, those two had been sparring ever since Jimmy took a knee. Nate has a rebel flag on his truck; it was only a matter of time. So, you know, not a shock. Anyway, Jimmy was giving it to him pretty good, then a few of the guys jumped in, along with The Duke, and pulled Jimmy off so nobody got seriously hurt. Jimmy was OK with that. He'd gotten in his shots. Nate tried to go at him again, but the guys held him back. After a minute or two, things calmed down. I hit the shower, and when I came back out, they were both gone. I never saw Jimmy again."

Jason flipped through his pages of notes. "Aside from Nate, are you aware of anyone on the team who had a grudge against Jimmy?"

Mahwah frowned and took a few seconds to think. "There are plenty of boys in there who weren't happy with Jimmy. We're a team in there, so we need to pull together. I can't say everybody loved him, but we all respected him. I don't think anybody, Nate included, would intentionally harm Jimmy. He's our QB. We need him. Some guys might want to make him stand up during the anthem, but kill him? No way."

"Do you know of anyone else – on the team or otherwise – who might have wanted to hurt Jimmy?"

"Well, you know, there were plenty of haters out there in the world who didn't like Jimmy or what he stood for. Or kneeled for. But I don't know anyone in particular."

"Thank you, Kevin," Jason said, standing and extending his hand. "Thanks for talking to us. Please don't talk to the other players about our discussion. We need to let everybody tell their stories without being influenced. You understand?"

"Sure, man. No problem." Mahwah rose slowly like he was doing a leg press, shook Jason's hand, waved at Mike, and hurried away in the direction of Muscle Beach, leaving Mike and Jason to ponder what they had learned.

Mike glanced at his watch, which read 10:10 a.m. "How many players and coaches do we have on the list Malone gave us?"

"Eighteen, plus The Duke and two locker room attendants."

"We're never going to get through them all like this. We'd better split up and then regroup at the end of the day." At that moment, Tammy reappeared on cue to fetch them the next player on the list. They split up the names, except for Nate, who they wanted to talk with last. Tammy got on her phone and quickly arranged for a second location inside the main building lobby where Mike could set up shop. She spent the day shuttling players to their meetings with the detectives. She also brought in lunch, fetched cold drinks, and otherwise made them as comfortable as possible.

At 3:30 p.m., Jason walked into the main building and found Mike's interviewing station in the corner, next to a potted palm. They compared notes and tried to piece together what had happened between Nate and Jimmy.

Mike waited for Jason to pull up a folding chair before speaking. "Nothing like a good love triangle, eh?"

"Sprinkle in a healthy dose of racism and you've got a nasty stew."

"I know the kneeling protest was controversial and divisive," Mike said with a puzzled expression, "but I wouldn't say the problems in the locker room amounted to racism."

Jason exhaled a slow breath, composing himself so he wouldn't speak too quickly. "So, Mike, I'm assuming the players didn't tell you how much of a redneck racist Nate Bedford is, right?"

"A few of the guys told me Nate and Jimmy didn't get along, and that Nate and several of the other players were not happy about his pre-game protests."

"You mean the White players?"

Mike paused. "Yeah, I guess it was the White guys who had a problem with it. Some of the Black guys told me they were not excited about it, but they didn't say anything to anyone."

"Mike, the White players aren't going to admit to being racist. They're also going to protect their teammates. The Black players aren't going to open up to you and tell you, either."

"Why not?" Mike asked, annoyed at the idea.

"Because you're a White cop, and they don't know you. They assume you're not going to take them seriously and that you're not going to do anything about it. They figure you'll report what they say back to the coach and GM, so they just keep it to themselves."

"But they'll talk to you?"

"Yes, they'll be more honest with me. And I can read between the lines on this better than you, Mike."

"I'm not sure—"

"It's no knock on your interrogation skills. It's human nature. I know how it is, so they know I'll understand, and believe them, and take them seriously."

"And they're not worried about you ratting them out to the coach or the GM?"

"No. I wouldn't do that."

"Neither would I," Mike said defensively.

"I know that – but they don't. Don't feel bad – or judge them for it."

"So, what did they tell you that they didn't tell me, exactly?"

Jason summarized what he had gleaned from his interviews. There had been tension between Nate and Jimmy ever since

Jimmy showed up in camp as a rookie. Nate was an old-school southern redneck who didn't like a Black quarterback being the leader of the team. The receiver kept it to grumbling and verbal sparring until Jimmy started taking a pre-game knee. Nate wasn't the only White player who thought Jimmy was creating unnecessary controversy and disrespecting the national anthem. It caused a lot of problems. Some of the other players started getting into heated discussions about police brutality and racism. But Nate was the worst. Most of the Black players Jason spoke with were surprised they hadn't had a fight sooner. But when the girlfriend got involved, that was the last straw.

"Yeah," Mike jumped in, "pretty much everybody knew about the girlfriend situation. It was pretty underhanded for Jimmy to sleep with Nate's girl."

"So, what? You're on Nate's side here?"

"I'm not on any side," Mike snapped. "I couldn't give less of a shit. But several players – including a few of the Black players – said that it was crossing a line and breaking an unwritten rule for Jimmy to fool around with Nate's girlfriend."

"OK, I get that. So, Candi Nelson . . ." Jason flipped through his notes. "She's a stripper who works at the Stiletto club up by the stadium. Some of the players hang out there in their off time. It's not unusual for the players to date the strippers. The girls like the attention, and they tend not to be looking for marriage. Candi started showing up at practices and at the players' entrance after games last season. It was apparently a pretty long-term thing, relatively speaking. A month ago, Nate and Candi showed up at a club in Manhattan and found Jimmy there. The two guys had a confrontation when Nate made a comment about Jimmy's date, who was White."

"I didn't get that from anybody," Mike admitted. "What I couldn't piece together is why Candi would hook up with Jimmy if she was such a steady girl with Nate."

"I'm a little fuzzy on that too, but it seems Nate yelled at her in front of her friends one night, shortly after the incident at the nightclub. Candi wasn't happy about it, so they broke up for a bit. Jimmy made some comment about it on the first day of OTAs and Nate flipped out, so Jimmy said something about Candi needing a big black dick and the other guys had to separate them. A couple days later, Candi shows up in a convertible and picks Jimmy up after the workout and they drive away. Candi stops returning Nate's calls and texts. Jimmy starts telling everyone how great Candi is in the sack, but then Jimmy decides he's had enough of Candi, who runs back to Nate's arms. That was on Tuesday."

"That jibes with what I got," Mike said, consulting his notes. "Then, on Wednesday after practice, Nate said something to Jimmy – or Jimmy said something to Nate – and the two went at it. I got a lot of conflicting descriptions of the fight, but everyone agrees Jimmy had the better of the boxing. Nate ended up on the ground bleeding. Jimmy was on top of him, landing some solid shots. The players stepped in and broke it up, along with our Duke guy. Nate yelled something and Jimmy yelled something and eventually Jimmy hit the shower and Nate left. That's the last time anybody saw Jimmy. Is that about what you got?"

Jason flashed a self-satisfied smile. "I got a little more than that."

"From the Black players?"

"Yes, from the Black players." Jason read from his note pad. "I have two guys who say Nate said he was going to 'kill you, you nigger motherfucker,' and said, 'I'll cut off your dick' as they were holding Nate back from jumping on Jimmy again."

"Amazing how none of the players I spoke to heard that," Mike deadpanned.

"Like I said." Jason left it there.

"None of my witnesses identified anybody else who was mad enough at Jimmy to want to actually kill him, although there's certainly plenty of crazies in the world who could have killed him."

"For sure. But most of those crazies aren't smart enough to pull this one off."

"Freezing the body and then dumping it on the carousel seems like a calling card for Crazy & Company."

Jason laughed as he reached for a bottle of water. "I guess it's time to talk to Nate."

# Chapter 8 – Terrible Teammates

NATE BEDFORD LOPED into the administration building wearing his sweaty workout clothes, with a white towel around his neck. He was as tall as Jason but thinner, with long arms and legs featuring boney joints. A blond crewcut made his square jaw stand out like a transformer robot. His skin was tanned and well-exposed by his cut-off, sweat-stained t-shirt. He flashed a sparkling smile that Mike supposed impressed the ladies, but quickly lost it when the two cops gave him only a poker-faced stare. He plopped into the chair opposite the two besuited detectives, crossed his legs, and relaxed into a reclining posture.

Jason launched into the questioning, treating Nate like a suspect, except without reading the man his Miranda rights. He and Mike had discussed the risks of not being able to use any admissions he might make against the advantages of not encouraging him to lawyer up. They decided they needed the information, and there was little chance of Nate confessing at the first interview.

"We've heard from a number of your teammates that you and Jimmy had a fight in the locker room at the end of the day on

Wednesday. Can you tell us what led up to the fight, and what happened in the locker room?"

Nate, who had been wearing a smirk, uncrossed his legs and sat forward with a more serious expression. "What'd you say your name was?" Jason knew Nate was from Alabama and he had the southern accent to go with it.

"I'm Detective Jason Dickson. This is Detective Mike Stoneman." Jason motioned toward Mike, who sat impassively.

"Sure. Well, I think I do recall Jimmy and I gettin' into it a bit. You know how it is sometimes, between men, right? We had a little disagreement, we decided to settle it like men. It was no big deal."

Jason glared at Nate, who was directing his answer toward Mike. "We understand the disagreement involved Jimmy's relationship with a young woman named Candi?"

Nate looked like he had just sucked on a lemon. "Yeah, well . . . it's true that Jimmy said a few things about my girl that got me riled up."

"Your girl?" Jason interrupted. "I thought Jimmy was screwing her?"

"Who told you that?" Nate shot back. When Jason didn't reply, Nate continued haltingly. "Well, I guess that was technically true. But she was my girl, and she's my girl now. Jimmy was cuttin' in on me, and I was pissed off at him. He got what he deserved."

"We heard it was you who got the business end of the punches. We heard Jimmy kicked your ass."

"That's a fuckin' lie!" Nate yelled. "I got in as many as he did. He was a bloody mess when they pulled me off him."

"We heard the other players pulled Jimmy off you – that you were on the ground and he was sitting on your chest. We heard the blood was all yours."

"That's bullshit! That's not how it happened."

"Well, tell us how it happened," Jason prodded, pleased he had the man upset and defensive. Suspects tended to say incriminating things when in such a state.

"He said something about Candi, and I yelled something back at him, and then he took a few steps toward me and said something like, 'Do you want a piece of me?' and I said, 'Sure,' and then I clocked him with a left and then I don't recall exactly who hit who next. But it lasted a minute or so and then the other guys pulled us apart and then Jimmy left. That's how I remember it."

Jason leaned forward. "When the guys were pulling you two apart, do you remember yelling anything at Jimmy?"

"Naw. I remember I was pretty upset, an' I may have been cussin' or yellin', but I don't know what I said."

"So, you don't remember calling Jimmy a nigger and a motherfucker?"

Nate flinched, but retained his good-old-boy smile. "Naw, I don't remember that."

"Isn't it true, Nate, that you and Jimmy had been feuding ever since Jimmy took a knee during the national anthem to protest police brutality against Black people?"

"Hey, his disrespect for the flag wasn't no protest."

"No?" Jason kept his voice even. "What do you think it was?"

Nate re-crossed his legs and sat back in the tiny chair. "I think he was just showboatin' and lookin' for attention. He thought he was so fuckin' smart. He was just embarassin' himself, and all the rest of us."

"So, you did have a disagreement with Jimmy over that?"

"Sure. I didn't take kindly to him pissin' on the flag, if that's what you mean."

Jason stood up, towering over the seated man. "Several witnesses said you threatened to kill Jimmy and cut off his dick. Do you remember that?"

"Oh, man, I don't know what I said. I told you that already. I don't know." Nate looked at Mike, as if searching for an ally. Mike kept his poker face firmly in place.

Jason sat back down and changed the subject. "What happened afterward? What did you do after practice on Wednesday?"

"Well, lemme see. I met up with Candi. She's my girl, no matter what anybody says. She picked me up and we went back to her place. We went back to her apartment an' we stayed in the rest of the night."

"You and Candi are back together?"

"Yeah. We are."

"What did you two do that evening at her place?"

"You know, man. We watched some TV, and maybe had a little roll in the sheets."

"Did you spend the night?"

"Nah. I left and went home. I had practice on Thursday morning, so, ya know, I had to get some sleep."

"Where do you live, Nate?"

"I'd prefer you call me Mr. Bedford, and I live in Jersey City."

"If Candi picked you up after practice and drove you to her place, how did you get from there to Jersey City?"

"In my truck. I left it at her place the night before. She drove me to practice on Wednesday morning."

"Did you spend Tuesday night there?"

"Yeah, I did," Nate said defiantly.

"Was that the first night you spent together after Jimmy broke off the relationship with her?"

"She dumped Jimmy! Not the other way 'round."

"OK, fine. So, you spent the night on Tuesday, but not on Wednesday, because you needed to get some sleep. I guess you didn't get enough sleep on Tuesday night, eh? Is that why she drove you Wednesday morning?"

"Yeah, somethin' like that," Nate said, smiling, as if sharing a masculine secret with the two detectives.

"Does your apartment building in Jersey City have a doorman?"

"Yeah, I think so, but I park in the garage and take the elevator, so I didn't see no doorman."

"What time did you get back to your apartment on Wednesday night?"

"I don't remember." Nate stared at the water bottle on the table next to Mike, not making eye contact with Jason. "Say, you mind if I grab that water?"

"Go ahead," Mike said, pushing the plastic bottle toward the wide receiver. Nate grabbed it and downed half the contents in one long swig.

"Did you see Jimmy again, after you and Candi left here on Wednesday?"

"No. I didn't. He skipped out on practice Thursday and was a no-show again on Friday. I never saw the – never saw him after that."

"What were you going to say, Nate?" Jason prodded. "You were going to call him a nigger?"

"Nah," Nate said, waving his hand toward Jason. "I was gonna call him a bastard."

"OK. Thanks for the honesty. We're going to need to talk to Candi."

Nate's face momentarily lost its confident smugness. "Candi don't need to be dragged into this. She wasn't there."

Jason watched Nate's eyes while he pretended to think about possibly not insisting on getting Candi's phone number. "I promise we'll be nice to her, Nate, but you've told us a story that includes her, so we're going to need to confirm it."

Nate's eyes flashed over to Mike, checking to see if he might appeal to the older cop. He didn't get any encouragement.

"OK, fine. I'll give you her cell number."

Mike handed over a pad of blank paper and a pen. "While you're at it, you can write down the license plate number of your truck. It will save us from getting it from DMV."

"Why?" Nate frowned as he stood up to receive the pad.

"It's just routine," Jason said simply.

"Yeah, well, fine." He wrote down Candi's number and his license plate number and handed the pad back to Mike. A moment later, he walked away without looking back.

After the glass doors had closed behind him, Mike said, "The fact that he's lying doesn't mean he killed Jimmy."

"Yeah, Mike. But it certainly puts him at the top of the suspect list, at least for now."

# Chapter 9 – The Power of the Pen

WHILE JASON WAS QUESTIONING PLAYERS under the pop-up tent, *New York Times* sports reporter Kristi Olsen was working her way around the practice complex. Like most days, she tried not to call attention to herself. She was an athletic 5'6", but chose to wear loose-fitting pants and a nondescript beige top with short sleeves. It kept her cool in the warm June sun, but showed off as little skin as possible. A wide-brimmed sun hat swallowed up her golden hair, which was confined in a bun. No jewelry adorned her ears or neck, only an ample treatment of sunscreen. Her black-rimmed sunglasses made her look like a kindergarten teacher out patrolling recess in the schoolyard. As a regular among the press corps, the players and team officials treated her like a piece of the furniture – which was just the way she wanted it.

She had noticed Kevin Mahwah ambling over to the pop-up tent where the two detectives had set up shop. Dexter Peacock, her reluctant byline partner on the Saturday story about Jimmy Rydell's murder, had clued her in about Mike Stoneman and Jason Dickson. They would have stood out regardless in their jackets and ties. When she saw Mahwah leave the tent and head over to Muscle Beach, she glided in that direction. The players liked showing off to each other, but they *loved* showing off their muscles to the public and the press. The team had set up Muscle Beach because the head strength and conditioning coach promised the players would spend more time lifting if they had an audience. He was completely right.

Kristi knew better than to try to conduct an interview inside the iron sanctum, but she casually walked by, got Mahwah's attention, and asked politely if she could catch him later for a quick quote. She knew Kevin was one of the more reliable team leaders when it came to both being accessible to the press and having something intelligent to say. Such athletes were rare and had to be cultivated. After Mahwah waved back at her to indicate his agreement and shouted that she should give him forty-five minutes or so, she circumnavigated the Muscle Beach area to see if there were any other receptive faces currently working out. Unfortunately, she didn't see Buzz Villano, who was face-down on a bench doing lateral arm lifts. When he came up for air, she quickly turned her head to the side. She knew what was coming and braced herself. She didn't change her path or her speed, but she battened down her emotional hatches.

"Hey, look! It's sweet Kristi Brinkley. Hey, babe – you wanna come over here and lift my weights?"

Kristi ignored the oaf and calmly walked ahead.

"Oh, come on, Kristi. Come sit on my face while I do my sit-ups." Renfroe, a tight end, burst into a deep, rumbling laugh, joined by several of the other nearby weightlifters. Mahwah was not among those partaking in the juvenile humor.

There were so many witty comebacks Kristi thought about in moments like these, but she knew better. Engaging with them only made it worse, and these boys were immune to any shame. Anything intellectual or subtle would go right over their heads, and there was nobody else there to appreciate it. Anything crude would only encourage their next volley and would further diminish her standing in their eyes. She was already thought of mostly as the token female among the team's beat writers. They didn't take her seriously, even though she knew more about football, strategy, and the business end of the game than any of them. But she kept that to herself. She had a job to do, and no matter what she had to endure, she focused on reporting as her primary objective. Payback would come in the form of her published words – but only when they were entirely based on the players' on-field performance.

As she stood on the walkway, considering her next destination, she felt a gentle tap on her shoulder. When she turned, she saw the warm, smiling face of Woody O'Meara. Kristi liked Woody, who was always a gentleman with her. She sometimes felt he treated her like his granddaughter, but he also sometimes tossed her little crumbs of information that he wanted to get out to the press. He liked to cultivate the impression that he was a doddering old man, but he was still sharp and shrewd.

"Do you have your sunblock on, young lady?" Woody asked with genuine concern.

"I do," Kristi said, "and several players have offered to rub on more."

Woody waved his hand. "As long as they don't do it without permission." He laughed at his own joke.

Kristi laughed briefly, but then he took on an unexpectedly serious tone. "Mr. O'Meara, I'm glad I ran into you. I want to tell you I'm sorry to lose Jimmy. Not just because of his talent, but because I respected him as a man."

"As did I," Woody responded. "Well, please keep up your good work." He waved and set off toward his office in the administration building.

Walking away from Muscle Beach, Kristi spotted a cluster of players on a side field. She picked up her pace and headed in that direction. Among all the beat writers, Kristi was the only one who ever paid any attention to Stuart Schwartz. He had been on the roster for seven seasons, making him the player with the longest continuous time with the team. Despite his seniority, few fans knew his name. For the coaches, however, he was a vital cog. He was integral to some of the most critical plays every game. He was the long snapper – the one who fired the ball back to the punter or the holder on field goal attempts. A mistake by the snapper could be disaster on a punt, and on field goals his snap had to be straight, hard, and true to cash in on three hard-earned points. The long snap was an art and a practiced skill that every team needed. Schwartz had been as reliable as anyone in the NFL, but snapper was not a glamorous role. The newspapers printed the snapper's name only when he screwed up. Schwartz had managed to remain entirely anonymous, which meant he was nearly perfect at his craft.

Kristi strolled up to the kickers and watched for a few minutes, after making eye contact with Schwartz. When the placekickers were ready to take a break, the snapper wandered over to the edge of the field. Kristi had helpfully procured a container of sports drink, which she handed to Schwartz.

"Did the cops talk to you yet, Stuart?"

"No. I don't think I'm on the guest list. We were still out on the field on Wednesday when the fight happened, so I'm not an eyewitness to anything."

"Are you hearing what kind of questions they're asking?"

"Mostly about the fight, I hear. But also about Candi and how Jimmy seduced her, and how mad that made old Nate. I hear that was the reason for the fight, so that makes sense."

"Have you seen Candi around today?"

"No. Nate drove his truck in this morning. It's not a big public day on a Sunday, plus I think she's working this afternoon."

"What do you hear about her and Nate?"

"Well, Kristi, you didn't hear this from me."

"Of course not," Kristi replied quickly. "Strictly off the record."

"OK. Candi and Nate got back together, and Nate went home with her after the fight on Wednesday. But after that, they haven't been together, and a couple guys say she had a black eye and a fat lip at the club on Thursday. She told them Nate hit her and she threw him out again. She hasn't been around the field since then, which is pretty unusual for her, so it's probably true."

"Thanks, Stu. I appreciate it." Kristi turned away and walked back toward Muscle Beach. She found a bench and sat down to make some notes. As she was staring at her notebook with a ballpoint pen in her mouth, a small cluster of players ambled past, headed to the locker room.

A second-year linebacker nudged his teammate, then called out, "Hey, Kristi, you'd look better with my dick in your mouth 'steada that pen." He laughed heartily, as did his mates. They slapped each other on their backs and rolled away down the path toward the players' sanctuary.

Kristi rolled her neck to the left, then right, then back, looking up at the puffy cumulous clouds meandering across the New Jersey sky. She removed the pen from her mouth and returned to her notes. She had a good lead and wanted to get a story tapped out on her laptop as soon as possible.

# Chapter 10 – A Cold Trail

WHEN MOST OF THE PLAYERS were either gone or hanging out in the locker room, Mike and Jason compared notes and waited for Tammy to fetch Duke Drepp. They had saved him for last, figuring he was the most able to wait. They heard Tammy's pumps clacking on the marble floor before they saw the mountain of muscles trailing after her.

Before he sat down, Jason asked, "So, Duke, tell us why you let Jimmy get into a fist fight. Wasn't it your job to keep him out of trouble?"

The Duke stopped halfway down into his chair and snapped back before his butt hit the seat. "Hey, I'm not washing his dick in the shower, man. It was in the fuckin' locker room."

"You spend a lot of time thinking about washing Jimmy's dick?"

Mike winced as metal chair legs grated across the tile floor with a screech, followed by a crash of metal against marble. After kicking over his chair, The Duke leaned forward, his waist pressed against the flimsy table and fire in his eyes. His nostrils flared like a bull's. "What the fuck is that supposed to mean!?"

Jason sat motionless, looking up into steel-blue eyes. "You mentioned Jimmy's dick, it seemed like you might be a little obsessed."

The Duke stepped back, found his chair where it had fallen, and regained his composure. When he had settled back down and crossed his legs, Mike took over the questioning.

"Mr. Drepp, please take us through what you remember about Wednesday afternoon in the locker room."

The Duke gave an account that sounded rehearsed, which was not surprising. He'd had all day to think about what he was going to say, which was why Jason wanted to get him off his guard at the start of the session. According to the bodyguard, he was hanging out with several of the players and kicking their asses at *Call of Duty*. When Jimmy got into it with Nate in the adjacent area, he didn't immediately intervene. He said Jimmy was handling things fine without him. He had drifted over to where the fight was happening. Several other players pulled Jimmy off Nate, and then The Duke jumped in.

"I didn't want Jimmy to mess up Nate too bad. That wouldn't help the team, and that's bad for Jimmy. My instructions are to make sure Jimmy doesn't get into trouble, and that would have been trouble."

"Fair enough," Mike said, ending the portion of the discussion where they already knew the answers. "Now, tell us about the rest of the day. Did you drive Jimmy back to his apartment?"

"Sure. I always do."

"What was Jimmy's mood during the ride home? What did he say about what happened?"

A vein on the side of the big man's temple was bulging and throbbing. The Duke clenched his jaw. "He was pretty quiet, now that you ask. He didn't say anything."

"No cussing about that redneck racist, Nate Bedford?" Jason prodded.

"He ain't no racist!"

"What did Jimmy think about that?"

"Like I said, he didn't say nothin'."

Jason sat forward for the first time since The Duke arrived. "Not ever? You're telling me in all the time you were hanging out with Jimmy, he never said a bad word about Nate?"

The Duke's fists were clenched in his lap. "I don't talk about what Jimmy says in private." He stared down Jason in silence.

"Well," Mike said in a soothing voice, "Jimmy isn't accused of killing Nate, so I guess it doesn't matter much what Jimmy said or didn't say. How about you tell us why you weren't around at the time Jimmy was murdered?"

"I had the night off," he said, sitting back once again and composing himself. "Jimmy said he didn't need me. He said he wasn't going out. I wanted to go see the new *John Wick* movie. So, I drove home, went to the theater around the corner, and watched the movie. Then I went home and went to bed. The next morning, I went to pick up Jimmy, but he never came down to meet me."

"How did you pay for the movie ticket?" Mike asked.

"Cash. I try never to use credit."

"Did you call Jimmy, or text with him that night?"

"Probably. We usually do to confirm the pickup time for the next morning. I don't really remember."

"OK, Mr. Drepp. Thank you for your cooperation." Mike stood up and offered his hand. The bodyguard's huge hand engulfed Mike's and squeezed hard. "We'll let you know if we need to ask you any more questions."

The Duke walked away, without offering to shake Jason's hand. When he was outside, Jason stood and stretched. "That guy is a racist bastard."

"That's a pretty harsh evaluation, Partner."

"You disagree? You have a more sensitive redneck radar?"

"I didn't say that. I just said it was harsh. Do we have any reason to question his story?"

"No, but I'm going to check out whether *John Wick* was playing at that theater Wednesday night. We've got his address from the GM's office, right?"

"Yeah, we have it." Mike pulled a sheet of paper out of a vinyl folio and handed it over. "You can have the follow-up on Mr. Muscles."

They both looked up when the front door opened again and Kristi Olsen walked through. Mike paid little attention; he didn't recognize her and figured she had some business in the administrative office.

Instead, she walked directly to the detectives, flashing a warm smile. "Detectives Stoneman and Dickson, I presume?"

Mike nodded but didn't reply.

"I don't suppose you'd like to share all the information you gathered today with *The New York Times*?" she said lightly, with a self-deprecating laugh.

Mike couldn't help but chuckle back. "You suppose correctly. I'm sorry, but I didn't catch your name."

"Kristi. Kristi Olsen," she said, extending her small hand with its naked, clipped nails. Mike gave it a short shake. "I'm the beat reporter for the paper, so I know most of the players pretty well. I also know who's sleeping with whom and which of the girlfriends are into threesomes, but I would never write about that because I have journalistic standards."

"I liked the piece you and Peacock wrote Saturday about Jimmy's death," Jason said. "Was that you, mostly?"

"It was a dual byline."

"Sure it was, but I've read Peacock's stuff and that didn't seem much like him."

Kristi inclined her head but didn't confirm Jason's speculation. "Do you have all the information you need about Candi Nelson?"

"What can you tell us about her that we don't already know?"

"That all depends on what you know, and what you're willing to share." Kristi raised one eyebrow suggestively.

"Ms. Olsen," Mike put on his fatherly good-cop voice, "I'm afraid we really can't comment on a pending investigation."

"Of course you can't," Kristi replied cheerfully. "But would you be interested in knowing whether Candi and Nate Bedford broke up on Wednesday night after he smacked her?"

"Who told you that?" Jason perked up.

"I'm afraid my sources are confidential, Detective Dickson. But I suspect that when you talk to Candi, she won't lie about it."

"Well," Mike said, "then we would have found out without your information. But thank you. If it's true, it's certainly interesting."

The fact that the detectives had not heard the news validated what Schwartz had told her. "I can also tell you she's working tonight. Do you know the place?"

"We do, thank you," Jason replied curtly, not wanting to get too deep into a conversation with a reporter.

"You're welcome," she said, smiling. "One more thing; no charge. On Thursday, when Jimmy was a no-show at practice,

I was poking around to see if anybody knew anything. Nobody did. So, I called his agent, Aaron Taylor, who said he hadn't heard from Jimmy. He said that wasn't unusual, but he was supposed to have a meeting with Jimmy on Friday. I asked everyone who was here on Friday. Nobody knew where he was and nobody had heard from him. I guess now we know why."

Mike nodded and thanked Kristi for the information. He said they would follow up on it.

Before she left, Kristi and Mike spent a minute talking about the Mets and their impressive rookie first baseman, Pete Alonso. Kristi confided that her colleague, the beat reporter for the Mets, thought Alonso was one of the sweetest and most unassuming young players he had seen come up to the majors since David Wright.

Mike told Kristi he was taking his godson, Tony, to the Mets game on Thursday night. Tony's father, Darin Curran, had been Mike's partner until he was injured on the job.

Kristi offered to set Mike and his godson up with field passes for batting practice before the game. She explained that the team's public relations manager, Jay Horowitz, was a good friend and an amazingly nice man. He would be happy to do a favor for the son of a hero cop. Mike thanked her.

"I'm hoping you'll have the chance to return the favor."

"You sound like Dexter Peacock," Mike said derisively.

"No. I don't." Kristi replied, then turned and walked away.

Mike and Jason packed up their notes, made their good-byes to Tammy, and headed for the Lincoln. As they pulled away,

Mike called in a DMV and EZ-Pass check on Nate's truck. Then he dialed Michelle. "Any update on the defrosting process?"

Michelle sounded disappointed. "No. Well, yes, some progress, but not enough for me to do an autopsy today. I'm hoping by tomorrow."

"So, no new information?"

"Sorry, Mike. Nothing. Maybe tomorrow."

Mike tapped the END button, then relayed the bad news to Jason.

Jason stared ahead, following the GPS directions coming from his phone to navigate them back toward I-78. "The trail is already cold," Jason said without any hint of irony.

"Frozen, more like." Mike stared out the side window at the manicured lawns passing by in front of enormous houses. He wondered how anyone could live inside all that empty space. "We'll try to get to Candi tonight, but I doubt she's going to have an explanation for what happened to Jimmy Wednesday night."

"Or why somebody froze his body, kept him on ice for a couple of days, then dumped him in the carousel in Central Park. Who does that?"

Mike continued gazing out the window, away from Jason. "Somebody who's worried about the autopsy? They froze the body to mess up our ability to get evidence from it?"

"Then why not just dump the body in the river, or burn it, or otherwise make it disappear? Why keep it for two days, then let us have it?"

Mike turned back toward his partner. "I have no fucking clue."

# Chapter 11 – Candi Land

THIRTY MINUTES LATER, Jason pulled the Lincoln into the continuous pothole that was the parking lot of Stilettos gentleman's club, off Paterson Plank Road behind the Meadowlands Sports Complex. On a game day, the place would have been hopping. On a warm June Sunday at six o'clock, there were only ten vehicles in the lot, more than half of them pickup trucks.

"I'm sure the dinner buffet's terrific," Jason deadpanned as they approached the chipped red paint that served as a door.

Inside, the space was large enough to handle 150 people, but was hosting fewer than a dozen. A thumping bass beat blared from ceiling-mounted speakers, accompanying a song Mike did not recognize. A large U-shaped runway stage dominated the front of the room, with chairs lined up along the brass rail and small tables scattered around the middle of the center lagoon. Larger tables with vinyl booths lined the outer walls. The rear wall was a long bar, where liquor bottles of all shapes and sizes shined against a giant mirror. Mike could see a buxom brunette in a bustier behind the bar, cleaning a drinking glass with a white towel. On the brightly lit stage, two girls gyrated around steel poles with bored expressions. A cluster of young men grouped together at one end, hooting toward a blonde wearing white stockings and garters. A smaller group was at the other corner of the "U" near a redhead, whose sequined bikini top lay crumpled at the base of her pole.

Mike turned away from the stage and scanned the rest of the room, where several other girls wandered between the tables soliciting the stray spectators for lap dances. A few were seated at the rear bar. One of the trollers changed course and moved in the direction of the new arrivals. Mike motioned to Jason to stop walking, waiting for the woman to arrive.

When she reached the pair of detectives, Mike stepped forward and held up his hand. Without any introduction, he called out above the thumping music, "Which one of you is Candi?"

The young woman, wearing a sheer nylon jacket with a blue boa, pouted at Mike's specific request for another girl, but pointed to a booth on the side where three ladies were hunched over bottles of water. Mike thanked her and walked slowly to the booth, with Jason trailing behind. After he asked again who Candi was, a redhead in a skintight scarlet body stocking raised her head and smiled at Mike, then at Jason. Mike thought she smiled more suggestively toward his partner. Candi shooed the other dancers away so the three of them could have the booth to themselves.

Mike jumped right in and advised Candi that they were NYPD, flashing his badge and saying he wanted to talk about Nate Bedford.

"You arresting me?" she asked, sitting forward so her barely confined breasts rested on the tabletop.

"No. You're not a suspect or under arrest. We just want to ask you a few questions." Mike had to speak much more loudly than he would have liked in order to be heard above the music. The song had changed, but the volume was still deafening.

Candi shrugged. "In here, I can't sit and talk unless you buy me a drink."

"Fine," Mike said, half to Candi and half to Jason. He nodded that Jason should go fetch the waitress and told him to get sodas for them, since they were still on the clock. Then he turned back to the buxom dancer. As he formulated his first question, he was also thinking about how he was going to describe this scene to Michelle later.

"Our information is you're dating Nate. Is that right?"

"No, Officer. You're behind the times."

"It's Detective," Mike said, again straining to be heard above the music.

"What?" Candi called back, holding a hand to her ear.

"Never mind. Are you saying you and Nate have split up again?"

"Whaddaya mean, again?"

"We heard you left Nate for Jimmy Rydell a few weeks ago."

"That's not true. Well, not exactly. I never broke up with Nate. I was pissed at him. And I did fuck Jimmy a few times, but that was just for fun – and maybe to make Nate jealous a little."

Jason returned, followed by a petite waitress with a tiny round tray and an even tinier mini-skirt. She flipped her bob of brown hair and set down their drinks – two tall, skinny glasses filled with ice and a tiny amount of soda for the detectives, and a martini glass with a zigzag stem for Candi.

"I didn't see you place an order," Mike observed.

"Tina knows what I want," she replied casually.

Mike moved over to allow Jason some room. "Miss Nelson – is Candi your real first name?"

"Yeah. It's actually Candice, but I've been Candi all my life. It just happens to be a great stripper name, too."

Mike half-turned toward Jason to invite him into the discussion. "Miss Nelson told me she didn't actually break up with Nate when she was sleeping with Jimmy, but she is now no longer with him."

"Is that so?" Jason raised an eyebrow. "What happened recently that's worse than sleeping with his quarterback?"

The volume of the music lowered several notches at that point. The dancers who had been on the stage were packing up their outfits and the few bills scattered on the hardwood. It seemed there would be a break in the performances, at least for a few minutes. Mike and Jason were happy they didn't need to shout to be heard.

Candi sipped her martini, leaving a bright red lipstick stain on the rim. "I ain't gonna stay with any man who hits me." She looked up with fire in her coffee-colored eyes.

Mike said, "Why don't you tell us what happened on Wednesday? You knew that Nate and Jimmy got into a fight, right?"

"Yeah. Nate told me he beat the shit outta Jimmy, but he looked pretty bad, so I didn't believe him. He had a cut lip and a bloody nose and his shirt had blood all down the front when he came out from the locker room. He jumped in the car an' I had to kick him out to clean up so he didn't get blood all over my seat."

"Then what happened?" Mike prodded when she went for another sip of her drink.

"We went back to my place an' he took a shower. We stayed in 'cause he didn't have any clothes to change into, so he didn't want to go out. That kinda sucked 'cause I didn't have nothing to cook, so I was kinda pissed off. We ordered a pizza. Then we had a few drinks and screwed for a while. He fell asleep and I called up one of my girlfriends and hung out for a while online." She paused and closed her eyes. When she looked at Mike, they had a misty glaze in them. "He woke up an' heard me talking and yelled at me for cheatin' on him again. I yelled back that it was just a girlfriend, but he was crazy. He grabbed me by the arm and . . . and then he hit me."

Mike stayed silent, not wanting to interrupt her narrative. He motioned with his hand that he wanted Candi to continue.

"I told him to get the fuck out of my house. Then he slapped me and I threw an ashtray at him. I picked up his dirty clothes and threw 'em out into the hallway and I got my phone and started to dial 9-1-1. I told him to get out or I'd call the cops. I don't let no man hit me." Tina, the waitress, walked by and Candi motioned for another round. If the detectives weren't going to ask for lap dances, she wanted to milk as much as possible out of them. "He called me a cunt, and some other things, an' then he left."

Mike nodded sympathetically. "I can't stand a man who'd hit a lady."

"Yeah, well, neither can I," Candi spat out.

"I'm afraid that, as a cop, I really need to know everything you can remember about what Nate said."

She drained her glass, seeming to think about the question. "He was pissed off and maybe still a little drunk. He had like half a bottle of Jack. I can't remember exactly."

"Did he say anything about Jimmy?"

Candi looked into Mike's eyes, hesitating. "Not exactly."

Jason intercepted Candi's next martini and tipped Tina, then carefully floated the new glass down onto the table. "What do you mean by 'not exactly?'"

Candi took a long sip from the fresh glass, then took out the toothpick and sucked the green olive off its end. "He called me a two-bit whore for sucking Jimmy's black dick."

"Did that piss you off?" Jason prodded.

"You bet your ass! Nate was fun and all, but Jimmy was a gentleman. He treated me so nice. I know he just wanted to make Nate crazy, but I was OK with that an' I had fun with Jimmy. I was so pissed off. I may have said something about Jimmy kicking his ass and how Jimmy's dick was bigger than Nate's . . . and how Jimmy's a better man than Nate will ever be. Or something like that."

"Did Nate say anything back?"

"Nah. He just called me a bitch and slammed the door. I was still holding my phone."

"What time was that, about?" Mike asked.

"I dunno. Probably around eleven-thirty or so."

"How'd Nate get home if you drove him there?" Mike cut in.

"He had his truck there from the night before. He wanted me to drive him to practice and pick him up after. I think he thought it would be a big 'fuck you' to Jimmy if he saw me choosing Nate, so it was fine with me. I guess I kinda liked the idea of those two fightin' over me."

"Not anymore, though?"

"Hell no! He's history. I haven't seen him since, an' I don't want to." She drained her second glass and set it down carefully on the wood surface.

"Do you know where Nate went when he left your place?" Mike tried to keep her talking before she had another drink.

"Nah. I heard him leave. He probably went to his place in Jersey City. But I can't really say. Now, one of you nice gentlemen want to have a dance with me?"

Mike politely declined the offer, explaining they were on duty. Tina appeared with an outrageously large bill for the two rounds of drinks, although neither Mike nor Jason had finished their first Diet Coke and their second round had never even arrived. They confirmed that the phone number Nate provided for Candi was accurate, then walked out of the dark club into the early-evening sunshine.

Mike studied the credit card receipt. "Sully's going to love it when I submit this one."

Jason chuckled. "Well, that's how these girls make a living – overcharging on the drinks for guys who want a few minutes of conversation."

As they carefully stepped over the detritus in the parking lot toward the Lincoln, Mike gave voice to what they were both thinking. "Nate left late Wednesday night, at least slightly drunk. He was pissed off that Jimmy beat him bloody and pissed off that his girl just threw him out, which he also blamed on Jimmy. At least, that's what he was probably thinking."

"You're right about that," Jason agreed.

"He got in his truck – angry and wanting to get some revenge – and he drove where?"

"We don't know, Mike. He could have gone home and slept it off. Or, he could have gone into Manhattan, found Jimmy, killed him, somehow got him out of the building without anyone seeing him, and dumped the body in a freezer."

"And then, two days later he retrieved the body and deposited it on the Central Park carousel? Does that make any possible sense?"

"The 'killing Jimmy in a fit of jealous rage' part does," Jason said, "but the rest makes no sense at all. It's still the big mystery here. Who the hell would kill Jimmy Wednesday night, then freeze him and dump the body in plain sight on Saturday?"

"I was thinking maybe somebody kidnapped him, but there was no ransom demand."

"Yeah. Lots of possibilities, Mike. But like you always say, our job is not to speculate – at least not until we have enough facts."

"You gotta stop quoting me to me, Kid."

Jason burst out laughing and unlocked the car doors with a click of his key fob. "I used to hate it when you called me Kid. But now that you're an old man, I'm thinking I like it."

"Screw you," Mike said with a smile as he got into the passenger seat. He checked his phone for email and tapped open a message from Central Dispatch. Somebody had run Nate's license plate while they were in talking to Candi.

"Check this," Mike said as Jason pulled out onto the street. "Nate's truck came up on the computer with a traffic stop at one-thirty Thursday morning. Wanna guess where?"

"Riverside Drive?"

"Close. The West Side Highway."

"Now what would Nate have been doing on the west side of Manhattan at that time of night when he lives in Jersey City and had practice the next morning?"

"We're going to have to talk to the uniforms who pulled him over before we go back to him. Add one more item to our list of things to do on this case tomorrow."

## Chapter 12 – Loose Ends

ON SUNDAY NIGHT, a little before midnight, a tall, muscular figure rounded the corner of Freedom Place and 71st Street. He walked purposefully down the sidewalk heading west, hugging the edge of Park Towers. The man was dressed in dark clothing and wore a knit hat, despite the mild June night. He slowed when he approached a huddle of shadows pushed up against the building over a metal grate that served as the exhaust from the building's HVAC system. In the middle of the block, there was only a security light above a nearby service door, along with the ambient light of New York City, to illuminate the scene. A wire basket filled with unrecognizable debris guarded the entrance to a rectangle of brown cardboard laying on the grate. A lump of blankets filled the interior of the paper shelter.

The man kicked the cardboard, creating a loud bang on the quiet street. "Hey!" he called out in a hushed exclamation. The lump of blankets moved, but only a little. He kicked again, twice, before the lump started to resemble a human figure.

"What the fuck?" Tiger called out. "I ain't botherin' nobody. Leave me alone, man." The young Black man crawled from his shelter, sleep in his eyes. Even in the darkness the circle of lighter skin on his chin, surrounded by a ring of wispy, dark hair, stood out. He squinted, trying to make out the identity of the large man towering over him.

"I got something I want you to do for me."

Tiger furrowed his brows. "Oh, hey. It's the middle of the night, man. What kind of shit you doin'?"

"It's a job. And it's right now. C'mon with me. Leave your shit."

Tiger hesitated, but then shook his head and grabbed his well-worn sneakers. By the time he fully emerged from his makeshift sleeping quarters, he had to run to catch up to the man in the knit hat. "Wait up, man!" the still-sleepy young man called.

The big figure didn't respond, or even acknowledge the plea. He kept walking back the way he had come, not at a particularly fast pace, but with long, confident strides.

"Whatcha want me to do?" Tiger asked. He fell into stride as they rounded the corner and headed south.

"I'll show you when we get there."

Ahead, a black SUV was parked on the curb in the first legal spot after the no-standing sign. The man opened the passenger door so Tiger could climb in. "Where we goin'?"

"I'll tell you in a minute."

Tiger sat back into the leather seat, then remembered to buckle his seat belt. The hulking vehicle pulled away and smoothly turned north onto Riverside Boulevard, then onto the ramp to the Henry Hudson Parkway. After his earlier questions generated such terse answers, Tiger sat in silence, enjoying the air conditioning.

As he watched the streetlights flash past, the boy thought about how lucky he was. He had only a vague memory of his mother. He had been in foster care since he could remember.

When he turned eighteen, he aged out of the system. His foster family, so proud of him when he graduated from high school, encouraged him to apply to a local community college. He moved out of his foster home to live with his girlfriend. But when he announced he didn't want to go to college, she packed up his stuff and threw him out. He was too proud to go back to his foster family, which wouldn't be getting any support from the state because of his age. So, he stayed on the street, not telling them about breaking up with his girl.

The Boys and Girls Clubs was the only place he ever really felt happy. The director of the lower Manhattan unit always treated him like an adult and challenged him to take responsibility for his life. It was there that he met Jimmy Rydell. Jimmy had shared stories from his own childhood. He had been lucky to find a foster family that was fully invested in his future. The fact that he had already been a star athlete didn't hurt, and Jimmy knew that. Jimmy took the scrawny kid under his wing and taught him about football and about life. He urged Tiger to take responsibility for his life.

When he moved out of his girlfriend's apartment, Tiger showed up outside Jimmy's building. Jimmy had encouraged him to go to a city-run shelter rather than live on the street, but Tiger had enough experience with the shelters to know it was safer for him on the sidewalk. Jimmy took care of him, allowing him to come up and use Jimmy's shower, buying him new shoes and clothes, and giving him $100 each week. The money was supposed to be for the coffee and bagels, which Tiger made sure he got every day, just the way Jimmy liked them. He kept the rest.

Then one day, Jimmy gave him a shoeshine kit. It was a wooden podium with a step, so Tiger could sit on the bottom step while his customer rested a shoe on the top. The kit came with rags and towels and polish. He stocked it with new supplies from the money he earned shining the shoes of the men and women who lived at Park Towers and the surrounding apartment buildings. He was polite, quick, gave a good shine, and didn't charge as much as the vendors in the business districts or the train station. Before long, he had a steady group of customers. With Jimmy looking out for him, the doormen at Park Towers left him alone.

The SUV exited onto Riverside Drive at 110th Street, breaking Tiger out of his ruminations. The driver pulled into a fire hydrant space on the northbound curb. He gruffly said, "C'mon," as he exited and walked across the mostly deserted street, toward the stone wall separating the roadway from Riverside Park.

Tiger scrambled out of his side and scampered after his driver, who had disappeared through a gap in the wall. The night was quiet, with only some chirping insects and a distant barking dog to interrupt the stillness. Tiger arrived at the dark gap, which led to a stairway slanting steeply down the embankment. Below the stairs, Tiger knew the landscape flattened out into a grassy expanse, crisscrossed by paved walking paths. He could only see dim outlines in the darkness, dotted with pools of light underneath the occasional street lamp. In the distance, a tall chain-link fence protected a group of tennis courts. Tiger could make out the dark surface of the Hudson River beyond. He couldn't see anyone, but there was only one way to go. Down.

When he reached the base of the stairs, Tiger stopped and looked right, then left. That was when he heard the swish and the thud and felt the pain on the back of his head. A flash of light pierced his sight as he fell, disoriented. He barely registered his knees scraping on the concrete as he crumpled. Instinctively, his left hand grabbed for his head, leaving only his right arm to prevent him from face-planting. A car horn sounded briefly somewhere to the south. He noticed the scent of cut grass. He must have bitten his tongue because he tasted blood.

He rolled, fighting the pain, down the gentle grassy slope. He struggled to his feet, trying to run. Then a second swish and thud. Another flash of light. Then darkness.

# Chapter 13 – Turning Up the Heat

Monday, June 3

THE MURDER OF JIMMY RYDELL was all anyone could talk about around New York City Monday morning. The Sunday papers had been jammed with a combination of obituaries, speculation about possible suspects and motives, and barely masked glee from Rydell's detractors. Wild theories emerged on social media and on the radio airwaves from Jimmy's supporters about the nefarious forces that might have conspired to take down a Black man who dared to speak up for social justice. The craziest theory, aside from space aliens, was that the NFL had put out a hit on Jimmy to silence him. The speculation about the rumored point-shaving scheme continued, although it was never clear how Jimmy's possible involvement could have resulted in his murder.

Kristi Olson wrote a lengthy article that appeared in the Metro section, not Sports. She recounted information from previous reporting about the rumored point-shaving investigation. Neither the league nor the FBI would confirm the existence of an ongoing probe.

The new article in *The Times* speculated that such a scheme, if it existed, would likely be organized on a large scale by crime syndicates in Las Vegas and around the country. Locally, the most likely connection would be the Gallata crime family. They had been involved in various illegal gambling operations for decades, along with loan-sharking, protection rackets, and drug distribution. Kristi analyzed every game from both local NFL teams from the past season and found nothing in any game consistent with a player, group of players, or coach throwing games or shaving points.

Meanwhile, Dexter Peacock had a companion article on the same page, blasting local law enforcement and NFL officials for failing to realize that Jimmy had been missing since Wednesday night. He wrote that the team had fumbled the ball by failing to report Jimmy as a missing person and that the police had failed to give the situation the proper urgency. Peacock's article speculated that the most likely motive for the murder was animosity against Jimmy based on his controversial social justice protests. Peacock claimed that Police Commissioner Earl Ward would be giving the case more resources if the dead quarterback were named Manning instead of Rydell. The Commissioner's office declined to comment, except to say that the police department was giving the situation the highest possible priority and that the team was cooperating fully with the police investigation. The NFL Commissioner and the Mayor gave similar no-comment responses.

Mike and Jason arrived early at the precinct. The Commissioner wanted a briefing and invited the public relations and communications departments, along with the mayor's press secretary. Everyone was interested. As Mike organized his notes at his desk, a half-dozen people walked past to give their two cents. Detectives Steve Berkowitz and George Mason, one of the other teams in the homicide division who worked out of the 94th Street location, came by together. Mason opined that there had to be a racial motive at work, given Jimmy Rydell's high-profile position at the forefront of the NFL player protests.

"You watch. It'll be some redneck racist kook who burns crosses on the weekend."

Berkowitz declined to speculate about the possible murderer, but was happy to list off three possible picks in the next year's draft who could fill the gaping hole in Gang Green's lineup. "After this, they're in the toilet for this season for sure. If they suck bad enough, they'll get the number one pick in next year's draft."

"You don't think Flacko can do the job?" came a feminine voice from behind. Mike turned his head and saw Detective Darla Meyer, holding a mug of coffee and flashing her usual friendly smile. Meyer had recently made detective and was doing a rotation through several divisions while the brass downtown decided on a permanent placement for her. She was starting a month in the Special Victim's Unit, which had two detective teams in the building. Since she was relatively available, Sully had assigned her to head up the review of the surveillance video from Park Towers. She had spent all day Sunday with a uniformed officer and a technician from the building's security team, watching digital video.

Before Berkowitz could respond, she continued. "Flacko threw for four thousand yards two seasons ago for Baltimore, in case you don't recall. He's got a Super Bowl ring for a reason. Sure, he's coming back from that knee injury, but he's a veteran. Chip O'Meara brought him in to be a mentor for Rydell, but also to be an experienced veteran who could take over if needed. Hell, he's better than Ryan Fitzpatrick."

Mason and Berkowitz spent a few minutes arguing the pros and cons of Flacko as both a near-term and long-term solution to the team's sudden quarterback problem. When Jason walked over, Meyer was already walking in the direction of the conference room.

"What did she say to get you boys so riled up?" Jason asked.

Berkowitz waved his hand in the direction of Meyer's departing back. "She's all weak in the knees about Flacko."

"So, if Meyer were a man, you would take her opinion more seriously?"

"I didn't say that!" Berkowitz protested.

"And you have some kind of problem with Darla being attracted to Flacko because he's White and she's Black?" Jason pressed.

"Well—" Berkowitz stopped talking, looking suddenly worried about how any answer might sound to his Black colleague. He cocked his head, then waved his hand at Jason with an, "Awww, forget it."

The discussion was interrupted by a uniformed officer standing at the top of the stairs, who shouted at Berkowitz. Somebody had reported a body in Riverside park at 111th Street and the responding officers needed a homicide team there, pronto.

"Great," Mason said with enthusiasm, "we can walk from here." Berkowitz didn't seem as excited about the prospect of a non-vehicular arrival at the crime scene, but didn't say anything. They both turned away just as Jason walked over to get Mike, telling him it was time for their briefing.

Mike chuckled as Berkowitz stalked away. "Even dead, Jimmy Rydell ends up in the middle of controversy, eh?"

"I'd expect nothing less," Jason said, returning the chuckle. "Let's go. We don't want to keep the commissioner waiting."

When they arrived in the cramped corner conference room, Sully was already hunched over the end of the ancient wooden table and staring into the silver speaker box. Sitting near the corner nearest to Sully, Detective Darla Meyer perched on the edge of her chair, staring earnestly at the captain. She turned her head only briefly to acknowledge the arrival of the more senior detectives.

A female voice, tinny and laced with static, escaped from the speaker. Mike recognized it as Kim Martinez, the press secretary for Mayor Douglass. She was asking whether detectives Stoneman and Dickson were there yet. Sully smoothly said, "Yes, they are. Are you ready on your end?"

"Just a moment," she responded, "Commissioner Ward is just coming in."

Sully smiled and motioned his detectives to sit, holding a finger to his lips to warn them against any chair-scraping as they took their seats. Mike and Jason had given Sully their summary as soon as they arrived, and Meyer had briefed them on her review of the surveillance cameras at Park Towers, so they knew what was coming.

Ward didn't wait for any pleasantries before launching into a tirade about how unfairly he was being portrayed in the press and how loyal he was to Mayor Douglass – the second Black mayor in city history. He pledged to provide all the support and resources needed. Nobody was going to accuse him of being racist. "Find the killer, and do it quickly," he bellowed.

When the commissioner was finished and grunted that he was ready to listen, Mike and Jason tag-teamed their way through a synopsis of their investigation and interviews so far.

"Great! So, when are we arresting Bedford?" the Commissioner asked enthusiastically.

Sully scowled and shook his head. He made eye contact with Mike, who was smiling and also shaking his head. Mike had predicted that Ward would insist on a quick arrest, while Sully had optimistically hoped the commissioner was enough of a cop to understand the problems associated with premature action.

"Sir, we've put in an urgent request with the DA's office to get a search warrant for his apartment and for his truck and phone. We've already traced him across the GW Bridge at eleven forty-five and we know he was pulled over on the West Side Highway at a quarter past one Thursday morning. Stoneman and Dickson are meeting with the officers who handled the traffic stop as soon as we're done here. We need to conduct the search first, then bring him in if there's enough evidence to support it."

Mike cut in. "Sir, we'll get the search warrant this morning, assuming Zimmerman doesn't encounter any resistance from the court."

"He'd better damned well not!" Ward shouted, as if Mike could do anything about it.

"Yes, Sir. I don't expect any problems there. The guy has motive and opportunity, but that's not going to be enough to convict him unless we've got more. We don't have any evidence that he was inside Jimmy's building Wednesday night."

Sully pointed at Detective Meyer, silently giving her a cue that she was up next to speak, then turned back to the speaker box. "Sir, we've had a team sifting through all the surveillance video from the apartment building. Detective Darla Meyer is here and can tell you what we found." He motioned toward Meyer, who looked like she was getting ready to face a firing squad.

Meyer hesitantly walked Ward through her day of finding basically nothing on the surveillance video. They observed Jimmy arriving through the lobby, taking the elevator up to his penthouse, and exiting the elevator. That was all on Jimmy. They watched all the video from the penthouse elevator and nobody else visited that floor until the following morning, when Jimmy's bodyguard went up to look for him. "There are more than twenty cameras in the building, so we're still sifting through, looking for something, but we haven't come up with anything relevant so far."

"So, how did Bedford get out of the building with Rydell's body?" the commissioner asked, as if the three detectives on the other end of the line hadn't thought of it.

Mike responded, "Sir, we obviously don't know. We also don't know how he got into the building without being seen. We're going to see if the officers who pulled him over searched the truck and whether they noticed anything to indicate he had a body inside. There are a lot of remaining questions, which is why we need to proceed deliberately so we don't miss our chance at the evidence that could nail him."

"Or somebody else," Jason added.

"Well . . . just do it fast!"

"No shit," Sully mumbled after pushing the MUTE button on the phone. Then, removing his finger, "Absolutely, Sir. We're on it with an all-out blitz." He hung up the phone before anyone else on the other side could try to get in a word. Turning toward Mike, he asked, "So, what the hell? How'd he do it?"

"Let's not assume he did it at all, Captain. There's a lot of smoke blowing in his direction, but so far no flames."

"He could have had help. Maybe somebody else did it for him." Sully stood and pointed at the phone, like it was the suspect.

"I don't think he's that stupid," Jason said, drawing a curious expression from Mike.

"I thought you had him pegged for a redneck racist idiot?" Mike said seriously.

"I do, but even a redneck racist idiot knows better than to hire a hit man and then drive his truck into the vicinity of the scheduled murder."

"I don't know," Mike parried, "I think he could be that stupid."

"Can it!" Sully shouted. "Just figure it out. And do it fast!" He stomped out of the room.

Meyer tentatively spoke up in the momentary silence. "I want to get back to the surveillance video. We worked all day yesterday but there are still some cameras we need to review."

"Get to it, Detective," Mike said enthusiastically. "It would be nice if things got simple."

"How many uniforms do you need to complete the review today?" Jason asked.

"I have the manpower I need," Meyer replied, more confidently. "There are only two positions in the security office at the building where we can view the video, so more bodies won't really help much. They apparently can't download all the files and give them to us until next week, even with a subpoena, so we're working through it as fast as we can. We canvased the residents pretty thoroughly Saturday and Sunday and nobody seemed to see anything. We'll keep that up today in case we missed anybody, but I think we have enough officers."

"Fine," Mike said, slowly standing as his chair legs scraped across the linoleum floor. "Let's get to it. Let us know immediately if you find anything remotely relevant."

"I will, Detective Stoneman."

Mike said, "You're a detective, too. You can feel free to call me Mike, or just Stoneman."

Meyer smiled. "Yes . . . Mike."

They all departed the conference room. Meyer hustled to the stairs to gather her team and get back to Park Towers. Jason trailed Mike back toward his desk. "You've mellowed toward the rookie detectives, I see."

"Don't push that," Mike snapped. "I treated you the way you needed to be treated at the time. Meyer needs a different approach. Don't get all jealous on me."

"Fair. What's our next move, while we wait for the search warrant?"

Mike thought about how to answer while he thumbed through several message slips on his desk. He developed a quizzical expression. "What the hell is *Birds of Britain*?"

"What?"

"Says here there's a guy waiting downstairs who's from Birds of Britain and he wants to talk to both of us."

Just then, Sully's voice called out and the two detectives walked over to his office door. Before they asked, he said, "There's a guy here from the insurance company that has the policy on Jimmy Rydell. The owner of the team is apparently a buddy of the mayor. He and the commissioner both want us to cooperate with the guy. He's some kind of big-shot investigator."

"Oh, Sully, for the love of—"

"Forget it, Stoneman!" Sully cut him off. "It's a done deal. Let him tag along. If he gets in the way, smack him around. I don't have any pull on this, so just pretend he's your FBI consultant on this case. You know how that goes."

Mike shrugged and turned without a word toward the stairs down to the front reception desk.

## Chapter 14 – Birds of Britain

A S THEY WALKED, Jason asked, "What's this guy's name?"

Mike glanced at the message slip. "Says here 'Gram Dickwith.' That ring any bells for you?"

"Not a tinkle."

When Mike pushed open the door leading to the waiting area, there was not much question which person was their visitor. The cramped space held the usual rabble of anxious folks waiting to retrieve loved ones from lockup, nervous-looking people waiting to be called in for witness interviews, and bored low-rent lawyers in wrinkled suits waiting to meet with clients.

In one corner, a man with a black brush moustache wearing a tweed jacket sat ramrod straight on the edge of his worn chair. He appeared to be about Mike's age. His black wing-tip shoes were polished to a military shine and were flat on the floor below long, gangly legs. He had a handkerchief in his breast pocket, the same paisley silk as his necktie. A gold tie bar at his starched collar, graying black hair slicked back along the sides of his balding head, and wire-rimmed spectacles completed a look that was entirely out of place.

"Mr. Britain?" Mike whispered at Jason, tilting his head in the man's direction.

Jason frowned, not used to being the second-best-dressed man in any room. By the time he and Mike reached the far side of the room, his better-dressed counterpart was on his feet, meeting Jason's eyes at a similar height.

"Mr. Dickwith?"

"Beckwith, actually, Detective Dickson. Graham Beckwith; Boyd's of Britain," he said in an elegant English accent. He extended his hand and gave Jason a perfect shake. Firm, but not showing off his strength; long enough to show no fear, but not lingering. One firm pump.

Mike extended his hand. "Mike—"

"Stoneman, yes," Beckwith said, giving Mike a similar shake. "Very glad to meet you, Detective. You and I are both scholars of the trade, as it were."

Mike nodded blankly, attempting to puzzle out the reference.

Beckwith sensed his confusion and clarified. "I teach the fine art of investigation to junior investigators at Boyd's." He smiled, pleased that his research into Mike's background had proven a useful way to get the upper hand in the introductions. "Good to meet you both. Let's get to it, shall we?" He raised both eyebrows, which were bushy and jet black, lacking the gray streaks of the rest of his hair.

Mike shrugged and motioned for Jason to lead the way through the security door and back to the bullpen. Mike walked to his desk, gesturing to Beckwith to take the guest seat opposite. The lanky Brit leaned over from his waist to a ninety-degree angle, inspecting the seat. He then removed the handkerchief from his jacket pocket and used it to wipe off the surface before sitting.

Jason leaned on the edge of the desk. "We're told your company wrote the life insurance policy on Jimmy Rydell. You're here to confirm the cause of death, right?"

"Right. I am the case investigator."

"Is investigator your corporate title, or is it more like a police designation?"

"A bit of both, actually," Beckwith said cheerfully, balancing on the edge of the chair as if preventing his suit pants from making excessive contact. "I was a detective inspector at the Yard, now retired. Claims investigator is my position with Boyd's, but not a title. I'm here to verify that the circumstances of Mr. Rydell's demise satisfy the terms of the policy. Normally, I investigate fraud claims – arson and falsified thefts and such. But in this case, my former police background prompted my employer to send me to evaluate the circumstances of the murder. There are potential variations here that could void the policy."

"Such as?" Jason raised his right eyebrow and leaned in.

"Such as if the policy holder was involved in the murder, or if the deceased was involved in criminal activity at the time of death."

"Well, Mr. Beckwith," Mike said, "so far we have nothing that points in either of those directions."

"Please, Detective, shall we dispense with formalities? Call me Graham. I find that in situations such as this, where we will need to work together in close quarters, the familiarity helps the process."

"Work together?" Jason's other brow shot up.

"Listen, um, Graham, we've been instructed to allow you to observe our investigation. But this is an NYPD operation here. You're here to watch, but you're still a civilian. We'll be happy to include you, but it's not like you're our partner. Is that clear enough?"

"Perfectly clear, Mike. I'm quite used to these situations. As I am frequently called upon to shadow police investigations, I assure you I will be quite invisible. Now, can you give me a rundown on the investigation?"

A flash of blue caught Jason's attention. When he looked up, he saw two uniformed officers standing next to the door to the conference room. He figured them for the two cops who had pulled Nate over on Thursday morning. They were due about this time. He waved at Mike and gestured in that direction.

"Graham, I tell you what. Our next task will be to interview those two officers. You come along and listen in. We'll see what else you need to know when we're done."

"Excellent!" The Englishman rose easily from his chair. Mike led the way toward the conference room. As Jason and Graham followed, the investigator remarked, "Detective Dickson – Jason – I must say I appreciate your professional dress. You seem to be the only one here who knows how to properly knot a tie."

Jason smiled. Maybe he had misjudged the man.

Inside the conference room, two officers fidgeted in their chairs. The first was White, with a classic cop crewcut and a muscular six-foot build. His partner, a Latina woman, flashed defiant black eyes. Her hair was wrapped into a tight bun and, judging by the muscles in her neck, the rest of her was wound just as tautly. They knew they were being called in because of the traffic stop involving Nate Bedford, and they were anxious about it. They both recognized Mike and Jason.

"Who's the suit?" the female officer, whose name badge read *Pinero*, asked suspiciously.

"How do you know he's not part of our homicide team?" Mike asked.

Officer Pinero hesitated, as if reluctant to speak up. Then, she lifted her chin and looked Mike directly in the eye. "I've never seen him before. He's got no gun holster under that tight suit jacket, and his watch is way too nice for an on-duty cop. Those shiny shoes haven't been on the streets and I know Detective Dickson is always the best-dressed dude in this house, so this snappy dresser doesn't work here. Who is he?"

Graham nodded and smiled. "Well done, young lady. I am Graham Beckwith, Boyd's of Britain. I am an observer to these proceedings."

Pinero looked at Mike, who nodded to her that it was fine to go ahead in Graham's presence.

Jason took the lead in the discussion about the traffic stop. The male officer, Russ Nelson, was driving the squad car. He explained that they were parked in a pull-off on the side of the West Side Highway south of the 96th Street exit when they saw Nate's truck driving northbound at 1:15 a.m. He was exceeding the speed limit and Nelson engaged their siren and pulled out behind him with lights flashing. At first, the truck sped up, but after a minute, the driver pulled over north of 125th Street. They followed standard procedure and asked the man to step out of the vehicle. Nate did not resist. They issued him a summons for speeding and reckless driving. He said he wanted to call for an Uber to take him home, so they called for a tow for his truck and waited with him until his car arrived. Then they resumed their patrol. Throughout the recitation, Officer Pinero did not speak.

"Did you conduct a search of the truck?" Jason asked.

"Yes, Sir. We conducted a visual inspection of the interior of the cab and rear seat, as well as the bed, which was not covered.

We did not observe any weapons, drug paraphernalia, or any other suspicious material."

"Tell me your observations about Mr. Bedford."

"Well, Sir, he was agitated about being pulled over. Once he was outside the vehicle, he was friendly and pretty calm. He was pissed off that he was getting a ticket, and he was embarrassed, I think, by the situation."

"Did you observe any blood or indications of injury, or of recently being in a fight?"

"He did have some dried blood on his shirt, Sir. And his face looked like he might have been bruised. But it appeared to be something that had happened some time before, not fresh. He wasn't bleeding. His hands weren't bloody. There was no indication he had been in a recent fight."

"Officer Pinero, do you concur with those observations?" Jason turned toward the female officer with a sympathetic expression, trying to indicate that she had permission to tell the truth, even if it contradicted her partner.

"Yes, Sir," she said stiffly, looking at Officer Nelson rather than at Jason. "He didn't seem to be any more nervous or agitated than anyone else during an average traffic stop."

Jason stared at her without asking another question, creating a prolonged silence. Officer Nelson filled the void. "It was all pretty routine, Sir."

"Was it?" Mike asked, then once again allowed the room to fall into silence.

"Yes, Sir," Pinero confirmed. "Pretty routine."

"Is there any chance there was a body stashed in that truck?"

"No, Sir," Nelson said confidently. "Plus, the truck was towed to the impound lot. They do a full inventory and search of any vehicle that's towed in there."

"Any indication of blood or other suggestion that a body could have been transported in the truck earlier that night?"

"No, Sir. Nothing we saw."

"Either of you have anything else to say?" Jason asked. Neither officer spoke. "OK. Fine. Please don't speak to anyone, including other officers, about that traffic stop, or about this interview. And don't talk to the press. If either of you gives a comment to a reporter, or if we see an article attributing a comment to someone close to the investigation, you'll both be directing traffic at the Queensboro Bridge for the next year. You understand?"

Both officers nodded as they quickly rose from their seats and headed for the door. Nelson exited first. As Pinero was stepping through, Jason called out, "Officer Pinero."

She stopped and turned her head, looking like she was desperate to get out of the room without answering any more questions.

Jason softened his expression and said, "I know how important it is for a junior officer to support her partner – as long as there's no information being withheld that's relevant to an important investigation. For now, I don't see anything important. Do I?"

"No, Sir," she said quickly, before turning and rushing out after her partner.

When Jason looked at Mike, he shrugged. Then, Graham spoke up unexpectedly. "The David Beckham treatment."

"Come again?" Mike said.

Graham smiled. "I understand that this man, Bedford, plays American football and is something of a celebrity, is that correct?" Mike and Jason both nodded their affirmation. "So, the David Beckham treatment – when an officer overlooks infractions due to the celebrity status of a suspect, particularly when no serious crime is implicated. It seems fairly clear Mr. Bedford was driving while intoxicated, but Officer Nelson was reluctant to arrest him for the offense. That would be embarrassing for him and, no doubt, for his football club. Officer Nelson issued a summons for a lesser charge but insisted he not drive his vehicle home in his compromised condition, and so allowed him to call for a taxi. Officer Pinero, as the junior member of the team, felt obligated to support her partner and go along with his lenient treatment. To do otherwise would expose them both to disciplinary action for filing a false report. But in the end, it's doubtful the suppressed details will be material to the investigation."

Mike pursed his chin and nodded. "I agree, Graham. What about you, Jason?"

"Agreed. But I think Pinero may be willing to share some additional details with us if it becomes relevant. I'm betting Nate Bedford wasn't as calm as the report suggests."

"You may be right." Mike stood and stretched his back. "What do we think it all means about Nate? Do we think he's dumb enough, even in a drunken rage, to drive into town and kill Jimmy, but then smart enough to dispose of the body somewhere it wouldn't be found, I guess in a freezer somewhere? And then be dumb enough right after that to drive recklessly up the West Side Highway on the way home?"

"Never say never, Mike. But no, I don't think so."

"If that's so, Detectives, then it would seem that all other theories are still in play. From what I'm reading there is some indication that Mr. Rydell may have been involved in an illegal gambling operation. And any number of people associated with the football club are glad he's dead."

"Mr. Beckwith," Mike said, forgetting to drop the formality, "I don't know how things work in the UK, but here in America, teams don't go around killing off the players who underperform on the field."

"Nevertheless, it's still a possible outcome of the investigation. Perhaps you might tell me what you know about the events leading up to that traffic stop?"

After Mike and Jason spent five minutes giving Graham the short version of the facts, he offered an observation. "Have you ruled out the existence of a freezer unit in close proximity to Mr. Rydell's apartment, where the body could have been stored by whoever killed him?"

"Not yet," Mike said. "But we can cover that when we go visit Detective Meyer and her video review team."

"Is that our next stop?"

"No," Jason said. "While we wait for the search warrant, we need to talk to Jimmy's agent. His office is in midtown. Then we'll get over to Jimmy's building and see if Meyer has any news on the video review. But first, Mike and I have a small detour here in the building."

# Chapter 15 – Inside Scoop

WHILE MIKE, JASON, AND GRAHAM were bantering in the precinct, Kristi Olson was prowling the practice complex in Florham Park. Woody O'Meara's office had issued an edict that nobody was to speak to anyone about Jimmy Rydell or about the events of Wednesday afternoon. They said it was because of an ongoing police investigation. Kristi knew the real reason was to shield the team from any negative publicity. She also knew football players were not particularly good rule-followers.

She spent an hour meandering around the complex, catching players here and there to get a quick quote about how sad they were after Jimmy's death and how optimistic they still were about the upcoming season. Nobody had a bad word to say about Jimmy. A few players, all Black, told her off the record about the fight and that they blamed Nate for initiating, although they didn't really think he murdered Jimmy.

She was hoping to catch William Due, a defensive lineman from Auburn. Due, who never wanted to be called "Bill," for obvious reasons, was an underclassman during Nate Bedford's final two years as a Tiger. She spotted him on Muscle Beach, then killed time on a nearby bench waiting for him to finish lifting. When he finally moved toward the locker room, she intercepted him on the walkway.

"Hey, William!" She made a show of stuffing her note pad into her shoulder bag, suggesting the conversation was off the record, without actually saying so.

"Hey, Kristi." He stopped walking and waited for the reporter to approach. "I'm not supposed to talk about Jimmy, you know."

"I know. I won't ask. But I've been doing some research about Nate and I know you two were teammates at Auburn." Kristi paused and looked up at the huge Black man, whose bulk belied incredible quickness and agility, which made him a formidable pass rusher. She was hoping he might be less than sympathetic about the conditions on his college team.

"Yeah, he and I were on the team together." The man looked down at Kristi with a quizzical expression.

"What were relations like between the Black players and the White players on that team – particularly between the Black underclassmen and the White seniors?"

The big man turned his head and gazed out toward the practice field, avoiding eye contact with Kristi. "I don't know. I was never at any other college, so I suppose it was like anywhere else. You know how it is. The upperclassmen always give the freshman a hard time."

"Were there any particular incidents that you remember?"

Due paused. "I don't know."

"Do you remember a freshman lineman named Jauwan Holmes? He had to leave the team."

"I'm not sure. You know, it was a while ago. I was just getting started on the team then."

"I know, William, but you're a pro now. You don't need to protect anybody anymore. You can speak up."

"What if I don't want to? I ain't gotta say nothin'. What's it gonna help now, huh?"

"Did you know about the incident – who was involved?"

"Nah. I didn't know. I heard some things, but it was just talk. It's not like anybody let us in on the secrets, you know. I don't want to get anything started. I got a career going here. I don't need no trouble. I'm not Jimmy. Come talk to me when I'm retired." He walked quickly toward the locker room, leaving Kristi behind.

On her way back to the parking lot, Kristi saw Dexter Peacock talking to the beat writer from *The New York Post*. She sidled up and said hello to Ted Ortloff, who had covered the team since the '80s and whose perpetually sunburned skin resembled a worn baseball glove. He smiled at her with a fatherly gaze. He was old enough to have never hit on her, and had even protected her a few times from handsy players. Peacock did not seem happy to see his colleague.

"Miss Olson, do you have anything helpful to report on the murder investigation?"

"Dexter, I don't think you want me to share scoops with *The Post*, do you?"

Ortloff excused himself and walked to his car, leaving Kristi alone with Peacock. "Well?" he prompted.

"Are you still going with the racial conflict angle?"

"Yes. It's the only legitimate story here. Aside from the murder investigation, for which we have very little."

"I thought you could get the scoop from your good buddy Mike Stoneman?" Kristi elbowed Peacock in the side gently.

Peacock snarled, "I'll tap that source only when it matters. Clearly, at this point, everything is speculation. But Mr. Rydell's lasting impact on the discussion about race relations and police brutality – that's a real story, regardless of who killed him."

"I agree, which ties into the research I did on Nate Bedford."

"Are you still trying to get confirmation that there was a fight between Bedford and Rydell?" Peacock suddenly seemed much more interested in his sportswriter colleague. Ever since he was thrown together with her on the Rydell story, Peacock had referred to Kristi as *the sports girl*, even when she was within earshot. Her craft did not impress him. He often called Sports *the toy department.*

"The racial tension in the locker room finally boiled over, but the background on Nate is critical to the story. I was planning on covering it in my daily, but if you want my help for your piece, I'd be willing to share the byline."

"I already shared a byline with you," Peacock derided. "Tell me what you have and I'll decide if it's something I want or if you should just run it without me."

Kristi smiled and sat down on the fender of a nearby car as she flipped through the pages of a thin notepad. "Nate is a descendant of Nathan Bedford Forrest, the first Grand Wizard of the Ku Klux Klan and a Confederate Army general. The family changed its name to Bedford to disassociate from the Forrest legacy. Nate and Jimmy had problems from the beginning – Nate didn't want to play for a Black quarterback. They had some very public disagreements about whose fault it was that the team was struggling offensively.

"The girlfriend of one of the other players confirmed for me that Nate was pissed at Jimmy for sleeping with Nate's girl, Candi. Jimmy had a reputation as a ladies' man, but other player's girls are supposed to be off limits. But Jimmy was looking for a way to tweak Nate because of his racist attitude and vocal criticism of Jimmy for taking a knee during the national anthem. So, Jimmy seduced Candi. Once you go Black, you never go back, right? It was a way for Jimmy to stick it to Nate. It didn't foster unity in the locker room, but Jimmy didn't care. He was tired of going along to get along. I have two sources who were in the locker room on Wednesday who say Nate swore he'd get revenge after Jimmy beat him up in front of his teammates."

"That kind of reality-TV garbage is not something I want in my story, I'm afraid. But the comment about Bedford threatening revenge on Rydell is certainly relevant to the murder story. Are you sure about the sources?"

"Absolutely sure. But you don't get them unless I get a byline. My ass is on the line with those players. I promised to keep their identities secret."

"And you have. I'm not giving you a joint byline based on one quote." Peacock turned up his nose and looked away, as if the conversation was over.

"Then you don't get the quote."

"I'll ask my editor to give you a tag line."

"Bullshit," Kristi said quietly. "I'm not taking an end credit that 'Kristi Olson also contributed.' My information is the key fact. All you have is speculation otherwise. I'm happy to let the editors decide, but we send in the story jointly. I want to see it before you file it."

"Don't you trust me?"

Kristi put a hand on her hip and leaned in. "Those of us who work in *the toy department* can't afford to trust."

Peacock fumed silently, before grudgingly agreeing.

"Great," Kristi said, hopping down from the car. "I'll let you work on it while I file my daily."

"I haven't got all day."

"Don't worry, Shakespeare. I'll be done before you are. I'm also working on some additional background on Nate. I have one source who says he was involved in a racist hazing incident in college at Auburn."

"Who's the source for that?"

"It doesn't matter. It's second-hand and it's not enough to publish. I need some corroboration. I'm working on it."

Peacock shook his head and walked briskly to his 1963 Mustang. He grabbed his laptop, engaged his phone's hotspot WiFi, and started typing. Fifteen minutes later, a tap on his partially lowered window jolted him from his concentration. He saw Kristi's smiling face peeking inside.

"Are you done already?" Peacock asked, unable to hide a hint of both admiration and jealousy.

"Sure. If I was on deadline I would have kicked it out faster, but since we had time, I didn't rush it. You ready?"

Peacock shook his head and glanced down at the four paragraphs on his screen. "I'm sure your high-speed copy is fine for the – for Sports. But I am working on something serious here." He glared at Kristi for a moment, then turned his attention back to his keyboard.

Kristi pulled out her phone and killed some time, wandering away from the car into the shade of a nearby tree growing on the edge of the lot. She peeked over her screen every few minutes, watching the celebrated journalist in the car as he agonized over each sentence.

The story hit the paper's website at 3:25 p.m. and ran in the next day's print paper on the front page of the Metro section. The byline was Dexter Peacock and Kristi Olson. The web article had more than 100,000 views by the end of the day and generated a lengthy thread of comments, mostly about racism. Many readers defended Nate Bedford's efforts to fight back against the Black quarterback's "unpatriotic" protests.

Kristi's daily training camp piece ran in Sports the next morning. The inside dirt about the sexual exploits in the locker room generated comments that doubled the reader engagement on the Metro section article. The local sports talk radio hosts – and several of the general news radio hosts – were fielding calls about the sex scandal for two days. The Sports editor sent Kristi a commendation about her excellent scoop, and copied the managing editor. Kristi received seven requests to appear on radio shows and nationally syndicated podcasts.

Local organizers put out feelers on social media about staging a march for social justice to coincide with Jimmy's funeral on Thursday.

# Chapter 16 – Perception and Reality

**M**IKE AND JASON LEFT GRAHAM WITH SULLY while they took a trip down the three flights of stairs to the basement. They needed to talk with Sophie in the records room. As they walked across the ancient chess-board-patterned linoleum tiles under the flickering fluorescent lights, a uniformed officer with a maroon expandable file folder walked toward them. The officer smiled and greeted them by name. Mike tried to read the name on the brass plate above his shirt pocket but couldn't make it out, so he awkwardly said, "Good morning, Officer." He mentally kicked himself for not remembering. He had certainly met the man several times around the precinct. Not for the first time lately, he muttered to himself that it sucked getting older.

Before Mike even saw her, he heard the jovial island accent of Sophie LaFontaine, queen of the records room. Sophie had thirty years on the force. She didn't give a rat's ass what anyone thought and she pitched the shit to all the higher-ranked officers without regard to their status. Jason had taken to using her as a sounding board, particularly regarding personal issues. Sophie looked like an aging, if overweight, Hollywood starlet. She had high cheekbones that were always well rouged, round lips covered with bright red paint, and oval eyes accented with blue and violet shadow and black eyeliner curved at the edges. Mike thought she resembled an old picture he once saw of the great jazz singer, Ma Rainey. Today, her long black hair was tied into an elaborate braid.

"Well, now, what brings you two celebrities down here to see ol' Sophie?"

"One thing I know about," Mike said and leaned over the counter to give the big woman a kiss on the cheek. "We're in the middle of a sticky one, Sophie, and we're up against some time pressure."

"I heard. That poor young man. So much life ahead of him, and now—"

"Yeah. It's a tough break for him. What we need, Sophie, is the report and the dashcam video from Officer Russ Nelson from Thursday morning – a traffic stop at about one-fifteen a.m. on the West Side Highway. We saw the data that's on the computer record, but we want to see the original written report and the video."

"Well, I'm sure I can handle that, Mike." Sophie turned to her computer console and typed a few keystrokes. While her eyes were fixed on the screen, she asked, "And what was the other thing?"

Jason leaned in toward Sophie. "I'm sorry to say that Mike here needs a reality check. We're investigating the murder of a Black man who was outspoken against police brutality. And you know Mike, he's a little bit sheltered and naïve about racism. He likes to see the good in people."

"Except for the scumbag criminals," Mike cut in.

"You see?" Jason stopped and tilted his head toward his partner.

"I see," Sophie responded, turning away from her monitor toward Mike. "I have a location on that report. I'll get the file in a minute. The link to the video will go to your email." She reached out her thick arm toward Mike and gently placed her open hand against his cheek. "Oh, Mike. I know you got no hate in ya. You always talkin' about fairness and justice. That's good for you. But you got to know how some men got hate in their soul. And it's not just some. Those folks are everywhere, including right here."

"You mean in New York?"

"No, Mike. I mean right here in the house. Some of 'em wearing blue and carrying a gun and a badge."

Mike developed an angry frown. "Who?"

"It ain't about me tellin' you who. It's about you seein' it for yourself when it's right before your own eyes." She removed her hand, climbed down from her high-boy stool, and went to retrieve the requested file.

Mike turned to Jason. "I'm not clueless."

"Not usually. But . . . sometimes. You were rough on me in the beginning, but I know – now – that you thought I got special treatment. You were bound and determined to treat me like a rookie and keep me in line. You weren't looking to set me up. You didn't refuse to work with me because I'm Black. I know that. I know Michelle feels the same way. But not being racist yourself is only half the battle. You need to be anti-racist. That includes taking action when it happens – not standing by and letting them get away with it."

"I don't—" Mike stopped himself from denying the charge and thought about it first. "I don't recall ever letting someone get away with being racist."

"That's the problem, Mike. You really don't see it. Remember when you told me I should always listen to Sophie?"

Before Mike could say anything else, Sophie returned, carrying a thin folder. "I made a copy for ya already, boys."

"Thanks, Sophie," Mike took the folder. "You're the absolute best."

"Don't you forget it," she called out playfully as they walked back to the stairs.

Back in the bullpen, Graham was again sitting gingerly on the edge of Mike's guest chair. The two detectives joined him there to review the incident report from Officers Nelson and Pinero. The form had two pages. Jason and Graham handed the pages back and forth while Mike accessed his email to get the video link. By the time Mike found the images of Nate's truck pulled over on the side of the West Side Highway, the other two were watching over his shoulder.

"Well, Beckwith, not that I doubted it, but it looks like you called it correctly. Does the written report include a notation of giving Nate a field sobriety test?"

"Yes, Mike," Jason responded. "There's an FST notation, but it doesn't say what the result was. The officers didn't mention that when they met with us, but it seems pretty clear they cut the star player a break. They let him off with two citations, but no arrest for driving while intoxicated. Maybe if they had arrested him, we'd have some additional evidence."

"Too bad for us the chap wasn't a Black man," Graham observed.

Mike furrowed his brow in annoyance at the comment from the foreigner. "What do you mean by that?"

"Nothing," Graham said quickly, his voice rising to a high pitch. "It's just, well, one has the impression that a Black suspect in that situation would have been cuffed and brought in, regardless of his athletic renown."

"Why would you think that?" Mike shot back, perhaps a bit more aggressively than necessary.

"It's just the impression one gets watching the news coverage from here in the States. Perhaps the impression is skewed somewhat. Do you think otherwise?"

When Mike didn't answer immediately, Jason said, "It depends on the officers. Some White officers might have treated the situation exactly the same. Some others, maybe not."

"Yes, such absence of consistency is the hallmark of the independent police force, I suppose. Fine. Well, forget I said anything. The only point here is that your suspect, Mr. Bedford, was allowed to go free mere minutes after the possible murder of Mr. Rydell. Too bad, but perhaps not so bad. He may now have a false sense of confidence about having gotten away with it – if it was him at all. In any case, no sense wasting time over spilt milk. Shall we get on to the next interview?"

Mike couldn't think of any reason not to agree.

# Chapter 17 – Professional Representation

YOU HAD TO BE IMPRESSED by the offices of International Sports Marketing Syndicate, LLC. Located on the 65th floor of a glass-and-steel office tower at the corner of 57th Street and Lexington Avenue, the décor was a combination of ultra-modern and classic sports. The walls were lined with framed jerseys and autographed bats, balls, helmets, and other memorabilia. The place oozed sports and money. Jimmy Rydell's agent, Aaron Taylor, was expecting them. When a fashion model in a white mini-skirt escorted the group to Mr. Taylor's office, the feeling of being impressed was only enhanced.

Taylor got up from behind a massive glass-topped desk and hesitantly greeted his three guests in the middle of the huge office, then gestured for them to sit on a collection of leather easy chairs. The agent looked impossibly young. His boyish features were fitted into an Italian-cut three-piece suit. Blue eyes glinted under a mop of shockingly red hair, made to stand out even more prominently by the young man's pale skin. He looked like he needed sunscreen to protect him from the halogen lighting. He also looked like he had never been alone in a room with two cops before.

After a round of introductions, Taylor asked whether they would like anything to drink. Mike and Jason both declined, but Graham asked for a cup of Earl Gray tea, with cream and no sweetener. Taylor gestured to the model, who clacked away on four-inch heels, leaving the door open behind her.

Mike took charge. "Mr. Taylor, as you know, we're investigating the death of your client, Jimmy Rydell."

"I'm sorry, Detective, but I really don't have anything to help you. Lord knows I want to know what happened – who killed Jimmy – as much as anyone. He was my best client. He was also my best friend."

"How long have you known him?"

Taylor's shoulders slumped slightly as he hesitantly told the story of his relationship with Jimmy Rydell. Mike had read many articles about Jimmy's story, but he had never seen anyone explain the role of Aaron Taylor.

The two had met in a foster home in Alabama. Taylor's parents died in a car crash and none of his relatives wanted to take him in, so he ended up in the state care system. Jimmy never knew his father and his mother was in jail, sending Jimmy into protective care. They were both nine years old when they got referred. Each bounced around from family to family for several years before they both ended up in the same house in Montgomery at age twelve. They were effectively brothers. Fortunately, that family, the Taylors, provided a stable environment. Jimmy and Aaron went through high school together. Jimmy was the star athlete. Aaron was allowed to hang around the teams because he was Jimmy's brother. Jimmy used the Taylor last name then, but he reverted to his birth father's name when they went off to college at Mississippi State. By then, Jimmy's mother had died.

Jimmy's success on the gridiron was well known, so Taylor skipped that, but explained how they had roomed together and remained as close as actual brothers. Aaron majored in economics and sports management. They had always planned for Aaron to be Jimmy's agent, but Aaron was no novice. He interned with two different sports agents during college and accepted a job at ISMS after he graduated early in January of their senior year, right after Jimmy won the Heisman Trophy. He admitted ISMS probably would not have given him the job if he weren't bringing in the likely #1 draft pick as a client. But he had worked hard and now had two other NFL clients, thanks to Jimmy's recommendations.

Aaron acknowledged that, with Jimmy dead, his position with the firm was precarious. He wasn't sure he could keep his existing clients without Jimmy's support. The kid was scared and didn't try that hard to hide it.

He also told them about Jimmy's devotion to the Boys & Girls Clubs. They had spent many afternoons and weekends there when they were both in foster care. He had contacted the local Clubs in New York and had spent hundreds of hours working with the kids. He had donated a million dollars from his first year's contract to the Clubs. "The man was a saint," Aaron said.

"We heard you and Jimmy were together last Wednesday out in Florham Park," Mike prodded. "What were you doing there?"

"I go out there a lot," Aaron said, fiddling with his cufflinks suddenly.

At that moment, the door opened and the model in the mini-skirt glided in holding a silver tray with a tea service, which she set down on a coffee table in front of Graham. All the men in the room watched in silence.

When she had gone, Taylor seemed more composed. "He's my biggest client, and I'm always in the market to make contact with other players, so I go out there a lot. Last Wednesday we also had a meeting with the GM."

"Tell us about that," Jason asked, drawing Taylor's eye contact in a different direction.

"I really can't divulge the contents of a confidential business discussion," Taylor said quickly, a rehearsed response.

Mike grunted. "Mr. Taylor, he's dead, so there is no confidential information anymore. Plus, we're conducting a murder investigation. I'm sure you would prefer that we not drag you out of here for an interrogation – or serve a subpoena on you here in front of your bosses. Am I right?"

Now Taylor was sweating, and again spinning his gold cufflink with the fingers of his left hand. "You – you can't do that," he said without much conviction. "I'm not a suspect. I had nothing to do with it. Why would I kill off my brother, and my biggest client?"

"I don't know. Why don't you tell us why you were meeting with the GM? We promise to keep it confidential unless there's something incriminating."

Taylor looked back and forth between Mike and Jason, not sure who he was supposed to be talking to – exactly what the detectives wanted. "Look, it's not a big deal. Chip wanted Jimmy to restructure his contract to help the team free up some salary cap space over the next few years. Especially for next year. That kind of discussion happens all the time. It's no big deal."

"Did you agree, about the contract restructure?" Jason asked.

"No, we didn't. Jimmy didn't want to do it, so we said no."

Mike picked up the metaphorical ping-pong ball that he and Jason were batting back and forth. "Why didn't Jimmy want to do it?"

Aaron turned again, getting visibly flustered. Mike almost felt sorry for the kid. He was in over his head. "Jimmy got a big signing bonus, but that's all kind of . . . assigned. He didn't want to give up salary this year or next year. After that, he'll probably be renegotiating for a new deal anyway. So, we didn't think there was any reason to, you know, move anything around now, or push anything out to future years."

"How did Chip O'Meara take it?" Jason asked.

Aaron stared out the window at his impressive view of the top of the Queensboro Bridge. He answered the question without looking at either detective. "I'd have to say he wasn't happy, but he's a professional, and I'm a professional, and so we left it at that. Jimmy had come up during practice for the meeting because I had another appointment that afternoon and we needed to get it done. So it was, like, right after lunch or something. But I remember Jimmy wanted to get back to the team. So, it was fine. Chip asked Jimmy to think about it and we scheduled another meeting for Friday."

"If I may?" Graham put his cup down with a clink as all eyes snapped to the Englishman. "Did Mr. Rydell have an accountant or personal secretary who handled his expenses?"

"No, why would he?" The agent seemed offended by the suggestion. "He had me and ISMS. I took care of him. The agency takes care of paying Jimmy's expenses and managing his money."

"I was wondering, you see. Because by my calculations, factoring in your ten percent fee along with the rent on his flat and my estimate of his general expenses and taxes, I would expect him to need to draw on some of his signing bonus money. If, as you say, that money was not liquid, then perhaps he took out some loans against future salary. Are you aware of anything like that, Mr. Taylor?"

"Well, certainly, if – I mean – I don't think you're correct, about Jimmy's expenses I mean. I'm not sure what figures you're using there, but I'm sure Jimmy's finances were just fine. ISMS always takes care of their clients. I take care of my clients, and especially Jimmy. I don't know – I'm frankly offended by the suggestion that I'd allow my client to be over-extended and need to take a loan."

"Let me ask this," Jason attempted to redirect the discussion. "How much of a commission are you going to get on the balance of Jimmy's contract over the next four years?"

Taylor closed both eyes, as if pained by the question. "The answer is nothing." He stood abruptly and began pacing behind the chairs where the other men were seated. "I got my commission on the signing bonus. The team has canceled the contract, obviously, and has no obligation to make any payments on the final four years. They'll get hit for the dead money, but I'll get nothing."

"What about life insurance?" Mike asked.

"That's why *he's* here," Taylor said, gesturing at Graham as he continued to prowl the room. "The team had a big policy, but the team gets the money. ISMS also has a policy on him, but much smaller. It's only one million. That's to hedge against the firm's expenses and marketing efforts. I don't get any of that, either. So, you see? Why would I have anything to do with killing Jimmy?"

"We're not suggesting you did," Mike said in his fatherly tone. It seemed appropriate considering that this kid was young enough to be his son. "We're tracking down leads and his finances are relevant, as are the contents of that discussion with the GM. You never know what's going to lead somewhere. Tell me a little more about the Boys Club?"

"It's the Boys & Girls Clubs," Taylor said acerbically. "Jimmy loved those kids. I did, too, but not like Jimmy. He felt like any one of them could be him at that age. But I don't see how that has anything to do with anything."

"Do you think there's anyone associated with the Boys – the organization – who might have had a grudge against Jimmy? Or gotten him into some trouble that you don't know about?"

Taylor stopped pacing and reached into a mini-fridge, from which he extracted a bottle of water and took a long swig. "I don't think so. Jimmy spent a lot of time down there. Much more than me. I guess anything's possible, but I don't see how."

"I'm so sorry," Graham broke in again. "You said something about *dead money*. Are you referring to the life insurance proceeds?"

"No." Taylor sighed, but seemed to appreciate having a question to which he knew the answer. "The dead money is the money the team already paid as a signing bonus. You see, there's a salary cap – the maximum amount the team is allowed to spend on player contracts each year. When you have a signing bonus, the total bonus is spread out over the life of the contract. So, if you pay a player twelve million as his bonus on a four-year contract, the salary cap hit is three million each year, plus that year's actual salary. But if you cut the player, or if he gets injured and can't play, then the remaining unaccounted-for money gets charged to the team's salary cap as if it was that year's salary. They call that *dead money*. I guess in this case it's a sick joke because it also applies if a player dies."

Graham seemed disappointed by the explanation. "So, there's no benefit to the team's finances if the player dies?"

Taylor looked confused. "It sucks for the team when they lose a star player. Finances are the least of it. I mean, they don't have to pay the salary for the rest of the term of the contract, so in that sense they save money. But they'll have to go out and get another quarterback, and that will cost as much or more than what they'll save."

"And, of course, they will recoup the twenty million death benefit on his life insurance policy," Graham observed. "Will that offset the, uh, *dead money*?"

"No. The team will get the cash, but that won't help the salary cap impact. The team will have a bunch less money to spend on players this year because of the dead money hit."

"How much did Jimmy have coming to him over the next four years on his deal?" Jason asked.

"He was scheduled to get five million this year, then six million next year, seven million in '21, and eight million in '22. He got thirty-six million as a signing bonus, so there's still twenty-four million that will hit the cap. It was supposed to be six million per year, but now that will get accelerated."

Mike scratched his head. "If he got thirty-six million up front as a signing bonus, how would it even be possible for him to have any financial problems?"

"He didn't have any!" Taylor shouted. "I'm telling you, he was fine. We paid his taxes on the bonus, then set up an annuity with the rest, which pays him out one million per year starting whenever he retires from football – well, would have retired. He still had plenty of income from the annual contract money, but I made sure he was set for life and couldn't squander his bonus money."

"How did Jimmy get cash when he needed it?" Jason asked.

"ISMS has a team of accountants who take care of our clients' routine expenses, taxes, and such. Jimmy didn't want to worry about those details, like most pro athletes. We set up a separate checking account for him where he could have funds he could easily withdraw for spending money and to make personal purchases. The rest was in an investment account from which the firm handled all his other payments."

"So, he didn't have access to the bonus funds at all?" Graham raised an eyebrow. "To him, in the short run, it's like the money never existed, is that it?"

"It was his nest egg. His safety net. God knows neither of us ever had one of those before. I convinced him it was the best way to go, and he trusted me." Taylor's voice trailed off at the end of his statement, as he gazed out the window again. He was clearly still in shock at the death of his friend and meal ticket.

"Well, like you said, it wasn't your fault," Jason tried to bring the kid back from his grief.

The young man in the expensive suit looked lost in his own office. He turned toward Jason. "Sure. Not my fault. But it sucks."

"It sucks more for Jimmy," Mike noted as he stood up. It seemed they were not going to get anything more from Aaron Taylor. "Do you have contact information for the guys Jimmy dealt with at the Boys and Girls Clubs? We may want to talk to them."

The question seemed to snap Aaron out of his fog. He hurried to his desk and tapped a few keys on his computer. Then a laser printer unit sitting on a nearby credenza whirred to life, spitting out a sheet of paper with the names and contact information Mike had requested. Jason lifted the paper from the output tray and it disappeared into his inside jacket pocket.

"Thank you for your time, Mr. Taylor. We're very sorry for your loss. I was really looking forward to Jimmy having a better season this year. It's a shame he never got to show us how good he could have been."

"Thanks," Taylor said blankly.

The fashion model who had shown them in appeared at the office door, no doubt bidden by some unseen electronic signal from her boss. They said their good-byes and were escorted away. As he passed through the door, the last one to leave, Mike glanced back at the young agent. Taylor was slumped over his desk with his head resting on his arms. Mike couldn't tell for sure whether he was crying.

# Chapter 18 – Where's Tiger?

AFTER A FRUSTRATINGLY SLOW DRIVE back to the West Side in the departmental Lincoln, the two detectives and Graham parked in the loading zone in front of Park Towers. During the trip, Mike had called the assistant DA, David Zimmerman, to see if they had their search warrant yet. He said he expected it any minute. Apparently, the judge had some kind of emergency and they were waiting longer than normal.

He had then called Michelle to inquire about the progress of thawing out their body. Her news was encouraging. She expected to be able to perform the autopsy by the end of the day. Finally, he had called Detective Meyer to see if the video review had turned up anything interesting. There was still a lot more to review, she said. Mike gave Meyer the contact information for the director at the lower Manhattan Boys & Girls Clubs. Mike instructed her to track him down, when she was done with the video review, and see if he knew of anyone connected to the program who might have had a grudge against Jimmy.

Inside the building, Mike wanted to speak to the weekday doormen who were there on Wednesday, the last time anyone saw Jimmy. After checking in with the building manager again, he called over Manuel, who was working on Wednesday, and Henry, whom they had spoken to on Saturday. Unfortunately, Manuel had no new information. The two of them together confirmed Jimmy's general pattern of staying in on weeknights and going out or hosting parties in his penthouse on weekends. Manuel confirmed that Jimmy came down every morning and got his bagel and coffee from Tiger. For the last two weeks, The Duke had picked him up every morning. He did notice that Jimmy seemed more beaten down by practice on Wednesday, but he remembered the player saying hello and calling him by name, as he always did. He was pretty sure Jimmy had food delivered at dinner time, then Manuel had finished his shift and gone home for the day.

When they finished, Graham asked, "Who is this person named Tiger?"

"He's a street kid who hangs around. Jimmy took a shine to him and has him run him errands and such. He brings Jimmy his coffee and bagel every morning."

"So, he's someone who spent some time with Mr. Rydell? Perhaps we should speak to him, don't you think? Where could we find this young man?"

Manuel shrugged. "I haven't seen him today." He walked toward the main entrance a few steps and called out, "Hey, Cesar, you seen Tiger today?"

"No. Not today. Maybe he's out in his house."

"House?" Mike asked.

"Yeah. The kid has a little campsite on the side of the building. He calls it his house. We can go take a look."

Henry led the group through a door behind the main desk into the breezeway that cut under the building and connected the exterior service entrance with Park Towers, and with the businesses that occupied the ground-level storefronts. Mike immediately noticed the lack of air conditioning in the nonresidential space. Neatly stacked boxes dotted the floor against one wall, labeled *kitchen, living room, kids' room,* and such. Someone was moving in. Sunlight washed inside the relatively dim interior through a large open door at the north side. The silhouette of a man pushing a hand truck piled with more cardboard boxes came toward them as they squinted into the brightness. When they emerged onto the sidewalk, the June heat hit them in full force. Jason extracted sunglasses from his coat pocket and smoothly transitioned to the sunlight. Mike held up a hand to shade his eyes. Graham seemed not to notice.

They turned left and quickly came upon the encampment. It was a familiar scene to the New Yorkers. A large cardboard box was propped up against the side of the building, mostly covering a ventilation grate. A disheveled pile of blankets and clothing peeked out from under the cardboard shelter. Mike noticed a thin, black wooden box pushed up against the building, next to a plastic milk crate containing neatly arranged brushes and tins of shoe polish.

"Looks like he didn't move his stuff out," Jason said.

"Yeah," Henry agreed. "His shoeshine kit is still here. He usually sets up shop out front on weekdays, looking to get some business from residents heading off to work. I didn't see him today in his usual place."

"OK, well, do us a favor and keep an eye out for the kid. When he shows up, give me a call." Mike handed the doorman one of his standard business cards.

Mike's phone buzzed. A moment later, he said to Jason, "We have a warrant. Zimmerman is having one of his guys meet us out in Florham Park so we can talk to Nate and then bring him along."

"Let's see how surprised we can make him," Jason said, clapping his hands.

Jason pulled the Lincoln into a parking spot in the shade of a tree. Graham had declined to accompany them to New Jersey, which was fine with the detectives. He said he wanted to spend some time "following the money," in reference to Jimmy's finances. He wasn't concerned about the investigation into Nate Bedford. If Jimmy's teammate murdered him in a jealous rage, the insurance would pay out without objection. Graham's focus was on theories in which either Jimmy was engaged in criminal activity, or the team was somehow responsible for his death. Either would void the policy and make Graham a hero. Anything else was irrelevant to Boyd's of Britain.

As they walked from the parking area toward the main building, where they expected to meet up with somebody from the DA's office with their warrant papers, Kristi Olson was walking toward them. She greeted the detectives and reversed course, falling into step with them back toward the team offices. Mike and Jason deflected her questions about why they were back and whether they had made any progress in their investigation.

"But you spoke to Candi, right? You got her story. So, I'm guessing you're here to talk to Nate again, huh?"

"We really can't discuss it," Mike politely put her off. "You'll have to excuse us." They had arrived at the door to the administration building, where they left Kristi outside. When they emerged a few minutes later with two copies of a search warrant tucked into Jason's breast pocket, Kristi was waiting.

"He's over at Muscle Beach," she said with a bright smile.

Mike wasn't thrilled about having to confront Nate in a public place, in full view and earshot of the press. He tugged on Jason's elbow and led him back inside. They passed the courier from the DA's office. He was on his way out, but they grabbed him and pulled him back. Moments later, Mike Fitzsimmons exited out a side door along with an intern from the team's Public Relations office. The pair navigated to the outdoor weightlifting area, found Nate, and advised him that his presence was required inside. Fitzsimmons was sweating bullets, worried that the player might bolt. He was not prepared to chase down an NFL wide receiver. Fortunately for him, Nate did not put up a fight. Kristi was surprised to see Nate going inside and objected when the PR intern told her the building was temporarily closed to the press.

Once again, Jason took the lead in questioning Nate. "We have a few follow-up questions for you. On Wednesday, after your fight with Jimmy, when they helped you up off the floor . . ." Jason paused to give Nate a look, challenging him to once again disagree with the characterization. Nate kept quiet this time. "We understand you lunged back toward Jimmy, like you were going to sucker-punch him when his back was turned. Is that right?"

"Hell no! That's a damned lie. Who told you that? I already got my licks in. I don't need help taking care of no n – no-good pretty-boy quarterback." Nate's eyes were wide. He glanced toward Mike again, as if pleading for something.

"Then, after Jimmy left, several witnesses heard you say you would get your revenge. Do you recall that?"

"I don't know. I guess I was pretty hot."

"So, you don't remember what you said?" Jason intoned the question as if implying Nate was either lying or an idiot. In truth, he thought both, but the object was to induce an answer from the witness, who might think silence was confirmation.

"I remember I yelled at him and told him to stay the fuck away from my girl."

"Is that when you yelled that you were going to kill him?" Jason raised an eyebrow.

Nate's face froze. Mike couldn't tell if he was dumbstruck that his teammates had ratted him out, or if he was just trying hard to remember. "I don't think I said nothing like that. I was pissed, for sure, but it's not like I was gonna actually kill him."

"So, then you left with Candi, right?" Jason leaned back, as if the tough part of the questioning was over. It wasn't, but Jason wanted Nate to relax and let down his guard.

"Yeah. Me and Candi went back to her place."

Jason was betting Candi had not told Nate about her interview with the detectives, so he played dumb and let Nate dig himself a hole. "Must be nice to have such a pretty girl tending to your injuries – giving you some good loving care, eh?"

"I didn't have no injuries," Nate shot back, defensively. "But, yeah, Candi got me a Band-Aid or two."

"I bet she made you feel better in a lot of ways."

Nate smiled. "Oh, sure. Ya know, I was all worked up, so we kinda let off some steam."

"Makes sense," Jason agreed calmly. "I recall you saying you had your truck there, at Candi's place?"

"Yep."

"You drove straight from Candi's apartment to your place in Jersey City?"

"I – well, ya know, I'm not sure. Things were kinda fuzzy that night."

"You'd been drinking?" Jason prompted, still reclining in his chair as if it were a casual question.

"I had a few beers."

Now Jason leaned forward toward Nate. His eyes were no more than three feet from the wide receiver. "Was that before you punched Candi in the face?"

Now, Nate was genuinely shocked, and his face gave away his thoughts. "Who told you that?"

"Don't deny it, Nate. You and Candi had a fight, and she threw you out and told you to never come back. Isn't that right?"

"That bitch tell you those lies?" The vertical muscles in Nate's neck bulged out on both sides.

"What's a lie, Nate?"

"I never hit her!"

"But you did have a fight?"

"No."

"Then why is she a bitch?"

"She's a bitch for telling you lies about me!"

"So, you didn't have a fight?"

"Well, yeah, you know, these girls are crazy. One minute all they wanna do is screw an' the next minute they're all pissed off about who knows what."

"So, she did throw you out?"

"I left. Okay? She was pissed off at me and I was pissed off at her, so I took off."

"And you drove into Manhattan."

"Yeah—" Nate froze. "I mean, I guess. I told you I didn't remember, but, yeah, now that you mention it, I guess I might have."

Jason showed no emotion, but quickly pushed out the next question. "You drove your truck to Jimmy's apartment building, didn't you?"

Now Jason and Mike watched as the gears inside Nate's brain cranked out a message that he was in huge trouble. He remained silent.

"You were pissed off at Jimmy; he had beaten you bloody in the locker room. You were pissed off at Candi and you blamed Jimmy for that, too, so you headed out to get your revenge, didn't you?"

"No! Maybe I was thinkin' that. Shit, I did drive down to Jimmy's sweet-ass penthouse, but I'm not a moron. I cooled off while I was drivin' and by the time I got there, I figured I was a little drunk and what was I gonna do? Break into his place? So, shit, I just turned around and drove home."

"That's when you got pulled over by the cops," Jason said.

Mike watched as recognition dawned on Nate that, of course, the detectives would know. "Yeah. Right. They stopped me. They were pretty decent an' didn't haul my ass in, but the guy cop told me I had to leave my truck, so I had to call an Uber to take me home."

Mike then decided the time was right to be the good cop. "Nate, why didn't you tell us all this when we first questioned you? This makes you look pretty bad."

"Hey, you never asked," Nate retorted with a smirk.

Mike laughed, as if impressed by Nate's clever avoidance of the damaging information. "We'll be sure to ask next time. Like, for example, right now. We're on our way to your apartment. Why don't you come along, so if we find anything that raises a question, you'll be right there to answer? How does that sound to you, Nate?"

"What?" was all Nate could come up with on short notice. "Wait. No. I don't think I'd like to do that. You can't just go snoopin' around in a man's home. Don't you need a warrant or something?"

Mike smiled his helpful-grandfather smile. "You are absolutely right, Nate. We do need a warrant. And we have one right here." He gestured to Jason, who removed the warrant copy from his inside jacket pocket and handed it to Nate. The player scanned the legal document, trying to decide whether it looked legitimate or might be a trick.

"Nate, we're going now, with you or without you. If you'd like to avoid having to change the lock on the door after we break into it, I'd recommend you come along and let us in."

# Chapter 19 – Forensic Failure

A FEW MINUTES BEFORE 5:00 p.m., Mike and Jason pushed through the swinging doors on the ground floor of the municipal building on Centre Street in lower Manhattan. They had stashed the Lincoln in a nearby loading zone. Jason planned to drive it to Brooklyn to meet up with Rachel for dinner, but first he and Mike needed to pay a visit to the county medical examiner.

The trip to Jersey City to search Nate's apartment had turned up Nate's bloody shirt, which was still in his kitchen garbage can, but nothing else of significance. The shirt might have some of Jimmy's blood on it, but after the locker room fight, that would prove nothing. Mike and Jason agreed that the guy wasn't stupid enough to leave it in his trash if he had worn it while killing Jimmy. Plus, even if he could have snuck in the side service entrance, somehow convinced Jimmy to let him into his apartment, then killed him in a fit of drunken, jealous rage, what had happened to the body? But they bagged the bloody shirt to send to the lab for analysis anyway.

They sent Nate's truck back to the impound lot for a forensics sweep but didn't expect much. They confiscated his phone, hoping there might be a stray text message or email. Nate, who had called his players' union rep by then, shut down his phone and refused to provide the unlock code.

They had checked off one more item from their to-do list, but they were no closer to placing Nate, or anyone else, at the likely scene of the murder. Michelle had texted Mike while they were driving back from New Jersey to say she had finally completed the autopsy on Jimmy Rydell.

Seeing the detectives enter her lab, Michelle stood up from her gray metal work desk at the far end of the room, under the huge poster of the periodic table of elements. She grabbed a file folder and met them halfway across the sterile space, where she motioned toward a countertop containing microscopes, heating units, and other equipment. Mike and Jason climbed onto high, barstool-like chairs, while Dr. McNeill stood on the other side.

"Why not sit at your desk for this?" Mike asked.

"Because I need to show you something I have on a slide," Michelle replied, gesturing to a nearby microscope. "You'll understand in a minute."

"Great. So, Jimmy finally thawed out?"

"Enough for me to do a proper examination, although I expect the tox screen is going to be inconclusive because of the time lag and the freezing."

"Why is that?" Jason asked.

Michelle explained that the combination of the passage of time – even in non-living tissue – and the effect of the freezing and thawing was likely to interfere with the results of standard toxicology tests. Cells would have broken down. Reactions had been altered. "It may prevent us from knowing for sure if he was drugged before he was strangled," Michelle said.

"So, you've confirmed strangulation as the cause of death?" Mike didn't try to hide his disappointment. He was hoping there would be something less obvious to help them with their investigation.

"Definitely," Michelle said, flipping open the folder so she could read her notes. She was pretty certain she had the important points memorized, but it was always best to be sure. "I found no wounds or injection points on the body. There were wide, discolored markings around his neck. You saw that already, but I confirmed the marks are consistent with strangulation using some kind of material around the neck."

"Rope?" Jason suggested.

"Not in the traditional sense," Michelle replied. "The marks are not consistent with a particularized force on a small surface area, like you would see where the surface of a rope, even a thick one, makes contact with the skin. This was more dispersed, wider, like a cloth – a scarf or maybe a towel or even a pair of pants. What I can tell you for sure is that it compressed the man's windpipe enough that it collapsed and cut off his breathing. All the other classic indicators of asphyxiation by strangulation are present. That's your cause of death."

"So," Mike prompted, knowing Michelle was waiting for the invitation, "what was it you wanted to show us?"

Michelle pulled a microscope toward herself, flicked on the light to illuminate the slide already in the mechanism, and adjusted the focus in the viewer. Looking up, she motioned for Mike to come take a look. She stepped aside so Mike could peer into the eyepiece.

After fifteen seconds and one slight focus adjustment, Mike pulled back. "You got me, Doctor. What is that?"

"I'm not sure. It's mostly rubber, but it's too small for me to give it a positive ID. It's yellow, though, as you can see."

"Where did you find it?"

"Under his fingernail."

"How sure are you that it has something to do with what strangled him?"

"I'm not sure, but there were other scratch marks on his neck, above the bruises made by whatever it was. They look like fingernail scratches, where he was clawing at himself – trying to break or get his fingers under it. It's likely he scratched it and a fragment broke off under his nail. I think I'll be able to match this to a sample of the original material, if we ever find it."

"Is there anything else of note about the autopsy?" Mike asked.

"No. Everything else was pretty normal. He was in great shape. Body fat level was miniscule. We'll run the tox screen, but I'm doubting it will help us, like I said. His stomach was empty."

"Time of death?" Jason asked.

"Uncertain," was the best Michelle could tell them. "The freezing and thawing of the body nullified most of the markers that indicate how long the body had been lifeless. Heat dissipation, for example, and the appearance of bruising, and blood settling – they were all thrown off by the freezing process. I can't tell you for sure if he died Wednesday or Friday. But there are no signs that the body was abused or tortured before death, so it doesn't look like he was kept alive. There are no markings to suggest he was bound or gagged and no other indications of being held captive."

"Any idea how long he was frozen?"

"No. Based on the body temperature when the corpse was brought in, I'd speculate that it had been out of the freezer for about six to eight hours. But I can't begin to speculate on how long he was frozen, or how long he was dead before he was frozen. Except, I'd guess it wasn't more than twelve hours."

"Based on the bruising?"

"That and the rigor mortis. Unless somebody took great pains to straighten out his fingers before freezing him, it's likely he wasn't dead more than twelve hours."

"The working theory is that he was killed at his apartment building on Wednesday night or early Thursday morning, then moved somewhere after death. Is that consistent with your findings?" Mike hoped for an affirmative answer, but knew how careful Michelle was with her opinions. It was what made her a great witness at a murder trial, but it sometimes drove detectives crazy.

"I'd say that theory is consistent with the physical characteristics of the body. Beyond that, I can't speculate." Michelle tilted her head to the side and shrugged. It was the closest she could come to saying, "You're probably right."

"Thanks," Mike said as he waited for any additional information. None came.

◆◆◆

Jason led the way back to the Lincoln. They were closing in on the longest day of the year and it was still bright and warm at 5:30 p.m. "You know, Mike, it's looking like this investigation is going to suck up all our time, plus overtime, for the rest of the week, at least."

"Yeah?" Mike said, asking with his tone why that mattered.

"What about Thursday night?"

Mike, who was just buckling his seatbelt, slapped his hand on the passenger-side door. "Crap. I forgot about taking Tony to the Mets game. He'll be disappointed if I have to cancel. And Marie – she'll be even more disappointed. She told me she has some big plan for her and Jenny while Uncle Mike takes Tony to the game. Well, I'll just have to make it work. Sully will be happy that the overtime will take a dip."

"OK, that works. I have some plans of my own for Thursday." Jason pulled the Lincoln out of the parking lot.

"Right. We'll have to make sure Thursday works for you. Jimmy's funeral is that afternoon, so most of our key players won't be available anyway. I still think you're moving too fast, but I'm happy for you – assuming she says yes."

"She'd better!" Jason laughed. "What time you want to get started in the morning?"

Mike scowled. "I can't do anything before nine. I have the mandatory departmental sensitivity training at 8:00 a.m."

"Good," Jason glanced over as he checked the traffic. "That training will do you some good."

"Bah. I've been through anti-harassment training a half-dozen times. It's fairly worthless. But Sully's been on my ass about getting it done so he can say all his detectives have finished it. Seems like a waste of time."

"Keep an open mind, Mike."

"Sure. Why not." Mike stared out the window. "By the way, I've been thinking about what we talked about this morning. I've been paying attention and I did notice two things today that struck me as racist."

"Two?"

"Yeah. Two."

Jason kept his eyes on the road. "When you saw those two incidents, did you call them out? Did you take any action to stop them?"

Mike was silent.

"That's the point, Mike. Noticing it is important, but it doesn't mean anything unless you do something about it. They might cover that in the training tomorrow."

Mike remained silent as Jason drove on in the Manhattan traffic.

# Chapter 20 – Important Decisions

THAT EVENING, Jason took advantage of having the departmental car by driving Rachel to Coney Island. He knew Rachel loved the boardwalk and the beach. They enjoyed the last few minutes of sunlight while walking barefoot in the sand, dodging the remarkably large number of New Yorkers who were pretending it was already summer.

The cold Atlantic water felt good on his feet as Jason walked closest to the water, holding Rachel's hand in his left, while holding his shoes in his right. Rachel stopped and leaned down to dig a small orange and white shell out of the sand. The twilight was fading into darkness and she could see the first stars on the eastern horizon.

"How did you and Diana like *Kinky Boots*?"

"Diana really loved going with me. Thanks for getting us the great seats. Maybe you'll take me back to see it again, so you can see it for yourself."

"I'm sorry I had to miss it. This case is pretty all-consuming."

"I guess I'm going to have to get used to that, huh? If I'm going to be with you, I'll have to live with the odd hours and the all-consuming cases."

"What do you mean, *if*?"

She disengaged her fingers from his and slapped him on his left arm. He gave an over-exaggerated groan and pretended to crumple over in pain. "Ow! You know you can't hit me there. I'm an injured man."

"Oh, you are such a baby sometimes." She reached out and gently rubbed the area around his healing gunshot wound. "You told me it was almost healed."

"Well, sure, unless somebody punches me there." He flashed his best smile and stopped to pull her toward him for a gentle kiss. She gladly complied, pressing herself into him, while holding her shoes out to the side.

When he lifted his head, he let his forehead rest against hers. "I'm a cop. There are some things that come with the job. Just like yours."

"My job runs in shifts. When the whistle blows, I'm done."

"Right." Jason pulled his head away. "Like that kid last week, the one you stayed with in the hospital for three hours waiting for his mom to arrive."

Rachel smiled at the memory and nodded her concession on the point. "He was so adorable. I couldn't just leave him there. My shift was over, so I was on my own time. And don't tell me you wouldn't have done the same thing." She raised an accusatory finger and wagged it at Jason.

"I'm not saying that. I just want you to know I wanted to be with you yesterday, and I would have been except that the investigation is so hot."

"I get it. I do. Don't worry. I know what I'm getting myself into. Everyone in the City is following the case." They resumed walking as Rachel kicked at the wet sand. "I wish I wasn't working on Thursday or I'd go to the march."

"What march?"

"There's going to be a march up the West Side to the church before Jimmy's funeral."

"Who's marching? And for what?"

"They're marching for Jimmy's memory. God knows he took enough abuse for kneeling and speaking out against brutality. It was probably some racist kook who killed him, right?" She turned to Jason with anger in her eyes.

"We don't know yet. It could have been, but we're a long way from being sure. I didn't know you were a big Jimmy Rydell fan."

"I'm not a football fan, but he's made a difference, and now to have him just taken out like that. He's younger than me. It's scary what can happen. It makes me so mad."

"I know. I feel the same way."

They walked in silence several steps before Rachel spoke again. "Jay? Is being a cop something you want to do forever?"

"What do you mean? Forever is a long time."

Rachel lowered her head. "It's just . . . I don't know . . . I was thinking that being a homicide detective is great, but maybe someday you'd take a different job that's not so . . . dangerous." She glanced up at Jason's face to see his reaction.

Jason blew out a breath in the direction of the ocean, away from Rachel. "It's something that I've been giving a lot of thought to lately." He looked directly into her eyes. "I don't think I want to spend the next twenty years chasing down bad guys with Mike, if that's what you mean. I can see myself moving up in the department. I can even see myself retiring someday and taking a civilian job. I mean, I might want to coach my son's Pop Warner football team someday."

Rachel brightened noticeably. "That's what I meant. But do you really think playing football is a good idea for kids? I mean, with all the concussion issues?"

Jason let out a loud chuckle. "I don't think we need to be concerned about making that decision right now."

"We?"

"I mean . . . you, or I, or you and I together . . . it's a decision that's a ways down the road."

"Yeah. Sure." Rachel lowered her head again so Jason couldn't see her expression as she smiled to herself.

"Speaking of Thursday, although you'll have to miss the Jimmy Rydell march, we're still on for dinner for your birthday. Mike is taking his godson to the Mets game that night, so even with this investigation, I'm sure I won't have to cancel that."

"Oooh, good. I'm really looking forward to *Le Renard Courrant*. I've read such great things about it. I'm still impressed you got us a reservation. And remember that my party's on Sunday, at my parents' house."

"I won't forget. I can't make any guarantees about how the investigation will be going by then—"

"Oh, no! You be there, investigation or no investigation. Daddy would be really upset if you don't make it."

"Then I'll be there. I wouldn't ever want to upset your father."

"Don't you forget it. He's really a pussycat once you get to know him."

"I'll take your word for it. So far it seems like he doesn't like me much."

"He has a tendency not to like any boy I bring home. It's a father thing, I guess."

Jason stopped again and put both arms around Rachel, who ignored the clunk of his shoes knocking into her lower back. "I will do my best to change his opinion of me, because I'm very much in love with his darling daughter."

They kissed, the soft waves lapping at their bare feet. The sound of screaming teenagers riding the Cyclone drifted across the beach, along with laughter from the boardwalk arcades.

"I love you, too, Jay. That scares me a little."

"I know. It scares me, too."

They kept walking, both thinking how good it felt to be together on the beach.

# Chapter 21 – Unconscious Bias

Tuesday, June 4

MIKE ARRIVED AT THE PRECINCT HOUSE on 94th Street at 7:55 a.m. on Tuesday, earlier than normal because he had a mandatory meeting. The police department training on implicit bias and bias avoidance had been rolled out at the beginning of the year. It was part of a program the Mayor had promised in his last election cycle to improve race relations between the NYPD and the minority citizens of the city. Commissioner Ward went along with it and made it mandatory for all department personnel. The deadline for having everyone complete the course was June 15th. Mike had skipped his first two scheduled sessions because they conflicted with his physical therapy appointments after his shoulder surgery. The second rescheduled session fell during the Christine Barker investigation, and he was too busy. He was still too busy now, but Sully had informed him that missing this one was not an option. He was even getting overtime pay for the hour, not that he needed any more overtime.

A mixed group of uniformed officers, detectives, and civilian staff crowded into the conference room on the 5th floor. Extra chairs had to be brought in. The whiteboard on the wall was mostly covered up with a brightly colored poster containing slogans and graphics intended to help with the presentation. Mike noticed that the upper-right corner of the board still showed the black outline of a square; the ink had dried on for so long that it would never completely erase. He sat up in his chair, took a swig of coffee, and paid attention when the presenter arrived.

An hour later, Mike descended the stairs to the bullpen on the third floor. Jason met him at his desk. "So, what did you think of the training, Mike?"

"I thought the instructor did a good job with it."

"What about the content? Did you learn anything?"

Mike paused to think about his answer, not sure how much ground he wanted to concede to his partner. "There were a few eye-openers for me, Jason. It wasn't a complete waste of time."

"High praise," Jason teased.

"Yeah, well, an old goat like me has a tendency to pretend things don't exist. Some of the material and statistics showed me that some people, including me, may have some attitudes that influence their behavior. They might not even realize it. I have to acknowledge that the information is important."

"That's progress," Jason smiled. "We'll make you woke yet."

"Don't get carried away," Mike retorted. "What's our first stop today?"

"First stop is the conference room. Birds of Britain is waiting for us."

Mike grimaced, but followed Jason toward the little corner room where Graham Beckwith was sitting primly in his chair, wearing his usual tweed jacket and sipping from a Starbucks cup.

"Our stationhouse coffee not good enough for you?" Mike couldn't stop himself from tossing out a friendly barb.

"Not at all, Detective. The Starbucks Teavana is remarkably adequate." He held up his cup in a mock salute. "Gentlemen, I'm keen to hear your update on the investigation, and I'm happy to share with you the fruits of my labor since we were last together." Graham paused, wondering if Mike or Jason would want to go first, but seeing no indication of that, he pressed on. "Right. I spent much of yesterday tracking Mr. Rydell's finances. As I'm sure you know, a man's spending patterns can be quite indicative of any unusual activity. Boyd's has a remarkable research department. In this case, there are several very interesting facts. The first is that our player – the, uh, quarterback – was making substantial payments to his employer, the football club."

Jason perked up, suddenly quite interested. "What kind of payments?"

"The flat where Mr. Rydell lived is owned by the New York American Conference Football Club, Incorporated. That would be his team, I believe. He was paying some eighty thousand dollars per month for his furnished living space."

"He was a subtenant?" Mike asked rhetorically.

"So it would seem," Graham said, then continued. "The base rent was not the only payment to the team. Apparently, management also set up an account for Mr. Rydell to take care of his other needs, including cleaning service, catering for parties, laundering of his clothing, and personal security."

"Personal security?" Mike said. "That must be The Duke. I thought the team assigned him to Jimmy to keep him out of trouble. The team was charging Jimmy? That's a little surprising."

"Well, someone was making the payments on behalf of Mr. Rydell without questioning the legitimacy of the charges. The peripheral expenses amounted to another thirty thousand dollars per month."

Jason whistled. "Wow. That's quite the umbilical cord for the team. That's, what, one point three million per year? I know Jimmy had a big contract, but that's like the team getting a refund."

"Exactly," Graham confirmed. "It seems the team purchased the unit when the building was constructed several years ago. Before Mr. Rydell, it was rented to another player who is no longer with the team. A Mr. Watson."

"The cornerback," Mike said. "He was the first-round draft pick two years before Jimmy. They traded him to Seattle. I guess they figured they could keep it rented out to their high-priced players and recoup the cost, plus make a nice profit. The big-money kids don't know any better, so they say, 'Sure, I'll live in the fancy Manhattan apartment with all the amenities covered by the team.' Why not? It's a pretty nifty deal. And they can afford it."

"It's like the old company store," Jason said. "Keep your employees indebted to The Man."

"C'mon, now, Jason. The kid was making much more than what he was paying. It's not like he was an indentured servant."

"No? Let's ask Mr. Beckwith." Jason looked at the Brit. "Have you done an analysis of Jimmy's budget?"

"Indeed," Graham said, smiling. "As I calculate it, after his taxes, agent's fee, and expenses, Mr. Rydell had only a small cushion. Perhaps in the area of one or two hundred thousand dollars net last year."

"Still a lot of money," Mike observed.

"Not if you're living the high life, like Jimmy," Jason said. "Plus, he had a bunch of legal issues and the lawyers he hired don't come cheap. And didn't his agent tell us he donated a million dollars to the Boys & Girls Clubs?"

"He did say that," Graham answered. "As I evaluate Mr. Rydell's accounts, I don't see where he had the available cash to make that kind of donation."

Mike ran his hand across his face, scratching at the stubble of his beard. He had neglected to shave that morning in his haste to arrive on time for the training class. "Taylor said that donation was out of his first year's pay. How does somebody spend that much money?"

"Maybe he didn't realize it," Jason suggested. "His agent's management company was taking care of paying all his expenses and managing his finances."

"Sure, but wouldn't his agent tell him not to make a donation he couldn't afford? And no wonder he didn't want to restructure his contract," Mike said. "He didn't have the money."

"Where does that lead us?" Jason asked, looking at Graham.

"Normally, gentlemen, it leads us to inquire where the money came from, and where it really went."

"You don't think it went to the Boys & Girls Clubs?" Mike asked.

"I make no assumptions."

"Good," Mike said, standing. "Neither do we."

The three men left the conference room, but before they got far, Detective Berkowitz walked up to Mike with a newspaper in his hand. "Say, Mike, what do ya make of the articles today about your boy, Jimmy?"

"He's not my boy," Mike replied testily. "But I haven't seen the paper today. What's in there?"

Berkowitz handed the paper to Mike, already folded to the page in the Metro section. The headline blared: **Rydell Murder May Have Link to Sports Gambling Syndicate.** The byline was Dexter Peacock and Kristi Olson. Mike scanned the story, while Jason and Graham peered over his shoulder.

The article, attributed to unnamed sources inside an ongoing FBI investigation, claimed that federal agents had been closing in on an organized nationwide syndicate engaged in a point-shaving scheme involving several NFL teams. Jimmy Rydell was identified as one of the players within the scope of the investigation. No details were revealed, and no other players were identified. *The Times* speculated that the reason Rydell's name had been leaked was because he was already dead. The article further speculated that Jimmy's murder could be connected to the investigation, and that whoever killed him dumped the body in plain sight on the Central Park carousel as a warning to other players that they should not cooperate with the feds.

The article also noted that, in connection with the murder investigation, the police had served a search warrant on Nate Bedford and interrogated him a second time on Monday. Nate was named as the prime suspect, although the article could not confirm whether Nate was also connected to the point-shaving scheme.

"That's a lot of speculation," Mike said, handing the paper to Jason, who was nearly done reading.

Graham took the paper afterward, creasing the center fold carefully. "Well, gentlemen, perhaps there is a connection between Mr. Rydell's finances and his link to this gambling operation?"

"You'd like that, wouldn't you?" Jason said.

"I neither like nor dislike the situation. My assignment is to establish the facts. But I will admit, my employer will be pleased if the death was the result of Mr. Rydell's involvement in a criminal enterprise."

"Don't you think that makes you a little biased?" Mike asked.

"Not at all, Detective Stoneman. It makes me good at my job."

"Well, we'll see where this leads."

# Chapter 22 – Fish & Stiffs

**M**IKE AND JASON SPENT the rest of the day on Tuesday unsuccessfully searching for other potential suspects. They trekked again out to Florham Park to interview the few remaining players and other team employees they had missed on Monday. That trip didn't uncover any important new information.

Graham met with Woody and Chip O'Meara to formally inform them that Boyd's of Britain was holding payment of the $20 million on Jimmy's policy while the police investigation continued. He reported to Mike and Jason that Woody understood and again pledged his full cooperation.

On the way back to Manhattan, Mike dropped Jason at 47th Street and 8th Avenue so he could dash over to the Diamond District before the stores closed. When he crossed 6th Avenue, Jason scanned the passing storefronts, looking for number 145. It turned out to be a massive, open room lined with rows of low glass display cases. It was one of the many rent-a-booth spaces where small business owners could set up shop amid hundreds of competitors and hawk their jewels to some of the most discerning customers on the planet. Jason's college economics professor would have called this *perfect competition*.

He swallowed his usual male pride and asked the proprietor of the first booth he passed where he could find location 47-D. It was pushing 4:00 p.m. and he was worried the sellers would start closing for the day. After another few minutes of searching the aisles, he still hadn't seen the sign for the All-American Gem Company, but he heard the unmistakable high-pitched voice of Ms. Helene DiVito Rosen. Helene fancied herself his personal jeweler after assisting in the investigation aboard the *Colossus of the Ocean* in May, where she and her companion, Henrick, had been selling baubles to cruise passengers. She had promised she could get him a great deal on an engagement ring if he ever needed one. Now was the time to see if she would come through.

Helene was helping a customer pick out earrings when Jason walked into her view. She smiled and made eye contact with the tall detective, who inclined his head to indicate that he could wait. When the other customer took a business card and walked away, Helene turned her attention to Jason.

Today, the former Mrs. Nick DiVito was dressed conservatively in a loose-fitting yellow blouse with bare shoulders. A string of pearls with matching earrings accentuated her long, shapely neck and her long blonde hair that was pinned up. Although she showed no visible cleavage, Jason's eyes could not help but stray to the massive mounds on her chest. She had once told Jason and Mike that her surgically augmented breasts were the nicest thing her now-deceased former husband ever bought her.

"Hello, Detective Jason Dickson," she said brightly, her voice arcing even higher at the end of her sentence. "I hope you're here for what I think you're here for." She stooped down to fetch a tray from under the display counter. Jason had called her two days earlier, so he didn't expect her to be surprised by his appearance. She carefully arranged the tray, containing rows of sparkling rings nestled in green velvet.

"I was hoping—"

"Oh, I know, Detective. I remember you and your beautiful lady, Rachel, who loves emeralds. It wasn't that long ago, and I have—"

"I remember, also," Jason cut her off. "But I was thinking I really should get a diamond for an engagement ring. Diamonds are what's expected, right?"

"Oh, no, Detective. These days, ladies like to have something unique and special. Diamonds are fine, of course, but I see lots of women coming in asking for rubies or sapphires or emeralds. And other stones can be set with diamond accents if you really want some diamonds. But that's not what your Rachel wants, I'm sure. She wants something elegant and simple, but pretty. Something that will catch people's attention. Let me tell you, if you get her a diamond, she won't be disappointed. But if you get her an emerald, you'll sweep her off her feet."

"How do you know Rachel so well?"

Helene smiled and dropped her head slightly, selecting a yellow gold ring with a shining green stone. She mounted it on a Tiffany-blue pedestal and sprayed it with a blast of steam from a tiny hose, making the stone sparkle under an overhead spotlight.

"It is gorgeous," Jason leaned down to closely inspect the gem.

"And emeralds are more affordable than diamonds. You can get a larger stone for the same money." She directed her soft blue eyes at Jason, beaming with excitement and anticipation as if she were the prospective bride.

Jason carefully plucked the ring from its display mount and held it up, scrutinizing the gold band against the bright lights. All around in the immense room, conversations, the clinking of glass and metal, and the hiss of steam sprays created a din. Jason, however, was oblivious.

"Can I ask you to put it on your finger, so I can see how it looks there?"

"Of course!" Helene chirped, snatching the band from Jason's fingers and sliding the emerald onto her left ring finger. She held her hand up so Jason could see, then placed it down on the counter so the lights would reflect off all the stone's facets. "It's really spectacular."

Jason nodded. "You're sure she'll like it?"

"Detective, if she doesn't love it, you bring her back to see me and we'll fix her up with something else. But that's not going to happen. I guarantee it."

Jason asked Helene to package up the ring and provided a credit card. As he tucked the small package into his jacket pocket, she leaned in and said, "She's absolutely crazy about you. It keeps me believing in love when I see couples like you getting married." She handed Jason a new business card that included her Instagram address. "I hope I get invited to the wedding." She winked, leaving Jason wondering whether she was serious.

That evening, Mike arrived at Michelle's apartment on Third Avenue ready to relax over dinner after a hectic day. Immediately upon opening the door, his mouth started to water as his nose was assaulted by the smell of baking bread, mixed with fish and spice. "Wow!" he called out, figuring Michelle was in the kitchen. When he caught sight of her, standing over a steaming pot on the stove, he burst into a grin. "That smells great. What are you making?"

The long wooden spoon in her slender hand never stopped stirring. Michelle had a floral apron covering her usual conservative work clothes. She turned her head to call back, "I thought you might like something we had on our cruise last month, so I got a recipe for Bermuda fish chowder. It lets me use some of that sherry pepper sauce we brought home."

Mike glanced at the little table at the edge of the living room, set for two. A bottle of Goslings Black Seal rum stood next to a tiny white vase containing a single flower. Mike immediately discarded his jacket and hopped onto a high stool at the half-wall counter separating the kitchen from the living room. As he watched Michelle take a loaf of bread out of the oven and inhale the aroma, he gave her a rundown of the day's events in the Jimmy Rydell investigation.

By the time they sat down with large bowls of the dark chowder and hunks of still-hot bread, Michelle was up to speed. They reminisced about their recent Bermuda cruise – only the fun parts, not the onboard murder investigation – and debated whether they liked the fish chowder at the Frog & Onion Pub better than the soup in the main dining room on the *Colossus of the Ocean.*

Mike marveled at how much had happened in their lives in the past year. They were a month away from the anniversary of Mike finally getting up the nerve to ask her out after a decade of working together. Now they were regularly spending nights together and had grown comfortable in their identity as a couple, which was no longer a secret.

Michelle broke off Mike's trip down memory lane by asking what the next steps would be in the Jimmy Rydell investigation.

"We have a few more loose ends," Mike said dejectedly, "but I'm running out of leads. I was hoping to get something from the surveillance video from the apartment building, but so far, that's been a big zero."

"Did you get anything yet from the phone company or from Jimmy's computer?"

Mike shook his head as he dipped a spoon into the thick soup. "Nothing important. I'm not sure if they cracked the hard drive yet, but we got a report from Verizon. We have a couple uniforms tracking down the numbers of his incoming and outgoing phone calls and text messages, but so far they haven't reported anything significant. His last text was sent at one a.m. Thursday morning."

"That's about what you figured. Who was the text to?"

"His driver, The Duke. Probably to confirm his pickup time for the next morning. It's too late for the phone company to get us the contents of the texts, so all we have are the stats. We'll see if there are any calls or texts to anyone unusual in the days before his murder. That's what we're looking for."

"You mean like a call to Fat Albert Gallata?"

Mike let out an involuntary laugh. Fat Albert was the head of the largest organized crime operation in the city. The Gallata gang had its hands in loan sharking, drug distribution, prostitution and human trafficking – and illegal gambling. If Jimmy had really been mixed up in a point-shaving scheme, it was a good bet the Gallata mob would be involved. "Sure. It should be that easy."

"Who else do you need to interview?" she asked just before slurping a spoonful.

"We may need to talk to the guy who runs the Boys & Girls Club where Jimmy spent a lot of time, but I don't have a lot of hope about that. The uniforms are still canvasing for witnesses around Jimmy's apartment building, but so far nobody saw or heard anything important. I'd still like to talk to the kid, Tiger. He was Jimmy's lap dog, apparently, but he's flown the coop and we can't find him."

"You think this kid knows something?"

Mike dipped another hunk of bread into a small dish of olive oil and pepper and held it suspended above the table. A drip of oil fell into his soup bowl. "It's a long shot, but he was living on the sidewalk outside the building. He had a shoeshine kit that Jimmy gave him, so he was always hanging around, hoping to score a shine. He would have been there that night, and he's Jimmy's friend, so it's possible. I put out an alert for the beat cops to flag him. You'd think a tall, lanky Black kid with a circular-shaped goatee wouldn't be hard to spot."

Mike popped the bread into his mouth, but stopped chewing when he saw Michelle's face. Her brows were furrowed.

"Mike. A Black kid, between eighteen and twenty-two, about six-one, skinny. Has short black hair and facial hair with a wispy beard shaped like a circle on his chin, leaving bare skin in the middle? Is that the description?"

"Yeah."

"I think he's in my morgue."

Mike had to finish chewing and swallowing his bread before he could speak. "When did he come in?"

"On Monday. No ID, so he's listed as John Doe. We're waiting for his fingerprint search to come back. The body was picked up in Riverside Park. Cause of death was blunt force trauma to the back of the skull. At least two blows. That's about all I can say based on the autopsy. Now I know what the black paste was under his fingernails."

"Shoe polish?"

"I guess so. I was waiting for a lab analysis, but I'd bet on it. We're waiting for somebody to claim him, or else we'll send him out for a pauper's funeral. What do you think it means that he was murdered?"

"I'm not sure," Mike sat back, suddenly not as interested in his soup, "but I'm betting it's no coincidence."

# Chapter 23 – A Mystery Man

Wednesday, June 5

WEDNESDAY MORNING, MIKE AND JASON went back to Park Towers with four uniformed officers. They dispatched their team to canvas the businesses on the ground floor and in the immediately surrounding area, looking for a freezer unit big enough to stash a body. If they found any, they would get samples to test. It wasn't much of a shot, but they needed to cover all the bases.

The morning papers were still laser-focused on the Jimmy Rydell murder. Social media was abuzz with competing claims of a racially motivated murder, a conspiracy involving drugs, a mob hit related to the point-shaving scheme, and a suicide that was falsely reported as a murder in order to incite a radical mob. The vacuum of actual facts was being filled quickly by a torrent of rumors, innuendo, and outright fabrications.

While they were still on the sidewalk outside the front entrance, giving instructions to the officers, Graham loped up to the group with his long strides. His tweed jacket seemed to be freshly pressed and his shoes were brilliantly shined. After the officers left, Graham greeted Mike and Jason cheerfully. "Good day, Detectives. Are we making any progress?"

"I hope so," Mike grunted as he walked toward the revolving doors. First thing that morning, he had received an email from Detective Meyer. She said she had something.

Mike, Jason, and Graham jammed themselves into the tiny security booth and stood behind an Asian woman wearing a Dave Matthews Band t-shirt, who was manipulating the controls on a console under a bank of four TV monitors. Detective Meyer was sitting next to her, looking bedraggled like she had been up all night. A pile of pages ripped from a spiral notebook lay on the edge of the counter at Meyer's elbow, covered with handwritten notes. Dates, times, and descriptions filled the pages in uneven columns. Meyer was giving directions to the young woman at the console.

"The center lobby shot at 18:13:32." She was struggling to keep her voice even. "Detective Stoneman – Mike – I want you to see this first." A moment later, she snapped, "Stop right there." The operator froze the monitor on an overhead shot of the main lobby. The image showed three men walking across the marble floor toward the elevators. In the middle, Jimmy Rydell was plainly visible. On his right, a large man walked close to him. The man had to be large because he was bigger than Jimmy, who was himself 6'2" and 225. He wore a black baseball cap and sunglasses, which obscured his face. His body was shrouded in a bulky gray hoodie. On Jimmy's left, also walking very close, Mike could make out a shorter, thinner man wearing a dark fedora-style hat. His face was similarly obscured, but he was wearing a green polo shirt with an NFL logo, the exact same shirt Jimmy was wearing.

"OK. You see these two men with Mr. Rydell?" Meyer swiveled her head around toward Mike and gestured at the screen.

"Yes. When was this?"

"This was a week ago Friday, five days before Jimmy's disappearance."

"Who are the two guys with him?" Jason asked.

Meyer turned her whole chair sideways to address the three men. But first, she spoke to the woman next to her. "Alice, find the other one now, the one from the street cam." Then, to Mike, "We don't know who the two guys are, which is a little weird. Normally, guests have to be screened by the doormen at the front desk. But as a favor to Jimmy, they sometimes let him bring in guests without making them sign in and without seeing ID, if Jimmy was with them. Usually it's a girl, but the doormen told me that sometimes he brought up teammates or other guys. Sometimes his bodyguard was with him, but not always. Anyway, that night Cesar the doorman saw Jimmy with these two guys and Jimmy said it was cool, so Cesar let them come in with him. I asked all the doormen whether they recognized these two guys from any prior visits, but nobody had seen them before. We have the two guys on the video leaving about an hour later, but the images are even worse – just their backs and the tops of their hats."

"What about the elevator cameras?" Jason asked.

Meyer shook her head. "They both stood in the elevator with their backs to the camera – like they knew it was there and didn't want to be photographed."

"That's pretty suspicious," Mike observed.

"I thought the same thing." Meyer turned back toward the monitor, which now showed a sidewalk. The same two men were in the frame, judging by the identical clothing. "So, I had the officers working with me check the businesses in the surrounding neighborhood, to see if any of them had exterior cams. We knew the time they were in the lobby, so we had a narrow time window to search. Luckily, there's an electronics store a block west of here that has an exterior surveillance cam. We caught this shot three minutes after they left the building. It was a hot day, so the big guy must have been sweating – see, he took off his hat."

They all peered at the slightly grainy image. The shorter, skinnier man still had his fedora on and his face was mostly obscured. But the large man had his hat in his left hand, exposing his full face and his entirely bald head.

"That's nice work, Meyer," Mike said, still staring at the screen and trying to recall ever seeing the bald man before.

Meyer smiled at Mike's praise. "Thank you, Sir. It seemed pretty standard to me. Anyway, we found this image yesterday afternoon. I wasn't sure if it was significant, but it seemed curious enough, so I sent the image out with an urgent request for ID based on facial recognition. We got back a blank and a notice."

"Notice?" Mike turned toward Meyer. "What kind of notice?"

"It was a negative on the ID, but had a notice that some information was withheld. You probably get that all the time, right?"

Mike looked at Jason, who gave him a shrug. "Actually, Detective, I've never seen that before. I've always gotten back either a positive ID, or a negative because the system couldn't find a match. What did the notice say?"

"Nothing," Meyer's voice cracked and she quickly pawed through her notes, looking away from Mike.

"Don't worry, Meyer, you had no way to know. If there's information on this guy but it's classified, we might be able to figure it out. That's good work. It may not be related to Jimmy's murder, but it's certainly interesting. Can you give us a printout of the image?"

Alice punched a few buttons and a nearby printer sprang to life.

When the three detectives emerged from the security office, Mike gently grabbed Meyer's elbow so they could talk. He congratulated her again on her work with the video, then gave her a new assignment. Now that they knew Tiger had been murdered, Mike told her to check in with Detectives Berkowitz and Mason, who were working the homicide case. "See if you can track down Tiger's movements in the days leading up to his murder."

After Meyer left to get back to the precinct, Mike said to Jason, "Are you thinking this bald guy might be in a database, but it's being shielded because of an active investigation?"

"That would make sense. And I'm thinking we might check in with our friends at the FBI."

"Exactly. This may be the connection we need to leverage a little federal cooperation. Maybe Agent Forrest can help cut through some red tape for us. And while we're talking, maybe he can give us a hint about Jimmy's involvement in the point-shaving scheme, if there really is an investigation."

"It's worth a shot. But I think you're going to need to take him to dinner or something, if you keep asking him for favors."

"Why is that?" Graham inquired.

Mike had momentarily forgotten there was an outsider listening. "Jason and I met him during a serial killer investigation a year ago. It turned out to have an overlap with an ongoing FBI investigation into a human trafficking arm of the Gallata crime syndicate. He helped us catch our guy and we got to be pretty friendly. Then about two months ago, he arranged to get us a loan of some high-tech surveillance toys. He's a good guy."

"I could arrange for a nice gift for the agent, if you'd like me to take care of it."

"That's alright, Beckwith. You don't want to be accused of bribing a federal officer."

"Well, I suppose. But if it will help, just remember that I'm on the team and willing to chip in."

"Great," Jason said with only a hint of sarcasm.

# Chapter 24 – Lunch Meeting

FBI AGENT EVERETT FORREST answered Mike's call and said he would prefer not to have Mike send him the image electronically. Mike suggested they meet in person, and they agreed to rendezvous at the Nom Wah Tea Parlor on Doyers Street. Mike, Jason, and Graham piled into the Lincoln and headed to Chinatown.

The little dim sum restaurant was tucked into a tiny street that curved between Mott and Bowery on which an assortment of one-story shops and eateries lined the pock-marked pavement. Mike knew the place well, as did Forrest. It was off the out-of-town tourist beat in Chinatown, and before noon they figured it would be nearly empty.

Mike waved to Mr. Tang behind the cashier's counter when they arrived and led the way to a table in the back, where Forrest was already seated and sipping tea from a white porcelain cup. After a round of introductions, Mike produced the printout of their mystery man and handed it over.

Agent Forrest was a fit six feet. He had very short brown hair, and dark eyes with wrinkles at the edges that made him look like he was perpetually squinting. He had a square jaw which enhanced his FBI agent gravitas when he was wearing a dark suit and sunglasses.

Forrest studied the grainy security cam image while Mike ordered tea for his group. When the waiter scuttled away, the FBI man whispered to Mike, "Where did you get this, Stoneman?"

"A block away from the apartment building where Jimmy Rydell lived, five days before his murder. We have him on a different camera walking into Jimmy's building with the now-dead quarterback that same day, but he was hiding his face. Our information is that he spent about an hour in Jimmy's penthouse, then left. We tried to get an ID, but the report came back unknown, with a notice about some kind of security hold. We were wondering if you could run it through your FBI database and see what pops up."

Forrest handed the page back to Mike. "I don't need to run it, Mike. I know who this is. But I'm afraid I can't help you, especially not with a civilian here." The agent looked at Graham, then back to Mike.

"I get it," Mike replied. He then escorted Graham to a different table at the opposite side of the room. Graham did not object. When Mike returned, Jason and Agent Forrest were already talking in hushed tones about the Rydell investigation. If they had been working on an anonymous murder, Forrest might not have been as interested and willing to help. But this was Jimmy Rydell – the case that even the FBI agents couldn't stop speculating about.

Forrest nodded to Mike upon his return. "Stoneman, I can't really help you; at least, not without some clearance. What I can tell you two is the reason you can't get an ID on this guy. He doesn't have an identity. We know him because he's some kind of bag man for Fat Albert Gallata. We've been trying to get an

ID on him for a year. We think he came in from somewhere in eastern Europe. He's got a little accent and our surveillance has picked him up making a few comments about Slovenia, although we're not sure he's from there. We followed him into a restaurant and retrieved prints off a wine glass, but they came up blank. Even Interpol doesn't know who he is. For lack of a name, we call him, Mr. Clean."

"Because of the muscles and the bald head?" Jason asked.

"Pretty much, and because he has this squeaky-clean profile. As far as we know, he has no credit cards, no driver's license, and only uses burner phones. He does odd jobs for the Gallatas and seems pretty tight with the boss. His name inside the organization is Igor, but we don't know if that's just a nickname. So, we're on him, and we don't want him popping up in anybody's facial recognition search."

"So," Mike hung his head, "he's basically off the radar. Is there any chance that his presence with Jimmy right before his murder could suggest a connection between Jimmy and the Gallatas?"

"You didn't hear it from me, Stoneman, but I'd say it's possible."

Jason leaned in and spoke so that his usually booming baritone wouldn't carry. "*The New York Times* is saying Jimmy may have been involved in a point-shaving scheme connected to organized crime, including the Gallata gang. Can you confirm whether this Mr. Clean guy is involved in that?"

Forrest shook his head. "I can't. I mean, I really don't know. I suppose if I knew I might not be able to tell you, but I'll tell you honestly that I don't know."

"Are you not investigating that?" Mike asked skeptically.

"No, not my team. If Fat Albert is into that operation, it's not a big part of his business. It's possible he was running some angle on his own, or maybe he was trying to get in on some larger action."

"It's a little frustrating when your suspects become our suspects, but you can't share info," Mike said.

"Yeah, I get that. But Mr. Clean isn't really off limits, he's just a ghost. We don't know who he is. He seems to live inside the Gallata complex in Queens. He comes out to run Fat Albert's errands and then goes back. He showed up twelve months ago. We don't have a constant tail on him because he usually takes the subway and we can't devote a whole team to following him around when he hasn't done anything criminal that we can figure out. For all we know, he's just muscle for Fat Albert."

"Let me ask you this." Mike raised a finger. "If we run into him on our own, are we clear to pick him up for questioning?"

Forrest hesitated, but then nodded. "Give me a heads-up if that happens, but sure. As far as the Bureau is concerned, this meeting never happened, so you have no reason to know he's a Gallata associate. But be careful. This creep is likely to be pretty dangerous."

"Can you get us any better photos?" Jason asked. "If you've been surveilling him, you must have some good shots of his face. That might help us track him. We'll share anything we learn with you guys."

Forrest cocked his head to the side, then stretched it in the other direction before responding. "I'll see what I can do."

Forrest got up and left the restaurant, raising a hand in a farewell salute to Graham, who promptly rejoined Mike and Jason.

"Did your federal colleague provide any useful information?" Graham asked as soon as he sat down.

"He can't share much, and what he can share is confidential. It's not that we don't trust you, Graham, but for now we have to keep it to ourselves. We don't have a name, but our federal friend has seen him before and calls him Mr. Clean."

"Is that an American reference?"

"Yeah. A big, muscular, bald cartoon dude on the label of a household cleaning product. He fits the description."

"Very well. Seems fine enough. Can he help us find this Mr. Clean?"

"Maybe," Mike said simply. "For now, while we're here, let's order some lunch."

# Chapter 25 – Baby Steps

*T*HE NEW YORK TIMES KEPT UP THE DRUMBEAT that Jimmy Rydell might have been involved in the speculative point-shaving scheme, although there was no evidence to suggest the scheme actually existed. At 2:18 p.m. Wednesday, the paper's website broke a new story under Kristi Olson's byline, adding fuel to the fire. *The Times* had enlisted a sports statistician to analyze the fourth-quarter results of every NFL game from the prior season. He concluded that scores by trailing teams resulting in back-door covers happened 28.7% more often than in the prior season. That proved nothing, of course, but it supported the speculation.

Mike and Jason set up shop in the corner conference room so they had a more private space where Graham could sit with them. The room quickly became crowded with football fan cops, who were more than ready to give their favorite theories. Mike and Jason kept quiet. When Sully called them in for an update, they left Graham holding court in the conference room, telling him there was some confidential case material they needed to discuss without him.

Sully made it clear that the publicity around the case was making the Mayor and the Commissioner anxious. He was not excited at all to hear that they had identified a potential suspect who was connected to the Gallata organized crime syndicate.

"I suppose you've told the Brit about this," Sully lamented, turning his head to look out the window at 94th Street.

"No," Mike said quickly, "we sent him away while we talked to Agent Forrest, so he didn't hear. We haven't told him about it."

Sully dragged his gaze away from the robin perched on a tree branch at the same height as the captain's third-floor window and looked back toward his detectives. "Good idea. Can you keep that up?"

"We can try damned hard," Mike winked at Jason, who nodded silently. "But if it turns out this guy was involved, and that Jimmy really was wrapped up with the Gallatas, then it's not crazy to think this point-shaving thing might have legs."

A wad of paper whooshed past Mike's head on its way from Sully's hand to the corner trash can. "That will make the insurance company happy, but everybody else will go apeshit. I'm not telling you to bury it, but please, for the love of God, make sure it's solid before you do anything to encourage those freaking reporters or the mayor will have a cow."

Jason got up, towering over his captain. "I'll tell you what, Sully. I'm not going to let anyone throw shit at Jimmy Rydell's good name unless we're positive. You can take that to the bank."

Sully nodded toward the door, then returned to the reports on his desk, leaving Mike and Jason to exit in silence.

Back in the conference room, the rampant, conspiracy-theory-laden speculation about whether Jimmy did or didn't shave points for the mob was still in high gear. Detective Darla Meyer's opinion was that a kid like Jimmy Rydell, with a huge six-year contract, was the least susceptible to the kind of leverage the mob, or anyone else, would need to use to get him to shave points.

One of the uniformed officers, holding a cup of coffee and leaning against the wall, called out, "Sweetheart, you need to go write some parking tickets and leave football to the men." Two other officers laughed. Meyer's back was toward Mike, so he couldn't see her face. He had a pretty good idea what it would look like.

"Officer Haggerty!" Mike barked from the doorway. All heads spun in his direction; everyone fell silent and froze in place. Mike was blocking anyone from scuttling out. Haggerty calmly took a sip of his coffee. He was a little older than Mike, with a larger paunch and grayer hair. His face was weathered, but his brown eyes were clear. Mike knew him. He had been a beat cop when Mike first arrived in the Manhattan North homicide division seventeen years earlier. He was still a beat cop, but spent most of his time behind a desk, reviewing reports and making assignments. He was what the department referred to as a Lead Officer – not a supervisor, but a senior staffer who directed the younger cops. He never made sergeant, but he had so much seniority that he was immune from any staff cuts and could pick his assignments. He was entitled; he had earned it through years of service on the streets. He was way past qualifying for retirement, but he hung on because he enjoyed his position.

"Hey, Stoneman," Haggerty casually replied, "you gonna tell us stories about your cruise?"

This drew another hearty laugh from the assembled group of cops. Mike took one step inside, still obstructing the doorway, with Jason at his shoulder. "No, Haggerty, I'm not doing any storytelling today. But I am going to ask you a question."

"What's that?"

"When did you become a detective?"

Haggerty squinted in Mike's direction, the wrinkles around his nose deepening as he scrunched his face. "I didn't."

Mike took another step toward the officer. "I didn't think so. So, I have another question. When did you become such an asshole?"

"What the fuck?" Haggerty's face changed from puzzled to angry in a blink. He took an instinctive step toward Mike.

"I'll tell you what the fuck. You're disrespecting a superior officer and you're being a prick."

"Who? You?" Haggerty now seemed confused again. "Like I can't bust your balls all of a sudden?"

Mike took the last step separating him from Officer Haggerty. He could smell the acrid coffee on the other man's lips. "Not me, shit-for-brains. You were disrespecting your superior, Detective Meyer. You want to tell me I should be out writing parking tickets? Huh?" Haggerty was silent. Mike could see him biting his lip. "You want to disagree with a detective, you do that, but you don't treat a woman – and a woman who outranks you – like a meter maid. You got that?"

"Yeah, sure, Stoneman," Haggerty held his ground, practically spitting in Mike's face as he responded dismissively.

"As a matter of fact," Mike raised his voice slightly, but perceptively, "you don't treat a meter maid that way. This isn't your junior high school locker room." Mike turned away from Haggerty's bad breath and addressed the rest of the room. "There's one woman here, and I expect you to treat her with the respect she deserves. And we have a guest here." Mike held a hand out toward Graham, who was seated placidly behind the table. "I don't want this gentleman to think the NYPD is populated by a bunch of Neanderthals who harass the female detectives. I'm sure that kind of behavior wouldn't be tolerated at Scotland Yard. Correct, Detective Inspector Beckwith?"

Graham, who had been observing the events carefully, looked at Haggerty as he said, "Oh, I should say not, Detective Stoneman. I am personally offended by the boorish behavior toward Detective Meyer and would expect appropriate disciplinary action to follow swiftly. I'll be happy to swear out an affidavit, if you'd like."

Silence followed Graham's statement. Mike made eye contact with the former English police officer, who subtly raised one eyebrow in response.

"Any of you officers have something to say to Detective Meyer?" Mike let the question hang over the room as everyone except Graham squirmed. Mike turned back toward Haggerty, still close enough to tell that he hadn't shaved that day. "What about you, Officer? What do you have to say to *Detective* Meyer?"

The officer reached with his left hand to grab his belt with a face like he had swallowed a turd. He looked Mike in the eye. "I apologize for the meter maid comment," he growled.

"Why are you apologizing to me? Did you call me a meter maid when I wasn't here?"

Haggerty scowled. "No."

"If you're gonna apologize, you need to apologize to the superior officer you disrespected."

"I – just – did," Haggerty spat out the words.

Mike took a step back and turned toward the table, where Meyer was still sitting with her back toward the door, her head inclined. Mike immediately regretted heading down this road without determining whether it was going to cause Meyer more harm than good. It was too late to ask her. "Detective Meyer?"

When Meyer turned her head to look at Mike, he exhaled. Her eyes were steel spikes directed at Haggerty. "Yes, Detective Stoneman?"

"As I was coming in, it appeared to me that Officer Haggerty here directed a sexist comment toward you. He insinuated that you weren't a detective because you're a woman. Is that the way you heard it?"

Meyer continued to stare down Haggerty. Without turning her head, she answered, "That's an accurate summary, Detective Stoneman."

Now Mike broke into professor mode. He taught classes at the police academy on evidence handling and interrogation techniques. He lectured to officers studying for the detective's exam on chain of custody, crime scene protocols, and de-escalation. His students called him *Culo de Piedre* behind his back – "Ass of Stone." He was accustomed to calling on unprepared student-cops.

"Officer Murray?" Mike selected the youngest officer present, figuring that he would be most likely to answer his upcoming question. The more veteran officers might be smart enough to dodge and claim to not remember. "Did you hear what Officer Haggerty said about Detective Meyer?"

Murray appeared to be right out of the Army, sporting a close crewcut above a square jaw and a defined chin cleft. His blue eyes darted from the senior detective to the senior officer and back again. "Yessir."

"And did you laugh at Officer Haggerty's comment?"

"Um – yessir. I did."

"How do you feel about that now, Officer?"

"I'm – I – I'm not proud of it, Sir."

"You wanna be a detective someday, Murray?"

"Yes, Sir!" Murray's eyes flashed to Mike, looking worried.

"When you're a detective – someday – how do you think you should treat Detective Meyer, your fellow detective? Do you think she'll deserve as much respect from you as you're giving me right now?"

"Yes, Sir."

Mike turned away from Murray and searched the back of the room where his homicide colleague, George Mason, was sitting next to Graham. "What about you, George? Do you think Detective Meyer deserves our respect?"

"Absolutely, Mike," Mason shot back in his Brooklyn accent.

Now Mike spun back around to face Haggerty. "What about you, Officer? Do you agree that Detective Meyer deserves your respect?"

"Yeah," Haggerty grunted.

"Yeah, what?" Mike softened his facial muscles, not wanting to spark a fist fight.

Haggerty's shoulders sagged slightly and he exhaled slowly. "Detective Meyer deserves our respect, Sir."

"I agree," Mike stepped back. "Now get out of here and go catch some criminals." The room cleared out except for Meyer, who stopped before reaching the door and faced Mike.

Mike held up an open palm. "I'm sorry if that embarrassed you, Meyer."

"No. It didn't. Thanks, Mike. I know that wasn't fun for you."

"Actually, by the end, it kinda was." He smiled, drawing a grin from Meyer.

"Ahem." Graham, who had been watching with amused interest, cleared his throat loudly. "While I found the verbal flogging of that reprobate entertaining, I would appreciate it if someone could explain the American football issue for me. How exactly would Mr. Rydell shave points for the benefit of the gangster gamblers?"

Mike looked at Jason. Jason looked at Meyer. "Detective Meyer? You seem to have a good understanding. Can you explain it to our British colleague?"

Meyer was surprised that the more senior detectives would give her the floor, but gladly explained how a quarterback, among all the players on a football team, could manipulate the score. Throwing an uncatchable pass rather than a completion, or even fumbling the ball or throwing an interception, particularly late in the game on a critical play, could thwart a scoring drive and leave his team stuck on a particular score, rather than building a bigger lead. "It would probably happen most in a late-season game when the team was eliminated from playoff contention, when they don't mind losing and enhancing their position in the next draft."

Graham held up his hand. "You mean to tell me that the teams at the bottom of the standings are rewarded?"

"Well, in a way, yes. They get the early picks in the next player draft."

"So, they aren't relegated to the lower levels?"

Meyer chuckled. "No, there are no lower levels. There's only one NFL."

Graham took a sip of his tea. "Seems like an incentive for teams to intentionally lose. I'd think that losing by a larger margin than the betting line would be commonplace."

"It does seem that way sometimes, but most of the time the players play hard and try to win. You'd be surprised how often an eliminated team takes out a team that's fighting for the playoffs in the last week of the season."

"So, if I were a gambler and I had some way to coerce a quarterback to lower his team's score, I could bet against the team and have an unfair advantage. Unless, of course, the other players overcome the quarterback's errors, or there are players on the opposing team who are similarly trying to lose."

"Well, yes, I suppose," Meyer mused. "But the point I was making is that Jimmy Rydell had a huge contract, and he was young and unmarried. I don't see how anyone could have leverage over him. It's not like he was in debt. They couldn't threaten his wife or kids – or parents. He was an orphan. So, how would someone be able to force him to shave points?"

Jason then explained that, according to Jimmy's agent, his signing bonus was sunk into an annuity and he was living off only his annual contract. He told Meyer about Graham's investigation into Jimmy's finances, which suggested that despite his $5 million salary, he might have been stretched. "Plus, if he was involved in any drug use or other illegal activity that would void his contract if disclosed, that could be the leverage point."

"Precisely!" Graham agreed.

Meyer shot Graham a reproachful frown. "But Mr. Beckwith, Jimmy didn't shave points. That's the big hole here. The last three games last season, after he came back from his injury, they won a game and covered the spread, then they lost big and there was nothing Jimmy could have done about it. Then, in the last game, they were losing by more than the spread until Jimmy led the team to a late touchdown that covered it. That's the opposite of shaving points."

"And yet," Graham pressed, "there is still a possibility that Mr. Rydell was involved in some kind of criminal enterprise."

"Sure. It's possible," Meyer conceded. "But not likely."

Mike decided it was time to change the subject. "Detective Meyer, any luck tracking down our boy, Tiger?"

"Actually, yes. That's why I came in here in the first place, looking for you. I found out the kid hung out at the Boys & Girls Club."

"Really?" Jason spoke up. "How did you get that?"

"Mike had asked me to contact the director because we know Jimmy spent a lot of time there. While I was talking to him, I mentioned the kid and gave a description and he immediately knew who I was talking about. He told me Jimmy met him at the club and took a liking to him. That's how Tiger ended up as Jimmy's gofer. Jimmy bought him a shoeshine kit so he could make some money and tried to help the kid out. Jimmy even paid for Tiger to enroll in a vocational school starting in September. He also told me about the million-dollar donation Jimmy made. He wanted to make sure that, no matter what else happened, people know what a big heart Jimmy had."

Jason sat on the edge of the wooden table, letting his leg hang over and dangle. "Did the club director have any idea how he ended up dead in Riverside Park?"

"No. But he told me Tiger almost never left his little campsite by Jimmy's building. The director and Jimmy both tried to get him to come to a shelter, but Tiger refused to leave. The director says Tiger never would have wandered forty blocks north on his own."

"So, we're thinking he got murdered somewhere near his homestead and then got moved to the park?" Jason suggested.

"Maybe," Mike said. "Did we do a forensic sweep of the area around his cardboard house?"

"No, we didn't – yet."

Mike turned to Meyer. "Detective, take a team over there and see if you can find any evidence suggesting that his box is a murder scene. It's a long shot this long after the fact, but you never know."

"Yes, Sir!" Meyer enthusiastically darted from the conference room.

"They need to get her a partner." Jason swung his leg down and landed it on the floor.

"Not my worry." Mike turned toward Graham, who was still sitting calmly. "I don't suppose you'd like to tag along with Detective Meyer, would you?"

Graham reached for his hat and stood up. "Actually, I'd be delighted to spend some time with the lovely detective." Graham hurried off to catch up with Meyer.

Jason walked out into the bullpen toward his desk now that they weren't babysitting Graham. Mike followed. As Jason shuffled through a small stack of message slips, he said, "Looks like somebody got a gold star in his anti-bias training class."

"You don't think I would have done the same thing last week?"

"No, Mike, I don't. I'm proud of you. You took action in there. It's not easy."

Mike turned away. "Well, I like Meyer. By the way, you all set for tomorrow night?"

"It's all set. I checked with Sophie and her niece, Dominique, has the . . . box." Jason took a long breath as he contemplated the reality of what he was about to do. "We have a reservation and Dominique will bring it to our table with the dessert."

"Very romantic. I hope she say yes."

◆◆◆

That night, over angel hair primavera at Michelle's dining nook, Mike recounted his confrontation with Officer Haggerty.

"Is that the first time you've done something like that?" She spun her pasta into a large spoon while looking into Mike's eyes.

"I suppose it was."

Michelle chewed slowly in silence, then sipped her red wine before dabbing her mouth with a napkin. "Was that the first time you ever heard a cop make a sexist or racist statement, or tell an off-color joke?"

"No, of course not. I've been around a long time, so you see a lot of stuff."

She bit her lower lip and took in a deep breath through her nose. "Mike, I'm really proud of what you did. I know you're a good person. And you spoke up to stop Haggerty today, which was great. It's a great start. I'm not going to tell you how wonderful you are for just once."

"I don't want you to," Mike said softly. "I'm starting to get it. For today, I'm batting a thousand. I'm not asking for a medal. We'll see how things go."

"I'll drink to that." She raised her glass and clinked across the table. "Oh, Rachel told me Jason is taking her out tomorrow to that new restaurant, *Le Renard Courrant.* I'm so jealous! It's supposed to be the hottest new place. That's pretty fancy for a Thursday night, don't you think?"

"I guess," Mike replied flatly. "I think Sophie's niece works there and it was the only day they could get a reservation. It's Rachel's birthday this weekend, right?"

"Oh, right." Michelle took another bite. "We're going to the party on Sunday."

"And remember, I'm taking Tony Curran to the Mets game tomorrow. Kristi Olson from *The New York Times* got me fixed up with pre-game field passes. Tony is going to love that. The poor kid needs something fun. And Marie is taking Jenny out somewhere for a girls' night. I haven't spent enough time with them, so I'm hoping tomorrow works out."

"Why wouldn't it?"

"This investigation. It's a hot potato, so if something breaks tomorrow, I could get stuck. Would you take Tony to the game if I can't make it?" He gave her an exaggerated pleading face with a frown and batted his lashes.

"Fine." She was unable to suppress a giggle. "Just stop looking at me that way!"

Mike tried to maintain his hangdog face, but broke into a smile after a few seconds. They ate their pasta and went over the autopsy results on Jimmy Rydell. They had been over it several times. Strangled by some kind of wide cloth. A yellow fragment under his fingernail. Michelle was still waiting for the lab results on the yellow substance. She was stumped. At some point, presumably after he was dead, his body was moved, then frozen. Or maybe frozen and then moved. There were any number of possibilities. Then he was left on the carousel, where he was sure to be found. Why? Why not burn the body, or dump it in the harbor? Why freeze it?

They went around and around for a half hour, until the wine bottle was empty and the dishes were washed. Michelle tried to read a book. Mike tried to watch the ballgame. They kept coming back to the case – hashing out different scenarios that got crazier as the night wore on. Finally, Michelle announced she was ready for bed.

"Let's not talk about the case anymore tonight," she pleaded.

"What should we talk about, instead?"

"How about if I give you something to take your mind off it?" Michelle flicked open the top two buttons of her blouse as she disappeared around the corner, toward the bedroom. Mike rose from his lounger, snapped off the TV, and followed. When he rounded the corner, he saw Michelle's blouse – and bra – lying on the floor, like a trail leading forward.

# Chapter 26 – Dirty Laundry

Thursday, June 5

THERE WAS A LARGE ENVELOPE on Mike's desk when he arrived Thursday morning. The return address read *Paul Pine*. Mike snatched it up and used a letter opener to tear open the top. Agent Forrest had come through again. Mike riffled through five 8x10 photos of Mr. Clean, in various locations and clothing. They were certainly surveillance photos taken with long-range lenses, but the clarity was excellent. Leave it to the feds to have the best equipment.

Jason and Graham agreed that the photos provided far superior images than the one from the electronics store's security cam. When Graham asked where Mike had obtained them, Mike said it was confidential.

They piled into the Lincoln and were inside Park Towers in five minutes. One by one, they pulled the doormen and other staff aside and showed them the photos. Nobody could say for sure whether they recognized Mr. Clean.

They were nearing the end of the staff list when a doorman they had not spoken to before stopped on one particular photo and studied it carefully. Sergio was a short, dark-skinned

Latino man with a thick moustache and a heavy accent. He stood erect in his doorman uniform and bore himself with confidence, which impressed Graham.

"I think I have seen this man. You see this?" He pointed to Mr. Clean's head, "see how he has a Yankee hat, but here," he gestured to one of the other photos, "he has a bald head. He looks like the substitute laundry man."

"What laundry?" Mike looked over toward the building manager, Mr. Stafford, and motioned for him to come over while they spoke to Sergio.

"I usually work the night shift. The laundry guy, Fred, comes very late – after midnight – to bring the clean and pick up the dirty."

Mike raised an eyebrow toward Jason. "You mean laundry from the residents?"

"Si, and also from the health club."

By this time, Stafford was standing next to Jason. Mike handed him the photo of Mr. Clean. "Sergio here says our guy looks like the substitute laundry worker. Does that make sense?"

"I guess it could," Stafford said, then turned to Sergio. "You're here late most days. Do you see the laundry guy come and go on the video?"

"Si," Sergio nodded crisply. "He buzzes the service door and drives into the loading dock. Somebody's on the desk watch if it's after ten, when nobody's in the security chair by the door. We open the door to let the truck out when we see him come back and pull out. The driver is Fred, and Tony on the weekend, but sometimes they send somebody else. Not always the same guy, but this guy," he patted his index finger on the photo, "he came once or twice, I think."

196| KEVIN G. CHAPMAN

"Are you sure?" Mike asked.

"Oh yeah, big muscular guy like that? I'm sure. One night, I was walking around the building when he came out with the dirty laundry, and he hit a bump and spilled out towels everywhere. I helped him out, right, and that Yankee hat fell off. Big bald guy makes an impression. It's definitely the same guy."

Mike grabbed Stafford's arm lightly, pulling the man toward him. "Do you have ID information on the laundry guys?"

"No. We have contact information for the company. They're bonded. Their employees have to have an ID badge that gets verified and lets them into the health club. We don't really keep track of which person comes on any given day."

Jason took the photo away from Sergio. "When was the last time you saw this guy come in for the laundry run?"

Sergio thought about it, his eyes darting to the building manager to confirm that he had permission to give out the information. "Last week, I think."

Three minutes later, they were again jammed into the little security office, looking at video. Alice was working the console again, but instead of Detective Meyer, it was Mike sitting next to her, giving instructions. They watched the video from the camera in the service breezeway from the prior Wednesday night into Thursday morning. At 1:05 a.m., the laundry truck pulled slowly into the tight corridor and backed into the loading dock. After a few minutes, a large rolling cart with canvas sides emerged from behind the truck, moving along the loading dock toward the service elevator about twenty feet away. They saw hands gripping the back edge of the trolly, followed by thick forearms. When the cart was fully clear of the truck, they could see the man pushing it. He was big, wearing white overalls over a white t-shirt that did little to disguise his bulging biceps. A dark baseball cap covered his head. They couldn't see the logo on the front as he was walking away from the camera's location, but they could see no hair protruding out the back or the sides from under the cap.

"Could be our guy," Jason said. "What does the regular guy, Fred, look like?"

Sergio was standing in the doorway, unable to fit inside the tight space. "He's my height and has black hair, very long."

Jason nodded. "Definitely not Fred."

They watched as the man waited for the service elevator and then rolled the cart inside.

"We have eyes inside that elevator?" Mike asked.

"Sure we do," Stafford snapped, "but that's a different file. Let's let this one roll and see what happens."

They watched as Alice fast-forwarded the video. The clock rolled ahead until the elevator door opened again and she reduced the footage back to normal speed. The laundry cart started to roll out, then stopped and pulled back, then rolled forward again across the threshold of the elevator. It was piled high with a disheveled array of towels, rising several feet above the lip of the cart. The big man shoved it from the rear, leaning down low and throwing his legs out far behind him for leverage until he worked up enough momentum to let the cart roll forward toward the back of the truck. They could see the white, interlocking NY logo on the front of the man's hat. He and the cart disappeared behind the truck, out of the camera's view. Two minutes later, the truck pulled forward, turned left, and slowly drove toward the exterior exit door. Mike could make out a beefy arm hanging out the open window, casually tapping on the frame as if keeping a beat with some unheard music. The clock read 1:39 a.m.

Mike asked Alice, "Does this file include the images from the same camera from other days?"

"Sure," Alice confirmed.

"Show us the video from the previous night, the Tuesday night, or early Wednesday morning."

Alice punched a few keys and clicked her mouse several times, and within a minute they saw the same camera view of the breezeway and loading dock area. The electronic clock in the lower-left corner displayed the date and time. Alice fast-forwarded until they again saw the laundry truck arrive. It appeared to be the same vehicle. They saw the same canvas-sided laundry cart emerge from behind the truck, this time pushed by a short, dark-haired man without a hat, wearing baggy white overalls. The cart contained the same crisply folded towels. The cart entered the service elevator at 1:05 a.m.

Alice advanced the video until the elevator door opened and the short man (whom they presumed to be Fred) rolled his cart, full of dirty towels, to the back of the truck, repeating the same pattern they had seen before. A few minutes later, the truck pulled away. The clock read 1:17 a.m.

"Thank you," Mike said. "Now, can we see the elevator cam?"

While Alice found the proper file and cued up the video, Graham inched toward the door and tapped Jason's shoulder to get his attention as he left the tiny room. Jason followed. When Mike had seen all he could see from the elevator camera, which wasn't much of anything they hadn't already seen on the loading dock, he strolled into the lobby. Graham and Jason were in a corner at the edge of the front desk talking softly. Graham gestured toward Mike, waving him over.

"Well, I think we've found our man, eh?" He smiled, showing his white front teeth.

Mike scratched his chin. "You think it's that easy?"

"Gentlemen, in my work for Boyd's I've investigated several high-value thefts that used similar methods. From what we all saw, there's little doubt that Jimmy Rydell, or his body, was inside the laundry cart when the bald man came out of the lift."

Mike adopted a poker face. "It's a bit cliché, isn't it? Using the laundry cart as camouflage to remove the body?"

"It's only a cliché because it's quite effective. I've seen the technique used to spirit fine art from a museum in Brussels and to conceal jewelry from an extremely prestigious establishment within an office complex. Rubbish collectors, laundry attendants, landscaping staff – they are effectively invisible and often have access to secure areas. In this case, there is precious little security in the first place, leaving the laundry extraction as the obvious choice for a criminal."

"I agree." Mike broke his stoic face and nodded his approval. "The weight of the cart?"

"Certainly, but also the size of the pile."

"It could be just a heavy laundry day."

Graham furrowed one brow and shook his head slowly. "I don't think so. On Wednesday, the pile was half again as high; that's too big an increase to just be a busy day on Wednesday compared to Tuesday. Between that and the additional weight, I'd say there was more than towels and bedsheets in that basket."

Jason held out his left index finger and pointed at Mike. "There's also the time."

"Yeah," Mike nodded again. "But since he was the sub, it's plausible that it would take him longer than the regular guy even if he wasn't killing Jimmy and hauling out his body."

"If he was already dead," Jason interjected.

"Yeah, true. He might not have been dead, but certainly unconscious if he was down at the bottom of that cart, covered with dirty towels. I'm betting on dead."

"So, did he go upstairs to Jimmy's apartment, kill him there, then drag him out in the cart?"

"Nah. The video from the service elevator shows him exiting with the cart on the basement level by the health club. Stafford says that's where the laundry drop is. He pushes the cart back in and rides back up to the loading dock a half hour later. Stafford and Alice are gonna check the cams in the passenger elevator that goes to the Health Club from the lobby, but there's not much chance the guy rolled the cart up to the lobby and then up to Jimmy's penthouse without anyone seeing him. My money's on Jimmy being in the health club and getting strangled there."

Jason started pacing around their little corner of the lobby as he spoke. "If Jimmy was in the gym, and let's assume he was alone, how does this goon come in and strangle him without leaving any evidence of a struggle?"

Graham pressed himself against the front desk to make room for Jason to pass by. "There are several plausible hypotheses to explain that. Mr. Rydell might have been working out with headphones on, listening to music, which allowed our baseball fan to sneak up on him. Or, the killer might have drugged him with chloroform or something similar, then strangled him. However, that is entirely speculative. What we suspect is that the bald giant is our killer. Our focus should be on finding him. At that point, the rest of the puzzle should fall together. If he's connected to a larger criminal enterprise, that would fully explain our situation."

"Well, let's not speculate on that either," Mike said quickly. "I'm also interested in how the guy knew Jimmy would be in the gym at one in the morning. I know he's famous for his late-night workouts, but why that night, and not Tuesday? And isn't it a coincidence that this all happened the same day Jimmy had his fight with Nate?"

"You think there's a connection there?" Jason asked.

"Maybe, but our first focus should be finding Mr. Clean."

Mike pulled out his cell phone and walked a few steps away, composing a text message to Agent Forrest. He had to be careful not to say anything that might get his colleague in trouble for disclosing information, but he needed to arrange a meeting without Graham. He hit the SEND button, then turned around.

"Jason, I'm going to see if I can stir up some information from a source I know. I can't take Mr. Beckwith along, so why don't you two take care of a few angles. First, let's get a forensic unit in here to sweep the gym. It's not likely there's anything to find this long after the fact, but let's try. Then, get the contact information on the laundry service from Stafford and track down Fred. Let's find out why he wasn't working last Wednesday night, and how Mr. Clean came to be there in his place. I'm betting the big guy isn't employed by the laundry service, but it's worth checking to see if they have any records for him."

Jason held Mike's eye contact and understood that he needed to keep Graham busy while Mike reached out to Agent Forrest. He agreed and led Graham back toward the security room. Stafford was still reviewing the elevator camera video with Alice, clearly furious that someone had breached his security systems. Jason figured Stafford had more incentive than anyone to find pieces of the puzzle if there were any to be found on the video. He also figured they already had everything that was going to be significant.

Mike hustled to the front door.

# Chapter 27 – Meeting Resistance

JASON CALLED FOR A UNIT of uniformed officers to lock down the health club as a crime scene. He and Graham patrolled the space while waiting for the forensics team, speculating about where Jimmy might have been and how Mr. Clean could have snuck up on him. It was clear the gym space was cleaned regularly. Stafford confirmed that the carpet was vacuumed daily and all the equipment was wiped down with disinfectant solution twice a day. They'd look for traces of blood or hair, but since they knew Jimmy was dead and that the cause of death was strangulation, the exercise had only a tiny chance of turning up usable evidence. Jason offered Graham a pair of latex gloves, but the investigator reached into his pocket and produced his own.

Graham speculated that Jimmy might have been lifting a barbell, flat on his back on a padded red bench. Mr. Clean could have forced the bar down on his neck, letting the weights crush his larynx. Jason thought the theory was inconsistent with the autopsy. In the area around the free weights, large balls, some heavy and some bouncy, sat in plastic rings. A dozen colorful jumping ropes hung like giant strands of licorice from a black bar next to rows of thick blue, red, green, and yellow rubber resistance bands. Graham removed a red band and stretched it, holding his arms out wide and letting the band press against his chest as he strained against the pressure. He did five reps, then replaced the red band with a blue one to see if it offered more or less resistance.

Jason saw him and called out, "Stop!" as he rushed over. "Stay away from the yellow bands."

"Is yellow special?"

"It could be when the autopsy includes a bit of yellow material under the deceased's fingernail."

"Ahhhh," Graham expelled a lungful of air. "I can see that. If you knew your victim would be here alone, the resistance band could be used as a kind of garrote. It would leave no blood. After the victim is deceased, you simply hang up the murder weapon with its neighbors, load the body into the laundry bin, cover it with soiled towels, and away you go."

"If it were me," Jason leaned down to visually inspect the huge rubber bands, without touching them, "I wouldn't put the murder weapon back on the rack. There are a bunch of them here. Nobody would notice if one was missing, unless they do a daily inventory, which I doubt. It would be safer to toss the band into the cart along with the body. Also, I'd probably throw in anything else that Jimmy brought to the gym. We never found his cell phone, so if he had it with him – which I would expect – then that would go in. Don't leave behind any evidence, right?"

"You're assuming a professional job, I take it, rather than his teammate lashing out in a jealous rage."

"Yeah. That's true. I'm not figuring old Nate for being careful and prepared. Plus, we saw Mr. Clean on the video; he's definitely not Nate Bedford. I'm not seeing the jealous nemesis as our perp here. Plus, it explains why Jimmy's body was naked."

"Because of his workout clothes?"

Jason nodded. "If they'd dumped him wearing his exercise shorts and a sweaty tank top, we'd have been looking at the health club from the jump."

Graham paced around the space, examining each piece of exercise equipment. "This scenario involves a carefully planned scheme. Our bald killer infiltrated the laundry service and came here as the substitute driver at least a few times before the night of the crime. He planned his exit strategy with great care, and apparently knew his intended victim would be alone in the gym. He managed the entire execution within thirty minutes, leaving behind no obvious evidence. That sounds like a professional, which suggests Mr. Rydell was the target of a criminal enterprise."

Jason straightened up and looked skeptically at Graham, gauging whether he was serious or just busting chops. "I can see why you'd think that. It would be in your company's interests. But we're a long way from reaching that conclusion."

"True, true, but you must admit it's a plausible explanation for the facts as we know them. If we're unsuccessful in proving an actual murderer or motive, it would be reasonable for the insurer to withhold payment pending a final determination, given the possibility."

Jason nodded with a resigned expression, but then stopped. "The problem with that theory – like all the others – is the appearance of the body. If Jimmy was the victim of a professional hit because he was engaged in a criminal enterprise, how do we explain the state of the corpse? A professional killer, having spirited the body out of the building in a laundry cart, would dispose of it without a trace. There are many ways. But here, we have two other facts – the body was frozen and the body was dumped at the carousel. And the boy, Tiger, was murdered. How are those facts consistent with a professional criminal enterprise?"

Graham opened his mouth and raised a finger toward Jason. Then he lowered his hand and closed his mouth without speaking. He turned and walked slowly away, as if thinking deeply. He walked once around a nearby weight machine, then stopped a few feet away. "In any case, if I were in charge of the investigation, I would certainly want to bring in Mr. Clean for some questioning."

"I agree. All we have to do now is find him."

◆◆◆

Building Manager Charles Stafford was motivated to help solve Jimmy Rydell's murder. It was going to be bad enough for the reputation of his building to be known as the site of a notorious murder. It would be even worse if he didn't cooperate with the police. As soon as Jason asked him to contact someone at the laundry service who could put them in touch with Fred, the regular driver, he jumped on it. In fifteen minutes, he had the manager, Thomas Norse, on the phone. Norse agreed to cooperate with the police without a subpoena after Stafford threatened to terminate their contract and move to their chief competitor in the surprisingly cutthroat world of New York City laundry services.

Fred Lanbow, the regular driver, would not normally start his shift until 9:00 p.m. But Norse called him and had him get over to Park Towers while Jason waited. Thanks to the efficiency of the New York City subway and the fact that Lanbow lived in the South Bronx, he arrived by 3:30.

They met with the driver in Stafford's office. Jason questioned Fred with Graham watching as if he were a second detective. Thomas Norse had already confirmed that there was no substitute driver matching the description of Mr. Clean. He also confirmed that Fred was on duty Wednesday night and was paid for his full shift. When Fred initially said he had made his usual run and picked up the laundry from Park Towers early Thursday morning, he was already fidgeting. Jason would have suspected him of lying even if he didn't already know for sure.

"Mr. Lanbow, would you like me to show you the surveillance video from one a.m. Thursday morning?"

Fred hung his head and wrung his hands together before looking up, tears forming. "Look, Officer, I can't lose this job. I got a family. It's a shit job, I know, and it don't pay much, but I need it." His eyes pleaded for some kind of mercy.

"It's Detective," Jason said calmly. "I have no interest in getting you fired, but I have a murder here and the primary suspect is a large bald man who drove your truck into and out of this building last Thursday morning. Now, you cooperate and I don't care what story you tell your boss. My investigation is not a public record. What I need from you right now is the truth. Otherwise, getting fired is the least of your worries. It appears you may be an accessory to a murder."

"OK. Alright. I get it." Fred continued wringing his hands, not looking at Jason. "That guy – the big bald guy – he sits down next to me at a bar I sometimes go to near Yankee Stadium, see. He starts talking to me like he knows me. He knows my name, and my wife's name, and my kid's name. He buys me a drink like he's my best buddy, ya know? Well, he tells me that he's got a friend who lives in Park Towers and, see, he says he needs to help his friend out by sneaking some stuff in and out. I told him it sounded pretty sketchy to me, but he says it's all innocent and not a big deal, but it's a big secret. So, he says he'll pay me five hundred bucks if I let him drive my truck in and do my delivery and pickup for me. Cash. He says he'll meet me, pay me, take the truck in and out, then meet me afterwards and give me the truck back and nobody will know."

"When he spoke to you," Jason cut in, "did he speak with any kind of accent?"

"Yeah, he did. He sounded strange, like maybe Russian or something."

"When was this conversation in the bar?"

"Maybe a month ago. Ya gotta understand, five hundred bucks is like a week's pay for me. I needed that money, and the guy seemed alright, ya know? So, sure, I said I'd do it. So, he calls me about a week later and says he wants to do it that night. He meets me a few blocks away and he's got a uniform. I'm like, what the hell, and I give him my ID card and the keys and he gives me $500. I tell him there's a GPS tracker in the truck and if he tries to steal it I'll be calling the cops and he says, ya know, no problem. I tell him where to go and where to park and where to drop off the cart and pick up the dirties. It's no big deal. He comes back a half hour later and says thanks and walks away and I take my truck and finish my route. No problem."

"That was last week?" Jason asked, puzzled. "You said it was three weeks ago."

"Yeah, that was the first time, like three weeks ago. Then he does it again the next week, one night. Same deal. Then last week was the third time. 'Cept that time it was different."

Jason sat forward, bringing his face within a foot of Fred's. "Different how?"

Fred shifted back in his chair, away from Jason. "Well, that time, he kinda – he wanted to keep the truck."

"Keep it?"

"Well, not keep it like, forever, but, ya know, he didn't want to give it back right away. He said he needed to run an errand with the truck. So, he gives me another thousand."

"He paid you another thousand dollars?"

"Yeah. Cash. So, I let him drive the truck away from where I was waitin' for him, and he was gone maybe another half hour or so. Then he comes back, tosses me the keys, and says thank you and he's gone. That's the last time I saw him."

Jason sat back and looked up at Graham. The investigator said, "How did this man communicate with you – to let you know he wanted to run his little switch on a particular night?"

Fred shrugged. "He called me on my cell."

"What did he tell you his name was?"

"He said his name was Alex."

"Like Alex Rodriguez?" Jason cut in. "Any last name?"

"He, ah, he didn't say."

"May we see the call record from your phone?" Graham held out his hand. Fred looked confused but reached into a pocket and hauled out his cell phone, which was at least four or five years old. The screen had a crack and the rubber case was marred with streaks of white residue. Graham examined it, then scrolled through the log of incoming calls until he saw a call from the prior Wednesday, received at 12:07 a.m. Graham extracted a small pad and pen from an inside jacket pocket and recorded the number.

After Fred got his phone back, Jason asked, "You said the truck has a GPS unit?"

"Yeah. Well, that's what my boss says. I never saw it or nothin' but it's supposed to be there. He says it records where I go and how fast I'm drivin' and such. I believe him."

"Thank you, Mr. Lanbow. You've been very cooperative."

Fred glanced around nervously. "Are you gonna tell my boss?"

Jason pitied the man, who had taken twenty-five hundred dollars in exchange for engaging in conduct he knew was shady, but which he had no reason to know would involve a murder. "I'll tell him only what I have to tell him. But if I were you, I'd fess up and tell him the truth. It's always better to take responsibility and apologize, rather than lie about something like this."

Fred nodded, but said nothing. Jason doubted he would take the advice.

After Fred left, Jason got back on the phone with Mr. Norse and asked about the GPS units. They were real, so Jason asked for a report on the route the truck took early Thursday morning after it left Park Towers. The manager said he'd have the report run and asked whether his driver had done anything criminal.

"No, I don't think so. He's not the brightest bulb, but I don't think he knowingly did anything criminal."

"You think we get bright bulbs to drive our trucks? Ha! That's a good one. Fred's a good driver. But if I find out he did anything—"

"That's between him and you," Jason cut him off, not wanting to get too deep into the conversation. "All I can say is that he was very cooperative and truthful with me, and I appreciate it. Thank you for your cooperation."

After Jason hung up, he and Graham kicked around the new information. It was all but certain the cell phone Mr. Clean used was a burner and not traceable, but the GPS data would show them where he had taken the truck. Since he came back in a half hour, that meant he had probably had a vehicle stashed somewhere nearby, transferred the body, and then returned the truck.

"Are there any exterior CCTV cameras that might reveal the getaway vehicle?"

"Could be," Jason conceded. "But if this was a pro job, any vehicle would be a rental or without plates and long gone by now. We'll check it out, though. You never know."

"We have a new prime suspect, eh?"

"You mean somebody other than Nate Bedford?"

Graham nodded. "I know he had a motive, but now that we've seen the video, it would seem Mr. Bedford is off the hook."

Jason's face hardened. "We don't know for sure that Mr. Clean wasn't hired by Nate Bedford."

"Oh, surely you don't think that? Three weeks before the fight at the practice facility, Mr. Bedford hired a professional killer who began setting up his plan, and then had him execute the kill on the exact day when Bedford looked the most guilty? Then he drove himself into the vicinity of the crime scene, knowing the murder was being carried out by his agent at exactly that time? Seriously, could he be so incredibly stupid?"

It was Jason's turn to open his mouth and then close it without speaking. Eventually, he said, "I've seen some pretty stupid people do some pretty stupid things, but I get your point. I'd say it's less likely that Nate is smart enough to set up a hit in the first place. You're right; he's not much of a suspect anymore."

"Which leaves the criminal conspiracy option higher up on the probability list," Graham announced with great satisfaction.

Jason started walking toward the exit. He needed to get back to the precinct, make a report to Sully, and then get to Brooklyn to pick up Rachel. "I can't argue with that."

While Mike was stuck in midtown traffic, stopped at an endless red light, he checked his text messages and saw a reply from Agent Forrest. It read, "In middle can't talk now if urgent can talk later." Mike pulled the Lincoln over into a loading zone so he could reply. He had hoped to catch Forrest today, but he had to pick up Tony and take him out to Citi Field by 4:30 p.m. if he wanted to catch batting practice. After telling Marie about the special pre-game field passes, he was committed. Then it hit him, and he sent back a text to Forrest.

*Had a big hit on cleaning solution.*
*Meet me @ Mets game tonight.*

It was a Thursday night game. The Giants were a draw, but there would be plenty of empty seats. It was the perfect place for a casual meeting that would raise no eyebrows, even if somebody saw them talking together. You bump into a friend at the ballpark, so you chat for a few minutes. Totally innocent. Forrest would have complete deniability about anything that happened. All he had to do was give Mike a clue about how to find Mr. Clean.

When he pulled back into traffic, he headed toward the Queensboro bridge, which he still couldn't bring himself to call the Ed Koch Bridge. He would be uncharacteristically early to pick up Tony. Maybe he'd have a few minutes to talk with Marie and Jenny. It had been nearly a month since Darin's funeral, and he hadn't come by to visit even once. It was about time to fix that.

# Chapter 28 – Dark Secrets

WHILE DRIVING TO QUEENS, Mike didn't see the article in *The New York Times* that hit the website late in the afternoon. Kristi Olson and Dexter Peacock had been busy. The reality was that Kristi had been very busy, and Peacock had insisted on writing a portion of the story and taking the lead byline. Kristi didn't mind too much – she was happy to get copy in the Metro section. The article was slated to run on the front page of the B section of the print paper the next day. Sports writers seldom appeared in such a prestigious location.

Kristi had a friend, Barbara DeMarco, who had been the star pitcher on the NCAA champion Auburn women's softball team in 2012. Barbara got a job writing for the sports page of the Montgomery Advertiser and met Kristi at a convention of female sports reporters. When Kristi called on Friday wanting some background on Nate Bedford, Barbara was happy to oblige. What she provided was dynamite. She couldn't be quoted by name, but she consented to Kristi referring to her as "a source close to the Auburn athletic department." Barbara's own source was inside the athletic department, and frequently inside her bedroom, but she wasn't about to reveal that.

The article recounted a scandalous narrative that everyone in the sports department agreed was entirely plausible. It was already common knowledge that Nate's father, William Bedford, was a white supremacist. His father was Nathan Bedford Forrest, the first Grand Wizard of the KKK. The unnamed source inside the Auburn athletic department claimed that, as a Junior, Nate was twice brought up on internal disciplinary charges related to race-based hazing and harassment of Black underclassmen. Both times, the head football coach and the athletic director intervened to suppress the facts. Nate was a star player and destined to become a high draft pick. Plus, his family had connections within the university.

The university president, Furman Beauregard Hicks, turned out to be a direct descendent of Stonewall Jackson. President Hicks's father, Nathanial Hicks, was a member of several fraternal organizations – as the KKK was called in those parts – with William Bedford. President Hicks had intervened in the disciplinary matters.

In one of the two incidents, a young Black football player named Jauwan Holmes was beaten so badly during a hazing ritual that he withdrew from school and never played football again. Barbara had done some digging and tracked down Holmes, who still lived with his parents and was under medical care for brain damage. The boy's mother told Barbara he had been injured in a car accident and that the insurance company had settled the claims for a substantial sum, which was how the family had been able to move into a plush home in the suburbs of Mobile. The family declined when Barbara offered to do an in-depth piece about the aftermath of the accident on a promising football player. Mrs. Holmes said they had signed a confidentiality agreement concerning the incident and that they did not want to talk about football.

Barbara was not able to find any police reports of an auto accident involving the young man. She speculated, and it was not much of a stretch, that the confidential settlement was with the university, in order to hide the tragic consequences of the hazing practices that still went on at southern colleges. The White AD and the White head coach, supported by the university president whose father was a known KKK member, had all conspired to cover up Nate Bedford's acts of violence toward his Black teammate. There was no reporting at the time about the hazing, the injuries to Jauwan Holmes, or the disciplinary charges against Nate. It had been a complete whitewash of the situation – until now.

At 2:30 p.m., the plaza outside Riverside Church was crowded with a cross-section of New York's celebrity elite, political power brokers, and ordinary citizens. Jimmy Rydell's death struck many chords. There were far more people than space inside the church. Two large projection screens had been erected to live-stream the funeral service to the crowd outside. The police had blocked vehicle traffic on the street. When two large black coach buses pulled up, the crowd surged in that direction to get a glimpse of Jimmy's teammates.

The team had cancelled all workouts and had strongly encouraged all players and coaches to attend the funeral. When Nate Bedford stepped off the bus, he got a mixed reaction. He waved and smiled, ignoring the scattered boos and calls for him to "go home" and that he was a "disgrace." Several of his teammates gathered around him as they moved toward the church doors.

Kristi Olson ducked under the barrier of the corral in which the press was confined and wormed her way toward the knot of players, coaches, and team officials. Halfway between the bus and the church, she managed to get close enough and called out to Kevin Mahwah, who helped her into the bivouac of bodies. She shared condolences and well-wishes with several players before achieving her objective of getting next to Nate.

"I'm glad you came, Nate. It's a nice gesture."

"Thanks, but I ain't talkin' to you."

"I don't want to talk about Jimmy," Kristi dismissed Nate's brush-off. "I need to give you a chance to give your side on a different story."

Nate stopped and turned. "Story about what?"

"It's a story about a teammate of yours from Auburn. Do you remember a freshman named Jauwan Holmes?"

Nate frowned as he processed the name through his memory. "I don't think so."

"My information is that you were involved in a hazing incident in which Jauwan Holmes suffered serious injuries and had to drop out of school. Does that ring any bells?"

Nate's frown turned to a scowl. "I don't know nothin' about that. I don't remember anybody called Jew-wan." He pushed to his left, between several people who were migrating toward the church doors, leaving Kristi behind.

Kristi pulled out a pen and made some notes on a small pad. While still looking down, she felt a tug on her elbow and a familiar voice shouting, "Kristi!" She looked up into the annoyed face of Chip O'Meara.

"Hello, Chip. I'm glad you made it for the funeral."

"Don't pretend to be nice to me, Kristi. I saw you questioning Nate. That's a pretty nasty thing to do on a day like this."

"Because Nate is so broken up about Jimmy's death?"

"That's not the point. This is not an appropriate place to be asking questions. You should know better. What were you asking him about?"

"About a hazing incident Nate was involved in at Auburn. Were you aware when you drafted Nate that he had been implicated in two serious misconduct investigations related to hazing Black underclassmen?"

Chip stared blankly, blinking his eyes. "Kristi, I can't believe you would dredge up such a thing today, at Jimmy's funeral. That's completely inappropriate. I have no official comment."

"What about off the record?"

He paused. "Off the record, I don't know what you're talking about, so I guess I had no knowledge. If I had been aware of any serious misconduct in college, I would always factor that into a decision to draft a player."

"So, if a player had beaten a Black underclassman into a coma, inflicting brain damage that caused the younger player to drop out of school, you'd consider it a character issue?"

Chip kept a poker face. "I really can't comment on such a hypothetical situation."

"Fine. I'll note that the team has no comment. But why not? Why won't you speak out about something like this?"

"Kristi, I need to show support for all my players. They need to know the team has their back. Even if there are problems, it's important. You remember when Alan Watson had that DWI arrest a few years ago? I said the team stood behind him and would support him, even if he was guilty. It's what any team does for its players. I support all the players, White or Black."

Chip hurried to catch up to the rest of the group he had been walking with and disappeared into the church. Kristi roamed through the crowd, looking for any of the Black team leaders. She spotted Elliot Williams, one of the offensive linemen on the Jet Fuel Squad. He was walking toward the doors with several Black teammates.

"Elliot!" she called out, getting his attention with a foot on the lowest stair step.

"Hey, Kristi, I really can't talk."

"It's not about Jimmy. I'm working on a different story – about hazing of Black players at southern colleges. You went to Texas Southern, right? Can you give me a minute?"

Williams backed down off the stairs, motioning to the rest of his group to go ahead without him. He moved off to the side, away from the flow of mourners surging into the church, and turned his back to the crowd, shielding Kristi from their view behind his bulk. "Look, Kristi, I can't say anything on the record. I don't want to go there. Not now. I got a career to think about."

"You think your old coaches can hurt you now if you speak up?" Kristi was genuinely confounded by this response, but she also wanted to appeal to the player's macho impulses and his sense of social justice – particularly on a day like this.

"It's not just them. It's a whole can of worms. I'm a free agent after next season. I'm not looking to get blackballed for being a troublemaker or an activist. I'm not Jimmy. I got a family."

"I get it," Kristi said calmly. "Can you give me anything? Attributed to an unnamed source? Did you get hazed by the upperclassmen at your school?"

"Off the record, no. Not me. They recruited me pretty hard. The coaches didn't want anything happening to me. But the walk-ons? And the small-town kids who needed their scholarships? Yeah. The upperclassmen – the White guys – they abused them pretty good."

"The coaches knew?"

"Sure. They knew. They thought it made 'em tougher. It built their characters. Funny how the White kids didn't seem to need their characters built up as much."

"Did anyone report it?"

"No. You didn't do that. The guys just took it and moved on. If they wanted to play, they had to prove they could be good team players. That's just how it is."

"Weren't there any Black coaches or Black administrators who would do anything about it?" Kristi found herself whispering.

"You can't understand how it is. I appreciate you trying, though."

"Would you be surprised to find out some of your current teammates participated in brutalizing Black players during hazing rituals in college?"

"No. That wouldn't surprise me. I guess it would surprise me if they didn't. It was part of being a team leader. Even some of the Black seniors did it. They took it when they were freshmen, so they dished it out when they were seniors. Like I said, that's just how it is."

"Did you?"

Williams lowered his head and shook it slowly. "Not me, man. I'd like to bust their heads – including the coaches. But there's some things you can't fight."

"I don't believe that," Kristi raised her voice. "It's my job to shine a light on it."

"You do that. Good luck. But leave my name out of it." Williams turned abruptly and headed back into the diminishing stream of funeral-goers. It was almost 3:00 p.m.

Kristi wandered back to the press area, pulled out her phone, and called the Metro section editor who was shepherding her story toward publication. She recited the quotes she had obtained so he could add them before he released the article on the website. When the funeral let out, she'd try for some additional quotes.

As six offensive linemen carried Jimmy Rydell's coffin out of Riverside Church at 4:35 p.m., more than a thousand protest marchers made their way up West End Avenue. The front of the crowd reached 110th street just as Chip and Woody O'Meara reached the bottom of the steps after exiting the church. The marchers carried signs reading "Justice for Jimmy" and "Take a Knee." Since leaving the organizing area around the Eleanor Roosevelt memorial just north of 72nd Street, the crowd had become more and more agitated. Afterward, some cable news channels would report that there were far-left radical activists in the crowd who were looking to start a riot.

The *Times* website published Kristi's story about the hazing at Auburn at exactly that moment. Word spread through the crowd like a flash fire. Only a few people had actually read the article off their Twitter feeds. The summary passed along from person to person was less than entirely accurate, but the gist of the story was pretty simple. Before five minutes had lapsed, most of the crowd was chanting "Bed-ford Sucks!" and "Racist Team" and "R-A-C-I-S-T."

When the front end of the marchers reached 122nd Street, they could see the stragglers of the funeral congregation milling about on the plaza in front of the church. Somebody shouted, "There's Nate!"

The marchers surged forward. The twelve uniformed officers from the NYPD who had been assigned to crowd control for the event were quickly overwhelmed. The increasingly angry protesters broke through the police line and rushed toward the group of football players, team officials, and political dignitaries who were making their way toward waiting buses and limos.

The police officers sent out a call for back-up. The reporters covering the funeral and the reporters covering the march captured video on their smartphones. Nate Bedford, it turned out, was already inside the team bus. Duke Drepp, who had been assigned as Nate's bodyguard after several death threats, was with him. They watched out the smoked bus window as the marchers surged toward the church. Fortunately for everyone, all the players were sheltered, and the church's reverend produced a megaphone and calmed everyone down before it turned into a riot. Six people were treated for minor injuries. There were no arrests.

# Chapter 29 – Polar Bear Parade

I T WAS A GLORIOUS LATE AFTERNOON at Citi Field in Flushing, Queens, home of the New York Metropolitan Baseball Club. With the temperature in the mid-70s and the sun still casting shadows over the right field corner, the Mets were taking batting practice. Mike and nine-year-old Tony Curran were standing on the warning track behind home plate with a group of twenty other fans with VIP batting practice field passes. Tony's eyes were fixed on rookie first baseman Pete Alonso, called the *Polar Bear*. Alonso was clubbing majestic fly balls over the outfield walls in all directions. Mike whistled as he watched one go into the Big Apple container in center field. Mike agreed that Alonso was impressive.

When Mike had arrived at the Curran home two hours earlier, Tony's mother, Marie, had not yet told her son about the surprise of special pre-game access. Since his father's death a month earlier, the boy had been understandably withdrawn. Marie said the ballgame date with Uncle Mike was the first thing he had been excited about in a while. Mike spent some time with Tony's younger sister, Jenny, who was nearly as excited about going out with her mom for the evening to have a girls' dinner and then go to a movie. He and Marie also spent time talking and, for Marie, crying. She didn't blame Mike for what happened. She knew the truth, but they didn't talk about it. Before Mike and Tony left for the stadium, Mike and Marie hugged for a long time.

Mike looked down at Tony's happy face and felt like he really was being *Uncle Mike*, like he should. He vowed to visit Marie and the kids more often, and to make plans to take Tony to a football game in September. For the moment though, he and Tony could just be happy, enjoy the almost-summer night, and root for the Mets.

When the last group of players finished their batting practice, they cleaned up the stray baseballs and gathered up their gear. Most headed for the dugout, but several wandered in the direction of the fans standing behind the yellow rope on the warning track. The VIP pass-holders would get a few minutes with some of the younger players who had drawn the pre-game meet-and-greet straws that night. One of them was Pete Alonso. He made his way slowly down the line of fans, signing balls and caps, shaking hands, and posing for selfies. Alonso had a huge smile, as if getting adulation from these fans was still new and cool for him. Maybe it was. He had already hit 20 home runs, nearly as many as the team's rookie record set by Darryl Strawberry, who won the Rookie of the Year award in 1983.

When Alonso reached Mike and Tony, the boy enthusiastically held out a brand-new official major league baseball which Mike had procured, along with a black marker. Mike had instructed Tony to hold out both the ball and the pen, with the cap off, and say "please" and "thank you" to the player. There was a ritual to asking for a big-league player's autograph that needed to be observed.

When Alonso handed back the ball, Tony said, "I hope you hit a home run tonight!"

Alonso chuckled and reached out to tussle Tony's hair. "I'll do my best, kid."

Tony wasn't done giving encouragement. "You're gonna set the record this year. I know it! You're awesome!"

"Thanks," Alonso said, looking at Mike to determine if he also wanted an autograph.

Mike reached out to shake the player's hand. "Keep up that attitude, Pete. You'll have this town eating out of your hand."

Alonso said "Thanks," then moved on to the next fan. By the end of the session, Tony had three autographs on his ball. He was on cloud nine when they made their way back through the belly of the stadium, down the brightly painted corridor and back out to the Jackie Robinson rotunda. Mike took Tony into the Delta Club dining room for some pre-game dinner. Tony continued to be thrilled by the outing and talked a mile a minute about the Mets, their players, the dominance of their pitching staff, and how far they could go if they stopped giving up so many unearned runs. Mike was impressed with the kid's knowledge and enthusiasm.

When the game started, the Mets took an early lead, although Alonso did not hit a home run. As the Mets ran off the field after the top of the third inning, Mike's cell phone pinged, indicating an incoming text message from Agent Forrest. Mike texted back that Forrest should meet him in five minutes in the wheelchair seating area at the top of section 116. Three minutes later, as the first Met was walking to the plate, Mike asked Tony if he would be OK sitting by himself while Mike excused himself.

Tony rolled his eyes. "Uncle Mike, I take the subway to school – I'll be OK."

Mike walked up the concrete steps to the top of the section. He spotted Forrest standing against the green-painted rail separating the concourse from the wheelchair area. He sidled up and assumed a position next to Forrest, without obviously greeting him. Anyone who saw them would think they were two random fans, both watching the game.

Mike spoke softly, without turning his head. "We have Mr. Clean on video at Jimmy Rydell's apartment building, dressed as the laundry service guy. He came in at one a.m. and left a half hour later with a big-ass laundry cart piled high with dirty towels. The cart seemed to be excessively heavy and loaded up way higher than normal. Jason tracked down the regular driver, who confirmed that Mr. Clean bribed him to let him make his pickup that night, then drove the truck away somewhere for a half hour before returning it. Sounds pretty clearly like he was disposing of a body. We have enough of his face on the video, so between that and the video of him in the lobby the week before, he's in the crosshairs. We have enough to bring him in for questioning, and probably arrest him. We'd love to do that, but we need to find him first. Any chance you can help make it happen?"

Forrest watched the game, without speaking. Outfielder Michael Conforto hit a foul ball that arched high behind home plate before landing in the seats below them. The crowd cheered. While the pitcher rubbed up a new ball on the mound, Forrest spoke, without looking at Mike. "Fat Albert knows we're watching him, but I'm not sure he knows we know Mr. Clean is one of his goons."

Conforto hit a deep line drive to right, but it was caught for the first out. When the crowd's cheers subsided, Forrest continued. "My bosses wouldn't be happy if it came out that I gave him up, even to you. You'd have to stage it so one of your cops just happens to spot him and haul him in. It can't look like a big, organized operation with lots of backup, like somebody tipped you off. I don't think Mr. Clean will bolt or try to put up a big fight, but I can't guarantee that. It would be putting some officers in a tough spot, trying to arrest him without back-up if he decides to resist. I can't take any heat for that."

"I understand," Mike mumbled, clapping his hands as Pete Alonso ripped a single into left field.

"So, here's what I can do for you, Mike. I can tell you that on Saturdays, the boss almost always has lunch at a place called Luigi's on Mulberry street. Mr. Clean usually goes with him and sits at an exterior table, watching for anybody from the rival gangs or cops coming inside after the boss goes in to eat. While he's there at the sidewalk table, somebody might spot him. You have a decent photo, so you have to use yours, not one of mine. If you put out an alert for your beat cops and one of them happens to recognize him, that probably wouldn't boomerang back to me."

Todd Frazier hit a long fly to left that brought the crowd to its feet and raised a roar that drowned out any conversation. The ball went foul, sending the Mets fans back into their seats.

Mike said, "Thanks," and backed away from the rail. He turned right and flashed his ticket to the usher. The old guy, whose name was Luke, nodded and smiled, but held up a hand to hold Mike back until the at-bat ended. Then Mike hustled down the steps to his seat. He glanced back to his right, but Forrest was gone.

When Mike arrived at the seat, Tony was bouncing up and down and holding up a baseball. Mike thought it was the ball with the autographs from before the game. "Careful, there, Tony, you don't want to smudge your autographs."

"No, Uncle Mike! It's a new one. I caught a foul ball!" Tony's smile couldn't be any wider as he held out the slightly dirty ball for Mike to inspect.

"That's great, Tony. Once in a lifetime." He put his arm around the boy as he sat down. They watched the Mets score two runs and go on to a 7-4 victory behind Seth Lugo. On the drive home, Tony recounted his leap across a row of seats to make the catch on Conforto's foul ball. Mike smiled and congratulated him on a great catch. "You keep working at it and maybe someday you'll make the big leagues."

# Chapter 30 – Best Laid Plans

W HEN JASON KNOCKED on the door of Rachel's house – actually Rachel's parents' house – twenty minutes later than he had planned, he heard her voice call out, "It's open."

Inside, he carefully draped his jacket on a hanger suspended from one hook of a teak coat rack. He called out, "Rachel? Sweetie?" then continued down the short entry hall and turned into the living room. Rachel was lying on the sofa, holding a plastic bag of ice against her face. "Holy shit! What happened?" Jason hurried across the room and knelt down next to Rachel, putting his hand on hers and reaching to stroke her disheveled hair.

She groaned softly and squeezed Jason's hand. The ice bag had dripped and left a wet stain down the front of her blue EMT uniform, which was unbuttoned, revealing a white t-shirt underneath. She lifted the bag away from her face, allowing Jason to see red, swollen skin with a small cut along her cheekbone. "I'm fine. I look like a UFC fighter, but I'm not really hurt."

"What happened?"

Rachel sat up and replaced the ice pack, which dripped more water down her front. She ignored it. "We had a call for a possible drug overdose. The guy was actually having a seizure. While we were trying to treat him, I was trying to take his pulse and he lashed out and punched me in the face. I don't think he knew what he was doing."

"Did the officers on the scene arrest him?"

"No! Of course not. He wasn't assaulting me. He was trying not to die."

"Did he make it?" Jason asked. He was trying to put on a concerned expression, despite his instinctive desire to throttle the complete stranger who hurt her.

"Yeah. We got him into the ambulance and dropped him at Bellevue." She dropped her arm, allowing the half-melted ice bag to slosh into her lap. "Then the new Neanderthal they have me partnered with gave me a hard time about coming home to take care of this. I almost slugged him." She reached out and stroked the side of Jason's face. "Listen, I know we were going to go out for dinner for my birthday, but I look awful and it was a really rough day. Can we just stay home?" Rachel's eyes pleaded with Jason.

"But – I –I got us a reservation at *Le Renard Courrant*. Sophie's pulled a hundred strings to get us the reservation. I know you were looking forward to it."

"Oh, Jay. I know. You worked so hard to get us in there. Any other night I'm sure I'd love it. But I can't go out looking like Rocky Balboa."

"It's not so bad," Jason quickly replied, grabbing the soggy ice bag and walking to the tiny adjacent kitchen. He tossed the bag into the sink and turned immediately back toward Rachel. "You'll feel a lot better if you get back up and get out where you can forget about the bad day. I'll even let you take all the selfies you want. I'll even smile." He flashed his best you-know-you-want-to smile and held out his arms, inviting her to come in for a hug, then leaned in for a soft kiss. They lingered in that position until Rachel finally took a breath.

"What time is the reservation?"

"It's six-thirty. We have just enough time to get there."

"I'll go get dressed."

"That's more like the party girl I love so much."

Rachel walked toward the bedroom, then reached up to touch her cheek and winced. But she had agreed. And it was almost her birthday.

In the cab to the restaurant, Jason felt his phone buzz. He knew Rachel would be happy to check her messages if he took out his phone, so he apologized and took a peek at the text. It was from Dominique, Sophie's niece.

> *Jason. So sorry. I have an emergency.*
> *My little boy is home sick. Don't worry. Jean-Luc will*
> *be covering for me tonight. He'll take care of everything.*

Jason stared at the message, then shoved the phone roughly back into his jacket pocket.

"Everything OK?" Rachel asked.

"Sure. Fine. Just a note from Sophie's niece. She won't be there tonight. Sick kid, I guess. She was apologizing for not being there. No big deal."

"OK. I was looking forward to meeting her. You always say such nice things about Sophie. We still have a reservation, right?"

"Sure we do." Jason put his arm around Rachel's shoulder and hugged her as she placed her uninjured cheek against his chest. Jason stared out the window and tried not to panic.

The cab left them on the curb in front of the red velvet rope holding back a line of people waiting to get inside. Rachel looked up at the opulent, neon-outlined placard hanging over the canopy sheltering the front door. The figure of a red fox wearing sneakers smiled down at her. She shook her head slightly at the absurdity of what could become the hottest restaurant in town. She had heard about the place on the local news and seen pictures of celebrities eating there. She suddenly realized she had no idea what the menu would be like, except that she assumed it was French cuisine.

Jason took her arm as a uniformed attendant pulled open the heavy padded door. Rachel had cleaned up nicely, opting for a silver mid-calf dress with a daringly plunging neckline. She figured it would draw attention away from her mangled face. She had covered the cut as well as she could with makeup and was satisfied that nobody would try to rescue her from Jason during dinner. The bruise might turn black and blue by morning, but for now she was passible. They made a striking couple – both tall, well-dressed, and looking elegant in the warm June evening.

When they reached the front desk, Jason stepped forward. A short, dark-skinned man in a tuxedo looked up from his reservation book and smiled. "How may I help you, Sir?"

"Are you Jean-Luc?"

"Oui, monsieur."

Jason leaned in and spoke softly. "I'm Jason Dickson. Dominique texted me to say she couldn't be here, like we planned, but she said you would take care of everything. So, she explained everything to you, right?"

Jean-Luc replied in a heavy French accent, although Jason wasn't sure if it was genuine. "Oh, yes, Sir. Of course, I will take care of everything."

"Great. Good. Thank you." Jason pulled back quickly and put an arm around Rachel. Within a minute, a smiling female server waved them forward and showed them to a table next to the window overlooking the street. They could see the lengthening shadows of passing pedestrians as the sun made its way toward New Jersey. Jason took Rachel's hand across the table and told her how beautiful she looked.

Rachel relaxed into the comfortable chair. They ordered sparkling water and champagne. Jason insisted, since it was her birthday celebration. "You only turn twenty-eight once," he said with a smile. "Look at it this way, even with the day you had, your birthday has to be better than Mike's fiftieth, right?"

Rachel laughed. "Oh, well, I don't know. There's still time for someone to take a shot at you before the night is over." They spent several minutes reliving their exciting experience aboard the *Colossus of the Ocean* only three weeks earlier. Jason absently rubbed the scar on his left biceps through his suit jacket.

Rachel pulled out her phone and took a photo of Jason, who smiled obligingly. Jason convinced her to take one joint selfie, although she swore she would never post it to Instagram with her "mutilated" cheek. She posted Jason's picture and smiled when she immediately got three envious comments.

All around them, excited diners pointed and spoke in hushed tones, noticing several prominent New Yorkers seated around the room. Crystal chandeliers reflected rainbows of color everywhere. Rich wood, leather, and thick carpeting created the ambiance of a European palace. Then the waiter brought them menus. At first, Rachel was excited by the banner at the top of the huge, leather-bound portfolio announcing: "healthy vegan French country cuisine." When she started reading the options, in French with tiny English subtitles, her smile faded. As the courses came to their candlelit table, their happy mood deteriorated.

The appetizers of fat-free mushroom *foie gras* and non-dairy *soupe a l'oignon gratinee* did not excite either of them. At least the bread was good. The service was billed as "relaxed" so that patrons could enjoy their meals without being rushed. Both Jason and Rachel wished their waiter would bring the food before the sun set. Jason wished he could have ordered duck or beef.

Rachel had ordered vegan sweetbreads. She thought it sounded safe. "It's sweet, so how far wrong can I go?" When the dish came, constructed of tofu and spices meant to simulate the internal organ meat of calves and lambs, she asked to share Jason's cassoulet, which was full of simulated duck and sausage. At least Jason's dish wasn't terrible.

When Rachel excused herself to use the restroom after their waiter cleared off the main course dishes, Jason stood up and waved in the direction of Jean-Luc at the host's stand. The small man saw Jason's gesture and smiled, waving back. Jason pointed to his watch. Jean-Luc waved again, then turned back to the next guest.

Jason sat back down as Rachel came into view.

"Did you get the check?" she asked with a glance toward the door.

"No. I ordered us dessert." Jason flashed his best smile.

"Oh, Jason. I'm not sure—"

Jason reached for her hand. "Sweetie, I want this to be the most memorable birthday ever for you. Just relax for a few minutes. Dessert has to be the best part of the meal, right?"

Rachel nodded and Jason asked how her sister and niece were doing, which perked her up. She was looking forward to seeing them at her birthday party on Sunday. As they exhausted the potential conversation about Rachel's older sister, who had provided her parents with their one and only grandchild, the waiter appeared and asked if they would like dessert.

Jason fixed an annoyed glare at their server. "I already ordered the crème brulée." When the waiter looked confused, Jason peeked at Rachel, who was giving him a reprobative stare. Rachel was touchy about treating servers with respect. She had plenty of friends who waited tables. He softened his expression. "Please speak to Jean-Luc. He took care of it." The waiter still seemed confused, but trotted off in the direction of the host's podium.

"Jay, really, I'd be just as happy to get the check."

"No. Sweetie, the *Times* said that the crème brulée here is the absolute best in town. You have to try it." Jason stole a glance toward the maître d's station and saw their waiter talking to Jean-Luc.

Jason relaxed when the waiter appeared, carrying a plate displaying a round porcelain dish of vegan, coconut-based crème brulée. Its sugar crust was browned to perfection and topped with a dollop of dairy-free whipped cream, accented with a plump blueberry and a triangle of dark chocolate.

Jason stared at the dessert offering, then looked up at the waiter, panic on his face. He looked over at the maître d's station to try to make eye contact with Jean-Luc, who was nowhere to be seen.

"Thank you," Rachel said as the waiter placed the dish in the center of the table and handed her a silver spoon. She dipped into the delectable dish, cracking through the caramelized sugar and scooping out the custard. She ate the spoonful with delight. "Ohhhh. This is good!"

Jason ignored the treat and searched the room with his eyes for Jean-Luc.

"Jay. Aren't you going to have some?" Rachel asked, putting down her spoon.

"Um. In a minute."

"Jason Dickson!" Rachel smacked her open palm on the linen-covered table. "You practically forced me to eat this, and I don't need the calories. So, you help me eat it or let's just go already."

Jason swiveled his head from side to side, desperately searching for the man who was supposed to have made the arrangements to deliver the emerald engagement ring on top of the dessert. Not seeing Jean-Luc, Jason turned back toward Rachel. Her eyes were angry. He stood up, then dropped to the floor on one knee. He grabbed Rachel's startled hand in both of his and held it tight.

"Rachel – I'm so sorry. This was supposed to be perfect, but it's gone to shit. Sophie's niece was supposed to take care of everything and Jean-Luc screwed everything up. It's all ruined now. I love you. I know what you need from me, and I'm ready to give it to you. I wanted to put a ring on it, but Dominique has the ring, and she's not here, and it all went wrong."

Rachel was dumfounded. "What are you—"

"I love you. I want to make you happy. I have a ring here somewhere, but I don't care about that. Rachel Robinson – will you marry me?"

Rachel stared with wide eyes.

At that moment, Jean-Luc appeared, rushing to the table, thrusting a small black velvet box toward Jason. "Monsieur, I am so sorry."

Jason snatched the box from the maître d's hand and otherwise ignored the small man, who backed away quickly. Jason held out the box toward Rachel, who was still frozen in place. He tried to open it, but its hinge was facing toward Rachel. He swiveled the box around and cracked it open, revealing the gleaming green emerald set in yellow gold, sparkling against the black velvet interior.

Rachel gasped, then looked into Jason's eyes. "OHMYGOD! YES!" she shouted, grabbing for the box with her left hand and reaching for Jason's arm with her right. She pulled him toward her as she stood up, squealing with delight. They hugged tightly, and every eye in the restaurant turned toward them. Several other diners started clapping and cheering. When he disengaged from Rachel's hug, Jason glanced around, embarrassed by the attention. He nodded toward the couple at the adjoining table, who were applauding particularly loudly.

Rachel pulled away and extracted the ring. Jason took it and slipped it onto her left ring finger. She then leaped toward Jason, jumping into his arms. They kissed several times in quick succession. Jason set her feet down, sporting a huge smile of relief. He glanced sideways toward Jean-Luc, who was slinking back toward his station and avoiding Jason's gaze.

Rachel's phone was already in her hand when Jason looked back toward his newly minted fiancée. She snapped two quick shots of her hand with the emerald ring, then turned back to Jason.

"I love it! Emeralds are my favorite. I'm so glad you remembered."

"Well, I saw how much you liked Mrs. Bloom's ring on the cruise, so I figured you would like this one."

Ten minutes later, Jason and Rachel emerged from *Le Renard Courrant* and stood on the sidewalk in the warm June evening. The red-coated doorman nodded toward Jason, then blew a whistle to summon a cab, which appeared instantly. When Jason settled himself into the back seat, Rachel was already on her phone, tapping keys frantically. Jason smiled, exhaled a deep breath, and leaned back.

Just before midnight, Mike walked through the door of Michelle's apartment at Twenty-Third and Third. Michelle was lying on her sofa, her legs extended and resting on a throw pillow. Mike hurried over, kissed her gently, then replaced the pillow with his lap and began massaging the balls of her feet. At Mike's request, she changed the TV channel to SNY to see the Mets highlights. Mike recounted the day with Tony Curran and how much fun both of them had.

Just before the sports highlight show went to its first commercial break, the announcer said, "Before we take a break, you have to see this catch by a young fan." The screen showed a foul ball lofting off Michael Conforto's bat and falling behind home plate. A boy leaped out, extending his gloved hand over the row of seats in front of him, and made the catch as he tumbled over the back of a seat. The kid then leaped up, holding the ball aloft and sporting a huge smile.

"Holy crap!" Mike called out. "That's Tony!"

Michelle paused the video, praising the wonders of their Verizon cable system, and replayed the clip, while Mike narrated. He explained that he was having his conversation with Agent Forrest and missed the catch in real time. He knew Tony had caught a ball, but he didn't know it was such a great catch.

"Oh, Mike!" Michelle exclaimed suddenly, "isn't it wonderful about Rachel and Jason?"

Mike pulled his gaze away from the TV and turned toward Michelle. "Did Rachel tell you something?"

"She sent out Instagram pictures of the ring!"

"That's great," he said.

Michelle fixed her eyes on Mike, staring into his. Mike held her stare without expression. "You knew!" she accused, the pitch of her voice rising above her normal controlled timbre.

Mike remained silent, calculating the probability of successfully denying his knowledge of Jason's plan to propose. He figured lying about it was not a good strategy. "Well, I wasn't sure it was going to happen tonight."

"Why didn't you tell me?"

"Jason swore me to secrecy."

Michelle opened her mouth to yell at Mike, but then held back. "I can keep a secret," she lamented.

"Sure. I know. But it wasn't my call. Jason made me swear not to tell you."

"Well, I'm thrilled for them," Michelle said, re-extending her feet and wiggling them in Mike's direction.

Mike turned back toward the television as he resumed his massage. Pete Alonso made a nice play on a line drive. "I'm really happy for them."

Michelle held out her phone to show Mike the photo of the emerald ring. "Did you know he was getting her an emerald?"

"Yeah, I did. She said she loved them on the cruise."

"Well, I agree. It's lovely. I can't wait to talk to her about it. They're such a cute couple. I'm so happy!"

"I agree. They deserve to be happy together," Mike responded carefully. "I'm hoping this doesn't mean I'm going to be getting a new partner."

"What do you mean?"

"Well, you know. Sometimes when cops get married, they decide that being a cop and being a husband are not a great match."

"You think Jason thinks that way?"

"Maybe. I'm not sure. I guess we'll have to see. There's time. It's not like they're getting married tomorrow."

"No," Michelle agreed. "But it's going to be fun for Rachel to plan a wedding."

"Sure," Mike agreed, turning his fingers back to Michelle's feet and his eyes back toward the TV.

# Chapter 31 – A Little Less Conversation

Friday, June 6

THE NEXT MORNING, Mike told Jason how grateful he should be that Mike successfully kept his engagement plans secret from Michelle. Jason thanked him for taking the bullet for him and gave his partner the quick version of the imperfect proposal.

"At least she said yes," Mike shrugged. "Years from now, it will either be the funny story about your proposal, or you'll both agree to tell the story as if everything went perfectly according to your original plan. Either way, it'll be memorable."

They spent the morning in the precinct, planning the Saturday sting on Mr. Clean. After much discussion, they decided they had to explain to Graham how they knew where Mr. Clean would be. It meant encouraging the criminal activity theory, but it couldn't be helped. As they expected, Graham was thrilled that the official investigation was going in this direction. He enthusiastically participated in the planning and even volunteered to assist, since there was no chance the mob boss's eastern European henchman would recognize the Brit.

They briefed Sully and asked him to pick them out a pair of uniformed officers they could count on to take down Mr. Clean. He had a pair in mind immediately and told them they could work it on overtime on Saturday, since the mayor was so interested in getting some closure.

When they emerged from the captain's office, Steve Berkowitz called out to Mike from the corner conference room and waved him over. As he and Jason approached, they could see a crowd inside.

As soon as Mike cleared the threshold, music filled the room. At the same time, a grainy video image projected on the whiteboard sprang to life. On the makeshift screen, Mike Stoneman stood on a stage, holding a microphone and belting out "A Little Less Conversation." Mike and Jason immediately recognized the karaoke bar aboard the *Colossus of the Ocean*. The other cops loudly broke into song and joined the video, laughing robustly.

Mike directed a suspicious glare toward Jason, who immediately held up his hands in surrender. "Not me, Mike. If you recall, you confiscated my phone before you went on stage."

"All right, you clowns, where did you get this?"

Berkowitz laughed and slapped Mike on his right arm. "Your buddy Dexter Peacock from *The Times* sent it over. Said he found it on the internet and thought we might enjoy it. And we did! I gotta hand it to you, Stoneman – you got moves!"

"All right," Mike bellowed. "You got me. Nice job. But what happens on the high seas is supposed to stay on the high seas. Now, will whoever obtained this video please do me the favor of deleting it before I have to start dredging up the personal dirt I have on each of you?" The group had another hearty laugh as the video and music were extinguished. Mike waved in disgust at the group as he and Jason walked back to their desks.

♦♦♦

That afternoon, they met with Officers Randy Siebring and Bill O'Dell, Sully's choices for their street team. They looked like linebackers. They were also sharp. The operation had to be quick and clean. They sketched it out on the whiteboard in the conference room, now lacking any projected video.

The plan was for Graham to approach Mr. Clean outside the restaurant and create a diversion. The officers would come in to break up the situation, as if they just happened to be driving by in their squad car. When they got the situation under control, they would "recognize" Mr. Clean from the APB that had gone out that morning, arrest him, and bring him in.

"Should be a piece of cake," O'Dell said like a soldier.

"Sure," Mike said, "it should be. But never underestimate the ways an operation like this can go sideways. Stay alert and expect the unexpected."

Jason stood and shook hands with both officers, telling them he was sure they would handle the situation well.

When the officers left to resume their regular patrol shift, the detectives and Graham remained to go over Graham's role. But before they got back to the diagram on the whiteboard, a uniformed officer arrived at the door with a thick envelope. Inside were the records from Jimmy's personal checking account. The whiteboard could wait while they dove into Jimmy's spending habits.

♦♦♦

Two hours later, the diagram of the plaza outside Luigi's restaurant had been replaced by rows of numbers, as Graham led the effort to understand Jimmy's personal finances. He had had plenty of money in his private account during his 2017 rookie season, but there were many large withdrawals of cash. There were also payments made on Jimmy's personal American Express card, which were automatically deducted from the account each month.

In January and February of 2018, after the season ended and while Jimmy wasn't getting paid, the account balance got low and was overdrawn twice. Each time, there was an infusion of funds from a direct deposit listed as ISMS. They figured these were transfers from the investment account held by his management company. "Funny how his agent didn't mention that," said Mike.

In early March, the account was nearly drained again by a cash withdrawal of $20,000. In early April, the balance was inflated by a deposit of $80,000. But this time, the deposit was a wire transfer from an account listed only as a series of numbers. After that, the balance fluctuated in relatively familiar patterns, including monthly infusions from the ISMS account, as had happened every month since the account was opened.

It was another puzzle. Why did Jimmy need $20,000 in cash? He hadn't bought a car. By that time, his license had been suspended, and he lived in Manhattan. It could have been some super-expensive jewelry, but they hadn't found anything like that in Jimmy's apartment. More curious was where the $80,000 had come from.

"Could be gambling winnings," Graham suggested. "If he was in with the point-shavers, that could be an explanation."

Mike and Jason had to agree it was plausible, but there were plenty of other possibilities. It wasn't evidence of criminal activity. But it was curious.

The three went back to their general speculation about how the murder went down. It seemed pretty clear that Jimmy had been strangled with the yellow resistance band in the health club. The forensics report on the yellow band they took from the gym at Park Towers had come back a dead-on match for the material found under Jimmy's fingernail. Afterward, Mr. Clean spirited the body out in the laundry cart. He then moved the body into some other vehicle, or straight into a nearby freezer. Either way, the body was chilled, and then ended up on the carousel.

Neither Graham nor the detectives could offer any theory to explain why Mr. Clean – or, more accurately, Fat Albert Gallata – would want Jimmy's body to be found, rather than making it disappear. That was the piece that didn't fit.

"There's also the murder of poor Tiger, the shoeshine kid." Mike pointed out.

Graham speculated that Tiger might have seen Mr. Clean on the night of the murder, prompting the thug to come back and take him out to prevent him from being a witness. That almost made sense, except even the feds didn't know who Mr. Clean was. Why would he be worried about being seen for a few seconds by a homeless kid? And why would he wait until Sunday night to kill him? And why dump Tiger's body forty blocks north in Riverside Park? Not even Graham could spin out a theory that explained all those facts.

Graham asked, "Was there anything in Mr. Rydell's phone records showing calls or texts to that burner phone or other suspicious numbers? I don't believe I saw those reports."

"I haven't seen them either," Mike responded absently. "The two officers sent us a summary of all the numbers and there was nothing significant. They tracked every number and they were all either teammates, his agent, his friendly driver and bodyguard, The Duke, or women who acknowledged having had consensual relationships with Jimmy. No burners and no mob bosses. I didn't look at the raw reports myself."

"Yes, I expected you'd have mentioned it if there were anything important."

They were at a series of dead ends. They all hoped the apprehension of Mr. Clean would lead them in a productive direction. At the end of the day, Mike was on his way downtown, while Jason was meeting Rachel at his apartment. They'd all meet in the morning in Little Italy.

That night, several politicians and activists organized another *Justice for Jimmy* march in the area around NYU. The police cordoned off the pro-Jimmy crowd in Washington Square. A procession of Black community leaders and several former NFL players made speeches in support of racial justice, while urging the crowd to be peaceful. A larger-than-normal percentage of the police officers working crowd control in that area were Black and Hispanic.

Meanwhile, the NYPD mounted patrols and a primarily White officer corps funneled a small anti-Jimmy crowd to Union Square. A few garbage cans ended up burning, but there were no arrests and no injuries officially reported. The late news shows featured split-screen images of the two groups, but there was nothing sensational or violent. The overtime bill for the city was more than $1 million. The Mayor was happy.

# Chapter 32 – Springing a Trap

FAT ALBERT GALLATA had earned his nickname as a boy, long before Bill Cosby's cartoon character was a persona to be avoided. By the time he was in high school he had cut down a bit on the pasta, but the name had stuck. In his adult years, he embraced it and decided that enjoying his meals was nothing to be ashamed of. Now that he was the head of the family business, he could have his tailor manage the details.

Fat Albert was now eleven months into his tenure as CEO of the organization and had proven to be a more astute businessman than his various lieutenants had expected. When the kid was suddenly thrust into the captain's chair after his father's sudden death in July of 2018, there had been a brief power struggle. Albert was aided by the turmoil in various arms of the Gallata operation after the murder of Justin Heilman, who had been viewed as a contender for the top job. Some of Heilman's closest allies were arrested by the FBI, which left his segment in disarray. Albert was able to stabilize the situation while insulating other tentacles of the business.

Perhaps, if Mickey "Slick Mick" Gallata had been taken out by a rival family, things would have gone differently. As it worked out, Fat Albert had settled in and was now firmly in control. On Saturdays, he enjoyed a leisurely lunch at his favorite restaurant in Little Italy. His security experts told him it was a bad idea to have such a predictable routine, but the boss figured the feds were already watching him closely enough that they would know where he was wherever he dined. If somebody else wanted to take him out, he was willing to take his chances that the owner, a longtime friend of the family, had his back. Besides, who would try to take him out with the feds watching? He did, however, bring two bodyguards along to keep watch over the entrance. Just in case.

On this particular early June Saturday, the weather was so wonderful that Fat Albert considered eating outside at one of the shaded tables along the sidewalk. It seemed like half of New York's population was out walking that day, enjoying temperatures in the 80s with low humidity levels. In the end, he went inside with a group of four other men and one eye-catching woman in a short red dress. His two bodyguards stayed outside. The first was Edward Bernedetti, known as *Eddie the Eagle*, because of his sharp eyes and quick reflexes in a fight. The other guard was the big bald guy they all called Igor.

Mike and Jason were huddled in the back of a panel van parked a half-block away, watching the events on a live video feed provided by the security system of the jewelry store across Mulberry street from the restaurant. The owner had been happy to reposition his exterior camera at the request of the NYPD. They were close by, just in case, but the plan was for them to remain invisible so that the arrest looked like a happenstance and not a coordinated operation.

"I'd feel better if we had a couple undercover cops sitting on that patio, and a few more in a car parked across the street," Jason said.

"Me, too," Mike agreed. "I'm just happy Sully signed off on this one. I'm sure he felt the same way about having plenty of back-up, but we can't have it look like the feds tipped us off. Forrest doesn't want Fat Albert to change his routine. If things go as planned, we'll have sufficient manpower."

Jason turned back to the small video monitor. "I know. I guess what I really want is to be there myself and not leave it up to Siebring and O'Dell."

"You're going to have to learn to live with being a recognizable celebrity cop, Jason. Since you got that hero medal, you've been on the TV news so many times, folks are going to recognize you. Maybe if you weren't so big, handsome, and well-dressed, you'd blend in more."

"Like you?" Jason turned his head and smiled.

"Exactly. Why do you think I work so hard to maintain this unimpressive physique?"

Ten minutes after Fat Albert and his dining party went inside, Eddie and Igor were settling into their little round table near the entrance. Nobody could enter without the two sentries seeing them. Their waiter brought a basket of fresh bread and glasses of iced tea. Both men were busy adding sweetener to their glasses when a tall man with a black moustache, dressed casually in slacks and a polo shirt, walked up and stood a few feet from their table. Graham Beckwith bent from his waist, studying the oversized menu mounted on an easel on the sidewalk as an invitation to passing pedestrians.

Choosing a moment when Mr. Clean was dipping a hunk of Italian bread into a saucer of extra-virgin olive oil, Graham stepped up to the table – closer than necessary – and said,

"Excuse me, gentlemen. Can you tell me whether this restaurant serves *authentic* Italian cuisine?" He emphasized *authentic* in his English accent as condescendingly as imaginable.

Eddie and Igor both looked up, scrutinizing the obvious foreigner with an attitude. Eddie dismissively said, "Get lost, jerk!" and returned to his iced tea. He expected the tourist to skulk away, and was surprised when he looked up a few seconds later to find the man still hovering over the table.

"I'm terribly sorry if I offended you, Sir. I merely want to ensure that I select an appropriate location for my last meal before I depart back to civilization. I can see the class of patrons here does not meet my standards, but I'm still curious about the quality of the food. Can you enlighten me on that subject, or are neither of you capable of forming a complete sentence?"

By the end of Graham's polite rant, both Eddie and Mr. Clean were staring daggers up at him. A grating screech accompanied Mr. Clean's chair being pushed backwards across the concrete sidewalk as the big man stood up. Today he was wearing a black baseball cap without any logo. The muscles on the man's forearms flexed as he drew himself up to full height, which was four inches taller than Graham. Mike and Jason had no audio, but could see that the plan was progressing nicely. They had correctly figured that Graham would be able to get under the skin of the two bodyguards.

Graham inched forward toward his larger adversary. "Listen here, you steroidal baboon, don't think for a minute you can intimidate me. I'll have you know I was a champion pugilist in my youth." He shook his index finger in Mr. Clean's face, making sure to land his last gesture with a light poke into the man's chest.

Mr. Clean lifted his right arm and swung a roundhouse toward Graham, who deftly ducked and hurled himself forward. He threw his arms around his larger foe, sending them both off-balance and toppling backwards, over the empty chair and onto the sidewalk.

"Go!" Mike shouted into his body microphone, which was connected to Siebring and O'Dell. They were in their squad car just around the corner from the restaurant, ready to cruise by and see the melee in the outdoor dining area.

Graham, who really had been a boxer in his youth, landed on top of Mr. Clean when they fell. He wrapped his arms around Mr. Clean's muscular chest and held fast, trying to keep in close enough contact that the man would not have any leverage for punches. Eddie the Eagle was standing now, watching the struggle but not wanting to intervene. His companion did not seem to be in any danger from the rude Brit, so Eddie was content to observe and make sure nobody else got involved.

The other diners immediately cowered away from the fight, grabbing their mimosas and Kir Royals to prevent spillage. A couple at the immediately adjoining table had already moved away in fear and surprise.

Mr. Clean managed to roll to his side and was trying to get on top, but Graham had his leg extended like a wrestler, establishing a leverage point. At that moment, everyone's head turned when the police siren popped loudly to life a few feet away. The two officers sprang from their vehicle and rushed to the scene, drawing their night sticks. O'Dell yelled out, "Alright, that's enough! Break it up!" as he leaned down to grab Mr. Clean's arm and pull him away from Graham. Officer Siebring stood next to Eddie, blocking him from intervening.

The events were progressing exactly as planned. As the two combatants got to their feet in the presence of the two officers,

O'Dell looked carefully at Mr. Clean, whose hat had fallen off in the scuffle. He barked out, "What's your name, Mac?" Mr. Clean stared at the cop but said nothing. "Hey, I said, what's your name?"

Siebring then called out, "Hey, Bill, I think this is that guy from the APB – the one the homicide guys are looking for."

That was when a green bottle of Pellegrino sparkling water, wielded by Eddie, smashed into the back of Officer Siebring's head, creating an avalanche of bubbles, water, and shards of glass. This was most definitely *not* part of the plan.

"Shit!" Mike reached for the handle and opened the rear door of the van. He scrambled out with Jason on his heels. When they rounded the corner and could see the outdoor seating area in front of Luigi's, they dashed headlong into the scrum.

Eddie the Eagle had run inside the restaurant, no doubt to warn the boss about the arrival of the police. The boss would want to know that the cops had some kind of bulletin on Igor. Siebring had struggled to his feet, rubbing the growing lump on the back of his head, and taken off after Eddie. This was contrary to the core instruction of the plan: "Just arrest Mr. Clean." Siebring would later say that he figured Graham and O'Dell could take care of themselves and that Mike and Jason would show up as their back-up.

Fat Albert and his entourage never came out of the restaurant through the front door. They no doubt had an emergency exit path out the back of the establishment.

As it turned out, Siebring's exit occurred just as Mr. Clean pushed Graham in the direction of O'Dell and tried to dash toward the street. Graham stuck out a lanky leg as he fell sideways, clipping the big man's knee. When O'Dell tried to grab Mr. Clean's arm, he spun around and head-butted O'Dell in the nose. Blood spurted immediately from O'Dell's face as he toppled backward, stunned. The other diners had cleared away and were huddled in clumps on the sidewalk, out of the danger zone.

Jason arrived at that moment and jumped in, putting an arm around Mr. Clean's neck in a headlock. Graham regained his balance and went for Mr. Clean's legs as the bald mound of muscle reached up with his left hand to grab the back of Jason's neck. Mr. Clean then lurched forward and pulled, trying to leverage Jason over his shoulder. He might have been successful if Jason hadn't leapt from the ground, lacing his legs around Mr. Clean's torso and keeping the headlock in place.

Siebring reemerged from the restaurant and dove in. He grabbed a pair of handcuffs from his belt and secured one to Mr. Clean's left wrist, which was still at the back of Jason's head. That prompted a roar of rage from the huge man, who snapped his arm down, bringing Siebring with him. Siebring lost his balance, and his hold on the other half of the cuff, and cracked his head on the leg of a metal chair.

Jason was still clinging to his headlock, while Graham struggled to find some way to contribute to the cause. Mike grabbed O'Dell's nightstick, which had fallen to the ground. He dodged over Siebring's legs and lunged for the loose handcuff. He grabbed the cuff, shoved the nightstick through, and grabbed the ends with both hands. Mike looked like he was waterskiing – holding the nightstick in outstretched arms and pulling Mr. Clean's arm like it was his tow rope.

Mr. Clean tried to pull Mike toward him, but Mike had his heels set and was leaning back. Seeing an opening, Jason let go of his headlock and brought down the full weight of his elbow onto Mr. Clean's outstretched arm with a crack and a grunt. Mr. Clean lurched to his left. Mike leaned back harder, falling backwards while stretching Mr. Clean's injured arm and throwing the big man off-balance.

Both Siebring and O'Dell dove back in, a bit wobbly and, in O'Dell's case, bloody. Between the two officers, Jason, Mike, and Graham, they managed to secure a second set of handcuffs onto the man's thick wrists and hold him down, amid much grunting and cursing.

Graham got up and dusted off his clothing, seeming no worse for the scuffle. He had deflected most of Mr. Clean's attempted blows. Continuing his role-play, Graham thanked the officers for their help and then scurried away, past the onlooking former diners and around the corner. By then a second squad car had arrived, which wasn't part of the prearranged plan. The newly arrived officers sorted out the stories and assisted in getting Mr. Clean into their car. Mike and Jason hustled back to the van without introducing themselves to the restaurant manager, who had come out and was yelling at everyone – the cops, Mr. Clean, his waiters, and the other diners.

The whole thing had lasted less than five minutes, but all the bystanders would be talking about it for days. One diner got the last bits of the fight and the arrest on a cell phone video, but without any police brutality to capture attention, it failed to develop a viral following on Twitter. By the time a reporter from New York One News arrived, the situation was back to normal and all the cops had left.

# Chapter 33 – Questions and Questions

MR. CLEAN WAS A ROCK. Mike and Jason had arrived at the precinct one block south of Canal Street ten minutes after the arrest. It was the closest station house, so the officers in the second squad car brought him to their home base. Mike and Jason prevailed on the duty sergeant to hustle Mr. Clean into an interrogation room, without booking him first. He was cuffed to the steel table in the middle of the room when Mike and Jason walked in.

Graham had shown up, but the officers insisted that he be taken to a nearby hospital to be checked out after his fight with Mr. Clean. He protested that he was fine, but they explained that there could be liability for the city if he had some serious injury that wasn't obvious and they needed to have him certified as fit for release by a doctor. Graham had grudgingly agreed.

After forty-five minutes, Mike suggested they take a break and left the room with Jason. They moved to the adjoining room and watched a video image of Mr. Clean, sitting in the chair motionless. If it weren't for the fan mounted in the corner, they would have wondered if the video had frozen. Mr. Clean had not said a word the entire time. He had not requested medical attention for his arm, despite obviously not being able to lift it. They couldn't verify whether he spoke with a Russian accent. He had not spoken. When Mike read his Miranda rights, the bald man just grunted and nodded.

"Maybe he doesn't speak English?" Jason suggested.

"No. He understands us fine. He's just clammed up." Mike rubbed his chin. "Let's let him sit for a while, then see if he's more talkative. I'm gonna go call Agent Forrest and let him know how things went down."

"You don't think he already knows?" Jason raised an eyebrow.

"Yeah, I figure he does, but it's good form." Mike walked out of the room into the hallway and pulled out his phone. Jason returned to the video monitor, studying their suspect and trying to think of some angle to get him to talk.

Before Mike returned, Jason's thoughts were interrupted by a knock on the door. He walked out and was met by the duty sergeant from the precinct, standing with a thin man dressed as if he had just stepped off a golf course. His pants were plaid and ankle-high, with argyle socks beneath. He wore a striped polo shirt and a white baseball-style cap on which the black letters "Titleist" stood out boldly. The sergeant introduced the golfer as Derek Offelman, a lawyer from the firm of Romano, Jefferson & Malone.

"He says he's the lawyer for your suspect," the sergeant barked out, cocking his head in the direction of the interrogation room.

Offelman introduced himself and asked whether his client had been charged.

Jason tried to assess the lawyer. Mr. Clean had not made a phone call; he had not even had a cell phone on him when he was searched. He didn't have a wallet or any ID, either. The only way this lawyer was his counsel was if somebody else had called the lawyer and knew where the cops had taken Mr. Clean. Not much mystery. "Did Fat Albert send you?"

The lawyer didn't blink. "I'm not familiar with anyone by that name, Detective Dickson. I'm not obligated to tell you who sent me or who is paying me. You may have heard of attorney-client privilege?" Offelman paused, as if expecting a response, but Jason gave him none. "Well, in any case, I'd like to see my client."

"That's fine," Jason said. "We have three suspects here in interrogation rooms. Which one is your client?"

"He's a big guy, six-seven or so, maybe two-seventy-five and all muscle. Has a bald head. Sound like one of your suspects?"

"Could be," Jason looked at the ceiling, as if pondering the question. "What's your client's name?"

"Detective, are we going to play games or are you going to make me file a *Habeas Corpus* motion?"

"You can't make the motion without identifying the corpus," Jason retorted.

"That may or may not be true," Offelman said, reaching into his pocket for a cell phone. He scrolled through some screens and then held up a photo of Mr. Clean. "Let's try this. Here's my client. Are you holding him?"

"What's his name?" Jason glared at the lawyer, who remained calm despite Jason's rather intimidating posture.

"Let me talk to him," was the only response.

"We have plenty of evidence to charge him with murder."

"Well, then I suggest you do that, immediately. We can have an arraignment this afternoon, at which time you will be obligated to produce the suspect in a courtroom. The judge will be very interested in the fact that the police refused to allow his lawyer to speak with him."

At that moment, Mike rounded the corner of the hallway and saw the gathering outside the interrogation room. When Offelman noticed Mike's presence, he turned away from Jason to face Mike. "Detective Stoneman! Excellent. Now we're getting somewhere. If you don't mind, can I ask you for a private moment – outside?" The lawyer held out an arm, extended back down the hall.

Mike and Jason exchanged a glance, then Mike said, "Sure, but my partner is coming with me."

Offelman pursed his lips. "I'm afraid I must insist on a private discussion – just the two of us. I promise not to bite."

"Fine," Mike said after a moment of thought. "We can step outside."

Five minutes later, Mike met Jason back in the viewing room. Jason was alone. Mike took off his jacket when he got into the room and handed it to Jason, along with his shoulder holster, phone, and service pistol. Jason was puzzled. "What's this for?"

"I need you to hold this stuff for me while I'm gone. I need to be back outside in thirty seconds, so there's not much time. This is going to sound insane, but that lawyer wants to take me to a private meeting with Fat Albert. He says it's critical to our investigation, but he needs me to go right now, to be sure I'm not wearing a wire and nobody is following me. He says Fat Albert will guarantee my safe return."

"You believe that?" Jason blurted out, taking Mike's jacket.

"I'm not sure. I guess the guy's got no reason to kill me, particularly after announcing that he'll be alone with me. The lawyer has no reason to make himself an accessory. We know something's messed up about this case. If I've got a chance to find out what it is, I'm going to take it."

"Sully will have a cow."

"I know. I'm not loving it myself. I want you to call Forrest and let him know what's happening. He may have surveillance on Fat Albert. I'll meet you back here or contact you as soon as I'm done talking to the boss."

"Mike, this is a bad idea."

"Yeah, you may be right. Wish me luck." Mike turned and hustled back out the door. Outside the station, Offelman was standing next to a dark sedan, holding open the back door. He gestured for Mike to get inside.

# Chapter 34 – An Unexpected Meeting

D URING THE RIDE from the Canal Street precinct, Offelman didn't speak. The car navigated the Manhattan streets toward Times Square, then stopped on 45th Street, between 7th Avenue and Broadway in front of Flannigan's Steak House. A politically incorrect cigar store Indian stood sentry outside the padded doors leading into the high-end restaurant. The last time Mike was there, he and Jason were investigating the death of a man who turned out to be connected to the Gallata operation, so it made sense that the place was affiliated. The driver, who had also remained silent for the ride, got out and opened the rear passenger door for Mike. He climbed out, looking back for Offelman.

The lawyer then finally spoke. "I'm not coming, Detective. There's no privilege that covers this conversation."

Mike nodded and allowed the driver to escort him inside. The interior of the steak house was dark; its windows, covered with thick curtains, made it seem like night even in the middle of a June afternoon. It was well before the dinner crowd, with only a few patrons eating at small tables covered with white linen and decorated with fresh flowers and sparkling cutlery. The driver nodded at the hostess and escorted Mike toward the back, entering the kitchen briefly before turning through a plain door that led to a private dining room.

The room had one large table, set for ten. At the far end, Fat Albert Gallata sat in a high-backed chair, looking like the host of an elegant dinner party. He wore a suit jacket with a dress shirt but no tie. He didn't stand when Mike entered. There were two other men there, more casually dressed. Both were taller and bigger than Mike. One of the men politely asked Mike to raise his arms while they patted him down and ran a long, thin probe up and down his legs, arms, and torso, obviously scanning him for both weapons and electronics. When one of the men nodded at Fat Albert, he waved for them to go, leaving Mike alone with the boss.

"Detective Stoneman, please – sit." Gallata motioned toward the seat to his right.

Mike walked to the indicated chair, making mental notes about his host. The man appeared younger than Mike knew him to be. His black hair was combed straight back across his head, as if trying to hide premature baldness. His face was plump and soft, not lined with worry. He had dark eyes that were open wide and seemed inviting and sincere. He stood and held out a hand with manicured nails when Mike reached his chair. Although he was not thrilled, Mike took the hand and gave one firm pump before sitting.

Food was already on the table. Fat Albert was halfway through a filet mignon that was oozing juice onto his plate, which also contained a pile of sauteed mushrooms and onions and a partially eaten baked potato. A glass of red wine with greasy fingerprints around the bottom of the bowl stood at attention nearby.

"Would you like something?" he offered, gesturing at the plates in the center of the table. There was steak, fish that Mike identified as Branzino, baked potatoes, green beans, and a partially full bowl of onions and mushrooms. It smelled wonderful.

"Not for now," he replied cautiously. "I don't know why I'm here, but I'm guessing it's not for an early dinner."

"Yeah," the fat man responded, reaching for his wine and taking a healthy draught. "I'm sorry for the hasty circumstances. You caught me off guard this afternoon. You interrupted me before I had my lunch, which normally would make me cranky. But, as you can see, I've managed a substitute."

"I'm sorry to have inconvenienced you, Mr. Gallata," Mike said almost sincerely. "Let's cut the bullshit. We picked up your goon because we have reason to believe he murdered Jimmy Rydell. Unless you're ready to throw him under the bus, I'm not sure why you had me come here."

"Naturally. I understand." Fat Albert picked up a wicker basket of dinner rolls and passed them toward Mike. "Come on, have something. I hate to eat alone."

Mike took a roll. He actually was rather hungry, and he was familiar with Flannagan's rolls, which were excellent. If Gallata wanted him dead, he didn't need to poison him. He took a bite, then said with a half-full mouth, "So, what is it you wanted to say to me?"

"First, Detective – may I call you Mike?"

"It's your meeting."

"Mike, first, I want to say that I appreciate how you took out the bastard who killed my father. We were looking for him as much as you were. I know cops sometimes get all sentimental and guilt-ridden when they kill a criminal. I can tell you with complete certainty that if Ronald Randall had spent one day in jail, he would not have seen the sunrise. I'm happy you didn't let him walk out of that warehouse. The papers may have called him the Righteous Assassin, but there was nothing righteous about that bastard."

"I'm glad you approve. I didn't do it for you."

"Sure. I understand, Mike, but I just want you to understand that I harbor no ill will toward you. You're a good cop, doing your job. We're all just doing our jobs."

Mike couldn't help himself. "Yeah, but my job doesn't include human trafficking and drug dealing."

"Hey, we're not here to argue philosophy. I understand you think you have some evidence that Igor killed Jimmy Rydell. In the normal course of business, you'd arrest him, charge him, maybe have a trial. You might even get a jury to convict him, since there is a certain amount of circumstantial evidence that might seem to point in his direction."

"You're right about that," Mike confirmed. He wasn't going to share any information with Gallata, but he wanted him to know that the DA would feel good about his case.

"I understand, like I said. The reason I brought you here, Mike, is to tell you you've got the wrong man."

"Sure. Why should I believe you?"

"You shouldn't, in most cases. But in this case, things are very unusual. I really like Igor. I like having him around. I will find him difficult to replace if he's locked up. And a trial would be very inconvenient for my operations. So, I'd like to make arrangements for you to let him go."

"Are you offering me a bribe?" Mike put his half-eaten roll down on his china plate and folded his arms defiantly across his chest.

"Not in the traditional sense, Mike. I'm not offering you money or anything like that. I'm offering you information that will lead you to the real murderer."

"Really?"

"Scout's honor." Gallata held up three fingers in the Boy Scout salute. "Unless you catch the real killer, my man is going to take a fall for something he didn't do. He may go down someday, but let's let it be for somebody he really did kill, hmmm?"

Mike said nothing. He just stared intently at his host.

"I know you need to get something here, and I'm willing to give it to you. But this meeting never happened. If you claim I said anything, I'll deny it. Nobody knows you're here, and you'll have no proof of it. But I'd still like you to agree that this conversation is off the record, so to speak. Can you do that?"

"Without knowing what it is you're going to tell me, how can I agree to anything?"

"I understand." Gallata cut himself a bite of steak and ate it slowly, letting Mike sit in silence. "Oh, what the hell. I'll trust you to be a man of honor, Mike. In memory of my father, I'm just going to tell you the truth."

"Thanks." Mike broke down and reached for the plate of Branzino. While he dished himself a small portion of the flaky white fish, Fat Albert told his story.

He explained that Igor had, in fact, been dispatched to kill Jimmy Rydell. Jimmy had been engaged in what Fat Albert described as a "business deal" and had breached his obligations. Jimmy had threatened to go to the feds and become a witness against the organization unless Gallata let him walk away from the deal. Mike asked whether the deal involved point shaving, but Fat Albert neither confirmed nor denied the underlying issue. He said he liked Jimmy, but the man had to die. He had failed in his obligations and he had threatened to turn into a rat.

Igor had made arrangements for entry and exit from Jimmy's apartment building by securing an understanding with the laundry delivery driver. They knew Jimmy had a bodyguard, and they wanted the hit to be clean, so they waited for a night when Jimmy was alone in the gym and put the plan into operation.

"How did you know Jimmy would be alone in the gym that night?" Mike interrupted.

"We have some tech at our disposal," was all Gallata would say. "The point is Igor did not kill him – when he got there, Jimmy was already dead."

"Already dead?"

"That's correct. Igor found Jimmy hanging from one of those big rubber bands, slung over a weight machine like he'd hanged himself. There was a little stool on the ground, like he made a noose, kicked away the stool, and said goodnight."

"Hanged himself? Do you really expect me to believe that he committed suicide?"

"No, I don't, and I'm sure he didn't, but we'll get to that. Igor wasn't sure what to do. He was worried Jimmy might have left a suicide note on his phone or something that would implicate me. He might have confessed to things we would rather keep private. So, Igor cut him down, gathered up all his stuff, and got him the hell out of there, like he had planned."

"That's it?" Mike finished a bite of the fish, which was delicious. He put down his fork with a clink. "You expect me to let your guy go free because you say Jimmy killed himself before Igor got there to kill him? That's a nice story, but no jury would buy it."

"I realize that, Mike. I'm not an idiot. I know Igor is technically guilty of a crime, since he did move the body." Fat Albert brandished his steak knife in Mike's direction, but not in a threatening way. "But haven't you been wondering how Jimmy's body turned up on the carousel in Central Park? I mean, if I wanted Jimmy Rydell to disappear, you would have never found that body."

"Yeah," Mike admitted. "That angle has us a bit puzzled."

"Well, Mike." Gallata cut another hunk of beef and skewered it with his fork, holding it up toward his face. "This is where it gets interesting."

# Chapter 35 – The Plot Thickens

THE STORY FAT ALBERT GALLATA TOLD was so bizarre that Mike had to admit it had a ring of truth. He'd had a truck scheduled to make a run from New York to Miami on Friday. The plan was to put Jimmy's body on that truck, in a freezer unit to keep it from smelling, and then to feed it to the fishes off the Florida coast. They could have done the same thing in New York, but with the feds having most of his guys and many of his locations under surveillance, it was safer to ship the body out of town. But, before the truck left, Fat Albert got a call.

"The guy says he wants the body back. Now, that was a pretty strange call to get. Who was this guy? And how the hell did he know I had Jimmy's body? The only person who could know was somebody who was there when Igor carted the body away and followed him. If he knew the body was inside my truck, outside a warehouse in Maspeth, and if he did some research into who owned that warehouse, and if he knew the right people to ask, I'm thinking it's plausible he might be able to link it back to me.

"But I figure he couldn't be a cop. That would have been a very different kind of problem – if the cops or the feds knew

Jimmy's body was in that truck. And he wasn't some innocent bystander. Any New Yorker who figured this all out would either be smart enough to leave it alone, or maybe brave enough to ask for money to keep it quiet. But, either way he wouldn't want the body. Anyway, the caller didn't want money, and didn't threaten to go to the cops. He only wanted the body back, and he wanted it to be recognizable, not all cut into pieces. So, I figure it has to be someone who wanted Jimmy's 'suicide' to be made public."

The fat man put down his silverware and wiped his mouth with a linen napkin. "So, being a businessman and recognizing an opportunity when one comes knocking, I asked for $100,000 in cash for the body. The guy agreed right away and we arranged for a dead drop. He didn't haggle. I got paid, and I delivered the body early on Saturday morning. I guess I should have asked for more."

"You gonna tell me who this guy is?" Mike asked, following along with the yarn skeptically.

"I still don't know," Gallata replied. "He got what he wanted. I got some cash. I got a dead Jimmy, so I was pretty happy with the whole arrangement. Except I wanted to know who was so interested in my corpse, so I had my guys follow them."

"Them?"

"They sent two guys. They put the body in the trunk of their sedan and drove it back to the West Side. It was like they weren't worried at all about being followed. They dumped the body in the corner of Riverside Park at 72$^{nd}$ Street, next to that new statue of Eleanor Roosevelt."

"That's near Jimmy's building."

"Yeah. It was like they wanted you cops to think the body had been there all along, but you didn't find it."

Mike was now fully engaged in the story. "How did it get to the carousel?"

"Igor didn't think it was a good idea for the body to be found so close to where he found it the first time. He figured whoever this was might be trying to set him up. So, after those schmucks left, my guys retrieved the body and moved it to Central Park. It seemed like they wanted the body to get found, so we made it easy. Hey, we made a deal – they wanted the body back, and they wanted to plant it somewhere it would get seen. Igor had to take Jimmy's gym clothes, so it wouldn't be obvious where he got whacked. Igor thought it was pretty funny, a dead guy in the swan seat."

"Hilarious," Mike deadpanned. "So, are you gonna tell me who the guys were who got the body?"

"I wish I could tell you, Mike. I really do. All my guys got was a license plate number." He reached into a pocket and extracted a blank business card on which the license plate number was scratched. "NXL 4573. It was a Toyota Corolla, dark gray."

Mike finished his last bit of fish and dabbed his mouth with a linen napkin. "So, what do you expect me to do with all this?"

"I expect you to trace that license plate and see where it leads. I expect you to find these idiots and convict somebody of killing Jimmy – somebody who's not Igor. And when you find the guy, you can let Igor walk. I need him back."

"I get it. I'm having a hard time believing it, but I get it. One question, though. When you were talking to this guy who didn't identify himself, did he give you any idea why he wanted the body back – wanted the body to be found?"

"No. I didn't ask and he didn't say."

"And one more thing." Mike took a sip of water. "Why'd your guy have to kill the kid, Tiger?"

"Who?" Gallata furrowed his brow in puzzlement for a moment. "Only tigers I know about are in the Bronx Zoo."

"You want me to believe you had nothing to do with it?"

"With what? I don't have a clue what you're talking about."

"I suppose I shouldn't expect you to admit to another murder."

Fat Albert drained the last ounce of wine from his glass, then turned a level stare toward Mike. "You're right, but I'm telling you, man to man, I don't know any kid named Tiger and if he's dead, my guys did not take him out."

"That's a pretty big hole in the story, if you ask me." Mike pushed his now-empty plate to the middle of the table. He noticed that no waiter had come into the room during the meeting. Fat Albert had his machine well oiled.

"You're the detective, Mike. You'll have to figure it out. I'm just reporting the facts."

"You should write for *The Times*. Is that all there is?"

Gallata held up his hands, palms up. "That's a lot, and it's all I got. Now, can I count on your discretion?"

Mike stood up. "If all this checks out, I'll consider it. I can't do anything about your underlying operation. That's your problem. Jimmy's not going to rat you out now, and you haven't told me what your business deal with Jimmy was, so I'm not a witness to anything. As for the murder, if I pin it on somebody else, then your boy should be off the hook, at least for murder. I'm not making you any promises or agreeing to do anything for you. But I'll do my job."

"That's all I ask," Gallata said, not getting up when Mike did. He reached for his wine bottle. "My driver will take you wherever you want to go. Good luck, Detective."

♦♦♦

Mike spent an hour on Saturday afternoon trying to explain his bizarre meeting with Fat Albert Gallata to his team and then to Sully. He and Jason decided it should be Sully's call whether to bring in the Commissioner and the Mayor. For now, he chose not to. Mike had already given Agent Forrest the abbreviated version. Graham was almost giddy about the apparent proof that Jimmy had been involved in some kind of criminal activity, but Mike pointed out that if somebody else had killed him before Mr. Clean arrived, the death may not have been the result of his involvement with Fat Albert's gang. That calmed Graham down considerably.

They all agreed that the story, as implausible as it seemed, actually explained the mysterious appearance of the body on the carousel. No conventional theory was consistent with that one undeniable fact. They still weren't sure how Tiger's murder fit into the puzzle.

At the end of the discussion, only three things were settled. First, they would charge Igor, whatever his real name was, and try to keep him in custody unless they actually found proof of another killer. Second, they would send a forensics team to Riverside Park at the Eleanor Roosevelt memorial to see if there was any evidence of Jimmy's body being dumped there, if only briefly. Third, they needed to follow up on the license plate number Fat Albert gave them. If he was telling the truth, that plate was the key to following the trail.

Sully would brief the Commissioner and the Mayor that night. If there was a different killer, they didn't want to tip him off that they were looking for him. The easiest way to do that was to leak to the press that they had arrested Mr. Clean. Of course, as soon as they charged him with Jimmy's murder, it would become public anyway.

When their briefing ended and the two detectives slowly got to their feet, still nursing aches and bruises from the morning's wrestling match with Mr. Clean, Sully held up his hand. "Stoneman, Dickson, I want you to punch out and go home. Get some rest. I'm calling in a second team of detectives to follow the car. Let's see what we have tomorrow."

"Good call, Cap," Mike said. "Jason and I both could use a break – and we both have something to do tomorrow anyway. Some rest will do us good."

"You're not going out on your own like cowboys again, are you, Stoneman?" Sully was instantly angry. Given Mike's recent history, the suspicion seemed justified. "If I hear that you're—"

"Don't worry, Sully," Jason cut in. "It's my girlfriend's – uh, my fiancée's – birthday party in Brooklyn. It will probably be far worse than getting shot at, but it won't make the papers. I promise."

Sully stopped waving his hand and worked on slowing his breathing. "Fine. Congratulations. Maybe she'll be able to keep you out of trouble. You two be looking for an email from me tomorrow afternoon."

They filed out, telling Graham they would keep him updated. Mike said he and Michelle would be at the party at noon and asked if Jason wanted a lift, since Mike still had the Lincoln.

"No. I'll be there earlier."

"Is this the first time you'll be talking to her father since the engagement?"

"Yes. First time."

"Well, don't worry. I'm sure he'll be thrilled that his little girl is getting married."

"Sure. You'd think that," Jason said, waving as Mike turned left and Jason turned right at the bottom of the steps.

# Chapter 36 – A Little Time Off

Sunday, June 9

SUNDAY AT 11:56 a.m., Michelle and Mike walked up the steps to the Robinson family rowhouse in Brooklyn. It had started to rain, leaving a tangy scent in the air as the accumulated dirt, gasoline, and other chemicals on the street mixed with the pounding drops. The block was well maintained with fresh paint on most of the homes, each having its own color scheme. The Robinsons' home was blue and white: Dodgers' colors.

Rachel's mother, Olivia, greeted them and welcomed them in. She guided them around the room, introducing them to various relatives whose names Mike tried his best to remember. Several of them wanted to shake Mike's hand and congratulate him on his recent notoriety, which he deflected. They managed to get a little time with Jason and Rachel. Michelle wanted to see the ring up close and gushed over how wonderful it looked on her finger.

Michelle's medical examiner eyes noticed the bruise on Rachel's cheek, despite the makeup intended to camouflage it.

Rachel quickly recounted the story of her unfortunate run-in with the seizure patient in hushed tones.

"Why are we whispering?" Michelle asked.

"Oh, it's my dad. He has this crazy idea that Jason hit me. Isn't that ridiculous?"

Michelle's face softened and she reached out to touch her friend's arm. "Sweetie, I see plenty of corpses with those kinds of bruises. It happens. But, obviously, Jason would never do anything like that. Wasn't your father impressed that Jason threw himself in front of a bullet to protect you?"

Rachel nodded. "He was, and I think he just likes busting Jay's chops, but it's a little tense."

In the kitchen, Jason was fixing a sandwich when Mike came in looking for a Diet Coke. They made eye contact without speaking. A few other party guests were there chatting and grabbing food, which was piled up on virtually every surface. Then, Rachel's father came in and glared at Jason.

Ernie Robinson was a thin, sinewy man who had worked for the NYC sanitation department for thirty years. He had a perpetual scowl in Jason's presence, but was nothing but smiles and hugs for his baby daughter. Jason always thought Mr. Robinson should be happy his EMT daughter was dating – and now engaged to – a cop. A detective, no less. Apparently, nobody was good enough for his princess.

Mike had not met the man before that day. Ernie immediately reminded him of a Black version of Jerry Stiller, playing George Costanza's father on *Seinfeld*. He was expecting Ernie to start talking about Festivus. He even had a similar, deep New York accent. Jason was not amused when Mike shared his observation later. As the other guests left the kitchen, Mike saw Ernie give Jason a look that he could only describe as a stink-eye. He nodded to his partner as he strolled back toward Michelle, with two glasses in his hands.

Ernie walked over to where Jason was standing, still picking out items for a plate he was preparing for Rachel. "I know I've been a little tough on you, Jason." The man was barely 5'6", but he could intimidate men a foot taller. "Rachel explained what happened. I believe her because I raised her to be an honest girl. But let me tell you, if I *ever* find out you touched my princess in anger, you'll answer to me. You got that?"

"Yes, Sir," Jason answered quickly and sincerely. "We both feel that way. I want to protect Rachel, and I know you do as well. We have that in common."

"Hmmph," Ernie grunted as he marched out of the room. Jason took in a heavy breath, steadied himself, and went back to preparing the plate for Rachel.

A few minutes later, Ernie caught Mike in a corner and grilled him for five minutes about Jason. He wanted to know if Jason had ever lost his temper during an encounter with a criminal.

"Don't worry, Mr. Robinson, Jason is one of the most under-control people I've ever worked with. Sometimes I wish he'd get ruffled, just to make me feel better." Mike chuckled at his own joke, but Ernie was not laughing.

"You mean, like he's hiding something?"

"No, not anything like that. Jason is thoughtful. He's smart – smarter than me about some things. He's also loyal. I can't give you details, but I'll vouch for him in any situation. If I had a daughter, I'd want her to marry somebody just like Jason."

Ernie thanked Mike but stalked away, seeming less than convinced.

They ate and drank until Rachel's mother produced a sheet cake emblazoned with a screen print of Rachel wearing her sparkly purple dress. From the front, it was very conservative. Mike and Michelle knew that in the back it plunged down to a dangerous point. Everyone sang heartily and Rachel blew out 28 candles. Rachel's friends and family congratulated her and Jason on the engagement and asked when the wedding would be. Rachel was looking at the following June. She had always wanted to be a June bride.

The party was an outpouring of hope, optimism, and love for Rachel. Mike and Jason were able to immerse themselves in the good feelings and forget about work for a few hours.

One of Rachel's friends asked Michelle whether she and Mike would be getting married soon. They both laughed and said they were far too old and were not thinking about marriage. Rachel's mother, Olivia, who was only a few years older than Michelle, suggested that they would both have the pleasure of vicariously experiencing the wedding by helping Rachel with the planning. Michelle was enthusiastic about that idea.

They spent ten minutes sharing stories about how wonderful Rachel was. By the time Rachel's sister joined them, Michelle was ready for a refill of her champagne. She asked Diana if she wanted one, but she declined.

Rachel immediately reached out and grabbed Diana's arm. "Honey, you love champagne. Are you . . . ?"

"Shhh," Diana said, looking around for her mother. "Don't you start. This is your party. I'm not going to upstage you. I'm so happy you're getting married. There's time to talk about me and Roy later."

"Oh, Sweetie!" Rachel sprang from her chair and gave her older sister a hug. "Have you told Mom yet?"

"No. And don't you dare. I don't want her to make a scene. As soon as the party's over, I'll tell her."

"OK, OK. I can do that.

Michelle and Rachel went to get fresh glasses of champagne. Michelle said, "Hey, have you told your brother yet?"

"Yes. I called him in Vegas. He's really excited. He wants to meet Jason. I'm hoping we can take a trip out to see him soon." They clinked their glasses and drank to the birthday and the engagement.

At 3:00 p.m., on the other end of the room, Mike checked his email. There was nothing from Sully. He was mildly disappointed to think the whole day might pass by without any update on the Jimmy Rydell case.

When they had a quiet moment, Jason pulled Mike aside. "Mike, Rachel's father is a foot shorter and a hundred pounds lighter than me, so why do I get the distinct impression that he'll kick my ass someday?"

Mike laughed. "Because he's tough as nails, he's a New Yorker, and he's Rachel's first love. If you ever make her choose between you and her daddy, you'll lose. So, you'll have to be nice to him and let him kick your ass if it ever comes to that. You can take it."

By 4:00 p.m., the birthday party was breaking up. Jason stayed with Rachel to help clean up, under the watchful eye of Ernie Robinson.

◆◆◆

At 4:42 p.m., *The New York Times'* website published a new article in the Sports section by Kristi Olson. The team had officially exercised its option to accelerate the dead money from

Jimmy's contract so that the entire salary cap hit would happen in the upcoming season. The article explained that this would cripple the team's ability to sign free agents in the upcoming season, but for 2021, Jimmy's death would free up a huge amount of cap space. So, next year, the team would have enough free cash to be a big player in the free agent market and also would be able to afford to sign a high draft pick. General manager Chip O'Meara also announced that the club had traded two veteran players for future draft picks, and would absorb the salary cap hit for their dead signing bonus money in the current season.

The article speculated that, without a starting quarterback and with few prospects for finding a top-shelf signal-caller before the start of the upcoming season, the team's prospects for winning were dim. In a similar situation a few years earlier, New Orleans had used the opportunity to dump salary and trade away highly paid players in preparation for a rebuilding program. The question was: Could a New York team afford to break down and rebuild without alienating their fan base?

# Chapter 37 – Financial Pressure

Monday, June 10

FIRST THING MONDAY MORNING, Mike and Jason got a briefing from Detectives George Mason and Steve Berkowitz, who had been tapped to track down their mystery license plate. While they drank their morning coffee and Graham sipped his Teavana, George gave a thorough report.

The plate belonged to a rental car, so it was easy enough to trace. National Car Rental was quite cooperative when the NYPD detectives explained that the vehicle might have been used for criminal purposes. The Toyota was rented at Newark airport, using what turned out to be a stolen credit card. The car was taken out at 2:00 p.m. and returned at 1:00 a.m. the next morning. "There's a security camera at the rental counter, but the guy who took out the car was wearing a pretty obvious disguise – a baseball cap covering his head, a bulky sweatshirt, and a bushy black beard. The cameras aren't sophisticated, so the image is pretty poor quality anyway."

They found the car in the rental lot at Newark. It had been rented again and returned once since May 31st. A forensics team combed over the car, which had been routinely cleaned in between rentals. There was nothing in the passenger compartment and no prints they could use, but inside the trunk they found some hairs. "Those are at the lab for analysis, but it's possible they could match Rydell."

"Our body snatchers weren't savvy enough to put down a tarp in the trunk?" Mike asked rhetorically.

"Maybe not," George responded. "Anyway, the GPS tracker in the vehicle recorded its route. It drove to Queens, then back to Manhattan, including passing by 72nd Street and Riverside, and then went back to Newark. We can't tell when it was stopped along the way."

Mike let out a slow whistle. "So, our perps were really dumb and used a tracked car, but we still don't know who they are."

"It does confirm Fat Albert's version of the facts," Graham observed.

Jason had developed a penchant for pointing out facts that ran contrary to Graham's favored theories. "Since these mystery men who wanted the body so badly were not affiliated with the Gallata family, it's actually *less* likely that Jimmy's murder was connected to criminal activity."

George reported that the forensics team didn't find anything in Riverside Park near the Eleanor Roosevelt memorial to suggest that the body had been there. But, since the GPS tracking on the car didn't put it anywhere near Central Park, Fat Albert's story was the only working theory for how it got to the carousel.

"We should go back to the point-fixing scheme," Graham suggested. "Perhaps Mr. Rydell's failure to perform his scheduled services for Mr. Gallata resulted in losses for someone who was angry enough to kill the player he blamed for his misfortune?"

Mike flashed his best that-seems-far-fetched expression. "Mr. Beckwith, gamblers lose big bets all the time, but they don't go around murdering the players for it."

"With all due respect, this is a country where organized crime figures are occasionally eaten by tigers, are they not?"

Mike shrugged. It was Fat Albert's father, Slick Mick, who had been eaten by tigers at the Bronx Zoo the previous summer. That murder had started the investigation of the serial killer dubbed the Righteous Assassin. Mike was surprised that the story had traveled across the Atlantic.

Jason said, "That's very rare."

"Nevertheless," Graham continued confidently, "we can't rule out anything, wouldn't you agree?"

Mike tossed his empty coffee cup toward the corner trash can, bouncing it off the wall and in. It left brown drops clinging to the wall. "I'd still like to know the real story here. We're getting little pieces. The problem is that Jimmy's dead and can't tell us. And speaking of tigers, I still wonder what information the shoeshine kid, Tiger, had that got him murdered."

"Do you really think the kid's murder is connected to Mr. Rydell's?" Graham asked.

"Pretty good bet. We don't have any evidence that it happened at Park Towers, but I don't believe in coincidences in a case like this. So, who does that leave who might have some of the puzzle pieces?"

Jason snapped his fingers. "I have an idea about that."

After a phone call and a cab ride, the two detectives and Graham Beckwith strode silently across the thick carpeting at the ISMS offices. The faint scent of lavender mixed with coffee welcomed them in. Muffled telephone conversations behind thick maple doors merged with honking horns and a passing siren sixty-five floors below.

When the blonde assistant opened the door to Aaron Taylor's office, Mike went in first and saw the young agent behind his desk. He looked scared. He was just a kid, a few years out of college, whose foster brother had been the number-one draft pick. Now, he was an inexperienced sports agent without a major client. He was screwed. As Mike watched Taylor put on a semblance of a professional expression, he was pretty confident that Jason's plan to exploit the situation was going to work.

When they were seated in the comfy chairs around the glass coffee table, Mike got right to business. "We've uncovered additional evidence that Jimmy was involved with the Gallata crime organization."

Taylor's face went blank. "You don't believe those newspaper articles, do you?" As he spoke, he jammed his right index finger under his flexible watch band and twisted it.

"What we have is much more substantial than what's been reported in the papers," Mike continued in a somber tone, like he was disappointed in Jimmy. "I know you were involved in Jimmy's finances. See, Aaron, it's looking more and more like you've got a problem here."

The agent's head, which had been pointed at the corner of the coffee table, snapped up. "Wh-what do you mean *I* have a problem?"

"Listen, Son, we're not trying to ruin your career. We're really not. But if we have to start serving subpoenas for your firm's financial records and dragging in your boss and your coworkers for questioning, I'm worried that it's not going to end well for you." Mike stole a glance at Jason to pass the ball.

"I'll tell you one thing," Jason picked up the thread. "We try to explain to executives that just because someone is under investigation, it doesn't mean they're guilty. Of course, sometimes you're not guilty, but that doesn't mean you're completely innocent. That's part of the problem. It's going to look pretty bad, no matter what."

Taylor's finger slipped out from under his watchband, which snapped back against the sensitive skin on the top of his wrist, causing him to wince. "I don't know what you're talking about." His eyes darted from Mike to Jason to Graham, looking for help. All the faces were cold stone.

"Aaron, you know what we're talking about. Your client doesn't withdraw twenty thousand in cash without his best friend and business manager knowing about it, am I right?"

"Jimmy was a very generous guy. He probably spent it on the kids down at the Boys & Girls Clubs."

Mike looked skeptically at the agent, noticing a bead of sweat that had formed below his right sideburn. "So, did the boys and girls decide to repay him by giving him eighty grand back?" Taylor dropped his head but said nothing. Mike continued the attack. "You see, Aaron, we're going to have to do a complete forensic analysis of Jimmy's finances to figure out where the money came from and where it went. But we have a pretty good idea already. The only question, really, is how much of it went through your accounts, and whether you get indicted."

When Mike stopped talking, Taylor remained motionless, his torso bent over and his head drooping between his knees. The room was so quiet Mike could hear the ticking of the grandfather clock in the corner, which had undoubtedly come with the office. Jason knew to let the silence do its job. Graham also knew enough to keep quiet.

Eventually, Taylor filled the vacuum. "I didn't know," he whispered. "You can't start digging in there. I'll get fired. It's not enough that Jimmy's dead? You gotta kill me, too?" He looked up, drops of sweat trickling down both sides of his face. He was pleading. It was exactly what Jason had hoped for.

Mike reached out and put a hand on the kid's knee in a comforting, fatherly gesture. "We have to follow the information, Son. If we had different information, we might be able to go in a different direction. If you're not guilty of anything, then you've got nothing to worry about – but you have to be straight with us. You're not protecting Jimmy anymore. You have to start protecting yourself." Mike patted Taylor's leg and snuck a glance toward Jason.

When Jason stood, he withdrew his phone and studied it carefully, then announced in an annoyed voice, "Mike, we can't mess around with this anymore. The Commissioner wants us to serve the subpoenas and start tearing this place apart. We're not getting anything from this piece of shit. He probably knew everything. Hell, he was probably the bag man who delivered the cash to Fat Albert's goons. When we dig into his accounts, we'll probably find more cash withdrawals and deposits. Let's get moving."

"No!" Taylor blurted out loudly, then lowered his voice, as if not wanting anyone in the office to hear. "No. Please. Don't. I wasn't involved."

"But you knew about it," Mike said – a statement, not a question.

"Yeah. I found out about it." Taylor sat up, then slumped back in his chair, looking exhausted and beaten. "I wasn't involved, I swear. Jimmy kept coming to me for money last offseason. I made the arrangements. I didn't ask why. Why should I care? He was doing great. I was doing great. I didn't really pay much attention. You know he made a million-dollar donation to the Boys & Girls Clubs at the end of his first season, right? That's Jimmy – he gave away more money than he had. I figured it was no big deal to advance him money against the next year's salary. The guys here said players do it all the time."

"Then he asked you to funnel money through your personal accounts, didn't he?" Jason pressed.

"You're gonna find out anyway. Yeah, he did. He was worried people might be looking at his accounts, so I gave him cash from my account. I wouldn't have had any of it if it weren't for Jimmy."

"How much?"

Taylor stared out the window at his spectacular view. "Ten thousand once. Fifteen thousand one other time. But then he stopped asking for money, so it seemed like he had gotten things together. We were still paying all his bills. He was still having parties and whatever, but there was no problem. He was one year into a six-year deal. Then, when the season started, he was fine. He started getting his regular checks from the team. Our accountants got back all the money we advanced him, and he paid me back what I gave him. I mean, the season didn't go so well, and he got hurt, which sucked. But he came back at the end of the season and he played well. So I was thinking this season would be cool.

"But then in April, I think, he had a party at his place. When everyone else was gone, he asked me if I could find him someone with the FBI and arrange for a meeting. I thought he was just joking around. How would I know someone at the FBI? Why the hell would Jimmy want to talk to an FBI agent? I told him to quit messing around. Then he told me. He was really scared. He'd had a lot to drink. I thought he was just crazy and ranting. He said he had fucked up bad. He admitted he had done some betting the year before, mostly on college basketball, and that was why he needed all that money. He met a guy who fronted him all kinds of cash so he could go to Vegas. He got into it with this guy, he said. He told me they threatened to tell the league about the gambling and the team could void his contract."

"Is that true?" Mike asked, since Taylor seemed to be struggling with the story. "Could the team void the contract?"

"Yeah, I think they could have. There's a clause about if he's convicted of a felony, but also if he engages in any gross misconduct, and the league has some pretty strict rules about gambling. I guess that's why he went to this bookie in the first place – because he didn't want to be seen making bets at the sportsbook in Vegas. Oh, man – you'd think he could get someone to do it for him, right? But Jimmy always had to do it alone."

Jason broke into the narrative. "I don't get it. Jimmy had been paid for the full season, so why didn't he pay back the money he owed to – whomever?"

"It wasn't money," Taylor muttered. He kept his head down, not wanting to look Mike or Jason in the eye. He had been beaten down by the recent events and knew his career as a sports agent was in tatters. "These guys, they wanted Jimmy to give them inside information about the team – about injuries or other things that could give them an edge. They wanted Jimmy to shave points." Taylor brought both hands up to his face and rested his elbows on his knees. He wasn't crying, but he was on the verge.

"Did you reach out to the FBI?" Mike asked.

Taylor raised his head suddenly. "No." Then his shoulders slumped. "Jimmy told me the guys pressured him at the very end of the season. The team was going nowhere – they were out of the playoffs at that point – and they wanted him to make sure they didn't cover the spread in either of the last two games. They said they'd leak the information about his gambling if he didn't play along."

"Wait," Mike cut in. "They did cover the spread in the final game. I remember. I was there with a buddy of mine. They were down eleven points in the fourth quarter. Jimmy drove the team down the field and threw a touchdown pass to Nate Bedford. It was right in front of where I was sitting. Then they went for the two-point conversion. Jimmy scrambled and ran it in. They messed up the onside kick and lost by three, but they were a five-point underdog at home for that game, so they covered."

"Yeah," Taylor said despondently. "Apparently the gambler guys weren't happy about that. A month or so after the season, some big dude ran into Jimmy at a club and told him he better get his will in order, 'cause he was a dead man. I guess it wasn't long after that when he told me about it. Jimmy decided to tell these guys that he wasn't playing along and that if they pushed him, he'd go to the feds. Geez. I guess he should have just talked to them in the first place. Threatening these guys was a bad idea. I should have told him that."

When Taylor had been silent for fifteen seconds and showed no signs of looking up, Mike prodded him gently. "I'm gathering Jimmy didn't tell anyone from the team about what happened?"

"No. No way. That bastard Chip would have voided his contract and tossed him away like yesterday's garbage. Christ, he was pissed off that Jimmy wouldn't agree to renegotiate his contract."

Mike raised an eyebrow. "You told us it was no big deal that Jimmy didn't want to renegotiate his deal."

Taylor shrugged. "Well, I guess I wasn't completely honest about that. So sue me. I don't give away my clients' secrets so easily. Yeah, Jimmy had been stretched thin on his finances as it was, so he didn't want to defer any money. I can't blame him, knowing what he was going through. He didn't know what was going to happen with these guys. He was hoping he could pay them off once the season started. But Chip – what an asshole! He was screaming at us about how Jimmy was letting the team down and how Chip couldn't make some deal he wanted to do because Jimmy was taking up too much cap room. He's a real douchebag. He actually said Jimmy was the worst mistake the team ever made and he wished his old man hadn't forced him to make the pick."

"And you and Jimmy just sat there and took that from Chip?" Jason asked incredulously.

"Fuck no!" Taylor was suddenly much more animated, defending his honor and that of his now-dead friend. "I told Chip if he didn't want Jimmy on the team, he should make a trade. It would have done Jimmy some good to get out of New York. But the dead money on his contract was still a problem for Chip. If he traded Jimmy, or cut him before the cap deadline, he'd have to eat the whole twenty-four million. I guess it really is dead money now. He's probably happy to have it all hit this year so he's clean for next year's draft. We'd all have been better off if Jimmy just had a career-ending injury – the team would have collected on its insurance policy, and the gamblers would have left him alone. Why'd they have to kill him?" Taylor now actually did start to cry, his left hand covering his eyes and wiping away the evidence.

The mention of the insurance policy made Graham sit up straighter. "I'm very sorry for the loss of your friend, but I must ask: did Mr. O'Meara say anything to you about the insurance policy?" He leaned forward, hopeful for some helpful information.

Taylor composed himself and looked at Graham quizzically. "No. Chip? No. He never said anything. He was only focused on the salary cap. He didn't give a crap about Jimmy."

Graham stood up and began pacing toward the window, looking out toward the 59th Street Bridge. "You mentioned something about a deadline. What was that?"

"It's just technical rules under the salary cap. If you cut a player or trade him, you have to accelerate his bonus money against your salary cap. That's the dead money. Jimmy got a thirty-six-million-dollar signing bonus. Remember, I told you we used the after-tax portion of that to fund an annuity for Jimmy's retirement years. Anyway, Chip and the team couldn't just cut Jimmy without getting hit with all the dead money. Chip was already having salary cap problems, which is why he wanted to restructure Jimmy's deal. If he had to lump on twenty-four million in dead money, that would have made it even worse for him."

"Yes, but what about this deadline?" Graham had something in his head and was not going to let it go until he got an answer.

"The deadline is just the date when you have to make a deal or cut a player. If you don't make the cut before the deadline, you have to pay a portion of the salary, and there's also the cap hit."

"Yes, Mr. Taylor. What is the salary cap issue?" Graham was getting impatient with Taylor; Mike felt the same way about Graham.

"Like I said." Taylor was obviously frustrated as well. "Since Jimmy died before the deadline – Geez, that's a rotten term, huh? I mean, well, he died before the deadline, so the team can take the whole twenty-four-million cap hit this year. That crushes Chip's ability to do any new signings for this season, which means the team's gonna suck. But without a quarterback they're probably gonna suck anyway, so I guess Chip doesn't care."

"And, if the death had occurred after the deadline?" Graham nudged.

"Then the cap hit for the dead money would be next year."

"And what is the deadline date?" Graham turned back toward the others, putting his back to the window. He was now backlit in the sunshine such that Mike could barely make out his face. He took a mental note – it was a nice technique. It wouldn't work in an interrogation room unless you had a bright light behind you, but here it was a good effect.

"June first."

"Thank you." Graham gestured with his left hand toward Mike, as if passing the floor back to the detective, and walked back in the direction of his chair.

"Thank you for being honest with us, Aaron," Mike was ready to wind down the interview, but needed to make sure his witness was not holding anything back. "I have to say you may be guilty of obstructing justice by not giving us all this information the first time we talked."

Taylor reached out a hand toward Mike, his eyes wide and pleading. "But—"

"Just listen," Mike cut him off, wanting to keep control of the situation. "It happens. People don't usually get prosecuted for lying to the cops when they're protecting somebody. I'm not making any promises about that. But if you're not being completely and fully honest with us now, you won't get any slack from the District Attorney later. So, if there's anything else you're not telling me, you'd better spill it." Mike fixed an intense stare into Taylor's eyes.

This time, rather than dropping his head, the kid stared back. "That's it, Detective. That's all there is. I screwed this up. I didn't protect Jimmy. Now he's dead, and I'm probably screwed whether you arrest me or not. But I'm telling you the truth. That's all I know."

"I believe you," Mike said, leaning forward and slowly standing, with a wince of pain from his balky left knee. "I'll tell you what you do now. You say nothing to anyone about what we just discussed. You go about your business, and we'll do our job and see if we can track down whoever killed Jimmy. If the DA needs you to testify, you'll testify. Until then, there's no need for us to make your life any more miserable than it already is – as long as we don't find out you're lying to us again."

"I'm not!" Taylor blurted out, before slumping back into the chair.

"Fine. I hope not. We'll show ourselves out." Mike waved for Jason and Graham to follow him toward the door. As he held it for his two companions, Mike looked back at the pathetic young man, still sitting in the comfy chair. He was staring into space, oblivious to everything except his own thoughts.

When they got back to the sidewalk outside the ISMS building, Mike sat down on a low marble ledge that formed a half-circle around the entrance. Jason and Graham remained standing. They all spoke in hushed tones, even though there were only a few passing pedestrians in the middle of the afternoon on a Monday. Bloomingdale's was a few blocks north, but there was not much for tourists to do on the plaza in front of an office building.

They had confirmation now of Jimmy's involvement in the point-shaving scheme at the behest of someone from the Gallata syndicate. It meshed, and now they didn't need to rely on what Mike had been told by Fat Albert in order to explain how the investigation got there. The DA would have Taylor as a witness, along with the banking records. Agent Forrest would be happy to get the information, and it would be nice for Mike to be able to repay the man's favors.

But the information still wasn't helping them narrow down the list of suspects. Igor was sitting in lockup, waiting to be charged with murder at the end of the day. And it didn't explain why someone would want the Gallatas to give back the body.

It was Graham who came up with a possible explanation. "The body was found last Saturday. That was the first of June, wasn't it?"

"Yeah, it was," Mike confirmed.

"So, the same day as the deadline for the dead money, as Mr. Taylor explained."

"What's your point?" Jason asked.

"Well, what we've been looking for is the thread that ties together the murder and the appearance of the body. We've been looking for a person with a motive not only to kill Mr. Rydell, but to have his body discovered. If Mr. Rydell had simply disappeared and his body had not been found, Boyd's of Britain would not pay out on the life insurance policy until there was a formal legal determination of death. Normally that takes some time, but the policy would eventually pay out. So, while the beneficiary of the policy has a motive for the body to be found, it's certainly not sufficient to risk being implicated in the murder."

"That's what we've been telling you." Mike didn't try to hide his annoyance. "And I've told you before that football teams don't go around knocking off their star players to collect on the insurance money. Plus, all the team would need to do is injure him so he couldn't play again. The insurance pays off the same as if he's dead, doesn't it?"

"Quite right," Graham conceded, "which is relevant, I'm sure. And yet, there is the issue of the timing." He paused, looking from Mike to Jason and back, waiting for one of them to jump in to agree with him.

"Wait . . ." Mike held out an arm. "You're saying that the team had an interest in the body being found before the cap deadline, so they could take the whole cap hit now instead of next year. If their quarterback is dead, they're not going to win many games this year, so Chip O'Meara would want to dump salary this year and eat as much dead money as possible to clear the decks for next year. If he somehow knew that Jimmy had been murdered, and knew where the body was, he would gladly pay the $100,000 to get the body so he could collect on the insurance and trigger the dead money. I agree it makes sense. It doesn't necessarily mean Chip had anything to do with the murder, but it would explain wanting the body."

"Who else could be responsible for the murder?" Graham challenged.

Jason was happy to rain on Graham's parade. "Nate Bedford, for one. We know he had motive and opportunity. What we could never figure was how he got the body out of the building. We now know how that happened, so it's possible that Nate got into the building and into the gym, found Jimmy there, and strangled him."

"How would he get in and past the security without being captured on camera?" Graham asked.

Mike jumped in before Jason could answer. "For that matter, even if we thought Chip O'Meara or somebody else from the team's front office might have been involved, who could have carried out the hit? Somebody who lived in the building and could have accessed the gym without having to get past security?"

"We haven't run background on every resident," Jason lamented.

Mike raised his hand again. "And how does that theory account for somebody killing Tiger?"

Graham furrowed his brows. "Perhaps it was unrelated."

"Like Hell it was," Mike said. "Let's get a cab and get back to the precinct. I think I need a whiteboard for this."

# Chapter 38 – Pulling on Threads

WHEN THEY WERE ON THEIR WAY back to the precinct on 94th Street, Mike had their cab let them off at Broadway and 92nd, where he picked up a large pizza for him and Jason. Graham ordered a plate of pasta. They trekked up to the 5th floor conference room, where there were fewer distractions and a larger whiteboard, then dove into the food and started charting out their investigation.

The grease had barely seeped through their thin paper plates when the old desk phone's shrill bell split their ears. Mike was chewing a glob of cheese and pepperoni, so Jason picked up the handset on a small corner table. He listened without speaking, then finally said, "Sure." He put the call on hold, hung up the receiver, and punched the button on the ancient speaker next to the boxy phone.

"Thank you, Detective Dickson. Is Detective Stoneman there now?" Kristi Olson's voice squeezed through the black holes in the silver box.

"This is Detective Stoneman," Mike barked out. "What can we do for you?"

"I'm sorry to interrupt, Detective. I'm working on a new story in the Jimmy Rydell murder case and I'm seeking a comment from the police department."

"Did you try the public relations department?" Mike tried to sound annoyed and dismissive, hoping it would dissuade Kristi from calling him directly next time. She'd probably done it at the suggestion of Dexter Peacock, who fancied himself Mike's best buddy.

"I wanted to give you the first opportunity to hear the facts – and to comment."

Mike rolled his eyes at Jason. "Fine. Please go ahead."

"I assume you saw our article on Friday about Nate Bedford's history at Auburn." She paused, waiting for Mike's response. When he remained silent, she pushed ahead. "I did a little more digging and, while I can't reveal my source, I can say that one of the other two players involved with the hazing incidents was Vernon 'Duke' Drepp. I knew that The Duke tried to make the team along with Nate after they graduated, but I didn't know they were particularly close until now. They were both involved in hazing a Black player to the point of brain damage and they protected each other by never talking about it."

Jason and Mike exchanged interested looks but didn't say anything.

"Should I assume from your silence that this is information you didn't have already?"

"I have no comment for you about our ongoing investigation," Mike replied without emotion. "Thank you, I appreciate the call. Tell me, when do you expect to publish this article?"

The line was silent, as if muted from the other side. Then, Kristi's voice came back at a lower volume. "We'll publish as soon as I get confirmation of a few key facts. I can't go with something like this without someone to confirm my main source, but I'm one hundred percent positive that the information is good."

"If you're not ready to publish, why are you asking for a reaction? Don't you usually wait until the last possible moment? Didn't Peacock teach you that lesson?"

"I don't need Dexter Peacock to teach me how to be a reporter," Kristi bristled.

"True. I won't argue that with you."

"Thanks. Well, now that the team has installed The Duke as Nate's bodyguard, I thought you'd want to know that little bit of their history."

Mike looked at Jason and Graham, all three surprised by the information. "That's very interesting, Ms. Olson. I appreciate it. I tell you what, why don't you give me a call back when you're ready to publish. I may be able to give you a quote then."

Again the line went silent for a moment. "I can't make any promises, Detective. As it is, my editor would probably kill me if he knew I was sharing unpublished information. But I'll consider it."

"Thanks," Mike said quickly.

"Wait—" Kristi tried to avoid letting Mike hang up. "There's one more thing. I saw a video clip of a fight at an Italian restaurant downtown on Saturday. Was that you and Detective Dickson? And did that incident have anything to do with the Rydell investigation?"

Mike shook his head, annoyed by the entire internet. "As I said before, Ms. Olson, I cannot comment on an ongoing investigation."

"Even for a reporter willing to share unpublished information?"

After making eye contact with Jason, Mike turned back to the speaker. "I tell you what, Kristi. I can't give you a comment on that question, but if anything important is going to happen over the next few days, I'll make sure to let you know where to be. How's that?"

"Thank you, Detective. I appreciate it."

The line went dead.

Jason, who had shed his suit jacket, reached out and deftly removed another mushroom slice from the pizza box. "I told you The Duke was a racist."

"You did," Mike conceded. "How does it help us?"

Jason went to the whiteboard. "Jimmy" was written at the top. He wrote "Duke" next to a box that already contained the name "Nate" and drew lines connecting each to Jimmy, and then a line between them. Over the next half hour, while the slices of pizza disappeared, they wrote and erased additional names, making connections, and speculating about relationships. The diagram had places for Fat Albert Gallata, Mr. Clean, Tiger, and Woody and Chip O'Meara.

Graham relentlessly pressed the theory that the team – either via Woody or Chip – enlisted The Duke and/or Nate Bedford to attack Jimmy with the intention of at least inflicting an injury that would end his career and allow the team to collect on its insurance policy. Mike and Jason continued to be skeptical, but more and more it seemed like the most plausible theory. If only they had actual evidence putting either of them at the scene of the crime.

As they were losing steam and Graham excused himself to the toilet, Detective George Mason knocked on the conference room door and brought in a stack of papers. Several pages were flagged with sticky notes and included yellow highlighting. Mason flipped through the pages, pointing to specific entries and talking with Mike. When Graham returned, Mike thanked Mason and walked over to the whiteboard. He drew a dotted line between The Duke and Nate Bedford and wrote "phone call" under the new line.

"What's this?" Graham asked.

"Detective Mason just brought me a printout we got from Verizon." He pointed to the stack of pages. "It's the records of Nate Bedford's cell phone calls. We haven't been focused on Bedford for the past few days, so George reviewed them when they came in and flagged a few key numbers. There's a call from Nate to The Duke's cell phone at 12:20 a.m. on Thursday morning, May 30th."

"To The Duke?" Jason shot his crumpled napkin into the trash can like a basketball. "The Duke told us he was at the movies that night, then went home. But while Nate was driving from Jersey to Manhattan, he called his old racist college buddy."

"It was pretty late," Mike observed.

"Sure, but he was a little drunk, and pissed off. He'll say he called his friend. How is that incriminating?"

Graham held up his index finger and walked to the whiteboard, picked up a green marker, and launched into a revised version of his favorite theory. "Nate was on his way to Jimmy's flat. When The Duke got the call, he wasn't at home sleeping. He was already at Park Towers, waiting for Jimmy to come to the gym. What if he told Nate to come over, then let him in through the service door?"

"How do we know they didn't plan it even earlier than that?" Jason suggested. "Nate may have been calling to confirm the preexisting plan."

Mike shook his head. "That doesn't jibe with Candi tossing him out of her apartment that night. According to her story, he wouldn't have left otherwise, so it's not likely The Duke was expecting him."

Graham frowned at the interruption of his narrative. "In any case, The Duke and Nate ambush Jimmy. The attack had been ordered by the club's management, which wanted to rid itself of a troublesome player and collect on the insurance policy. The Duke and Nate strangle Jimmy. They stage the scene to look like a suicide, then Nate leaves to drive home."

"Wait," Mike cut in. "You're still assuming management was involved. Maybe it was just Nate and The Duke conspiring to take Jimmy out on their own. It turns out they had a history together. Maybe The Duke was just waiting for an excuse to hurt Jimmy because of his social justice protests. His boy, Nate, called him that night, pissed off about the fight, and they decided on the spot to go take care of Jimmy."

"But," Jason picked up the story thread, "The Duke was interrupted by Mr. Clean – Igor – who rolled in the laundry cart. That's been puzzling me. How did Fat Albert and Mr. Clean know to show up on that particular night? The regular driver, Fred, said it was the third time Mr. Clean called him and wanted to swap in for the delivery. How did he know Jimmy would be alone in the gym?"

Mike ran a hand over the stubble on the side of his face. "Fat Albert said something about the FBI not being the only people with tech. Maybe they had a bug in Jimmy's apartment, or a hidden camera in his hallway, so they could tell when he was going to the gym late and when his bodyguard wasn't there. If it were me, I'd want to catch him alone and not have to try to kill him and his bodyguard together. The Duke is a pretty imposing dude, and Jimmy's no pushover even when he's alone."

"That's true," Jason agreed, "but what happened the other two nights Mr. Clean made his delivery run? Why didn't he kill Jimmy either of those nights?"

"Maybe," Graham offered, "The Duke turned out to be there, or maybe Jimmy ended his workout early those nights, or maybe there was somebody else there, like one of the desk attendants, and Mr. Clean aborted the attempts."

"That would make sense," Jason jumped back in, "but how did The Duke know Jimmy would be alone in the gym that night?"

"Maybe Jimmy told him he was planning a late workout, or maybe he was banking on Jimmy's general routine."

Jason asked, "How long will it take us to get a warrant for a cell site analysis on The Duke's phone? We could place him in Jimmy's neighborhood instead of up in Washington Heights at the time of that call."

"It would take a couple of days," Mike muttered, "and it wouldn't prove much other than that The Duke wasn't telling us the truth about going home after the movie – if he ever even went to see the movie. It would give us grounds to question him, but that's about it."

They continued to construct hypothetical sequences of events, drawing and erasing lines on their whiteboard. As Graham was writing "Laundry Van" next to Mr. Clean, Mike sat up straight and slapped a hand on the table.

"Crap! Why didn't I see this before?"

"What," Graham turned, the dry erase pen still in his hand.

"If The Duke had been acting alone, or in concert only with Nate, then the arrival of Mr. Clean would have been a godsend.

He – or they – would have been thrilled for Mr. Clean to dispose of the body, leaving no trace and creating a perfect suspect for us to focus on. Think about it. They staged it as a suicide to provide some plausible way that it wasn't a murder. They had no way of removing the body, so that was their way of throwing us off. They were expecting that somebody would find the body swinging from the resistance band in the morning. But if somebody showed up out of the blue and carted away their corpse, they would be thrilled. There would be no reason for The Duke to follow the laundry van in order to determine where Mr. Clean took Jimmy's body. He would have simply counted his blessings and gone home. He would have to figure nobody would ever see that body again."

"Unless he knew his boss would be unhappy with a missing Jimmy, and would want to have a body," Jason said. "The Duke must have known about the insurance policy. It's not impossible that he would want somebody to find the body so the team could get the insurance money."

Mike conceded the point. Graham continued to maintain that direct involvement by team officials in advance of the murder was the more plausible theory.

Mike and Jason had to acknowledge that coordination with some team official seemed more and more likely. They basically agreed on the hypothetical remainder of the story. The Duke, for whatever reason, followed the laundry truck out of the building, then followed Mr. Clean to the drop site. There, Mr. Clean transferred the body to a freezer unit inside the bed of an 18-wheeler, which was supposed to be headed to Miami on Friday.

"So, are we pretty certain the O'Mearas had to be involved at the point where somebody needed $100,000 to pay off Fat Albert to get the body back?" Jason asked.

Mike frowned. "That's assuming the information we got from Fat Albert is accurate. I'm not saying it's not, but it's an assumption. Plus, The Duke could have gotten the money from Nate."

Jason shook his head. "What motive does Nate have to want the body back? It would seem to be a terrible idea to give the body to the police. Why would Nate do that? Would he risk being linked to the murder through the payoff money, just to help The Duke look good with the bosses?"

Graham pressed his point. "The team needed a corpse to establish death, both to collect on the insurance and to trigger the acceleration of the dead money against the salary cap. So, once The Duke reported the successful murder, but advised Mr. O'Meara – one of them – about the absence of the body, someone did a little research and established that the site where the body was stored was connected to the Gallata organization. Someone pulled some strings and managed to contact the boss, Fat Albert, to offer him a nice sum of money to return the body. This, I believe, is much more plausible as the efforts of the well-connected owners rather than the singular effort of a simpleton bodyguard and a jealous teammate. Don't you think?"

Neither Mike nor Jason could dispute the point. Graham then completed his circle. "The team sent out their guys, probably including The Duke, to drop off the cash and retrieve the corpse, and the body ended up, through the now-known circuitous route, on the Central Park carousel on the first of June."

Mike carried his plate and a few stray bits of crust to the garbage can. "Why would the team wait until so close to June first before putting this plan into action?"

Jason tapped on the table, then stood up and walked toward the whiteboard. "It may be that Chip still hoped to convince Jimmy to restructure his contract, to help relieve pressure on the salary cap for this year. It was that day when Jimmy and Aaron Taylor told Chip they wouldn't agree. We know now that Chip was angry about Jimmy's refusal. And it was the same day that Nate went after Jimmy in the locker room. So, while Mr. Clean may have been planning his hit for a while, maybe Chip or Woody made the final decision at the last minute. With the deadline looming, they figured it was better to punt this season, take the cap hit immediately, and rebuild for next season."

"They had already embedded The Duke as Jimmy's bodyguard," Mike said. "If Chip needed to arrange for something to happen to Jimmy, The Duke was right there, waiting for the call."

"We should get a subpoena to scrutinize the banking records of both Chip and Woody O'Meara, as well as team accounts. If we find a $100,000 cash withdrawal on the last days of May, that will be compelling evidence." Graham looked at the two detectives for confirmation.

"Of course," Mike agreed. "We'll get on that immediately."

"Mike," Jason interrupted, "we're leaving out a piece of the puzzle. How does any of this mesh with somebody killing Tiger?"

"Hmmm. You're right. Where does that fit?" Mike stared at the whiteboard. The box containing the word "Tiger" had one line leading up to Jimmy, but no other connections on the diagram.

It was Graham who came up with an idea. "What if Tiger was acquainted with The Duke? The boy spent time with Jimmy, and The Duke would have been there often. In the mornings, when The Duke was retrieving Jimmy and driving him away, Tiger was there with the morning's coffee and pastry."

"Bagel," Jason corrected.

"Yes, yes. Bagel. In any case, the boy knew The Duke. So, in our scenario, The Duke would have been following Mr. Clean as he spirited the body away. How would he do that?" Graham looked at his colleagues, wondering if someone would respond.

Jason finally did. "He would take the stairs up from the health club to the breezeway as soon as Mr. Clean entered the service elevator. He could have seen the laundry truck pull out. The truck would have been driving slowly inside the breezeway, then it would have exited through the big garage door to the street. The Duke could have run through the service door before it closed and followed the van. But he couldn't chase the van on foot."

"No." Mike picked up the trail. "He wasn't supposed to be there. He would have wanted to get in and out without anyone seeing him. He had to come in through one of the side entrances or the service entrance to avoid the doormen. He would have left his Escalade there so he could get out after killing Jimmy."

"Precisely!" Graham agreed. "The Duke would have left the building in a rush, having an urgent need to follow the laundry van. He wouldn't have known that Mr. Clean would drive only a short distance before meeting up with the regular driver. The Duke would have been rushing, likely running. If someone who knew him saw him running by, jumping in his SUV, and speeding away at one-thirty in the morning, that would be a memorable event, don't you think?"

Mike's eyes lit up as he realized where Graham was going with this. "Tiger would have been inside his cardboard house, right outside the service door. He might have seen The Duke tearing out. Maybe The Duke parked his truck on that side street and used the service entrance to get into the building in the first place. If he came running out and burned rubber in pursuit of the laundry truck, the kid would notice. He's now a witness, so The Duke has to go back and clean that up by getting rid of Tiger. He either kills him and then dumps his body in the park uptown, or maybe lures the kid up there somehow – like you said, they know each other."

"He wanted to tell us about it," Jason said softly, almost to himself. "Mike, remember on Saturday, when we were leaving the building? Tiger was there. He said something about wanting to talk to us. But The Duke was there too, and maybe Tiger wouldn't have wanted to say anything in front of him. We waved him off and told him we'd be back. The Duke probably heard that. Maybe he didn't even realize Tiger saw him until that morning, which is why he didn't kill the kid until Sunday night."

Mike walked back toward the door of the conference room, thinking. "As crazy as it sounds, I can't say it's impossible." He turned and faced Jason and Graham. "If he were the killer, it would make sense for The Duke to stage the scene to look like a suicide. Jimmy was already on the edge with his gambling involvement. Maybe The Duke knew about that. He could even leave a suicide note, which Mr. Clean would have removed along with the rest of Jimmy's things."

"Wait!" Jason interrupted. "Think about that. If I were trying to stage a suicide, I wouldn't try to write a note by hand. It wouldn't be in Jimmy's handwriting. Besides, a young guy like Jimmy would probably post his suicide note on Twitter."

"Yeah, but then somebody would instantly call 9-1-1." Mike was still pacing around the small room.

"OK," Jason joined Mike in pacing. "Let's try to think like The Duke, as hard as that is to imagine. If it were me, and if I had Jimmy's phone, I'd send myself a text message with the suicide note. Then, the next morning, I'd show up at Park Towers. Jimmy's body would have been found hanging in the gym by then, and I'd show the cops the suicide text. That would wrap it up. Jimmy's phone would be there next to the corpse, and when we cracked open the phone, or got the records from the carrier, there would be a text to The Duke with the suicide note."

The three men stood in silence for a moment, all thinking about how much sense that made. Graham reached up to the top of the whiteboard and drew a dotted line from Jimmy to The Duke labeled "text?"

Jason tapped the table. "Mike, wasn't there a text message to The Duke on Jimmy's phone?"

Mike got up from his chair and headed for the door. He returned in less than five minutes with a folder containing printouts covered with handwritten notes from the officers who reviewed Jimmy's phone records. Mike had already pulled out the last page. He put it on the table and pointed.

"The notes say that this number here is 'VD.' Vernon Drepp. It looks like he texted his bodyguard at 1:02 a.m. on May 30th." He looked up at two very interested sets of eyes. "The Duke said Jimmy texted to confirm the morning pickup time. That made sense, but it might also be the suicide note, right?"

"Is it possible to retrieve the actual message?" Graham asked.

"No." Mike didn't mask his disappointment. "Verizon text messages get deleted after a few days. Obviously, we have the statistical data, but we can't get the actual message."

Jason pulled out his phone and started tapping. "I'll send Zimmerman an email and have him work on a subpoena for The Duke's phone. Maybe we can retrieve the text directly from his device. And while we're at it, we can get the cell site data for that night."

"Sure," Mike said, "we should do that. But I have to believe The Duke is smart enough to delete the message from his phone as soon as the suicide plan went sideways when Jimmy's body wasn't in the gym the next morning."

"Is the existence of the text along with the cell site data and all the other circumstantial evidence enough to arrest The Duke?" Jason asked.

"Arrest? Maybe. But it's not enough to convict anyone. There's plenty of evidence pointing to Mr. Clean. Which seems more plausible? That Fat Albert and Mr. Clean knocked him off, or that The Duke killed him minutes before the mob hitman arrived? The DA has to prove guilt beyond a reasonable doubt. I'd say there's plenty of doubt about which story is true, at least based on the evidence we have now. Even if we find a $100,000 cash withdrawal in Chip O'Meara's bank account, that doesn't prove anything because Fat Albert is never going to admit that he solicited or received the payment."

Jason slammed a dry-erase pen down on the table. "You're right. It's going to be impossible to get a conviction unless one of them confesses."

Mike scrutinized the diagram on the whiteboard. "Maybe we try a hard count – see if somebody'll jump into the neutral zone before the snap."

Graham stared at Mike, completely baffled. "I'm sorry, is that a Star Trek reference, or does the term have another meaning?"

Jason slapped the Brit on the back, perhaps a bit harder than necessary. "Don't worry, my soccer-watching friend, we'll explain it to you."

# Chapter 39 – Under the Bus

Tuesday, June 11

TUESDAY WAS THE NEXT-TO-LAST DAY of Optional Team Activities at the Florham Park facility. After Wednesday's workout, the players would disperse until they returned in July for the formal beginning of preseason practices, followed by preseason games. Mike commented during the ride out to Jersey that, for a sport with only sixteen games in the season, the players spent a lot of the year wearing their team's colors.

Graham was in the back seat. Mike and Jason had discussed not bringing the investigator along, but decided that he would add some leverage to their planned discussion with Woody and Chip. Mike had enlisted Commissioner Ward to reach out to his buddy, the NFL commissioner, to help arrange the meeting. Since the league had put pressure on the NYPD, it was only fair that the NYPD put some pressure on the league to aid in the investigation. Woody and Chip had been told to bring both Nate Bedford and Duke Drepp to the meeting. Mike wanted them all in one room, even if it was on their home turf.

They parked outside the administration building, next to a County Sheriff's car in which two uniformed deputies were seated. Mike walked over and spoke to them for a moment, then rejoined Jason and Graham. It was starting to rain. After more than a week of dry, hot weather, this was the third day in a row with some rain. A distant rumble of thunder growled across the practice field, sending a member of the field staff scrambling to gather up stray gear. Mike heard a shrill whistle from one of the practice fields. Two figures wearing bright red vests threw simultaneous passes. Nobody was wearing pads. The players didn't seem worried about the possibility of lightning.

As they rounded the corner of the building, Mike saw Kristi Olson sitting alone under the overhang at the front entrance. She had a laptop computer perched on her knees, sheltered from the rapidly increasing rainfall. She looked up at the approaching group and waved. "Hello, Detective Stoneman. What's on your agenda today?"

"Hello yourself, Ms. Olson," Mike replied politely. "I'm afraid I can't comment on our activities. But I'm impressed by your articles. You not only dug up some facts we didn't know, but you've gotten most of the investigation facts right. A rare feat."

"Thanks!" Kristi called brightly.

"Are you still working on that other angle we talked about yesterday?"

"Yes, I am. I'm waiting for a call any moment now. I appreciate you giving me a ring today so I could be here. What am I waiting for?"

"Maybe nothing. We'll see. I may be able to give you something when we come back out."

Kristi watched the three men disappear into the building. She peered through the glass, watching them ascend the steps to the second-floor executive offices, then went back to writing her daily update.

Inside, Woody O'Meara's personal assistant met them at the top of the stairs and escorted them to Woody's office. Mike remembered why he had been impressed the last time. Looking across the wide room, he could see the main practice field spread out across the row of floor-to-ceiling picture windows, each one six feet wide and separated only by thin columns. The rain was pouring down now. It was like being in the owner's box at the stadium – which, in effect, it was. The room was covered with field turf, just like the stadium. In front of the massive mahogany desk, an oval team logo on the carpet left no doubt what domain they had entered.

Woody rose from the leather-and-chrome chair behind his desk and walked around to greet his guests. He smiled and shook hands with the detectives and Graham like a politician greeting potential donors at a fundraiser. He invited them to take seats in the padded chairs opposite the dark leather sofa. On the sofa sat Nate Bedford, The Duke, and Chip O'Meara. Next to them, in a separate chair, Mike recognized Craig Linderman, the team's general counsel, who had attended the last meeting.

Nate was in his practice clothes, tight compression shorts and a green tank top, and had a white towel draped around his neck. The Duke wore his usual dark shorts and tight white t-shirt. Chip, apparently not taking after his old man, had on a full business suit. Woody, in slacks and a polo shirt, settled into an armchair at the end of the football-shaped coffee table. Not quite neutral ground, but symbolically not on either side of the table, Mike noticed.

After the visitors declined refreshments and Woody's assistant left and closed the heavy door, Mike got right down to business. "Thank you for meeting with us, Mr. O'Meara–"

"Oh, now, please call me Woody. Everyone else does." He smiled with a sincerity and disarming friendliness that made Mike forget for a moment that he was a billionaire and a cutthroat businessman.

"Fine, Woody. Like I said, I appreciate you assembling your group here for us so we can give you all an update on the investigation and ask a few follow-up questions. Jason, please give these folks the rundown."

Mike eyed the men sitting opposite him on the sofa. The Duke looked relaxed, almost bored. Nate was sitting forward, listening carefully. Chip crossed his legs and looked at his father, not making eye contact with either Mike or Jason.

"We have evidence suggesting that Jimmy was murdered in the health club of his building." Jason paused, as he and Mike – and Graham – observed their reactions. Only Nate showed a change, seeming surprised and interested. "We further found evidence that Jimmy's body was moved that same night. We believe the killer staged the body, using a yellow exercise band, so it would appear Jimmy hung himself from a weight machine. The killer wanted it to look like a suicide."

Again, Nate reacted visibly, furrowing his brow and pursing his lips in a silent, "Wow!" The Duke cocked his head slightly, looking directly at Jason. Chip didn't show anything.

Woody sat forward in his chair. "You mean it's possible Jimmy wasn't murdered at all?"

"That's one scenario," Jason replied. "But there is some evidence we need to examine, which is why we wanted to talk to you all today." Jason paused again, scanning the men on the sofa. "Mr. Drepp, am I correct that you have a cell phone issued to you by the team, as part of your professional services?"

For the first time, The Duke's expression changed. He turned his head slightly toward Chip, then back toward Jason. "Yeah. Sure. I got a phone."

"May I have it, please?" Jason extended his hand over the edge of the coffee table toward The Duke.

"Hey, now, just wait a minute," Linderman cut in. "You're asking one of our employees to give up private information here. Do you have a warrant for that?"

"No, I don't." Jason turned to Woody. "Mr. O'Meara – Woody – we're attempting to get to the bottom of the situation. That phone is company property, which means the company owns its contents. Your corporate privacy policy – posted on your website – clearly says employees have no expectation of privacy when using company electronic communications devices. Will you consent to me inspecting two specific items on that device?"

"Mr. O'Meara," Linderman said, "I'm here to protect the company's interests and I don't—"

"I understand," Woody cut off his lawyer. "Look, the police can get a subpoena and we can come back tomorrow and have the same meeting, right?" Linderman shrugged. "We have nothing to hide here. Duke, give the man your phone."

A concerned look passed over The Duke's face as he looked at his boss's boss. "Mr. O'Meara, Sir, I – there might be some stuff on that phone I don't think—"

"Don't worry," Jason said, "I'm only looking for one text message and one phone record. I won't be looking at your porn or your emails. I promise I'll give it back."

"Fine," Woody announced, ending the discussion. "Give it to the man." He motioned to The Duke, who looked at Woody apprehensively, but pulled out his phone and put it on the table.

"Please unlock the phone."

The big man's forearm muscles bulged in and out as he clenched his fist, but he took the phone and swiped in his security pattern, then handed it to Jason.

As Jason punched icons and swiped the screen, holding it close to his chest, Mike took the lead. "Most of the time, a phone user can delete information they don't want us to find. Of course, we can usually get it directly from the provider. In a few days, Verizon can tell us everything we need to know, but we're hoping to cut down the time it will take. Jason here was a forensics tech in the Army. He learned all the tricks to recover deleted material, and he takes CIA-level classes twice a year to keep up on all the new security tricks with these smartphones. It's really valuable in our line of work, as you can imagine. With any luck, he'll be able to recover what we're looking for."

"And what is that, exactly?" Woody asked. He seemed genuinely curious and not at all apprehensive. Graham and Mike were observing the reactions from the sofa; The Duke appeared quite concerned and kept glancing between Chip on his left and Nate on his right. Nate was looking at The Duke. Chip was looking at the lawyer, trying to make eye contact. The three had clearly not been told to keep their poker faces in place.

Mike leaned toward Woody, who was on his immediate right. "You already know that Nate here had a little dust-up with Jimmy in the locker room back on May 29th." Woody nodded. "What you probably don't know is that Nate also had a disagreement with his girlfriend later that night. She threw him out of her apartment, after he had been drinking heavily. She's waiting to press charges for assault and battery against Nate for hitting her twice and breaking her nose."

"Hey! That's a lie. I only slapped her once! There's no way she had a broken nose," Nate yelled.

Woody cast a disapproving glare at his wide receiver. The lawyer reached out, gently put a hand on Nate's shoulder, and leaned in to whisper in his ear. He was undoubtedly telling Nate to keep his mouth shut.

Mike paid little attention to the side conversation and continued to answer Woody. "Regardless of the number of times Nate hit his girlfriend, she tossed him out. He jumped in his truck and drove to Jimmy's apartment building in Manhattan. We know Jimmy was alone that night. His bodyguard here," Mike nodded toward The Duke, "wasn't with him. That made it much easier to kill him. What we don't yet know for sure is whether Nate knew Jimmy was unprotected." Mike turned his head slightly so he had a view of the sofa. "So, what Jason is looking for is a record on The Duke's phone showing a call from Nate, or to Nate, that night. We want to know if Nate confirmed where The Duke was, and whether he was or wasn't providing protection for Jimmy."

Nate and The Duke turned their heads simultaneously to look at each other. The Duke shook his head very slightly at his old college teammate.

Jason held the phone close to his face so that nobody else in the room could see the screen, which displayed The Duke's call record from earlier that day. The record from May 30th had, in fact, been deleted, but Jason had memorized the information from the Verizon logs back at the precinct.

"Here it is," Jason announced loudly, looking over the top of the device at the men on the sofa. "There's a call here from Mr.

Bedford's phone at 12:20 a.m. on Thursday, May 30th. The call lasted two minutes. So, the question is, what did you two talk about after midnight that night?" Jason looked at The Duke. Mike looked at Nate. Both men were still looking at each other.

"Detective," the lawyer broke in, "at this point it appears you are questioning these men in connection with the investigation of a serious crime. They have the right to remain silent and the right to counsel. I must protest and instruct them not to answer."

Jason was prepared for this and smoothly responded. "Mr. Linderman, you are correct. All citizens have the right to remain silent. It seems to me that they are already represented by counsel."

"I am not their counsel," Linderman protested. "I'm counsel for the team. I can't act as individual counsel for anyone here – not even for Mr. O'Meara."

"Oh, so when you advised them not to answer, that was not legal advice?"

Linderman turned his head toward Woody, looking like he had just bitten into an overripe lemon. "I made that statement as a concerned friend, not as their lawyer. I am not their lawyer."

"I didn't think so." Jason turned back toward Nate. "So, like I said, you have the right to remain silent. But, if you remain silent, my partner and I will take that into account when we decide whether to arrest you and walk you out of here in handcuffs in full view of the press guys out there. And your employer, Mr. O'Meara, is entirely within *his* rights to void your contract and fire your ass if you refuse to answer questions that involve team business. So, you can refuse to answer, but you'll have to suffer the consequences. Since this guy here is not your lawyer, he's not going to give you any advice, so it's up to you. What do you say, Nate? What did you and The Duke here talk about that night on the phone?"

Nate's head swiveled between Jason, Woody, and The Duke. He grabbed the corner of his workout towel and wiped the sweat from his forehead. It was fully air-conditioned inside the plush office, but Nate seemed to be feeling the heat.

"Don't say nothin' to these guys," The Duke said, his voice calm.

Nate looked confused. He could read the slightest twitch of body language in an opposing cornerback, telling him that his adversary was planning to take an outside angle off the snap. He could then instantly flash an open hand toward his quarterback, letting him know to throw the inside slant. He could keep all the patterns and options for the entire playbook in his mind during a game. But there was no playbook for this situation. Here, he was on his own. "Mr. O'Meara, Sir, you wouldn't hold it against me if I just kept quiet here, now, would you?"

Before Woody could formulate an answer, Mike jumped in with the next arrow in their pre-planned attack. "Before you answer that, Sir, I have to tell you something else you may not know."

Woody, whose placid face remained impossible to read, nodded toward Mike.

"You read the article in *The Times*, I'm sure, about Nate being involved in some brutal hazing of Black players when he was at Auburn."

"That's not true!" Nate called out, again earning a firm hand on his shoulder from Linderman.

"Well, the article mentioned some other players involved who were not named. These were guys who thought nothing of beating a Black freshman to the point he had to withdraw from school and never played football again. They are the worst kind of racists – they beat up a Black teammate like it has no consequences. And their coaches and the school officials are just as bad – enabling the racists by looking the other way and letting them get away with it, which only feeds the monster."

"I ain't no racist!" Nate shouted. Jason suppressed a smile. Getting Nate riled up was an essential part of the plan.

"Shut up, Nate!" Chip snapped, glaring around The Duke's imposing chest.

Mike pressed forward. "So, Woody, what you don't know is that one of the other players involved in the Auburn hazing was your own Vernon Drepp." Mike kept his eyes on Woody, avoiding the temptation to peek at the reaction from the sofa. Jason had that covered.

The Duke's neck snapped in Nate's direction.

"Is that true?" Woody asked, staring at the pile of muscle in the middle of the sofa.

"It wasn't like that. It was a long time ago." The Duke tried to keep his emotions in check, but once again, Jason could see the muscle in his forearm flex repeatedly.

"So, you see," Mike said, "These two have been KKK members together, like their fathers, since their old college days."

"I ain't no KKK member! That's a fuckin' lie!" Nate shouted.

"No?" Mike snapped right back. "We all know you hated it when Jimmy took a knee during the anthem to protest racism. You deny that?"

"No I don't! I don't stand for nobody disrespecting my flag!"

"Are you telling me you and your buddy here didn't talk about hurting Jimmy if you thought you could get away with it?"

"That's a damned lie!"

"So why did you call him after midnight that night when you were in your truck on your way to kick the shit out of Jimmy?"

"I wasn't – I didn't – Oh, I don't give a shit. I got nothin' to hide. I was just callin' The Duke to see if he was up for something. I was pissed off at Candi and I was thinkin' maybe if he was up, we could go get a drink somewhere."

"A drink?" Mike raised one eyebrow. "You hadn't already had enough to drink that night?"

"I don't know. Hell, maybe. But The Duke was with some girl, so I said no problem and that was it."

Jason picked up the questioning, which was also part of the plan. They figured, like before, that Nate would react badly to being questioned by a Black cop. "But you did go to Jimmy's apartment building, didn't you?"

"I—" Nate stopped himself when The Duke elbowed him in the ribs. "I don't remember if I ever got there or not. I think I might have gone, but I figured it was a waste of time, so I turned around and went home."

"And got pulled over for drunk driving," Jason pressed.

Woody's face turned even more disapprovingly serious. "Is that true, Nate?"

"No. Hell no! I got pulled over, sure, but I didn't get no DUI."

"No, because the White cop who pulled you over recognized you and let you off with just a reckless driving citation. But they impounded your truck and wouldn't let you drive home. Why would they do that if you weren't drunk?"

Nate jumped up from the sofa with the agility of the professional athlete he was. "I wasn't drunk!" He took a step toward Jason.

"You're lucky you didn't get stopped by a Black cop who would have put your ass in jail."

Nate balled his fist and leaned forward. "Don't you talk to me like that, you–"

The Duke grabbed him by the back of his shorts and pulled him back down to the sofa. He landed with a squeak as the entire piece of furniture slid backwards an inch.

"We found a shirt in Nate's apartment with Jimmy's blood on it," Jason continued. "Nate knew Jimmy had no bodyguard that night. He was alone. All Nate needed to do was get to him, and we think we know how he did that. He used Jimmy's friend, Tiger – a kid who lived on the street and ran errands for Jimmy. Tiger would know how to sneak somebody into the building to visit Jimmy. He did it all the time. And he'd recognize Nate as a teammate of Jimmy's. Isn't that right, Nate? Tiger let you inside that night, didn't he?"

"I don't know what the hell you're talkin' about!" Nate's southern drawl was getting more pronounced the angrier he got.

"Well, let's see if I can recover the text message." Jason turned his attention back to the phone, still in his hand. He held it up and swiped a few times, then tapped it.

"What text?" Nate demanded.

Mike knew it was time to take over the storytelling. "We think the killer might have used Jimmy's phone to send a text message, so it would look like a suicide note. We're thinking the note would go to someone Jimmy texted frequently, like The

Duke. Do you recall, Duke, if you got a text message from Jimmy's phone that night?"

The Duke looked at Mike, clearly pondering his response. He glanced over at Jason, who seemed to be intently studying the phone and kept tapping it. He looked at Nate, then at Chip, as if searching for some support, but not getting any. Then he stood up suddenly, slid past Nate's knees, and took a few steps toward the big windows overlooking the field. It was raining even harder now. Most of the players had departed the practice field. He turned around, backlit against the window.

"I can't protect you anymore, Nate." Mike noticed that when The Duke said this, he was making eye contact with Chip. "I did talk to Nate that night. He was drunk and sounded crazy. He told me he was on his way to kill Jimmy. He wanted my help. I tried to talk him out of it. It was Nate's idea to beat up those guys in college. I was his buddy, so I went along with it. It's his father that's a Klansman. He sent me the suicide note in that text from Jimmy's phone. He told me he did it, and I promised to keep it a secret. I'm sorry, Buddy. I can't lie for you anymore."

As Mike and Jason had planned it out, they had hoped one of the two men would feel enough heat to throw the other one under the bus, either because he deserved to be there or as camouflage for his own guilt. Jason wasn't really a wiz at recovering deleted material from smartphones, but their suspects wouldn't know that and the prospect of Jason unearthing the previously deleted message just might smoke something out. The next move was going to be to tell The Duke they had already obtained the cell site information on his phone and could place him near Jimmy's building. Mike had bet a dollar that Nate would point the finger at The Duke. Jason took the opposite side. Graham had bet them both that somebody would implicate Chip, or possibly Woody. At this point, it looked like Jason would be getting two bucks. None of them had anticipated how Nate would react.

It is difficult for normal humans to appreciate the quickness of an NFL wide receiver. Jason had played linebacker in college; the scholarship got him his degree, but it had been many years since he was an active athlete. Nate was twenty-six and in peak condition. So, when he launched himself off the sofa, it happened too fast for anyone present to react.

"You bastard!" Nate yelled as he covered the ten feet between himself and The Duke in a blink.

The Duke had just enough time to take one half-step back and lift one arm before Nate connected with his torso like a human missile. Nate used the tackling technique he had been taught since grade school: head up, lead with the shoulder, wrap your arms. The Duke did not have sufficient leverage to keep his balance and immediately toppled backwards, with Nate's full weight driving him.

Sixty square feet of plate glass window exploded with a crash heard in every corner of the practice facility. All heads that weren't concentrating on catching a pass or kicking a ball at that exact moment turned in the direction of the administration building. The intertwined bodies of Nate and The Duke hurtled out into empty space, surrounded by shards of glass. They plummeted downward onto the canvas awning protecting the building's entrance from the falling rain. The awning had been in place for several years, enduring sweltering summer heat and brutal winter cold. It held up well enough against drops of rain, but it was no match for 490 pounds of human bulk. It sagged, absorbing most of the kinetic energy, then ripped. The two men fell to the concrete walkway with a thud.

# Chapter 40 – Muscle Beach Party

UNDER THE CANVAS AWNING, Kristi Olson sat against the wall. She had finished her daily training camp report and was holding her phone, responding to reader comments on her Twitter account, when she heard the crash directly above her. The appearance of a mound of grunting arms and legs on the ground within an arm's length made her scream and jump away. When she reached the edge of the protective awning, she screamed again and recoiled from the rain of glass fragments showering down around her. She ducked back under the ripped awning and pressed herself against the wall, still clutching her phone.

Nate ended up on the bottom and let out an "ooof" as he hit the ground. He didn't let the impact of the fall interrupt his desire to tear The Duke a new asshole. The two men rolled to the right, arms locked around each other while each attempted to gain the upper hand. The Duke aimed his left knee toward Nate's groin, but didn't have enough space to land a disabling blow. Nate grabbed the short hair on the back of The Duke's head and pulled, prompting a yelp from the bigger man.

The rest of the men upstairs in Woody's office froze in the first moments after Nate and The Duke crashed through the window. Linderman, who was closest to the window, sprang from his chair and looked through the jagged maw. Jason also rushed to the window. Chip was glued to the sofa. Woody stood up but didn't move. Mike took three steps toward the window, then was the first to bolt for the door. As soon as the others realized where Mike was headed, they stormed down the stairs toward the front entrance.

Nate and The Duke rolled onto the wet grass. The rain was pelting down now. Only the kickers, holders, and snappers were still out on the main practice field, working on bad-weather kicks. They were all straining their eyes to see what was happening over by the administration building.

"I thought you were my friend!" Nate grunted. When The Duke stopped on top for a moment, Nate lifted his knees and rolled backward, raising his hips with rock-hard abdominal muscles, sending The Duke's bulk over his head. Nate spun sideways and scrambled to his feet. The Duke, who had landed heavily on his back, took a moment to recover, but then rolled and pushed up into a standing position.

Nate ran at The Duke, extending his arm in an attempt to clothesline his opponent's neck. The bigger, but slower, man spotted Nate in his peripheral vision a split second before the receiver arrived. The Duke twisted his body just enough to make it a glancing blow rather than a take-down.

Nate's momentum took him past The Duke in the direction of Muscle Beach, which was deserted because of the rain and the threat of lightning. He spun around to face the man he had considered his best friend, but who had thrown him to the wolves like a leftover bone. "You're a gutless, backstabbing scrub!"

The Duke barked out a derisive laugh. "What are you worried about, Dipshit? You didn't do it, so they can't convict you. Just deal with it. I know you wanted to snuff that selfish bastard too. You're glad he's dead." As he grunted out the last word, he charged toward Nate in a bull-rush, using his larger bulk to its maximum advantage. Nate stepped back but bumped into a metal rack where free weights sat in notches on the opposite side. The Duke's momentum sent both men into the rack, which slowly toppled over creating an iron-on-iron cacophony.

By that time, the kicking squad members had abandoned their practice and were walking in the direction of the commotion. Jason was first to reach the front door of the administrative building, just at the moment when the free weight rack toppled. He pointed in the direction of Muscle Beach and started running, his wingtips sloshing through the wet grass.

A stream of blood mixed with rain ran down the back of Nate's head from its impact with the metal rack. The wide receiver slid off the overturned structure onto the padded flooring of Muscle Beach. As he rose, The Duke landed a left hook on his cheek, sending him spinning away off-balance, stunned by the force of the blow. He steadied himself on a large structure with pullies and ropes hanging down from overhead beams. As The Duke charged forward again, Nate reached up, grabbed a rope in each hand, and pulled himself off the ground. He kicked both legs into The Duke's chest, stopping him cold and sending him reeling back.

As Nate got both feet back on the ground, The Duke grabbed a weighted bar and swung it like a baseball bat. Nate raised his left arm, which absorbed the blow with a sickening crack. Nate screamed in pain and darted to his right to escape the range of the swinging rod.

Through the pain in his arm, Nate yelled, "What did you do, man? Was that fucking text from Jimmy?" He reached for the shaft of a barbell, poised over a bench covered in bright red vinyl. There were no weights mounted on the bar, but it still weighed twenty pounds on its own. He held it with both hands as The Duke swung his rod, absorbing the blow with a loud clang. Then, Nate's face went blank. "That was your truck. On the street outside Jimmy's building. You were there. You lied to me, you fucker! It was you that killed Jimmy! You crazy bastard!" Nate moved sideways between two weight machines, toward the far side of Muscle Beach. His left arm hung limp at his waist and throbbed. Hot blood oozed down the back of his neck. He was having trouble seeing clearly.

The Duke circled to his left, holding his rod and looking for an opening.

"C'mon, Bro," Nate pleaded. "I wouldn't rat you out. Hell, I would have helped you. We just shut up and the cops got nothin'. Chip'll run interference for us. He never liked Jimmy anyway. He's probably happy. He's—"

The Duke swung his rod again, but Nate twisted and took the blow on his back, which sent him rolling off the edge of the Muscle Beach padding onto the moist grass with a splat.

The Duke reached for a barbell on the bottom of a nearby rack; this one had single sixteen-inch weight rings on either side. He hefted it over his head and ran toward Nate. "It's you or me, Bro. I'm not going down for killing that fucker!" He grunted, then pulled the barbell down from over his head and onto Nate. The bar contacted with Nate's neck, driving him backward and sending his injured head slamming into the ground. The weights on either side sank three inches into the soft, rain-soaked earth. The bar across Nate's neck pressed against his throat but did not crush his larynx. He was pinned, but not dead.

Nate tried to reach up with his one functioning arm, but he had no leverage to pry off the bar, now securely locked into the ground. He looked up at The Duke, who grabbed a fifteen-pound dumbbell that had rolled off the padded mat. He picked it up and advanced toward Nate.

At that moment, Jason reached the edge of Muscle Beach closest to the administration building. The weightlifting area, now littered with fallen racks and scattered equipment, was sixty feet square. Jason could see The Duke holding the dumbbell. He had seen Nate fall but did not know where he had landed. Jason drew his service pistol and shouted, "Freeze!"

Nate, still pinned to the turf, started screaming. His voice croaked out past the pressure of the bar on his neck. "It wasn't me – it was The Duke. He killed Jimmy. I saw his truck – he was there!"

The Duke yelled back, "Shut the fuck up, moron!"

Nate did not. "He told me! He did it!"

"I said shut up!" The Duke raised the dumbbell and took a step toward Nate.

A pair of arms grabbed The Duke from behind, holding him back. Stuart Schwartz, the long snapper, had drifted over to Muscle Beach and decided it was time to intervene. The kickers and punters were right behind him.

Jason maneuvered around the obstacles across Muscle Beach until he stood six feet from The Duke, now struggling like a sumo wrestler with Schwartz, two placekickers, and two punters. The smaller men were hanging off The Duke, who was wielding his dumbbell in an attempt to swat away his attackers.

Mike arrived next to Jason a few moments later, his own gun drawn. Linderman and Chip lagged far behind, with Woody and Graham bringing up the rear of their procession. All were soaked by the heavily falling rain.

Mike moved to his left, while Jason kept his gun poised. At the moment, he had no clear shot with all the other players engaged with The Duke.

"Drop the weapon, Duke!" Jason called out, circling to The Duke's left and staying out of range. He knew he wouldn't shoot with the other men so close, and without sufficient provocation.

Nate was still croaking, "Duke killed Jimmy!" although his volume was getting lower as he struggled to breathe.

Chip stepped forward, his suit now stained with rain and his slicked-back hair pressed to the side of his head. He was breathing heavily from the sprint. "Duke, put down the damned weight. That's an order. Stu! Let him go and step back. Let the police handle this!"

Schwartz, who was hanging onto The Duke's back, loosened his grip and let The Duke go. The other players also dropped off and stepped back. The Duke dropped the dumbbell on the grass. It landed on its end with a *thwack* and sank a half-inch into the turf, now muddied after the trampling of a dozen feet. He stood, frozen, looking at Chip. By now, Mike had circled around to a point where he and Jason were at a 90-degree angle on two sides of their suspect.

Linderman rushed to where Nate was still trapped under the barbell and started tugging, attempting to free him. When Schwartz jumped in to help, the bar lifted up with a slurping sound as the weights were extracted from the squishy ground. Linderman put his arm around Nate's shoulder to help him sit up and came away with blood staining his shirt. Then he lowered Nate's head back to the ground, slowly.

"Call 9-1-1," Linderman called out. "Nate's bleeding pretty badly." Graham pulled out his phone and dialed for an ambulance.

Jason yelled, "On your knees, Duke! Hands on your head! You're under arrest for the murder of Jimmy Rydell."

"Fuck you!" Duke spat back, again looking at Chip.

Chip stepped forward, within a few feet of Jason. "It's over, Duke. I can't protect you anymore." Then Chip turned toward Mike. "I'm sorry, Detective. I've been trying to protect my guys. When Duke told me he knew where Jimmy's body was and that he could get it for me, I didn't believe him. But I knew somebody was in big trouble. Duke admitted to killing Jimmy. I'm not sure if Nate was involved or not."

The Duke took two steps toward Chip. Jason yelled again for him to freeze. Now Chip was directly between Jason and The Duke, who shouted, "You bastard! You planned it!"

Chip spat out a cough-like laugh as he stepped away toward Mike. "Please, why would I want Jimmy dead?"

"The dead money and the insurance." The voice belonged to Graham, who had completed his 9-1-1 call. "And after Jimmy was dead, you had to make sure the body was found."

Mike trained his gun on The Duke's legs. If he had to shoot, he didn't want Nate or the cluster of people around him to be in the line of fire.

Woody shouted, "Now just wait a minute. We don't know that The Duke killed Jimmy."

"Yes we do. He admitted it." The voice belonged to Kristi Olson, who was standing slightly off to the side, on the edge of Muscle Beach. She held up her cell phone. "I got it on video."

"There you are, Detective," Chip said to Mike, "you can arrest him. I'll fully cooperate."

"You bastard!" The Duke took a stride toward Chip. Mike yelled for The Duke to stop. When the huge man kept moving, Mike fired, causing everyone but Jason to flinch. Blood burst forth from The Duke's exposed right calf muscle. He roared in pain but kept moving.

Jason had a shot. He squeezed his trigger, aiming for center mass, but just as he fired, The Duke stooped down to the ground. He grabbed the dumbbell that was stuck in the turf while Jason's bullet sailed over his back. Chip, seeing the rage in The Duke's eyes, dashed to his right – blocking Jason's line of fire.

The Duke took one huge stride, swung his right arm, and planted the hexagonal end of the weight squarely into the side of Chip O'Meara's head. The general manager crumpled to the soggy grass, a crimson stain immediately mixing with the raindrops.

Jason now had a clear shot and fired, connecting with The Duke's hip. Mike also fired into his left leg. A moment later, Schwartz and the two kickers rushed forward and jumped on The Duke, holding him down while Jason got out a pair of handcuffs.

The players were still sitting on The Duke's legs when the two uniformed sheriff's deputies rushed onto the scene. Mike and Jason had arranged for them to be close by, in case they needed some help making an arrest. When the deputies heard the window break, they had exited their car, but they were under instructions not to come inside until called. When they heard the first gunshot, they figured back-up was needed. One officer joined the players who were securing The Duke. The other administered first aid to Nate. Mike instructed the deputy to stay with Nate when the paramedics showed up and to consider him under arrest.

There was no first aid to be administered to Chip. His father knelt in the rain, holding one hand over his mouth, next to the body of his dead son.

The rest of the press corps showed up right behind the deputies. They had all been inside the press room, staying out of the rain and watching an afternoon baseball game. When somebody near the door heard the first gunshot and peeked out, they all piled out and arrived late to the party. The reporters immediately started asking questions and taking photos in the rain, despite Mike's shouts to stay back and keep the crime scene clear. There wasn't much evidence that needed to be preserved, but it was Mike's instinct.

Over the next half hour, the reporters pieced together the story, but only Kristi had a video.

A rain-soaked Graham Beckwith walked over to Mike and Jason after the scene was secure. "Well, that was more excitement than I anticipated. I suppose I can start drafting my investigation report now."

"You do what you need to do," Mike replied. "We'll file our report, and we'll see what the DA decides to do with The Duke – if he lives – and Nate. Things may not be quite as clean and tidy as you'd like them to be."

"Yes, well, we'll see. In the meantime, you both owe me one American dollar."

"How's that?" Jason asked.

"I'd say that The Duke quite clearly implicated Chip O'Meara in the murder of Jimmy Rydell."

Standing there in the rain, listening to an ambulance siren growing louder, Mike and Jason couldn't help but laugh.

# Chapter 41 – Holding Out for A Hero

MIKE AND JASON HAD HOPED to get somebody to slip up slightly under pressure. They would have been happy for The Duke or Nate to give away some small fact, or make some tiny admission that would help them build a case. Instead, they got the lead story on the national news.

The first minute of the video, licensed by *The New York Times* and credited to reporter Kristi Olson, was jumpy and blurry. Kristi was running to find a position with a good angle to record the fight. Once she found a stable spot, the recording documented The Duke and Nate demolishing Muscle Beach. She recorded all the way through the final confrontation, including Mike's first shot, Jason's missed shot, and The Duke murdering Chip O'Meara. The impact of the dumbbell against Chip's head was pixilated out. The audio did not pick up Nate's croaked cries while pinned under the barbell, but earlier The Duke could clearly be heard saying he wasn't going down "for killing that f---er." The f-word was bleeped out, according to the newspaper's policy.

It was the most-viewed video of the year on the paper's website. Kristi's article, including her firsthand reporting and some quick interviews with Stu Schwartz and the other players involved, ran on the front page. She did not share the byline.

Over the next week, Kristi doggedly pursued every lead in the case, including a profile on Candi Nelson, the full exposé on Duke Drepp's involvement in the racial hazing at Auburn, and the likely involvement of Chip O'Meara in a conspiracy to murder Jimmy Rydell. She got Aaron Taylor to acknowledge that Chip was enraged when Jimmy refused to renegotiate his contract and told Jimmy he "would regret it." The police had quickly obtained Chip's bank account records, showing a $100,000 withdrawal on May 31st, which Kristi speculated was payment for the hit on Jimmy. They also found a draft suicide note in the deleted files on Chip's personal laptop computer. Mike arranged to send that information to Kristi ten minutes before a press release went out to all media outlets.

Kristi's articles never definitively accounted for the whereabouts of Jimmy's body between Wednesday night and Saturday morning, but the assumption was that it was part of a scheme to disguise the identity of the killer. A source, who preferred to remain anonymous, said there was another man, large enough to have been another football player, who helped remove Jimmy's body from the Park Towers health club. The police would not confirm the existence of this other man.

Kristi interviewed the director of the lower Manhattan Boys & Girls Clubs and wrote a long article about all the money and time Jimmy spent with the disadvantaged kids. She included a profile on Tiger, whose real name was Tyrone Green, and whose murder seemed to be linked to Jimmy's killing. Although the police were not pursuing charges, Kristi speculated that Duke Drepp likely took out Tiger, who may have been a witness. A memorial that included many stuffed tigers sprang up in Riverside Park at 110th Street, where Tiger's body was found.

Kristi's reporting did not reach any conclusion about whether Nate Bedford was an accomplice to the murder. Nate maintained his innocence. The Duke's statements during the fight at Muscle Beach seemed to point toward Nate being a racist, but not a killer.

In all, Kristi wrote five major articles attempting to piece together what really happened to cause the murders of Jimmy Rydell and Chip O'Meara and the career-ending injury to Nate Bedford. Dexter Peacock lobbied to have his name on the articles, but the editor-in-chief declined. The paper later nominated Kristi's series for a Pulitzer Prize for local reporting.

Nate Bedford recovered from his head wound and his broken forearm, but was deemed a concussion risk and retired from football. He reached a settlement with the team over his injuries and collected on an insurance policy for a major portion of the balance of his contract. The district attorney agreed not to charge him as an accessory to murder in exchange for his testimony, if necessary, at any future trial of Vernon "Duke" Drepp. The publicity about his involvement in the racist hazing at Auburn killed any chance he had for sponsorship or spokesperson work as an ex-NFL player. The President of the college resigned, and three football coaches were fired after an internal investigation stemming from Kristi's articles.

The Duke survived his gunshot wounds, but was immediately arrested. The District Attorney charged him with the murder of Chip O'Meara and several counts of assault and attempted murder on Nate. His lawyer, who took the case *pro bono* hoping for big publicity associated with a sensational trial, ended up negotiating a plea agreement that included a 20-year prison sentence. The DA was happy to avoid a circus trial over Jimmy Rydell's murder, knowing that as part of pretrial discovery he would have to turn over the video of Mr. Clean on the scene of the murder, seeming to cart out Jimmy's body, and the other evidence pointing to Jimmy's involvement in the point-shaving scheme, all of which would point to Mr. Clean as the murderer. It would have been a tough job convincing a jury, beyond a reasonable doubt, that it was The Duke and not Mr. Clean, who killed Jimmy. Since they had The Duke on video murdering Chip and attempting to kill Nate, there was no need for additional charges.

The speculation about Jimmy's involvement in the still-unconfirmed point-shaving scheme died down, which made the NFL commissioner happy. The protests seeking *Justice for Jimmy* also petered out, since the killer was in custody. That made Mayor Douglass happy. It also made Police Commissioner Earl Ward happy, which made Sully happy.

Beginning that August, the NFL relaxed its internal policies regarding pregame protests for social justice. It was a small but important step. Scenes of Black and White players linking arms and taking knees together in support of reforms to reduce police brutality became routine. What had been a loud cry of condemnation from some media outlets about disrespect for the national anthem was reduced to a fringe whisper, at least for a while.

In the immediate aftermath of the Florham Park skirmish, Mike and Jason took some criticism for failing to subdue The Duke before he killed Chip O'Meara. While Mike could have aimed for The Duke's torso, or fired multiple shots to stop him, nobody within the police department was going to start an internal investigation based on their failure to prevent the murder of a man who was most likely the mastermind of the conspiracy to murder Jimmy. Internal Affairs quickly determined that Mike and Jason both fired their weapons with good cause and did not endanger any of the bystanders.

After Chip O'Meara's funeral, Woody announced that the team would be making a substantial donation to the Boys & Girls Clubs of greater New York to establish the Jimmy Rydell scholarship fund and to build athletic facilities for disadvantaged youth. The first project would be a football field to be called the Tyrone "Tiger" Green Memorial Field. Woody also introduced Aaron Taylor as the director of a newly formed charitable foundation bearing Jimmy Rydell's name. Despite everything, Woody still had a soft spot in his heart for Jimmy because of what he went through as a kid, and Aaron shared those same experiences. Aaron was already the executor of Jimmy's estate, including the $22 million annuity which Jimmy had directed be used to support foster kids. Woody had the idea of using that as seed money to start a new organization to support young athletes who were part of the foster care system. Jimmy's money would be supplemented by funds from Woody's own charitable foundation. As the director, Aaron would draw a modest salary and would be able to spend his time advancing Jimmy's legacy.

After two months of incarceration without having been charged with any specific crime, the man known as Igor was put on a plane at JFK bound for Prague. The federal authorities still did not have a positive ID for him. They decided that deportation was a superior option to prosecuting him for battery and for unlawfully transporting a corpse. Interpol advised that the authorities in the Cech Republic wanted to interview him.

Three weeks later, Agent Everett Forrest sent Mike a text reading: "The fat man got a delivery of household cleaner."

♦♦♦

The Friday after Chip's death, Mike and Jason were in the bullpen, sifting through the files on the three new cases to which they had been assigned now that the Jimmy Rydell file was closed. At 11:45 a.m. Mike heard someone clearing his throat. He looked up and saw the smiling face of Graham Beckwith, holding a long black umbrella with a shiny metal tip.

"Mr. Beckwith!" Mike exclaimed. "I expected you to be back in London by now."

"Well, Detective, I decided to take advantage of some holiday time and have been enjoying your fair city. Your theater district has some exceptional venues. I'm on my way to my flight home and wanted to stop in. Do you and Detective Dickson fancy a pint before I go?"

Sully gave permission for an early lunch and the three men adjourned to the One-Ten bar on Amsterdam Avenue. Over craft-tap ales for Mike and Jason and a Guinness for Graham, they exchanged good wishes for the future. They also talked through a postmortem on the Jimmy Rydell matter.

Graham had filed his report, which admittedly included some speculation and deduction. He believed Duke Drepp's exclamation that Chip had planned Jimmy's murder was sufficient to conclude that Chip, acting on behalf of the team, had caused Jimmy's death. The statements on Kristi Olson's recording made lone-wolf action by The Duke seem unlikely. They all agreed that Nate probably was not involved, although joint action by Nate and The Duke was not entirely impossible. The $100,000 withdrawal from Chip's bank account was certainly the payoff to Fat Albert Gallata to get the body back, although paying the ransom on the corpse did not necessarily prove that Chip had ordered a hit on Jimmy.

Boyd's of Britain would likely refuse to pay the $20 million. There would be litigation. Graham expected to be back in New York at some point to testify, and said he hoped they would have the opportunity to spend some time together. He suggested trying out Luigi's Italian restaurant in Little Italy. They all toasted to that idea.

Two months later, on a sweltering Friday morning in August, Mike and Michelle were in the front row of a small audience, sitting in rickety folding chairs outside the entrance to the Fire House that housed the EMT unit where Rachel worked. They fanned themselves with their paper programs and hoped the proceedings would move along quickly, while there was still a little shade. Jason was next to Michelle. Next to him, Ernie and Olivia Robinson wore smiles as bright as the August sun.

Rachel stood next to a podium, where a man in a casual business suit stood at a microphone. Henderson Wainwright was the man who had a seizure and smacked Rachel in the face on the day of Jason's proposal. It turned out he was a hedge fund manager. He credited Rachel with saving his life. He was announcing a $500,000 donation to the city's EMT squads, in honor of Rachel. He said she was a true hero, and everyone in attendance agreed.

After the ceremony was over, they all went for lunch at the Nom Wah Tea Parlor on Doyers Street. Olivia Robinson, Michelle, and Rachel talked about plans for the upcoming wedding.

342| KEVIN G. CHAPMAN

While the ladies discussed options for upcoming clearance sales on wedding dresses, Ernie asked Mike and Jason if they were planning on going to any football games during the upcoming season. Woody O'Meara's team was in tatters, although he had hired a new general manager – an Asian woman who had been one of Chip's leading assistants. She became the first Asian and the first woman to be a GM in the league. However, they were playing preseason games with an aging backup quarterback, which did not bode well.

"We've been invited to come to any games we want this year," Mike said. "I've had about a dozen people send me emails offering me free tickets. We're not allowed to accept, of course, because of ethics rules. But Woody said he'll sell us the cheapest tickets in the stadium and then invite us to be his guests in the owner's suite, which I think we'll get approval for. We have a friend in Internal Affairs who can review it for us."

Jason reached for a plate of steamed pork buns. "I know a guy who has season tickets. He tailgates with a big group in section L-11 before all the home games. The head guy is called Frank the Flagman and he has thirty flags he flies over the tailgate area. It's the best pre-game party in the lot, and we're invited. That one doesn't require departmental clearance." He bit a healthy chunk out of the steamed bun and happily chomped away.

Ernie asked Mike if it was true about the point-shaving, and that Jimmy was involved with organized crime. He said he never really liked Jimmy as a player, he objected to his excessive lifestyle, and he was embarrassed by his off-field incidents. But he always thought Jimmy had a good heart, and he was touched by the time and money the man gave to needy kids. He also thought Jimmy was brave to take a stand against police brutality and protest for social justice, even when it made him a target and maybe got him killed.

"Ernie, there are some things I'm not permitted to tell you, even here among friends and even if you are going to be Jason's father-in-law. But I'll tell you this. I never met Jimmy Rydell, and I had a pretty negative impression of him before he died. But the more I found out about him from the people who knew him, the more I realize things were more complicated than I thought. He made some bad decisions in his life. He reminds me of a partner I once had. We can all do better, but they were both people I'd be proud to call friends."

Ernie turned to Jason. "You marry my baby and you'd better not make any bad decisions."

Jason smiled and raised his glass of Diet Coke. "Here's to making only good decisions."

Rachel looked across the table at the men having a toast. "What are you all toasting to?"

Jason gazed into Rachel's eyes. "To you, my brave and very beautiful fiancée; may nobody ever give you another black eye."

They all raised their glasses and drank to Rachel.

Then Rachel stood up. "This day was really special. Thanks to all of you for being here. I wouldn't be here at all without the love and support of all my friends and family. So, a toast to all the wonderful times we have ahead of us; may we all be together like this as often as possible."

Everyone raised their glasses again and called out, "Hear, hear!"

[The End]

Please consider making a donation to an organization in your area that supports foster kid and disadvantaged or underprivileged youth, whether through athletic programs, other recreational activity or other much-needed programs. For readers in the New York City area, consider these very worthy organizations:

The Boys & Girls Clubs of America.
https://www.bgca.org/

The Marty Lyons Foundation
https://martylyonsfoundation.org/donate-today

The Victor Cruz Foundation
http://www.victorcruzfoundation.org/

The Harlem Jets
https://www.harlemjetslacrosse.org/

The Colin Kaepernick "Know Your Rights Camp"
https://www.knowyourrightscamp.com/

Thank you for reading *Fatal Infraction*. I truly enjoy hearing from readers about their reactions to my characters and stories. I welcome critical comments and suggestions that can help me improve my writing and urge every reader to **please leave a review**. Even a few words will go a long way and I will be grateful. Post on Amazon, Goodreads and/or BookBub to let other readers know what you think. And send me an email directly via my website at www.kevingchapman.com to tell me your thoughts about this book.

Keep reading to find a sneak preview of book #5 in the Mike Stoneman Thriller series – *Perilous Gambit*. Visit the Mike Stoneman Thriller series page to preorder book #5 or pick up copies of books 1-3 in the series (along with the free short story, *Fool Me Twice)* today!

And please tell your friends (and book club members) about this book. As an independent author, I need all the word-of-mouth plugs I can get. Keep reading books by indie authors; there are a lot of great writers out there just waiting for you.

Kevin G. Chapman
July 2021

# About the Author

Kevin G. Chapman is, by profession, an attorney specializing in labor and employment law. He is a past Chair of the Labor & Employment Law Network of the Association of Corporate Counsel, leading a group of 6800 in-house employment lawyers. Kevin is a frequent speaker at Continuing Legal Education seminars and enjoys teaching management training courses.

Kevin's second novel, *A Legacy of One*, originally published in 2016, was a finalist for the Chanticleer Book Review's Somerset Award for Literary Fiction. *A Legacy of One* is a serious book, filled with political and social commentary and a plot involving personal identity, self-determination, and the struggle to make the right life decisions. *A Legacy of One* has been significantly revised and updated and will be re-published in 2021.

Kevin has also written several short stories, including *Fool Me Twice*, the winner of the New Jersey Corporate Counsel Association's 2012 Legal Fiction Writing Competition, which was the genesis of Mike Stoneman. *Fool Me Twice* is available as a stand-alone short story and is FREE on Amazon, Kobo, Nook, and other ebook retailers, or you can get it directly from Kevin's website. And, of course, book #5 in the Mike Stoneman Thriller series, *Perilous Gambit* is in production for publication (hopefully) in late 2021.

Kevin lives in Central New Jersey and is a graduate of Columbia College (class of '83, where he was a classmate of Barack Obama), and Boston University School of Law (magna cum laude '86). Readers can contact Kevin via his website at KevinGChapman.com

## Book Club discussion questions for *Fatal Infraction*

1.  What was your reaction to Jason's attempts to open Mike's eyes to racism around him?
2.  How do you think Mike handled his own attempts to become more sensitive to racism (and sexual harassment) issues?
3.  How do you feel about how Kristi Olsen handled the sexual harassment?
4.  Did the discussions about racism and sexual harassment in the story make you think about the issues any differently?
5.  What do you think Nate's role really was in Jimmy's murder?
6.  Did you think Chip was involved before Chapter 39 ("Under the Bus")?
7.  Do you think Woody knew what Chip was doing?
8.  How did you feel about Jason's proposal to Rachel? How do you think that relationship will progress?
9.  What would you like to see happen in the future between Mike and Michelle?

# AUTHOR'S NOTE & ACKNOWLEDGEMENTS

As always, I must credit my insightful wife, Sharon, for brainstorming the plot ideas and character development points in this book. Sharon has a fantastic vision for where my characters are going and she sees inconsistencies in the story that I sometimes miss. I could not write these books as well without her.

I also thank my brilliant editor, Samantha (Samanthachapmanediting.com) whose careful reads, sensitivity, and great ideas give me the editor that every author wants. The final product has been polished and improved significantly in the editing process. Just ask my beta readers. And kudos to my cover designer, Peter from bespokebookcovers.com. Peter outdid himself with this eye-catching cover. Every cover designer should be so patient and helpful. Also kudos to Jiawie "Peter" Hsu from Fotolux in Princeton Junction, NJ (my local photo shop) for making me beautiful prints for my publicity posters.

My beta readers provided me with invaluable perspectives and ideas as the book was in development. Thanks so much to Cindy Thiel, Kay Barton, Mimi Bailey, Amy & Kevin Knarr, Joanna Joseph, Buzz & Beth Barydan, Gayle Wilson, Barbara Dena, Roxx Tarantini, and Matt (M.C.) Thomas for giving me critical feedback and suggestions early on. And special thanks to Gayle, Mimi, and Nancy Lee for being beta listeners for the audiobook.

I also thank Nicole McCain and Chuck Monsanto for being my sensitivity readers. Nicole and Chuck gave me valuable double-checks on the racial issues in the book. And an extra special "Thank you" to Irene Paterson, Lain Andrews, and Irene Paterson, who were my British dialogue checkers and who corrected many, many potentially embarrassing errors that would have reinforced negative stereotypes about American authors for my British readers. The character of Graham Beckwith was fun to write, but is not intended to mock

Englishmen. If you want to be a beta reader for a future book, just send me a note via my website or and I'll put you on the beta reader list.

I also pay tribute to my AXP Typokillers, who combed over the finished manuscript and rooted out more than 50 errors, large and small, to make the final text as clean as it can be. (But, if you find a flaw, please let me know so I can fix it.) All authors should use the typokillers. Thanks Sandy Wilson, Lonnia Helton, Deena Guptil, Sheila Whitney, Sandra Yeaman, Kim Hine, Heidi Farmer, Barb Stoner, and the typokiller army commander, Amy Vansant.

Last, but not least, a huge thanks to Kristi Ackert, sportswriter for *The New York Daily News*, who consulted regarding the experiences of a female sportswriter. Even decades after women were permitted to interview male athletes in professional locker rooms, the treatment of female reporters leaves tremendous room for improvement. Kristi's insights and willingness to share were invaluable to this book.

If you're a Mike Stoneman fan, join me on Facebook (Mike Stoneman Thriller Group) and send me a note to get on my newsletter distribution list or onto the Whiteboard Squad (my social media army). Find me at www.KevinGChapman.com

<u>The Mike Stoneman Thriller Series</u>

*Righteous Assassin* (Mike Stoneman #1)
*Deadly Enterprise* (Mike Stoneman #2)
*Lethal Voyage* (Mike Stoneman #3)
*Fool Me Twice* (A Mike Stoneman Short Story)

coming soon:
*Perilous Gambit (Mike Stoneman #5)*


Other novels by Kevin G. Chapman

A Legacy of One
Identity Crisis: A Rick LaBlonde Mystery


Visit me at www.KevinGChapman.com


<u>Connect with Kevin</u>:

**Kevin's website: https://www.KevinGChapman.com**

**Facebook page: Mike Stoneman Thriller Group**
https://www.amazon.com/gp/product/B08BZMDSVT

**Email:** Kevin@KevinGChapman.com

# PREVIEW
# Perilous Gambit
# (Mike Stoneman Thriller #5)

## Chapter 2 – Alarming discovery

MIKE STONEMAN WAS PERPLEXED and getting frustrated. He was staring into the bottom Dr. Michelle McNeill's bedroom closet. Michelle, the county medical examiner, was running late, which was unusual for her, but not her fault. The body that came into the morgue late that afternoon was a high priority. Michelle completed the portions of the autopsy process that required her personal attention, and left the remainder to her assistant, Natalie. But, by the time she arrived at her Third Avenue apartment, she needed to hustle if they were going to make their pre-theater dinner reservation. Mike's assignment was to fetch her silver two-inch pumps. They were supposed to be on the rack on the floor on the left side of the closet.

When Mike could not locate them, he was confused, since Michelle was the most organized person he knew. Other shoes were there in the rack, but not the silver pumps. Mike decided to open the right side of the double door. As it swung outward, Mike noticed two things. The missing silver pumps where there, on the hardwood floor just inside the threshold. But what really caught his eye was the dress covering the entire inside surface of the closet door.

It was sheathed in clear plastic, as if just returned from the dry cleaner, and hanging from a swiveling hanger hook draped over the top of the door. The dress was a shining white, covered with tiny white beads and lace fringes. It had long sleeves with white silk gloves dangling from its lace cuffs. There was no question. It was a wedding dress.

Mike had seen the inside of Michelle's closet enough times to know that this dress had not been there as recently as a few days earlier. He grabbed the silver shoes, carefully unhooked the dress hanger, and carried them both down the narrow hallway.

Michelle was looking into the bathroom mirror, applying makeup at an efficient but unhurried pace.

He set the shoes down on the floor. "Here you go. And, by the way," He held up the dress. "Is there something you want to tell me?"

Michelle didn't look away from the mirror, where she was applying mascara. "Oh, Mike, you didn't touch Rachel's dress, did you?"

A very relieved Mike exhaled, not conscious of how tense he had been. "No. I mean, it's still in its plastic. But – why is Rachel's wedding dress hanging in your closet?"

Michelle was now brushing eyeshadow on her lids. "We picked it up this morning at the Vera Wang sample sale. She didn't have time to take it back to Brooklyn before her shift, so I said I'd hold it here for her. She's was supposed to be here a half hour ago, but then again, so was I. I guess we're both running late. I hope she gets here before we have to leave. I'll text her as soon as I'm finished."

After returning the dress to its place, Mike walked to the living room and sat down, trying to assess why his heart was still racing after seeing the wedding gown. He glanced at his wristwatch. If they were going to make it to the restaurant in time to have dinner and still make the curtain for *Wicked*, they needed to be down on the street hailing a cab in the next few minutes. At that moment, the house phone rang, indicating that someone was ringing up from the lobby.

"I'll get that," Michelle called out, emerging from the bathroom wearing the silver pumps and looking ready to leave. "It's probably Rachel."

Michelle picked up the white phone hanging on the wall, looking like a leftover from the 70s. As soon as she brought the receiver to her ear, her expression changed from calm to concerned.

"Rachel, what's the matter? . . . Slow down, Honey . . . What? . . . Never mind. Just come right up."

"What's that all about?" Mike asked.

Michelle stood frozen, the phone receiver still in her hand, tethered to the wall unit by its short coiled cord. "I'm not sure. Rachel's coming up. She was distraught – almost hysterical. I've never heard her sound like that. Something's very wrong."

\* \* \*

To find out why Rachel is distraught, pick up your copy of *Perilous Gambit* (Mike Stoneman Thriller #5). Order on amazon.com or visit my website at www.kevingchapman.com.

Printed in the USA
CPSIA information can be obtained
at www.ICGtesting.com
LVHW041350090823
754555LV00006B/167